TO DARKNESS AND TO DEATH

TO DARKNESS AND TO DEATH

Julia Spencer-Fleming

MINOTAUR BOOKS

A Thomas Dunne Book

New York

To my father, Lt. Melvin Spencer, USAF

my father moved through dooms of love

through sames of am through haves of give,

singing each morning out of each night

my father moved through depths of height

—E. E. CUMMINGS

and to my father, John L. Fleming

My father didn't tell me how to live; he lived,

and let me watch him do it.

—CLARENCE B. KELLAND, 1881–1964

"The Day Is Gently Sinking to a Close" appears in *The Hymnal*, 1919 ed., published by the Church Pension Fund.

The quotes at the beginning of each section are from *The Book of Common Prayer*, 1979 ed., published by the Church Publishing Company.

A THOMAS DUNNE BOOK FOR MINOTAUR BOOKS.
An imprint of St. Martin's Publishing Group.

www.thomasdunnebooks.com
www.minotaurbooks.com

The Library of Congress has cataloged the hardcover edition as follows:

Spencer-Fleming, Julia.
 To darkness and to death: a Clare Fergusson/Russ Van Alstyne mystery / Julia Spencer-Fleming. — 1st ed.
  p. cm.
 ISBN 0-312-33485-0
 EAN 978-0-312-33485-7
  1. Fergusson, Clare (Fictitious character)—Fiction. 2. Van Alstyne, Russ (Fictitious character)—Fiction. 3. Adirondack Mountains (N.Y.)—Fiction.
 4. New York (State)—Fiction. 5. Missing persons—Fiction. 6. Police chiefs—Fiction.
 7. Episcopalians—Fiction. 8. Women clergy—Fiction. I. Title.

PS3619.P467T6 2005
813'.6—dc22

2005041318

ISBN 978-1-250-01606-5 (trade paperback)

First Minotaur Books Paperback Edition: December 2012

D   10   9   8   7   6   5   4   3

Acknowledgments

I want to thank my husband, Ross Hugo-Vidal, who heroically sat through every children's movie made in the summer of '04 in order to give me time and space to write. If it weren't for Ross, this book would still be a large pile of index cards.

Thanks to my children, Victoria, Spencer, and Virginia, for taking their mother's erratic working hours and long absences during book tours in stride. I owe a debt of gratitude to everyone at St. Martin's Press, especially my editor, Ruth Cavin, who helped me shape a huge stack of manuscript into the story I wanted to tell, and to Toni Plummer, who dealt with my raving phone calls with humor and good grace.

If any of you aspiring authors out there wonder if an agent is worth his fee, the answer is yes, yes, a thousand times yes, in the case of Jimmy Vines and his hardworking assistant Alexis.

Several people read *To Darkness and to Death* in manuscript form, and their suggestions made it a much better book. Thanks to Roxanne Eflin; my parents, John and Lois Fleming; Ellen Pyle; and Mary Weyer. Several other people gave me food, drink, and a place to stay while I roamed about the country talking about my books: Thank you, James and Robin Agnew; Evonne, Dan, and Michelle McNabb; Daniel and Barbara Scheeler; May Lou Wright and Judy Bobalik. And thanks, as ever, to Les Smith, for giving me a longing to inquire into the mystery.

The Day Is Gently Sinking to a Close
—Christopher Wordsworth, 1863

The day is gently sinking to a close,
Fainter and yet more faint the sunlight glows:
O Brightness of Thy Father's glory,
Thou eternal Light of light, be with us now:
Where Thou art present darkness cannot be;
Midnight is glorious noon, O Lord, with Thee.

Our changeful lives are ebbing to an end;
Onward to darkness and to death we tend;
O Conqueror of the grave, be Thou our Guide;
Be Thou our Light in death's dark eventide;
Then in our mortal hour will be no gloom,
No sting in death, no terror in the tomb.

Thou, Who in darkness walking didst appear
Upon the waves, and Thy disciples cheer,
Come, Lord, in lonesome days, when storms assail,
And earthly hopes and human succors fail;
When all is dark, may we behold Thee nigh,
And hear Thy voice, "Fear not, for it is I."

The weary world is moldering to decay,
Its glories wane, its pageants fade away:
In that last sunset, when the stars shall fall,
May we arise, awakened by Thy call,
With Thee, O Lord, forever to abide,
In that blest day which has no eventide.

MORNING PRAYER

When the wicked man turneth away from his wickedness that he hath committed, and doeth that which is lawful and right, he shall save his soul alive.

Ezek. 18:27

Saturday, November 14, 5:00 A.M.

Cold. The cold awoke her, creeping underneath her blanket, spreading like an ache along her hip. She tried to move, to burrow into some warm space, but the cold was beneath her, and then there was a hard, hot twinge of pain in her shoulders and she had a panicky moment of *Where? What?* She tried again. She couldn't move her arms. They were pinned behind her back, her wrists fastened by something sticky and implacable.

Scream. Her cheeks and lips didn't move. Her eyelids felt glued together, but she blinked and blinked until the sting of cold air brought tears to her eyes. Open, closed, the darkness was the same. The darkness, and the cold.

Her brain didn't want to make sense of anything she was feeling. Was she drunk? Was this some sort of game? What had she done? She couldn't remember. She remembered dinner. She had chickpea stew. Homemade bread. Red wine. She could picture the table, laid with her mother's best china. She could remember looking down the long table to where her father's picture hung on the wall, thinking, *I know he'd approve. I know he would.* But then what? Nothing. A blankness more frightening than the cold blackness around her. Because it was inside her. A hole in her mind.

She suddenly remembered a trip to Italy they had taken. She had been ten or eleven then. It was the summer after Gene's mother had died, the only summer they didn't come up to the camp. Daddy had hired a driver to take them on the drive through the mountains to Lake Como, but the morning they were to leave Pisa, he had canceled. An American had been kidnapped. She had been whiny, bored with the university town, eager for the water-skiing and boat rides she had been promised. Daddy pulled up a chair and explained they couldn't risk it. That they would make very good targets. That was the word he used, targets. *Because we're American?* She had asked. *Because we're rich,* he had answered. It was the first time, the only time he had ever said that. *Because we're rich.*

Kidnapped. Oh, God. She squeezed her eyes shut against a spill of hot tears and wished, for the thousandth time, that her father was still alive. To make everything all right.

5:15 A.M.

R ing. Ring. The phone. She snarled, rolled onto her stomach, and pulled her pillow over her head, but the damn thing wouldn't give up. Once. Twice. Three times. With an inarticulate curse, she reached out from under the covers and grabbed the receiver. "H'lo," she said.

"Reverend Fergusson? Did I wake you?" She was spared coming up with an answer worthy of the question, because her caller went on. "It's John Huggins, Millers Kill Search and Rescue. I'm calling you on official business."

I'm so glad it's not personal, she thought, but the only thing her mouth could manage was "Me?"

"You signed up, didn't you?" She could hear the rustle of paper over the line. "Air force training in survival, search, and rescue? Nine years army helicopter pilot? Physically fit, has own gear?"

She shoved the pillow beneath her and propped herself up on her elbows. The only word her sleep-sodden brain latched on to was "pilot". "You want me to fly?"

"Not hardly. We got a young woman reported missing. Went out for a walk last night, never returned. Her brother called it in this morning after he discovered her bed hadn't been slept in."

This morning? She squinted at the blackness outside her window. Didn't look like morning to her. "Why me?"

"Because we're down to the bottom of the list." Huggins said, his voice laced with exasperation. "Two-thirds of the crew are off on loan to the Plattsburgh mountain rescue. They got an old lady wandered away from her home and a pair of hunters who haven't reported in for three days. Can you do it or not?"

The bishop's visit. She pushed away the last of her muzzy-headedness. Half the congregation of St. Alban's would be at the church today, preparing for the dog-and-pony show that was the bishop's annual visit. She should be there. But . . . the search and rescue team needed her. She did sign up. *And hiking through the woods is a lot more appealing than counting napkins and polishing silver,* a treacherously seductive voice inside her pointed out. "Sure, I can do it," she said. "Where should I meet you?"

"A place called Haudenosaunee."

"What's that? A town?"

"Naw, it's an old-time estate. What they call a great camp. Inside the Blue Line."

"The Blue Line?"

"Inside the boundary of the Adirondack State Park." Huggins sounded as if he were having second, maybe third thoughts about calling her.

She rolled out of bed. There was a pencil and a pad of paper on her nightstand. "Give me the directions," she said. "I'll be there as soon as I can."

5:15 A.M.

Ed Castle was sitting in the dark. There was no reason for it, really. He had crept out of his unlit bedroom to avoid waking his wife, but with their door safely shut, he could have snapped the hall lights on. Or turned on one of the lamps in the living room when he unlocked the gun cabinet and tucked his rifle under his arm.

Maybe it was because for so many years he had been up early winter mornings, long gone before his family awoke or the sun rose. Tiptoeing past the doors that had once led to his daughters' bedrooms, he felt a tug, like a hook from out of the past embedded in his heart, and he had wanted to open the doors once again to see them sleeping, all silky hair and boneless limbs.

In the kitchen, he had started the coffee and found his Thermos by touch and the green glow of the microwave clock. He thought maybe he'd need some light to find the box of cartridges he kept hidden behind Suzanne's baking tins on the top shelf, but he hadn't. Now he sat in the dark and thought about the years of his life, which were doled out, it seemed to him, winter by winter, tree by tree, marked by a chain tread and a scarred path leading into the woods. Leading to where he could not see.

The light snapped on, starting him upright in his chair. Suzanne stood in the orange and gold halo of the hanging tulip lamp, zipped into her velour robe, her graying hair every which way. "What on earth are you doing here, sitting around with no lights on?" She stepped toward him, her slippers shush-shushing over the vinyl floor. "You didn't get a call about a fire, did you?" Ed was a member of the Millers Kill Volunteer Fire Department.

"No." He shrugged. "I was thinking about when the girls were little. This was the only quiet time I had back then."

"Well, you're going to get a chance to relive those days." She crossed to the counter and opened a cupboard to retrieve her coffee cup. "I'm watching Bonnie's boys while she's finishing up that big sewing job, and Becky's coming home for the weekend."

He grunted. She waved the pot in his direction, and he held out his mug. "She coming up here to gloat?"

"Stop that," Suzanne said sharply. "She didn't force you to put the business up for sale. You can't make the Adirondack Conservancy Corporation the bad guy in all this. It was your decision."

"I wouldn't have had to make any decision if the ACC wasn't going to cut off my lumbering license." He buried his nose in his coffee cup. "I can't believe my own daughter turned into a damn tree hugger."

Suzanne seated herself at the table. "It's your own fault. You used to sneak her out to your cut sites when she wasn't big enough to tie her own shoes."

One half of a smile crooked his cheek. "You used to carry on something fierce about that."

"A lumbering camp is no place for a four-year-old."

He laughed. "Remember how she would stomp around in a fit if she couldn't come with me?"

"Uh-huh." Suzanne looked at him pointedly over the rim of her cup. "So now she's grown up into someone who loves the woods, is hot-tempered, always speaks her mind—and you can't figure out where she gets it from." She snorted. "The only thing she doesn't favor you in is her hair."

Ed ran his hand over his nearly bald scalp and grinned.

Suzanne rolled her white crockery mug between her hands, a gesture he had seen her make on a thousand cold mornings like this one. "What's really bothering you?"

"Sellin' off the business."

"Thought so."

"I know it makes sense. If this land trade-off goes ahead like it's supposed to, by this time tomorrow the van der Hoeven wood lot is gonna be off-limits to lumbering. By this time next week, the crew and I'd have to head fifty miles north to the nearest open woods. A hundred extra miles a day. Six hundred a week. With fuel prices the way they are, Suze—"

"I know."

"Not to mention the increase in the insurance premium once we start putting that many open-road miles on our trucks."

"I know."

"And we'll be getting hit with more maintenance on the trucks."

"I know."

"I just don't see how we can take the increased cost and survive." He looked down at the rifle resting in his lap. It had been his dad's, along with the timber business. For a moment, he felt cut loose in time, unsure if he was sixty or sixteen. The gun, the woods, the coffee, even. All the same in his father's time. In his grandfather's.

"I always hoped to keep it in the family somehow. Maybe leave it to Bonnie's boys. They love the woods."

She nodded. "They do. On the other hand, do you want them risking their necks sixty hours a week to bring home twenty-five thousand a year?"

He looked at her, surprised. "You never complained."

She laughed quietly. "I was a lumberman's daughter. I knew what I was getting into when I married you."

He put down his coffee and took her hand. The feel of her skin under his thumb was another bright spot against time and the dark. "I called the boys on the crew yesterday. Told 'em I wasn't going out this winter. It's a hell of a thing to do, to tell a man he ain't got the job he's been counting on. But if I sell out now to one of the larger companies, I can get a good price for the equipment. Not great, not with fuel prices high and interest rates low, but decent. Good enough so's we could get a place in Florida. Become snowbirds. Would you like that?"

He watched her roll the thought around in her mouth, tasting it. "It'd be nice," she finally said. "Wearing short sleeves all the time. Gardening year-round."

"No more dark mornings," he said.

She smiled a bit at that. "I'd miss seeing Bonnie and the boys, though. And it would be odd having Christmas where it's sunny and warm." She looked at him more closely. "What are you going to do? I can't imagine you not timbering."

He glanced down at the old rifle in his lap. That was the question, wasn't it? "Man and boy, I've hauled wood out of those mountains forty years now. I don't know what I'll do if I'm not a lumberman. But change is coming, Suze." He rubbed his thumb over her hand again. "And if we don't change with it, we'll get left behind."

5:30 A.M.

Dressed in insulated camos and a blaze-orange vest, Russ Van Alstyne padded downstairs in his stocking feet. Every chair, sofa, and table in the parlor was piled high with meticulously folded draperies, glossy stripes and chintzes that made the room look like a dressmaker's shop gone mad. He shifted a deeply ruffled swag to grab the new Lee Child novel he'd been reading last night and heard the dry crunch of tissue paper stuffed into the folds. No wrinkles for these babies. Unlike him. Straightening, he caught sight of himself in the mirror above the mantle. *I don't look a half-century old,* he thought. *Do I?*

The smell of coffee drew him on to the kitchen. Even in heavy wool socks, the drafts along the two hundred-year-old farmhouse's floor chilled his feet. He stepped into the unlaced boots waiting for him by the mudroom door before pouring himself another cup from the coffeemaker. Boxes of rings and hooks and other curtain-hanging hardware took up all the available space on the kitchen table, so he stood by the sink, looking out the window into the pale darkness, Jack Reacher's adventures abandoned on the counter.

Upstairs, a whirring sewing machine fell silent. A moment later, he heard the stairs creak. "Can I help you load any of this stuff in the car?" he called out.

"Not yet," his wife said, toting what looked like a ball gown through the kitchen. "Let me get rid of this, and I'll be right back." She kneed open the mudroom door and clattered down the steps into the unheated summer kitchen they used for storage. That room led to the barn, where Russ had spent most of the last summer prying up the uneven plank flooring and laying down heavy-duty joists, making it a usable garage for the first time since the horse-and-buggy days. He was actually looking forward to the first big storm of the season, just for the novelty of getting into his truck without knocking snow off first.

"Okay, birthday boy, you ready?" Linda Van Alstyne peeked around the mudroom door. "I couldn't wrap it, so this is all the surprise you get." She emerged into the kitchen cradling a pristine quilted canvas rifle case.

"Whoa," he said.

"Take a look inside." She handed it to him. He unzipped the case. Nestled in the well-padded interior was a .378 Weatherby Mark V.

"Oh. Honey." He drew it out reverently, running a hand along the gunstock walnut, smooth and warm to the touch, like a living thing. "It's beautiful." Rosewood and maple gleamed in the kitchen light. He drew his fingers across the bolt sleeve, etched with scrollwork from another century. "I don't know what to say. This is amazing."

Linda dimpled at him, glowing with cleverness. Dressed in a sweatsuit, her face showing the strain of the past weeks' work, she was still gorgeous, all extravagant curves and touseled blond curls. His very own Marilyn Monroe. "How on earth did you know what to get?" he asked.

"I asked Lyle MacAuley for a list of recommendations." His deputy chief was an avid hunter. "Last time I went to New York to buy fabric, I got it. I'm glad you like it."

"Like it? I love it. I didn't think I'd ever handle a Weatherby outside of a gun shop." He glanced up at her. "Are you sure we can afford it?"

Her dimples vanished. "Russ."

"Don't get me wrong. I love it, I really do. But Weatherbys cost an arm and a leg. I don't want you to be shorting your budget just to get me a pretty gun."

"Stop worrying about the money. I've got more business than I can handle right now with this commission from the Algonquin Waters resort. And if I can pull it all off in time for their grand opening tonight, I'll be able to pick up tons more business."

"Yeah." He replaced the gun in the carrying case. "If that's what you want."

She tugged a dishrag off the faucet and swiped the immaculate counter. "Don't start with me. This is absolutely the right direction to take the business. No more running up curtains for one room or even one house at a time. The spa has almost five hundred installations, counting the interior accent decorations.

That's a year's worth of work. It's my chance to step up to a whole different level."

"I just don't like to see you working so hard—"

"Russell! Hello? Is this the man who can't take a vacation because the police department might fall apart without him?" She tossed the rag into the sink and faced him head-on. "For years, I've been supportive and understanding when you've left dinner on the table to run to a crime scene, or when you've stayed out until 4:00 A.M. working a case, or when you've missed Thanksgiving or Christmas because you're taking someone else's shift. Now it's your turn. I've finally found something I love to do, something I'm good at, something people will pay me for. You've always had that. I haven't. You should be happy for me."

"I am. I know when we retired from the army it was hard on you. I'm glad you've found something to do with yourself." She opened her mouth disbelievingly, and he winced. "I didn't mean it like that. It's just . . . you're spending all your time at the spa these days."

"Have you run out of groceries? Is the house a filthy mess? Are the monthly bills unpaid? I'm keeping up my end, so get off my back."

"Linda." He was making a hash of this, but some shambling monster of marital discord made him open his mouth and wedge his foot deeper in. "It's not the time. You're . . . I hate that you're working with John Opperman." He couldn't stop his voice from tightening when he said the resort developer's name.

She shoved one of the wooden chairs against the table. "Mr. Opperman has been both a perfect gentleman and a generous employer who's committed to hiring locally. If he had gone with a big commercial furnishings company, he'd have his curtains up this morning, instead of having to wait and wonder if I can pull it off before the opening ceremonies tonight." She stalked into the living room. "I have to load the rest of this into my car. You can help, or you can go. Whatever." She scooped up a stack of quilted shades piled so high they looked like bedding for a princess and a pea.

"For chrissakes, give me those. They must weigh a ton." He relieved her of the stack. "I've dealt with Opperman. He smiles at you and he talks real smooth, and all the time he's got the knife out, waiting to stick it in."

"You haven't dealt with him. You've investigated him. Of course you think he's the bogeyman." She shook out a plastic bag and slid several tissue-stiffened swags inside. "One of his business partners was murdered. His other partner tried to kill him. I'm sorry if the case didn't turn out like you thought it would, but honey, it's been over a year. The trial has come and gone, and Mr. Opperman wasn't implicated in any way. Don't you think it's time to let it go already?"

He stomped through the kitchen with unnecessary force.

"He could have taken the insurance money and run," Linda went on. "Instead, he built the resort. He gave a lot of local people jobs, including yours truly." She trailed him through the open mudroom door into the unheated summer kitchen. "Let's face it, honey, you divide the world into two categories, criminals and potential criminals." Her words made vapor puffs in the cold air. "I've worked with him. Believe me. He has a clear conscience."

In the barn, Russ lifted the back gate of her boxy old Volvo wagon and slid the quilted shades in. "Careful of those sheers," she said.

"Jeffrey Dahmer had a clear conscience, too, you know."

She dropped her swags in the back and slammed the tailgate. "You. Are. Impossible." She stomped up the barn steps, strode through the summer kitchen, and let the mudroom door swing in his face.

"Honey," he started, but she held up her hand.

"I don't know why you've been such a grouchy old bastard lately, but it's going to stop." She threw open the refrigerator and pulled out an insulated lunchbox. "Here. I made you a lunch. Take your pretty new gun and go shoot something."

"Honey . . ." He tried again.

She paused in the doorway between the kitchen and the living room. "And don't think all this talk about how terrible Mr. Opperman is will get you out of going to the grand-opening party tonight. I expect you to be here, wearing your tux, car keys in hand, by seven-thirty tonight. Do us both a favor and work out your aggressions on the deer, okay?" She leaned against the doorjamb, crossing her arms over her chest. "Okay?"

"Okay."

He was rewarded with the dimples again. "You're impossible, but I love you."

"I am impossible," he agreed.

"And . . ."

"And I love you, too."

She disappeared into the living room. God, she was still so beautiful. When he had married her twenty-five years ago, he had wanted nothing else than to grow old with her. And now, that had happened. He was fifty years old today. Fifty years old, and in love with another woman.

5:45 A.M.

Clare pulled over to the side of the dirt road and fished her flashlight out of the glove compartment. Her sweet little Shelby Cobra, which had been such a bargain because it was rebuilt, didn't have a working dome light. She thumbed the light on and studied the directions John Huggins had given her. She kept her right foot tromped down hard, because her car also didn't have a functioning parking brake. The timing chain had broken twice since she bought it, and the muffler was about to fall off in a shower of rust flakes, but the Shelby went like she had a 455 rocket, and the heater was a regular blast furnace, a fact she was grateful for on this below-freezing morning.

Okay, she had gone off the paved road and had already passed two dirt roads to her left. Huggins had warned her that the multiple access roads to the Haudenosaunee land would be confusing. According to her directions, she had another half mile to go, and then a right turn into a dirt road marked with stone pillars should bring her to the main camp.

Sure enough, in a matter of minutes she was turning past two riverstone obelisks and wending her way even higher into the mountains over a switchback road drifted deep with dead leaves. She was just starting to worry that she had taken a wrong turn despite the directions when the trees crowding in on both sides of the road opened up and her tires crunched onto gravel.

Her first glimpse of Haudenosaunee surprised her. She was expecting something grand, an Adirondack-themed fantasia with peeled-birch Gothic trim and a rack of antlers over the door. Instead, she faced a simple, two-story log building with a deep-eaved roof and a broad porch that looked more like Wyoming than New York State to her. The house—camp?—fronted a gravel drive almost as wide as it was long. On the far side of the drive, opposite the porch, the trees had been thinned rigorously, leaving a dramatic view of the mountains rolling away to the north. Meant as a summer house, then. One thing Clare had learned in her almost two years in Millers Kill was that no one built a house facing north if he could help it. The view was bracketed by a three-bay garage on one end, also constructed from logs. Its doors, like the house's door and shutters, were trimmed in Adirondack green.

Huggins's black Dodge Ram was parked out front among several other pickups and SUVs. Clare pulled in beside them, a midget in the Land of the Four Wheel Drive.

The clammy chill of the predawn air seized her as soon as she got out of the car. She ducked back in to get her parka and gloves from the passenger seat and nearly cracked her head when someone called, "Reverend Fergusson?" from the camp house's shadowy front porch.

"Yeah, it's me," she said.

"Glad you could make it." He stepped off the porch into the gray light, a compactly built man in a blaze-orange jacket. "Don't know if you remember me, but I'm Duane." He shook her hand.

"Sure," she said. "You're one of Russ's—one of Chief Van Alstyne's part-time officers, aren't you?"

His teeth gleamed in the half-light. "Part-time police, part-time rescue, part-time EMT, full-time pain in the neck, my wife tells me. You got something orange or reflective in there?"

She pulled her Day-Glo green running vest out of the backseat. "I thought this would do."

"Good enough. We don't want you getting shot up by somebody mistaking you for a buck."

She shrugged the vest over her parka while following Duane back to the house. "Is that a real problem?"

He glanced up at the lightening sky. "A beautiful Saturday in November? These woods'll be full of hunters by daybreak. Which could work to our advantage in finding the missing girl. Provided nobody shoots her or us first, of course." Duane led her up the porch steps and opened the door. "We're meeting in here."

Clare tried not to goggle as they entered the house. The outside may have been spartan, but the interior was everything she had hoped for. Turkish carpets covered polished floorboards, twig rocking chairs sat before a crackling fire in a massive stone fireplace, and the walls were hung with Hudson School landscapes and animal heads. She expected Teddy Roosevelt to stride into the room and welcome her at any moment.

Instead, she got John Huggins. "Fergusson! Come on over here. You'd been any later, we would have had to leave without you."

Huggins and the five other members of the search and rescue team were clustered around a dining room table whose shining mahogany surface was cluttered with topographical maps and grease pencils.

Huggins slid a map toward her and continued from where he had apparently left off. "Okay, I want regular check-ins on the radio. We've notified the Fish and Game folks; they'll be telling anyone they come into contact with. If you run across any hunters or hikers, give them the girl's description and remind them of the emergency signal—two shots into the air. But tell 'em to get close and make sure it's the girl—otherwise we'll have excitable fools blasting an alarm every time they spot an old log. We'll regroup and take a break in about three hours." He waved a hand at the men. "You may as well get started. I'll brief Fergusson here." He turned to her. "You bring a GPS unit?"

"Nope," she said.

He made a noise indicating that this lapse didn't surprise him. "Duane, give her a unit and a radio. You do know how these things work, right?"

"The global positioning system enables the carrier of a unit to position him- or herself on an exact latitudinal and longitudinal coordinate by receiving and relaying information through the global satellite system," *Chief*. Huggins reminded her of an old-school crew chief she had worked with in the Philippines who had always referred to her as "the girl" despite the fact that she outranked him. Clare had spit-and-polished him into a grudging acceptance. She figured the same approach might work for Huggins. She flicked on the unit, glanced at the coordinates, and ran one finger across the topo map. "Here we are."

Huggins grunted, but from the corner of her eye she saw Duane grin.

"Who are we looking for? And what are the parameters? How young is the girl?"

"Twenty-six." A rusty voice behind them startled her. She turned to see a thirtyish man detach himself from the deep shadows framing the thick-walled fireplace. Flickering firelight made a crazy quilt of light and darkness out of his face, and as he drew nearer, she saw it wasn't an effect of chiaroscuro. Fire itself, at some time in the past, had shaped half his face, leaving behind taut, glazed skin and ropy keloid scars. "It's my sister. Millie van der Hoeven."

Clare blinked, realized she was staring. "Um, hi," she said. "I'm Clare Fergusson."

He took her hand. The left side of his face was perfectly normal, although he was looking haggard and worn at the moment. The scars ran down his neck, disappearing behind the collar of his plaid flannel shirt, and she guessed the rough, creaking tone of his voice was due to damage, not just emotion over his sister going missing. "Eugene van der Hoeven. You're the priest at the Episcopal church in town, aren't you?"

"Yes, I am," she said, surprised he knew of her. "I haven't seen you around." As soon as the words were out of her mouth, she could have kicked herself.

"I don't get into town much." His head twitched almost imperceptibly to the right. Clare could guess why.

"Mr. van der Hoeven, can you fill Reverend Fergusson in on what happened?" John Huggins's usual brassy tone was downright respectful.

"My sister Millie—Millicent—has been staying with me for the past three months or so. Last night, after dinner, she said she wanted to take a walk. When I got up this morning, she still hadn't gotten home."

"What time did she leave the house?"

"Around eight."

"Didn't take her cell phone?"

"It's still plugged into the recharger in her room."

Clare glanced at Huggins. "That's kind of late to go wandering out into the Adirondack forest, isn't it?"

Eugene frowned, considering. "Is it? I didn't think so. Anyway, she had a flashlight. And there are trails all through these woods."

"Didn't you worry when she didn't show up at bedtime?"

"I was readying myself for bed when she decided to take her stroll." He gestured toward an oak-and-glass gun case mounted on the far wall. "I had planned to hunt this morning."

You and every other man in Millers Kill, Clare thought. She turned to Huggins again. "Is Millie in good shape? Any physical issues that might slow her down? Is she familiar with being in the woods?"

Eugene van der Hoeven answered. "She's in excellent health. I've known her to readily hike ten miles in a day. As for familiarity, she summered at Haudenosaunee every year from the time she was born until she went to college."

"We're guessing she got disoriented in the dark," Huggins said. "If she was smart, and it sounds like she is, she hunkered down under some brush and is waiting on daylight. We're working the search with the starting assumption that she walked for up to two hours before she realized she was lost."

Clare bit off an expletive before it could escape. "That's a six-mile radius."

"Maybe more." Huggins rocked back on his hiking-boot treads. "Hopefully, she figured out she was in trouble after forty-five minutes and she stayed put after that. But I'm not in the hopeful business, so we'll plan for the worst."

6:00 A.M.

Russ downshifted and let his truck grind its way farther up the logging road, bouncing from rock to rut. He figured he was a few minutes away from permanent kidney damage when he spotted a gleam through the trees. Around the last bend, where the road petered out into brush and stumps, Ed Castle had parked his Ford Explorer. Russ pulled up behind him and got out. "Did I keep you waiting?" he asked.

"Naw. Perfect timing. Official daylight's in fifteen minutes. Then we can get started. This gonna be your year, is it?"

"You bet." Russ hauled his pack with his lunch and Thermos out of the cab and settled it over his shoulders. "Twelve points or bust."

Ed snorted a laugh. Russ had been hunting with the man for three falls now and had yet to bring down a yearling stag, let alone one with a twelve-point spread of antlers.

He filled one pocket with spare cartridges and then unzipped his new gun case. Ed whistled as Russ withdrew his Weatherby. "Will you look at that," Ed marveled. Russ held it out for the older man to inspect. Ed rested his own gun against the truck and took the Weatherby reverently. "This is a beaut."

"Birthday present from my wife."

"Now that's a woman. Know what I got for my last birthday from my wife? A dinner out at a restaurant where I had to wear a tie, and a fish on a plaque that sings songs when you walk by it." He stroked the Weatherby's stock lovingly. "You treat this woman right."

"I try."

Ed handed the rifle back to Russ. "Ready?"

"Lead the way."

They walked in silence for a while, watching as branches etched themselves in detail and bittersweet berries flushed from gray to orange in the gathering light. Russ loved the woods this time of year, loved the dry, half-musty smell of the fallen leaves rustling underfoot, loved the snap of the cold and the tracery of frost on tree bark and pine cones. Here and there, a lone oak still held its foliage, and he and Ed brushed under tanned leather leaves, acorn hulls crunching beneath their boots.

"So," Russ said. "Haudenosaunee. I haven't hunted here since I was a kid. Have you heard it's a likely spot?"

Ed shook his head. "More of a busman's holiday for me. I harvest timber from the estate. Or I did. They're setting to close it to timbering after tonight." He glanced up at Russ. "You know about the land deal they've cooked up for this place?"

"Yeah." Russ stepped over a mossy rock. "Some big wood products company is buying the whole estate and then turning it over to the Adirondack Conservancy Corporation. I'm supposed to go to the damn party where they sign the papers tonight."

Ed's eyebrows shot up. "How'd you rate that?"

"Linda was invited. Her business is doing all the curtains for the resort."

"Right, right, that's right. My oldest girl, Bonnie, she does sewing for your wife, you know. Don't think she was invited to the party, though."

"I'd give her my invitation if I could wiggle out of it. Unfortunately, Linda has me in the crosshairs. So I have to show up in a rental tux and make small talk with a bunch of suits." He took a deep breath of the thin, cold air. "Not my favorite way to spend an evening. But my wife cuts me a lot of slack. I owe her."

"I hear that."

They walked on for a while, quiet again, eyes scanning for a telltale flash of white or a trace of spoor. It was true dawn now, rose-gold light shafting high into the treetops from the east, brightness hanging in the air. The deer would be on the move, heading back to their beds, pausing to snatch a mouthful here or there before retiring to sleep away the day.

Over the rise of a slope, the heavy forest opened up to a long glade. Rotting stumps sprouted saplings and mushrooms, and the grass was still shaggy and green under a rime of frost. Spindly young birches and maples shone in the dawn light. The forest was reseeding itself.

"I did this," Ed said. "Cut it eight years back." He gestured upward. "It goes way up, between these two hills."

"How many acres are there?"

"To Haudenosaunee? Two hundred fifty thousand."

Russ whistled.

"Ayeah. It's been my primary harvesting area for a good ten years now. Used to cut in forest that was close enough to make it easy to get to, up past Tenant's Mountain, but Global Wood Products bought it up a decade ago. We'd leased the yearly rights from Haudenosaunee, from way back when it was my daddy and old Mr. van der Hoeven. When I was younger, I didn't understand why my dad didn't do more in these woods, since he paid for the license. But as one piece of land and then another shut down to timbering, I was grateful he'd held this place close to his pocket."

"Isn't the company that's buying the land for the conservancy GWP, Inc.? Is that Global Wood Products?"

"It's their American subsidiary. All these big foreign companies got themselves an American subsidiary these days."

"So why aren't they harvesting the timber themselves?"

"Oh, they may some time in the future. Right now, it's more valuable as a tax write-off to them. It works like this, see. If you're the owner, you pay six, seven dollars an acre on these woodlands in property tax. That's sumpin' like two hundred thousand dollars a year for Haudenosaunee. And the owner pays that whether he's taking timber from the holding, or building vacation homes, or just sitting on it watchin' the leaves fall. The Adirondack Conservancy Corporation loves getting their hands on great big tracts of land like this one. But they're hard-put to buy 'em, unless the owners can afford to give 'em a break on the price. So the ACC teams up with a business like Global Wood Products. The business buys the land and gives the conservancy the development rights to it. GWP takes a big yearly tax write-off, and the conservancy gets to save the woods from guys like me, as they'd say."

"Why doesn't GWP harvest the timber?"

"Don't be fooled—they hold on to the logging rights. They just agree not to exercise 'em for a decade or two and to give the ACC first option to buy 'em outright. Gives 'em a place to put their profits, while locking up some choice timber for the future."

"And meanwhile, the giant corporation gets a reputation as a warm and fuzzy, environmentally friendly kind of place."

"Yeah. And nobody notices that they're getting rid of all the little guys in the timber products business at the same time."

Russ looked at him sharply. "Little guys? Like you?"

Ed shrugged. "Looks like it." He let his gaze drift out over the green and sun-splashed glen he had created. "What the hell. I had a good run. Everything ends eventually." Then his breath caught. He pointed.

At the other edge of the clearing, a young buck emerged from the wood, lured into the open by the rich feeding. Russ had a glimpse, for a moment, of the way it all worked: the man felling trees to make his living, the cleared land running thick with grass, a new feeding ground for the deer. Eventually the trees would grow over it all, and the cycle would begin again. Or not.

Ed nudged him, gesturing, *Take your shot.*

Russ shook his head. He swept his arm, indicating the clearing. *You made it. You take it. It should go to you.*

6:15 A.M.

Officer Mark Durkee straightened his hat as he walked up the driveway toward the entrance of 52 Depot Road. He knew the current tenant, Mike Yablonski, from three disturbing-the-peace calls and a suspicion-of-dealing relating to a large quantity of pot that had circulated through Millers Kill last fall. He knew the man he was here to pick up from Christmas and Thanksgiving dinners.

Mark pressed the buzzer for Apartment B. And pressed the buzzer. And pressed the buzzer. On the fourth ring, he heard a slam and someone clumping down the stairs inside. "For chrissakes, I'm coming! Shut up already!" The door flung open, revealing Mike Yablonski, barefooted, wide-eyed, in sweats and a saggy T-shirt. "Uh," he said.

Mark noted Yablonski neglected to look through the window or even pause to unlock the door before opening it. Not the habits of a drug dealer—at least, not one who hoped to remain in business. Chief Van Alstyne might want to drop him from the watch list. "I'm here for Randy," Mark said. He skipped the pleasantries; he wasn't this man's friend, and he didn't want Yablonski thinking he was.

"Oh. Yeah. Sure." Yablonski leaned forward, looking at the battered blue pickup parked in front of Mark's squad car. "You taking his truck, too?"

"He can come back and get that later. I'm just delivering him home to his wife."

"Sure. I'll go get 'im. You can, um—"

Mark put his foot in the door. "I'll wait here."

Yablonski looked at Mark's shoe. "Yeah. Sure." He trudged up the stairs. Mark examined the walls, old horsehair plaster cracking and bulging away from the lathes. The hallway smelled like cat urine. He crossed his arms, drawing his uniform jacket snugly over his shoulders. The only reason Randy wasn't living full-time in a dive like this was because he had had the good sense to marry a smart woman. Mark's wife's sister. Too bad she hadn't been smart enough to avoid a loser like Randy Schoof.

He heard voices, faintly, from above. "C'mon, man, time to get going. Your brother-in-law's here." Then stumbling steps. Finally, Yablonski appeared, one arm wrapped around Randy's waist, supporting him on his ham-sized shoulder.

"Hey. Mark." Randy waved blearily as his buddy helped him ascend the stairs. "Whaddya doin' here, man?"

"Lisa called me."

"Did I . . . did I forget to call her?"

Yablonski answered. "No, man, you called her last night after you decided not to drive home." The big man looked at Mark, as if seeking approval. "That's what you're supposed to do, right? Stay over, 'stead of driving."

"That's right." Mark reached for his brother-in-law. "C'mon, Randy. I told Lisa I'd bring you home."

"I knew I called her. I always call her. I don't want her to worry."

"Yeah, you're a saint, all right."

Yablonski stepped back, giving Mark space to maneuver Randy out the door. "Hey," he said. "Anybody ever say how much you two look alike?"

"No," Mark said. In truth, he had heard the remark more than once, and it pissed him off every time. Yeah, he and his brother-in-law were both several inches shy of six feet. And they both kept their dark hair short, Mark in the high-and-tight of his academy days, Randy in an angry-white-guy buzz. And they both had more than a few muscles, Mark from regular weekly workouts in his basement gym, Randy from swinging a chain saw and unloading crates and whatever other backbreaking work he could find to keep him in cigarettes. But all anyone had to do was look at the tattoos crawling up and down Randy's arms, at his idiotic Yankees rally cap, at his jeans flopping past his boxers. Nothing could be further from Mark's spit-polish and shine, as he pointed out to anyone tittering about the Bain girls marrying mix-and-match husbands.

He deposited Randy in the squad car and went around to the driver's side. Yablonski was still standing in the doorway. Mark stopped. "Thanks for letting him stay the night," he said grudgingly. Whatever else he thought of Randy's companion, Yablonski had kept Randy from driving drunk. That was worth thanks. "Sorry about waking you so early. I'm on my way home after my shift. This was my only chance to get him."

"No prob. I was planning on hunting today, anyway. You kept me from being later than I would've."

Mark nodded. He slid behind the wheel of the squad car and chucked his hat onto Randy's lap. "Don't throw up on it," he warned as he reversed out of the driveway.

"I'm not going to throw up."

"You look like you're gonna throw up."

"I'm not gonna throw up."

Randy reeked of old cigarettes and stale alcohol. Mark navigated the twists and turns out of town silently. As he drove west, toward the mountains, the rising sun exploded across his rearview mirror. He tilted the mirror and rolled down his window. Cold air battered his face. Randy mumbled something.

"What?"

"I said thanks. For picking me up. I got kinda messed up last night."

Mark considered pointing out that Randy had gotten messed up considerably before last night, starting with dropping out of school at the end of tenth grade.

"I'm losing my job."

"Which one?"

"Working for Castle Logging. The old man called me yesterday morning. Said he was sorry, but he wasn't going to be able to cut the costs of moving the operation up north. So he's putting the business up for sale. Says he'll give me a good reference if I find a job with another timberman."

"Jeez. I'm sorry to hear that." Randy's lumbering job ran from whenever the forest floor froze hard enough to support the weight of trucks and skidders until the thaw threatened to mire the heavy vehicles in their tracks. Usually late November through April. Getting laid off so close to the start of the season would make it hard to find a place on another crew. "Does Lisa know?"

"Yeah."

"What'd she say?"

"She said I'd find something." He slammed a shaky fist against the edge of the door. "Find something. Like what? There's nothing around here in winter except lumbering."

"Take it easy on the car. It's not mine." Mark turned off Old Route 100 onto a dirt road that would shave five minutes off the time it would take to get to the Schoofs' house. They were about as far away from Mark and Rachel's Cossayuharie home as they could get, tucked up in the mountains, inside the Adirondack State Park. "There's plenty of work around here in winter. Retail in the mall—"

"At minimum wage plus a buck or two. Cutting timber paid sixteen thousand in a season. There's nothing else I can do that'll get me that much money."

"Why don't you try going back to work at the mill?"

"Reid-Gruyn? Christ, they're in as bad shape as the lumber industry. Plus, they'd want to put me on the overnight shift like they did last time I worked there. That sucks."

Mark didn't comment on the fact that he worked the dog shift. From the dirt road, he turned onto a county route, startling a passing SUV, whose driver slammed on the brakes at the sight of his black-and-white. "You got a trucking license for Castle, didn't you? Why don't you see if there are any local carriers hiring?"

"Staying up twenty hours in a row and never seeing my wife? No, thanks. Besides, I like working outdoors, not behind a wheel. I just got the license so old man Castle wouldn't have to spend the bucks to hire an outside delivery service. Fat lot of good it did me."

Then go hire yourself out as a compost heap, you complaining sack of shit.

The turn-off to the Schoofs' house was hard to see, just a narrow gravel way shrouded in bony bushes that grasped at Mark's car like witches' fingers. He jounced over a few ruts, then pulled into the clearing in front of the house. He hadn't reached the end of the drive when Lisa bounded out the kitchen door. In her red woolly jacket and matching hat, she looked like a cardinal against the graying house and the November trees. Mark pulled alongside her and killed the engine.

"Hey, babe." Randy staggered out of the car into Lisa's arms.

"Are you all right, baby?"

"Yeah. Still kinda out of it. I'm sorry I didn't come home. I was feeling so lousy about losing my job that the guys started buying me quarter shots to cheer me up."

Lisa looked past Randy's shoulder at Mark. "I gotta ask you another favor."

"What's the problem?"

"I'm supposed to be cleaning at the Haudenosaunee estate right now. My piece-of-crap Ford fell apart last week, so we're down to just Randy's truck. Could you give me a ride?"

Mark's heart sank. He was hoping to catch some quality time with Rachel before she left for her shift at the hospital. Sometimes, if Maddy was still asleep when he got home, they had time for a quick one before Rachel had to shower and get dressed.

His dismay must have shown on his face, because Lisa added, "I'll trade you a favor."

"Like what?"

"I know Rache would love to do something special for your anniversary," Lisa said. They had been married right before Christmas, which had seemed romantic as hell at the time but which in practice meant they ignored their anniversary in the rush of preholiday shopping, cooking, and cleaning. "I'll stay overnight with Maddy, and you two can go to a bed-and-breakfast."

"Yeah? That would be great. Okay, you got it." He suddenly felt a lot cheerier. A bed-and-breakfast. He'd find one with a big fancy four-poster and a fireplace in the room. And a restaurant within walking distance, so they could have a bottle of wine and after-dinner drinks without worrying about driving. He was sprawled across the bed and Rachel was peeling off her clothes in the firelight when his sister-in-law's voice brought him back to reality.

"We gotta go right now." She grabbed Randy by the jacket shoulders and kissed him. "Go to bed and sleep it off, baby."

"How are you going to get home?" Mark asked.

"Randy can come get me on his motorcycle. You'll be okay by noon, won't you, sweets?"

Randy grunted over his shoulder as he shuffled toward the door.

Mark swung back into the squad car, and Lisa dropped into the passenger seat. "Thanks so much. I really appreciate it."

"It's not a big deal," he said.

"Yes it is," she said, "and you're a good sport. You're my favorite brother-in-law."

"I'm your only brother-in-law." He grinned despite himself. He liked Lisa; he always had. Both she and Rachel had inherited their dad's relentless work ethic and their mom's broad streak of common sense. Which is why he still couldn't figure out what she was doing with Randy Schoof. "Are you two going to be okay? With Randy losing his lumbering job?"

"Sure. He'll find something else. He turns jobs up all the time during the rest of the year. I'll see if I can pick up a few more cleaning jobs in the meanwhile. Mrs. Reid, the lady I clean for Thursdays? She says she'd be glad to recommend me to her friends."

Mark kept his mouth shut as he pulled onto the paved road. He and Rachel had both argued with Lisa before. She ought to be in school. She ought to be working a real job, with real benefits and pay that counted toward Social Security instead of cleaning houses under the table. Her answer was always the same. Randy needed her. He needed her steady income. He needed her to do all the things around the house he didn't have time to do. As far as Mark could tell, Randy needed Lisa to wipe his ass for him.

They drove in silence along the winding mountain highway. Dead leaves swirled behind the squad car and rattled into drifts at the edge of the road. The woods were dark now, the colors of October fallen away, the weathered trunks of the deciduous trees rising among the mournful evergreens like smoke from a funeral pyre.

"Slow down. The entrance is right here."

He slowed and turned between two riverstone pillars. There was no indication they were the entrance to the fabled Haudenosaunee, only a mailbox on a wooden post and a sign reading PRIVATE WAY. The road to the great camp wasn't much different from Lisa and Randy's driveway, except that the dense firs and tangled brush were kept back far enough to allow a plow to get through. And you'd need a plow, not a snowblower, Mark realized, as the road wound on and on with no sign of a house. "How long is this drive?" he asked Lisa.

"A couple miles." She looked at him. "What did you expect? It was built to be a wilderness camp. Mr. van der Hoeven told me the paved county road wasn't built until the eighties. Before that, this went six miles and hooked up with Lower Egypt Road."

The trees and brush opened at last to reveal an expanse of gravel, a staggering view of the mountains, and a sweeping two-story log palace. "Wow." He whistled. "It's huge."

"What the heck?" Lisa leaned forward. "What are all these trucks doing here?"

Mark surveyed the ragged row of pickups and SUVs. He was about to ask Lisa where she wanted him to let her off when he spotted a tiny car tucked in behind the bigger vehicles. "Wait a sec." He drove toward the sports car. "This is Reverend Fergusson's car."

"Who?"

"She's the rector over at St. Alban's." He slowed as he passed the back of the car. THE EPISCOPAL CHURCH WELCOMES YOU, read one bumper sticker. The other one told the world MY OTHER CAR IS AN OH-58. "Yeah, it's hers all right."

"How do you know what a minister's car looks like?" Lisa grinned at him uneasily. "Please don't tell me you're finding religion."

"Not me. But I think my boss is."

Lisa raised her eyebrows. He ignored the implicit question. It wasn't anybody's business that the chief had been getting in and out of this car, despite having a perfectly good truck at home. He didn't approve, but he sure as hell wasn't going to gossip about it.

"So, you want me to walk you to the door? Check out what's going on?"

It took him a moment to decipher the expression on her face as reluctance. Getting a ride from her off-duty brother-in-law was one thing, but she didn't want to appear at her employer's door escorted by a police officer asking questions. "Um . . . ," she said.

He grinned, letting her off the hook. "Okay, I get the picture. Give me a call later if you need a ride home."

"Randy'll come and get me."

Yeah. 'Cause he's just so reliable. He watched her whisk around the corner of the house, presumably headed for the kitchen door. He had done what he could. Some people . . . you just couldn't get through to them. His eye fell on the red Shelby Cobra, its chrome winking in the early sun. Some people . . . were going to shoot themselves in the foot no matter what you did.

6:45 A.M.

She opened her eyes and saw it was light. It must have been growing brighter for some time now, but after her first thrashing panic attack, she had drifted into a stupor of defeat. She didn't want to—she couldn't—think about what was happening to her, what might happen to her. So she went away, inside her head, tuning out her body and her surroundings.

But now it was light. Suddenly, she was aware of everything. Her arms were numb. Her hip felt bruised, her neck muscles bunched and painful. Her stomach growled. She had to pee.

She rolled across the wooden floor, out of the blankets that had enclosed her. She was wearing one of her flannel shirts and sweatpants, but whether she had dressed herself or someone else had was a mystery. She had on socks and hiking boots, and her ankles had been wound about with duct tape in a wide figure-eight. Probably the same stuff that covered her mouth and held her wrists pinned behind her back. Somehow, she had expected something more exotic. Not the old handyman's standby.

She twisted fully onto her back and contracted her stomach. She slowly jackknifed into a seated position. The effort left her trembling and breathing heavily through her nose. If she could just get to her feet . . . she tried rolling forward, but her knees wouldn't spread far enough. She wiggled from side to side until she flopped over again, but she couldn't get her feet beneath her. Tears of frustration stung her eyes. She rolled, contracted, got herself seated again.

She was in a small room. *Cell.* Unfurnished, except for the tumble of blankets that had kept her warm and a five-gallon bucket. She could guess what that was for. One wall, to her left, was post-and-beam timber, with a small and solid door set well into a massive lintel. The other wall curved around her in a perfect half circle, its dressed stone pierced with three . . . *arrow slits.* A tower. A stone tower. She was being held prisoner by the sheriff of Nottingham. Beneath her duct-tape gag, she started to laugh. She laughed and laughed until her breath caught in short hitches and she was gasping, flaring her nostrils, sucking down oxygen.

She finally settled herself down. She was sweaty from her contortions and her panic attack. She wrenched her wrists up and down, hoping her skin was slick enough to slip beneath the duct tape. Nothing. She snorted in disgust. At least she was warm now.

Then she looked around again. The stone walls, the arrow slits. She realized where she was. And suddenly she was very, very cold.

6:45 A.M.

L eft. Right. Left. Right.

Clare forced herself to keep her steps even, her head moving methodically as she climbed up the increasingly steep slope. Tramping through the woods on a fine and frosty November morning was great. It was the actual searching part of it that was, well, boring. After an hour, she had given up on the idea that she was going to stumble over a tearfully grateful Millie van der Hoeven at any moment. She was, she had to admit, too impatient to be a naturally good searcher.

So to compensate, she plodded. She looked from side to side with mathematical precision. She called out, "Millie? Millie van der Hoeven!" every five minutes by her watch. She tried to keep her attention focused on where she was and what she was doing, rather than worrying about tomorrow's visit from the bishop. Everything was going to go fine. Glenn Hadley had waxed the woodwork until you couldn't lean against the old rood screen without slipping to the floor. The altar guild was coming in today to polish the silver—oh, God, the locked cupboard. Where the good stuff was stored. She thought of the little key, hanging from her key chain. Which was in her car. Did Judy Morrison have a copy?

The scratch and tug of brambles drew her back to the present. She was taking the path of least resistance through the undergrowth, but a tangle of blackberry stopped her. She backed off and thrashed sideways through a thigh-high stand of brown, papery fern to where the trees grew taller and the vegetation was scarcer. This was ridiculous. No one would have fought her way uphill through this in the dark of night. Even if she thought she knew where she was going.

"Millie! Millie van der Hoeven!" It wasn't even seven o'clock and she was already well and truly grubby, one leg slimed where she had slipped on some rotted leaves, her clothing pocked with tiny burrs and clinging seeds, riding along in a last-ditch attempt at procreation. Despite the freezing-point temperature, she had worked up a sweat, and she guessed a mirror would reveal dirt grimed on her face. She would have to scrub herself down as soon as she could—she could just imagine meeting the diocesan deacon like this. The bishop's front man, he was scheduled to arrive today to make sure all was in readiness for the visit. Normally that meant transporting the bishop's elaborate vestments and going over the paperwork of candidates for confirmation, but Clare had received a letter just last week from Deacon Aberforth inviting her to a "chat" Saturday. Attendance, she gathered, was not optional. It was probably routine. She was closing in on her second year at St. Alban's; they were in the middle of a capital campaign. He was probably just taking her temperature. Unless . . . *unless someone told him about you and the chief of police,* a voice in her head pointed out. It sounded like Master Sergeant Ashley "Hardball" Wright, the man who had tormented her and taught her and toughened her up during her survival training. *When you're behind the lines, don't forget about friendly fire,* Wright said. *It may be coming from your team, but it'll kill you just as quick as your enemies.*

She shook off the thought. Looked left, right, left again. Maybe the missing woman was over the next rise. Maybe.

7:30 A.M.

Shaun Reid pretended to sleep. His wife moved through the darkened room quietly, slipping into her running gear, easing herself onto her side of the bed in order to tie her shoes. She leaned over him and kissed his temple softly. He let that rouse him enough to open his eyes.

"Go back to sleep," Courtney said. "I just wanted to give you a kiss. I may not see you until this afternoon. After my run, I'm doing some shopping and then heading straight over to St. Alban's."

He made a sleepy, inquiring noise.

"Tomorrow's the bishop's visit. Please don't tell me you've forgotten. I'm chairing the preparation committee. How will it look if my husband doesn't come to church? Just this once? For me?" She kissed him again before rolling off the bed. "I dropped your dinner jacket off at the dry cleaners. Make sure you pick it up before they close."

He closed his eyes and kept them closed, listening to the tread of her running shoes disappear through the hallway, down the stairs, through the foyer. When he heard the *thunk* of the front door, he opened them again.

The bishop's visit. Maybe he should go. The last time he had been to church was their wedding, seven years ago. But what the hell. He needed divine intervention at this point. *Dear God, I'm in deep shit. Give me a shovel.*

An acid twinge scorched his stomach. He heaved himself out of bed and headed for the bathroom. He had a few antacids left in the giant economy-sized bottle he had bought. Last week. He needed to see his doctor, get a prescription, but he had been too pressed for time. Pressed for time. And now he was almost out.

He shook four tablets into his palm and knocked them back, crunching them into powder before swallowing. He winced at the chalky-sweet taste. He examined himself in the mirror. Christ, he looked terrible. Like he hadn't slept in a week. Maybe a month. He bent over the sink and splashed cold water in his face. He couldn't meet Terry McKellan looking like he was on the edge of a breakdown. Confidence. That's what he had to project. Energy. Resoluteness.

He checked himself out again. Tried a smile. Maybe caffeine would help.

In the kitchen, he plugged in the machine and shook a mound of ground coffee into the filter. He thought about cereal or toast, but his stomach roiled in protest. When the coffee was done, he took a cup into his office. His desk, his papers, his open laptop drew him unwillingly, in the way that a gruesome accident demands you slow down and stare. He set his mug beside the computer and turned the machine on. A spreadsheet sprang to life. He went over the numbers again, as if the cobbler's elves might have come in and done some creative accounting for him while he slept, but no such luck. They were exactly as they had been last night, as they had been at yesterday's board of directors' meeting, as they had been since GWP, Inc., had pinned Reid-Gruyn in its massive sights and indicated it might be interested in acquiring the operation.

Shaun had thought he was safe. He had thought they were too small to draw any of the big boys' attention. Too specialized. With too slim a margin of profit. That was what was going to sink them, now.

"We're not saying that we like the idea of selling up to GWP," Clyde McAllister had said at the directors' meeting. "But let's face it." He pointed to the spreadsheets in front of him. "If we have to start importing pulp from Canada, the additional costs are going to cut our after-tax profits to the bone. The next slack time or economic downturn, we'll have to start eating our own belly to survive. We have to recommend the takeover be placed before the shareholders."

Where were all the directors that jumped through hoops at their CEO's command? Why didn't he have any? Just a group of stone-faced men and women, people who had known him since childhood, for chrissakes, telling him it was their responsibility to the shareholders. Tolling a death knell for the business he had inherited from his father, and his father's father, and his father before him.

His hand closed over a short stack of correspondence. Replies from merchant banks in New York, declining to invest in upgrading the depreciable assets, declining to lend the business capital, declining his corporate applications for loans that would let them buy back stock. Terry McKellan was his last hope. If Shaun could get a personal loan, enough to increase the family shareholdings from 49 percent to 51 percent, he could stop the buyout dead in its tracks.

"If it weren't for the sale of the Haudenosaunee woods, Shaun." That had been Elaine Parkinson. "If we weren't losing that source of pulpwood, we wouldn't be entertaining this motion. But the new numbers don't add up."

He had read a science fiction story once about a girl who stowed away on a spaceship that was bringing medicine to some far-off planet. The ship had just enough fuel to make it—without the added weight of the girl. So the pilot had shoved her out the airlock. He had been regretful and all, but hey, it was the good of the many against the good of the one. It had been titled "The Cold Equations." That was what he was in the grip of: cold numbers. Estimates of the cost of pulp imported from Maine, from Canada, from the northernmost reaches of New York. Cold places, where the forests grew unbroken for a million acres and lumbermen drove in in the dead of winter so their ten-ton machines wouldn't mire on dirt trails. Places he could fly to in an hour, or two, or three. But you can't fly lumber out. You haul it, board inch by board inch, and every foot of the way costs: the taxes, the insurance, the man-hours, the fuel.

His board of directors had read all the cold numbers. And they were willing to throw Reid-Gruyn out the airlock.

He opened a drawer and swept the politely worded turndowns into it. He turned off his laptop. Time to hit the shower. Put on his most expensive casual clothes—no suit; he wanted to look affluent, not desperate—and go see the corporate loan officer of AllBanc. His last chance. He paused in the doorway. *I'm looking for that shovel. Any time now.*

8:00 A.M.

She counted off the exits as she drove past them. Tuxedo. Half Moon. Clifton Park. Saratoga Springs. Every mile Becky Castle put between herself and Albany felt like another stone rolling off her shoulders. She was headed home for the weekend. Home to the mountains. She triggered the cruise control and jammed her finger on the radio scan button until she found a bouncy country song she loved. *"Just before dark, jump in the car . . ."* she sang, wishing she had a convertible so her hair could whip all around. Except they didn't make hybrid convertibles yet.

Before ski season and after leaf peeping, the Saturday morning traffic was light on the Northway. She had missed the turning leaves, missed them entirely this year, cooped up in the Adirondack Conservancy Corporation's office in Albany writing grants and copyediting the *Your Adirondacks . . . and You!* brochure. It was not what she had envisioned when she had joined the conservancy. Not by a long shot. She had pictured herself in the thick of things, carrying a green banner, saving land for future generations. Now, thanks to Global Wood Products, Inc., she was going to get her chance.

Becky was the one who had put it together. She was the one with the personal contacts with the Haudenosaunee heirs. She was the one who had sold the idea to her higher-ups at the Adirondack Conservancy Corporation. She was the one who came up with a list of prospective buyers, researched the tax advantages, met with the executives of GWP. She was the one who had wrangled, cajoled, kissed up to, persuaded. And tonight, she was going to be at the head table with the conservancy's president and lawyer, at a ceremony that would take a quarter of a million acres out of private hands, restoring it to the "forever wild" state called for in the New York constitution.

She grinned as the Glens Falls–Queensbury sign disappeared behind her. She was, no lie, officially Hot Stuff. Suddenly she couldn't wait to talk with Millie. She fished her phone out of her bag and speed-dialed her friend's number. The phone rang once, twice, three times, then Millie's voicemail clicked on, asking her to leave a message.

"Hey, girlfriend. What are you, sleeping late? I'm in my car, headed for Millers Kill, so give me a call when you get this. Love ya!"

As her thumb hit the end-call button, she realized she should have told Millie she was coming to Haudenosaunee this morning. Maybe she could reach her using the camp's phone? Becky scrabbled through her bag, hauling out a bottle of water, her camera, a Baggie of yogurt-covered raisins. She finally found her address book, flipped it open, and laid it on her knee. She entered the number and pressed the send button.

The phone barely had time to ring. "Hello?"

Becky blinked at the unfamiliar female voice. "Hi. I'm trying to reach Millie van der Hoeven?"

"I'm afraid she's not here." The voice on the other end seemed to deflate.

"Have I reached Haudenosaunee?"

"Sorry. I mean, yes, you have. I'm sorry, I should have said. I'm Lisa. I'm Mr. van der Hoeven's . . . I clean house for him."

"Okay. Can I leave a message for Millie?"

There was a long pause. Becky wondered if Millie's brother, Eugene, had hired some sort of mentally disabled woman to work for him.

"Look, when I said she wasn't here, I didn't mean she's gone out shopping or anything," Lisa said. "I mean she's missing. Supposedly she went out for a walk last night and never came back. There's a search and rescue team out looking for her right now."

The Northway stretched out ahead of her, long and gray and undulating over rise and hollow. "Missing?"

"Are you a friend of hers?"

"Yeah. I'm . . ." What was she? Were there special categories of friends that got information? And others who would have to wait to read about what happened to her? Becky went for the easiest, the longest-running, choice. "I'm her college roommate."

"If you leave me your number, I can make sure someone calls you. When we know something."

Becky shook her head. "I'm going to be at Haudenosaunee later this morning."

"She'll probably be back by then." Lisa's voice was hearty and hollow. "You can talk to her yourself."

"Right." The sign for the Millers Kill exit flashed by. Her heart thumped. She braked too fast, and a station wagon swerved past her, horn blaring. Becky signaled, swiveled to look behind her, and veered into the right-hand lane. "Thanks," she managed to say into the phone. "Talk to you later."

"Can I say who—" But she had cut off the signal and dropped the phone into the passenger seat before the housekeeper could finish her sentence.

She took the exit and turned northwest, to the road that would lead her to Fort Henry and Cossayuharie and Millers Kill. Missing. Millie. The woman who had hiked the Appalachian Trail through New York and New England. Who ice-climbed in British Columbia. Who had summitted the Grand Teton from her adopted home out west.

Something has happened to her. With that thought came another, one she was ashamed of. *The deal. The deal will fall apart without her. And then where will I be?*

The questions hung in the stale air around her. She lowered her window, letting the icy air whip through her car. She wanted to concentrate on her friend, on the edge of worry coiling low in her stomach, but she was picturing herself standing on a platform with the president and CEO of GWP, Inc., and her bosses from the Adirondack Conservancy Corporation. They were all waiting . . . waiting . . . waiting.

She stopped for a red light. Early shoppers trickled into the Super Kmart parking lot. Through the windshield, she could see the road to Bonnie's house, just past a nursery shuttered down against the coming winter. She flicked on her turn signal. She needed comfort, and encouragement, and reassurance. That meant she needed her big sister.

Bonnie was almost twelve years older than Becky, the long gap between them punctuated by several miscarriages their mother didn't like to talk about. When Becky was a little girl, her sister had been like another mother to her, a young, fun version who painted Becky's nails and taught her to dance to Adam Ant's *Strip*. In her teens, thrashing against the confines of their small town and their parents' overburdening protectiveness, Becky would escape to Bonnie and James's house, to play with their little boys and complain endlessly to her sister. Becky was long past that stage, and long gone from Millers Kill, but her career as an environmental advocate was a touchy subject with her parents, and she still looked to Bonnie as the conduit, the place where the family's lines of communication crossed.

The Liddles lived in a small ranch, flanked by houses that had been identical when they were built in the 1950s. A half century of tinkering by owners had personalized them, although their tightly controlled lawns and greenery still gave them a certain sameness. Becky parked behind Bonnie's Taurus, walked up the drive, and let herself in.

Her younger nephew, Patrick, sprawled pajama-clad on the couch, gazing slack-jawed at a hyperkinetic Japanese anime on the tube. "Hey," Becky said.

His eyes snapped into focus. "Aunt Becky!" He jumped up and hugged her.

"How are you, Squirtle?" The nickname wasn't going to fit him much longer. It looked like he had shot up at least three inches since she last saw him.

He wrinkled his nose in scorn. "Nobody's into Pokémon anymore, Aunt Becky."

Uh-oh. Better rethink her Christmas gift. "Where are your folks?"

Patrick collapsed back onto the couch. "Dad's taking Alex to a meet. Mom's sewing."

Just then, her sister bellowed, "Patrick! You had better be in your clothes, young man. You're going to Grandma's in five minutes!"

"Okay, Mom!" Patrick didn't move.

Becky crossed through the kitchen to the sun-splashed addition James had built four years back. It was a dining room–family room–sewing room ell, and she could hear Bonnie before she could see her, the sewing machine whirring, her sister muttering under her breath.

"Don't let me startle you," Becky said.

Bonnie whipped around in her chair. "Good grief, what are you doing here?"

"I'm on my way to Mom and Dad's." Becky slid a pile of folded fabric to one side and made herself at home on the built-in bench. The bright fabric, the sunshine, the hominess of the room lifted her spirits again. She smiled smugly. "I'm going to be at the signing of the Haudenosaunee land transfer to the conservancy tonight."

"Believe me, I know. Mom hasn't stopped talking about it. Neither has Dad."

"Is he still pissed at me?"

"Who knows. He's tearing what hair he has left out over selling the lumbering company. But he's also bragging about 'our college girl.'" Bonnie turned back to her machine. "While you're wining and dining with the upper crust, be sure to check out these curtains. Made by yours truly."

"You're making curtains for the new hotel?"

"Linda Van Alstyne got the contract. There are two other seamstresses besides me on the job."

"Shouldn't they be done already? I mean, the grand opening is tonight."

Bonnie looked at her sideways. "Thanks for the reminder. Yes, they should already be done. I've got at least two carloads to run up to the spa, and I still have to take Pat to Mom's."

"He can come with me."

"Really? That would save me a half hour."

"Sure. I don't have anything to do until later this morning." She opened her mouth to tell her sister about her other responsibilities for the Haudenosaunee land transfer, then closed her trap. Her sister got the brunt of their parents' opinions on Becky's life. Bragging about how great she was would be uncool. She needed to be sensitive to her sister's position. Like Millie, who had always been careful not to draw attention to the fact that her family was richer than Croesus. Millie.

"I tried to call Millie this morning, and she's gone missing."

Bonnie raised her eyebrows without taking her eyes off the raw silk gliding beneath her needle.

"According to the housekeeper, she went out for a walk last night and got lost. The search and rescue team is looking for her."

"What's the big deal?" Bonnie stopped the machine. "She's probably out there somewhere with a knapsack on her back. Val-de-ree, val-de-rah." She pulled the curtain forward and snipped the trailing threads with her scissors.

"She wouldn't just go wandering off. Not on the most important day—" Becky broke off before she could complete the sentence. *Of my career.*

"That sounds exactly like something she would do. That girl's got all the dependability of a mountain goat." Bonnie stood, shaking the curtain out. "Help me fold this."

"That's not true. She's taking responsibility for her brother Eugene. She wants him to come live with her in Montana." Becky took the end of the drapery and brought it up to meet her sister's hands. "Why do you dislike Millie?"

"I don't dislike her. I think she's a spoiled little rich girl, and I think she's been a bad influence on you."

"On me?" She and Bonnie each took an end and brought it up. They met in the middle.

"She can afford to spend her life living in trees to save old-growth forests and traveling the country to every ecoprotest meeting there is. She doesn't have to work for a living. But you do."

"I have a job! A good one. I have a health plan!"

Bonnie folded the curtain over her arm and laid it on a pile of similarly colored chintz. "You spent two years living hand to mouth after college, following Greenpeace ships around. Stuffing envelopes for fund-raisers and writing grants for crackpot back-to-the-land groups. Is that why Mom and Dad sacrificed to send you to school? They wanted you to have a better life."

"I like my life. I'm doing work that's important to me and to the world around me. It pays enough for me to live the way I want to. I don't need a lot of money or things."

"Oh, grow up." Bonnie twisted around. "Patrick! If you aren't dressed with your bed made now, you're never watching TV again!" She turned back to Becky. "Someday you're going to be married and have children. Believe me, when you have to tell your kid that he can't go to the college of his choice because you can't afford it, you'll feel differently."

Becky bit her lip. "Alex?"

Bonnie scooped up a stack of curtains. "He got accepted at Cornell. But the aid package wasn't enough." She nodded toward another pile of cloth. "Grab those, will you?"

"So where is he going?"

"State University at Plattsburgh. Between the loans and the track-and-field scholarship, we can manage it. I hope. If the car lasts another four years and we don't have any medical bills."

Becky followed her sister. She was amazed to find Patrick fully dressed in the living room. He had even remembered to brush his hair. "Get your Game Boy if you want to bring it to Grandma's," she said. "I'm driving you."

"All right," he said. "Can we stop at Kmart? There's this game cartridge I want to look at."

"Maybe," she said. She carried the curtains out to Bonnie's car and shoved them in alongside the rest of the piles and boxes.

"It's game cartridges and braces and shoes and class trips." Bonnie leaned, on one hip, against her aging Taurus. "It never ends, Beck. And then when the kids are gone, you have to think about yourself, about whether you can retire, whether you can afford to move to a place where you can walk around outside in the winter without worrying about breaking your hip."

"You mean like Mom and Dad."

"God only knows, I understand the lure of those woods. It's kept them scraping by for forty years. But it's sucked so much life out of them. Dad may be cussing and kicking about selling out, but I think it's the best thing to happen to them in a long time. If he can get a decent price for the business." There was an edge to Bonnie's voice. In the cold sunlight, Becky could see the lines around her eyes.

She shifted from foot to foot. The deal she was so proud of, the deal that was going to make her a player in the conservancy and in the national arena of land preservation, was the reason her dad was selling Castle Logging. She wanted everything she was going to get from this deal, but she also wanted her parents to be healthy and solvent and living in the same house they had always lived in, not forced into retirement. "I'm sorry," she said, not really sure what she was sorry for.

Patrick bounded out of the house. "Go back and get a coat on!" his mother yelled. Bonnie let out an impatient breath. "Don't worry. It's me. It's been—things have been tense with them lately. Everything will be okay."

Because Becky wanted to, she tried to believe.

8:45 A.M.

R uss had been prepared for the sight of Haudenosaunee. He knew the history of the camp, and although he had never been a visitor before, he had seen black-and-white photos of the World War II–era construction, deliberately simple in a time when both men and materials were hard to come by. He had been prepared for the glorious view of the mountains, where the trees and brush had been cut away to expose range after range fading into the northwestern sky. What he hadn't been prepared for was the number of vehicles parked in the drive.

"What the hell's going on?" Ed Castle asked, descending from his SUV. They had pulled in along one side of the drive, closest to the road out, intending to thank Eugene van der Hoeven for opening his land and to let him know about the fine six-point buck dangling off an old bike carrier bolted to the back of Ed's Explorer.

Russ walked past his hunting partner toward the row of trucks. He pointed toward the nearest, a wide-bed pickup with double rear wheels supporting metal gear lockers. "This is John Huggins's." He glanced at the next truck. "Uh-huh. And here's a search and rescue sticker." He turned toward the log house. "Let's see what the search and rescue team is doing here, shall we?"

Russ let Ed lead the way. The older man rang the doorbell. The wait for someone to answer was long enough for Ed to turn to Russ with a worried frown, but then the door opened, cutting off whatever it was he might have said.

"Ed Castle. Hello."

"Eugene." Ed shook hands with the man in the doorway. "Good to see you again. I've been hunting on your property today, brought a friend of mine. I don't know if you've met him. Russ Van Alstyne. Police chief down in town."

Russ had heard the stories, of course, so the face that turned to him wasn't too much of a shock. "Mr. van der Hoeven." He extended his hand. "You've got good hunting land up here."

Van der Hoeven's grip was cool and dry. "I like to think so. Did you take anything?"

Russ shook his head. "Afraid not. But Ed here harvested a beauty."

"Six points." Ed rocked back and forth on his heels, every orange-and-camo-clad line of him radiating satisfaction. "We field-dressed the old boy and hung him up, and after having to do some work, Russ decided he'd had enough."

Russ smiled good-naturedly. "No use letting the meat sit around getting old. Gotta get it home and butcher it."

"It's just as well." Eugene looked toward the woods visible from his front door with an expression of resignation. "The search and rescue team is out there searching for my sister. Any game in the area is gone to ground today."

"Your sister?" Russ spoke more sharply than he had intended to.

Eugene looked at him for a moment, then stepped back from the door. "Why don't you two come in?"

Ed made some noise about their smell—dressing out a buck wasn't a clean process—but Russ followed van der Hoeven in without comment. He didn't think a little fresh blood from a healthy deer made them offensive. He had seen and smelled far, far worse in twenty-seven years as a cop.

The interior of the great camp should have felt welcoming. The wood and rugs made patches of quilt-warm color, and the spindly antiques were balanced by genuinely comfortable chairs and sofas, but there was something off-putting about it. Cold. Maybe it was the sheer size of the place; the living room–dining room was almost as big as the footprint of Russ's house.

"I set some coffee and pastries out for the searchers. May I offer you anything?" Van der Hoeven waved toward a sideboard that would have filled up half the Van Alstynes' kitchen.

"No. Thanks."

Ed wasn't as reticent, grabbing a muffin out of a basket made of looping silver wire set next to a coffeemaker.

"So what's this about your sister?" Russ asked.

"Maybe I should have rung up your people instead of John Huggins." Eugene's gaze was unfocused, as if he were looking into the misty past. "But I reasoned the only thing the police could do would be calling out the search and rescue team."

"Are you sure she's lost?"

"It's the only thing I can think of." Van der Hoeven ran a hand over the back of his head, smoothing his overgrown hair, bunching it into a little ponytail in his fist. "Millie and I were having dinner last night—"

"Millie is your sister?"

"My younger sister, yes. Our older sister, Louisa, lives in San Francisco. Anyway, after dinner, she said she was going to take a walk. I was tired, and planning on getting up early to hunt, so I said good night. When I arose this morning, she wasn't in her room. Her bed hadn't been slept in. I took a quick turn around the paths and buildings nearest to the house, and as soon as it was obvious she wasn't anywhere nearby, I phoned search and rescue."

"What time did your sister go out on her walk?"

"We dined at eight, so it must have been close to nine."

Russ looked at the dining table, a shining mahogany plain dominating the room. Hell of an overkill for two people. "Kind of late to be taking a stroll in the woods, wasn't it?"

"The lady on the search team said the same thing."

Russ raised his eyebrows. He hadn't heard of Huggins adding any new members to the team. Let alone a woman.

"I'll tell you what I told her," van der Hoeven went on. "Millie knows this land. It's been in our family since the time of the Civil War. She and I have roamed these woods and hills since we were first able to walk. It wouldn't intimidate her any more than an after-dinner stroll around the block would scare you." He bunched his hair in his hand again. "However, that's not to say she couldn't get lost. I've done it myself on more than one occasion, and thank God it's always been in daytime and I've managed to run across a familiar marker to lead me home." He looked toward the door, as if expecting his sister to burst in at the next moment. "I have confidence in her woodsmanship. As soon as she realized she was lost, Millie would hunker down and make a shelter."

She'd have had to. It must have been in the midtwenties last night. The temperature was probably just breaking freezing right now. Still, if she had the sense to pull some pine branches over her as a windbreak and bury herself in dead leaves, there was no reason to suspect she wouldn't come through okay. Scared and cold, but okay. Unless . . .

"There's no chance she might have taken off by herself? Driven into town to meet someone?"

Van der Hoeven shook his head. "Her car's in the garage." He pronounced it oddly, accenting the first syllable.

"Could someone have come up here to meet her? After you were in bed?"

"No. Well . . ." Van der Hoeven paused. "It's not impossible, but it's damned unlikely. I don't have many guests." His head twitched to the left. "And my sister doesn't live here. She's just visiting."

"No old friends looking her up?"

"None that have made themselves known to me."

Russ thought that was a damn funny way to answer the question. Then again, van der Hoeven was clearly ill at ease with other human beings. Russ was framing a polite way to pry further into Millie's personal life when the front doorbell rang. Eugene gave him a pained look before excusing himself. Poor bastard. He was probably seeing more people today than he normally would in the course of a year.

Ed Castle sidled up to Russ, brushing muffin crumbs off his face. "What's with the third degree?"

Russ shrugged. "There's a woman missing. It's my job to ask questions."

"I thought you were off today?"

Like Linda. Like anyone with a normal job; you're either working or not working. "I'm off in the sense that I don't have to be at my desk or on patrol. I'm on duty in the sense that I'm always on duty. Crime never sleeps and all that."

Ed grunted.

At the door, visible from their slice of the living/dining room, a pair of men were stamping their boots and brushing off their jackets before entering the great camp. Russ heard Huggins's voice booming off the rafters. "Mr. van der Hoeven! Hope you don't mind us showing back up. 'Fraid we're empty-handed. Mind if we use the facilities and help ourselves to some more coffee?"

Eugene was murmuring something about his housekeeper making them breakfast while the guys on the rescue squad walked warily through the door: Russ's part-time officer Duane; Dan Hunter, who worked at AllBanc; Huggins's cousin Mike; and at the tail end, the "lady searcher" Eugene had mentioned. She tugged a knit toque off, and her hair, the color of sunshine through whiskey, fell to her shoulders in a messy tangle. Her oversharp nose and blunt cheekbones were red from the cold, her lips were colorless and chapped, and her parka and stained twill trousers hid any suggestion of her figure.

When he had first seen her, he had thought her plain. He could remember the thought, remember his sober assessment of her face and form. When had she become beautiful to him? She laughed at something Duane said and, laughing, turned, and that was when he met her eyes.

Oh, love.

8:45 A.M.

The radio hanging from her shoulder crackled. "Fergusson?"

"Fergusson here."

"See anything?"

"A lot of trees. No sign of Millie van der Hoeven, though."

"Okay, come on back. We're gonna debrief and take a break."

"I'll be there." She thumbed off the radio. She was glad she had her GPS unit and her map. From where she stood, the forest stretched out vast and quiet, seemingly unbroken and eternal. She knew she walked on Haudenosaunee land, that lumbermen and hunters and hikers all came here, shaping it and leaving their marks, but slipping between the grave gray alders and the massive toad-colored oaks, the idea that humans could own this land, that anyone had ever set foot where she was stepping now, seemed unreal.

She hiked over a rotting log, crushing coffee-brown pulp and meaty fungus beneath her boots. The smell, rich and wet, mingled with the odor of pine sap. A flash of movement caught her eye, and she whirled, just in time to see a gray fox vanish like smoke into the earth.

With no slow and careful searching to delay her, the walk back was much faster than the walk out. The trail became more and more pronounced. She passed one trailhead to a waterfall—marked on her map—and one to the tumbledown 1860s camp house, ditto. She thought about taking a detour to get a look at either of the sights, but her stomach growled in protest. If her conscience wouldn't keep her on the straight and narrow, evidently her appetite would.

The trees thinned, and she saw the rest of them, hurrying along the trail toward the low rock wall that encircled Haudenosaunee's back garden. Duane, straggling behind the others, waved. "Hey, Reverend."

He waited while she passed through the gate, crossed the still-thick grass, and skirted a flagstone patio running almost the length of the house.

Tarp-covered shapes marked the outdoor table and chairs, and empty chains hung loose from a wooden frame. She imagined a wicker swing, too delicate to last outside through the long Adirondack winter.

"Pretty nice, huh?" Duane thumbed toward the French doors. "How'd you like to come out here for a barbecue?"

"Right now, I'm more interested in checking out the bathroom," she said, heading around the corner toward the thrum of voices at the front of the house. She and Duane strode past the brown stalks and seed pods marking the graves of perennial borders. They crunched across part of the gravel drive, mounted the steps, and came to a halt, stymied by a logjam of searchers, all trying to squeeze through the front door at the same time. She turned for a look at the long mountain view and saw Russ Van Alstyne's pickup parked at the edge of the drive.

Her heart made a ridiculous, giddy ger-thump. She breathed in deeply. Okay, there was a missing person. Eugene van der Hoeven must have called the police. Although, come to think of it, Russ had told her he wasn't going to be on duty Saturday. Maybe the department was overwhelmed and had to call him in? Logical thoughts, none of which wiped the foolish smile off her face.

Walking into a home where there's been a tragedy grinning your head off is just plain tacky, her grandmother Fergusson chided. Everyone would think she knew something, had seen something. She swallowed her smile and pressed forward behind Duane with as much sobriety as she could muster.

A petite, dark-haired woman, clad in jeans and a sweatshirt, held the door wide. She looked at the trail of leaf rot and dirt accumulating on the floor with dismay.

Eugene van der Hoeven stood apart from the search team clustered around the table, conversing with two men in leaf-print camouflage and hunter-orange vests. The taller of the hunters was half-turned toward her. Russ's eyes widened a fraction, then eased. The corners of his mouth crooked up in what might have been a smile. *Happy Birthday,* Clare mouthed. She ambled toward the men.

"Chief Van Alstyne."

He nodded his head. "Reverend Fergusson. I didn't expect to see you here."

"I volunteered for the search and rescue team last year. John Huggins finally got down to the bottom of the list and called me in." She glanced at the older man next to him: gray-haired, what was left of it, and close to her height, but broad, with powerful shoulders and a chest like a tree stump.

"This is Ed Castle. Ed, Reverend Clare Fergusson."

Clare's hand was enveloped in a calloused grip. "Pleased to meet you," Castle said. "Sorry it had to be under such circumstances."

"Are you"—she looked back and forth between them—"here to help the search?"

"We've just found out about the missing girl." Russ glanced at Eugene. "Ed and I were hunting on van der Hoeven land. We stopped in to pay our respects."

"Mr. van der Hoeven," Huggins called from the dining room table. "If I can have a minute of your time?"

Van der Hoeven ducked his head toward Clare, paused, as if he were about to make a remark, then slipped away.

"Poor guy," Ed Castle said. "This must be real hard on him."

"His sister missing?"

"Yep. But I was thinking more along the lines of him having to put up with all these people. He's a real private guy. Likes to keep to himself."

"How do you know him?" Clare said.

"I've had the license to harvest timber offa Haudenosaunee for twenty, thirty years now. Had it from old Jan van der Hoeven, and now from his kids. 'Course, it'll all be smoked once the Adirondack Conservancy Corporation gets their hands on the property."

"How's that?"

Ed Castle told Clare the details of the impending land sale. She glanced back at Eugene van der Hoeven, bent over a topo map. "He's going to stay in this house, right? I mean, he didn't talk like a man whose home is being sold out from underneath him."

"Dunno," Castle said. "Alls I know is, no timbering licenses from the new owners. Buncha tree huggers. Don't realize how important harvesting is to the health of the forest. Think it all happens naturally."

"Fergusson!" Huggins's head popped up from the huddle. "Bring that map of yours over here."

Clare complied, squeezing in between Duane and a slim redheaded man, spreading her map next to the others. She pointed out the ground she had covered.

"We need to rethink our strategy," Huggins began, only to be interrupted by a low rumbling from Duane's midsection.

"Sorry." He grinned. "No breakfast."

"You all need some food," Eugene said. He sounded embarrassed, as if he had invited them there for a cocktail party and had forgotten the drinks and nibbles. He stood up, looking around the room. "Lisa? Lisa!"

The dark-haired young woman appeared in a far doorway. "Let's get these people breakfast. Can you rustle up eggs and bacon and toast, whatever we have?"

"Me?"

The entire male contingent stared at the housekeeper expectantly. Clare rolled her eyes. They looked like a pack of hounds with their ears pricked, waiting for the sound of the can opener. "I'll help you," she said loudly. No one else leaped in to volunteer.

Snorting, she strode toward the door. Lisa jumped out of her way and fell in behind her. "Thanks," she whispered. "It's not that I'm not willing. I'm just not much of a cook. Especially not for a gang like this."

The doorway led though what had probably been called a butler's pantry into the kitchen. It was roomy, meant for serious cooking for large numbers, but its vintage fifties decor had outlived the institutional look and was now funky. Clare prised open the refrigerator. "Let's see what we've got." She pulled out eggs, milk, and bread. "Let's make French toast. It'll go farther and fill people up more." She emptied the vegetable bin of a few oranges, an apple, and a single bunch of grapes. "See if there's any canned fruit in the pantry. We can mix up a big macédoine."

Lisa scurried to the pantry. Clare laid the ingredients out on the pristine white counter and started opening up cupboards, looking for bowls and frying pans.

"I really appreciate this," Lisa said, setting canned pineapple and pears and a jar of maraschino cherries on the other side of the sink.

"You do windows but you don't do meals?" Clare straightened, a nest of mixing bowls in her hands.

Lisa smiled. "You got it."

"Have you worked for the van der Hoevens long?"

"About four years now. What are we going to do with these?" She held up the cans.

"Let's drain 'em, then empty them into a bowl. Then we can chop up the fresh fruit and add that." Clare made a sound of satisfaction and emerged from a lower cupboard clutching two heavy-duty cast-iron skillets. "So you weren't here last night when Millie and Eugene had dinner."

Lisa shook her head. "I come in Wednesdays and Saturdays. Usually I don't see much of Millie."

Clare turned on the water to scrub her hands. "You don't?"

"She doesn't actually live here," Lisa explained. "Her home is in Montana. But she's been staying with Mr. van der Hoeven for the past few months. Working on this deal to sell the land and . . . stuff."

There was a noticeable pause. "Stuff?" Clare said, drying her hands on a faded cotton towel.

Lisa kept her eyes on the apple she was peeling. "You know. Environmental stuff."

Clare touched the younger woman's arm. "Lisa. If there's anything we should know that might help us find her . . ."

Lisa turned, apple in one hand, knife in the other. "I don't want to get in trouble. I don't want to get one of the van der Hoevens in trouble, either."

"What is it?"

Lisa dropped her head, frowning furiously, as if weighing a series of pros and cons. Finally she looked up. "I'll let you look. You can tell me what you think." She crossed the kitchen, past the back door, to a built-in desk beneath a wall-mounted phone. She opened the desk drawer, scooped out several envelopes and papers, and laid them atop a stack of wooden crates waiting to be unpacked by the kitchen door. The boxes were stenciled VAN DER HOEVEN VINEYARDS. Having your own vineyard. Now that was one perk of wealth Clare actually envied. She picked up the papers. They were pamphlets, giving information on "extreme eco-activism" and "defending your mother earth against all enemies, domestic and foreign." She looked for the organization name. She whistled.

"The Planetary Liberation Army." She looked up at Lisa. "No wonder you were worried. This is the group that firebombed a research lab in California last year. Killed three people."

Lisa nodded grimly. "I saw this special about them on MTV News. It said they also blew up an SUV dealership in Michigan." She held up another pamphlet. "This one is all about the evils of big, gas-guzzling, four-wheel-drive trucks."

"They'd have a field day with the search and rescue guys," Clare said, picking up a typewritten letter. It was addressed to Millie van der Hoeven. It thanked her for her cash donation and her interest in aiding the PLA in its mission. It suggested any further discussions be held in person.

"These started showing up after Millie got here at the end of the summer. I found 'em in the drawer when I was looking for a piece of paper to write down a phone message. I didn't say anything to Mr. van der Hoeven, 'cause I figure it's nobody's business." At Clare's look, she frowned. "I didn't want to cause bad blood between the two of them. He thinks her environmental causes are crazy enough without this."

"What do you think?" Clare asked.

Lisa shrugged. "Maybe she had some sort of secret meeting with them? It says meet in person."

"But why wouldn't she have returned already? You'd think the last thing she'd want to do would be to draw attention to herself."

Lisa looked into the middle distance for a moment. "If I was going to do something illegal—like blow up a car dealership?—I'd think being lost in the woods was a great idea. Get someone to pick me up, do the dirty, then get dropped off at one of the access roads that lead onto the property. Come wandering out, tired and cold and hungry. Who's to say she hasn't been lost the whole time?"

"You don't like her very much, do you?"

Lisa raised her eyebrows in surprise. "I don't know her well enough to like her or not. But, you know, nowadays, you gotta be on the lookout for terrorists everywhere. There's no reason they might not go after Millers Kill."

Clare thought Millers Kill would fall pretty far down on the list of possible targets for an environmental terrorist group. But then again, she would have thought that about an SUV dealership in Michigan. And wasn't one of the dealerships in Fort Henry selling Humvees now?

Clare held up one of the pamphlets and the letter. "Can I keep these? If the police get involved—" Lisa's dismayed face stopped her. "Not that they necessarily will. But I'd like to show this, unofficially, to the chief. He's a friend of mine. He might have some ideas about finding her."

Lisa was shaking her head. "I don't want to get anybody in trouble. I know how the cops are. Nothing's ever unofficial."

"Have you thought that it might be the other way around? What if Millie met with these people, decided she didn't want to take part in whatever they were planning, and they're holding her against her will?"

"Riiight." Lisa's face showed what she thought of that idea. She swept the pamphlets off the wine crate and held out her hand for the remaining papers.

"Please?" Clare said.

Lisa sighed. "Oh, all right." She shoved the pamphlets into the drawer. "But you don't mention my name. I didn't show these to you, and I don't know anything about it."

"Deal." Clare sniffed. One of the skillets was beginning to smoke. "We'd better get back to breakfast. 'Cause God knows none of those men is about to feed himself."

9:05 A.M.

The duct tape wasn't coming off. She had tried stretching it, rubbing it against the edge of the door lintel, working her hands back and forth until her wrists were raw. Nothing.

Using the bucket had been a nightmare of complications. It had taken her five tries to stand upright, a feat she accomplished finally by rocking back and forth on her aching arms until, in a kind of reverse somersault, the velocity of her forward roll brought her to her feet. She hopped all the way to the wall to keep herself from falling forward. Standing, she discovered that the stretch of duct tape between her ankles served as a shackle, and she was able to shuffle slowly to the bucket. Getting her sweatpants down was a matter of plucking with her almost-numb fingers and hopping up and down, but when she lowered herself over the pail, she lost her balance and tumbled over. She had to go through the whole rigmarole again, this time with her sweats sliding around her thighs and the bucket rolling across the floor.

Once she was erect, she shuffle-walked to the bucket and, with tiny kicks and nudges, shoved it against the wall. She couldn't figure out how to get it upright with her hands behind her back and her feet only inches apart, so she thudded painfully to her knees and head-butted it into its final position. It was there she discovered she could get to her feet by leaning hard against the chilly stone wall and forcing her feet under her. She kept her arms and back to the wall this time when she squatted. When she was finally able to relieve herself, it felt like a victory on par with winning the Tour de France. Civilization one, barbarism zero.

Scootching her sweatpants back up with the help of the wall, she considered what to do next. At least using the bucket had given her a goal. Now she was down to two choices: collapse into a motionless heap or find some way to get out of her cell. Since she had already done the motionless heap thing, an escape attempt seemed to be in order.

That was when she discovered that duct tape, the handyman's friend, was a lot more resistant than she had ever realized.

All right, if she couldn't saw, stretch, or slither herself free, maybe she could get out while still bound? The arrow slits were at an easy height; standing, she could look out any one of them and see sunshine and bare-branched trees and sky. They opened wide into the cell, maximizing light, but their external openings were narrow enough to repel invaders—or prevent determined children from killing themselves while playing King Arthur and the Knights of the Round Table. Besides, even if she could wiggle her way between the constricting stones, where would she be? The view from the arrow slits showed the tops of the trees. And she knew from painful experience there was no handy fire escape.

She dismissed the curving wall with its deceptively open windows and considered the door. She had read a book once where someone freed himself from a locked room by removing the door's hinge pins. These hinges were large, faux-medieval things, stretching a quarter of the way across the face of the door. The pins holding them in place were topped by pointed iron finials, reminding her less of the Middle Ages than of the tops of flagstaffs. She shuffled to the oak slab, turned around, and slid down until her hands touched the triangular top of a pin. She pulled it. Nothing. She twisted it. It moved. She twisted the other way, then tugged and pulled, her thighs straining with the effort of squatting. The pin moved upward. She felt like Galileo—*e pur se muove!* It moves! Excited, she tried a mighty wrench. The pin slid another inch and stuck fast. Beneath her duct-tape gag, she groaned in frustration, then bit the sound back. She wouldn't be discouraged. She would be . . . smart.

She attacked the pin again, this time twisting and teasing and scraping it upward, bit by squeaky bit, her arms shaking, sweat slithering under her flannel shirt. More and more of the narrow metal dowel rose from the hinge until she could feel it wiggling loose, and with a final pivot and pull she had it. She bent forward and straightened, her long thigh muscles complaining the whole way. She stood upright, swaying slightly, letting her heart, which she hadn't realized had been pounding, slow down to normal. Letting her legs stop shaking, letting her shoulders relax.

The hinge pin was cold and heavy between her fingers. She let it go. It rang and rang again against the stone floor before coming to rest next to her boot.

"One down, one to go," she said, and that was when it hit her. She whirled, staggered to catch her balance, and stared at the door. Stared at the top hinge, the uppermost hinge, the curlicued, black-iron, hand-forged hinge whose pin sat at the same level as her head. Her hands, taped behind her back, twitched. The pin might just as well have been on the ceiling for all that she could reach it.

The disappointment, the *unfairness* of it, pressed against the back of her eyes like knuckled fists. Tears of rage spilled down her cheeks, scalding her skin. She keened in her throat, a strapped-down, inexpressible sound that made her even more angry—she couldn't even shriek and howl, goddammit!

She kicked one hobbled leg in fury. The duct tape yanked against her ankles, and the lower hinge pin rolled across the floor with an old, hollow sound of iron on wide wooden planks. She blinked. Sniffed hard. Stopped crying. Looked at the pin, six or seven inches long, slender enough to conceal in her sleeve. But heavy. One end flat, circular. The other—pointed. She looked again at the door with its unreachable hinge. Okay. She didn't have way out.

She had a weapon.

9:20 A.M.

Clare was finally seeing a look of admiration on John Huggins's face. Unfortunately, it was for her cooking.

"This is great," he said around a mouthful of French toast. "You have to do this for our annual firehouse breakfast fund-raiser."

Clare made a noncommittal noise that was swallowed up in the clink and clatter of forks hitting plates and spoons stirring coffee. She cleared away an empty jam jar and the denuded butter plate and headed back to the kitchen. Maybe if she rooted way in the back of the fridge, she could find another stick of butter. She was head-down, checking out the produce bin, when she heard the door open and close. Whoever it was simply stood there. Saying nothing.

It struck her what she must look like, presenting rump-out like a primate in a *National Geographic* special. She jerked her head from the refrigerator and whirled around.

Russ lifted his eyes to meet hers. "Hi."

"Hi." She gestured toward the Frigidaire humming behind her. "I was looking for more jam."

He grinned suddenly, wiping ten years off his face. "Don't let me stop you."

"Huh." She cocked her head. "What, exactly, did you come in for?"

He stepped toward her, and she could swear that she felt the air moving, giving way. He stopped before he got too close. He was good about that. They both were. "I thought you might need some help."

She wiped her hands on her pants. "I think that's my line." She pointed toward the pantry. "Take a look in there, will you?"

He nodded, ambling to the pantry and clicking on the light. "So what do you think of Haudenosaunee? I bet you love this kitchen."

Cooking was one of her passions. He knew that, of course. "It beats the pants off of mine, that's for sure." Hers had been installed in the rectory during the reign of the last rector of St. Alban's, an elderly celibate who had, Clare suspected, lived on TV dinners and casseroles donated by the ladies of the parish. "I'm a little disappointed, though. I expected something grander from a great camp. You know, an Adirondack Victorian extravaganza."

"The style you're thinking of 's called haut rustic," Russ said, emerging from the pantry clutching a jar of blackberry jam. "The old Haudenosaunee had Victorian extravaganza in spades. Unfortunately, it turned out to be a firetrap."

She leaned on the granite-topped work island. "How do you know?"

"Everybody in Millers Kill knows at least the bare bones of the story. The van der Hoevens were downstaters who made a bundle in the Civil War, and the head of the family liked to hunt. But he liked to do it in comfort. So he dragged his wife and kids and the servants and the dog up here—in those days it was by private rail and boats and portage—pitched a dozen tents, and oversaw the building of Haudenosaunee." Russ put the jam on the island top and hitched up onto a stool. "At first it was a big, plain log building, styled like the communal hunters' lodges that were popping up throughout the mountains."

"Sort of like this building," Clare said.

"Sort of. Anyway, twenty years later, it was rebuilt in the grand Adirondack style by a van der Hoeven trying to please his pretty young wife. There are pictures in the historical society—I guess the best way to describe it was Swiss chalet meets twig Gothic."

"Did it work?"

"Did what work?"

"Did he please his young wife?"

"She couldn't have been that impressed, because she took off for Europe with their son and stayed there for the next few decades."

"Oh, that's too bad."

"Well, the son returned from Europe right before the First World War broke out."

"Good timing."

"This would have been Eugene's . . . let me see . . . great-grandfather. Can't remember his name."

"You're really good with all this local history."

He smiled like a shyly pleased schoolboy. "I did a report on it in high school. Even then, I was into old houses." Russ had extensively rebuilt his Greek Revival farmhouse. *The house where he and his wife live,* she reminded herself.

"That van der Hoeven thought what the place needed was Old World elegance, so he added on turrets and towers and battlements and the like, trying to turn a Swiss-Gothic chalet into a castle. Even in his day, when rich people were building privies shaped like Versailles and carriage houses that looked like the Tower of London, it was considered a great big ugly heap."

Clare looked around her at the clean lines of the current Haudenosaunee. "Is that when the family built this house?"

"No, that came when Eugene's grandfather tried to modernize the old building. Evidently the older van der Hoeven wasn't content to merely build castles. He wanted to live in the Middle Ages." Russ tapped his temple meaningfully.

"You mean . . . ?"

"No running water, no electricity, no central heating. He actually disconnected the bathrooms that had been state-of-the-art in 1880 and installed drop toilets."

Clare made a face.

"Yeah. So when his son inherited the place, he decided making the fourteenth century fit for human habitation wasn't worth the trouble, and he had this house built."

"What happened to the old camp?"

Russ's blue eyes clouded over. "It burned down."

Comprehension dawned. "Is that what happened to Eugene?"

He nodded. "Whoever says money solves all your problems never met the van der Hoevens."

She was climbing onto the stool kitty-corner from Russ when the letter and pamphlet crinkled inside her pocket. *Speaking of problems.* She pulled them out. "Take a look at this." She held them out to him. "Have you ever heard of this organization?"

He scanned the letter and unfolded the brochure. "One of the radical environmentalist groups, right? Like Earth First? Volunteers living in trees, that sort of thing?"

She shook her head. "More like spiking the trees and then blowing up the loggers' equipment. The Planetary Liberation Army believes in direct action."

"That'd be pretty direct, yeah." He read the back of the pamphlet. "I don't see anything here about the Adirondacks. And I've never heard of them operating in our area." He looked up at her. "Where'd you get these?"

She had thought out her answer when she persuaded Lisa to let her keep the documents. "They were here in the kitchen." She opened the drawer and tossed the remainder of the pamphlets on the stack of wine crates, just as Lisa had done. "I was opening up drawers, looking for utensils and stuff." There. Absolute truth. "These are more in the same vein."

He ruffled through the brochures. "These could be anybody's."

"The only people who live here are Eugene and Millie. One of whom is now missing."

"You think this may have something to do with her disappearance?"

"She gave them money. It's not like mailing in your annual donation to the Sierra Club. These folks aren't sending her a preprinted thank-you letter and a calendar."

He glanced at the paper again. "If she's the outdoorsy, save-the-earth type, she probably gets solicitations from every group under the sun. Lord knows, my mom does." Russ's mother was an environmental activist whose various causes and concerns came close to giving her son an ulcer. "Adirondack Conservancy, Stop the Dredging, Mothers Against Nuclear Waste Disposal—Mom supports 'em all. It doesn't mean that she's plotting to blow up Nine Mile Point."

Clare flipped her hand open. "But what if she were? Millie van der Hoeven, I mean, not your mom."

He looked at her skeptically. "And this is based on?" He flapped the brochure at her. "One letter inviting her to talk and a diatribe about the evils of development? That doesn't make her a terrorist."

"I'm not saying she is. But we have this supposedly woods-wise young woman who goes out for a walk after a late dinner. She's spent every summer of her life right here in these mountains. And she gets lost? On the same day that she's supposed to sell her family's land to a multinational wood products corporation?"

"Which is then signing it over to the Adirondack Conservancy Corporation. They're not going to be clear-cutting the place. They're going to put a stop to all development. And logging. The PLA people should be doing the happy dance over this. If they know about it."

She thought about what Lisa had said. About how being lost in the woods could make a convincing alibi. "It may not have anything to do with Haudenosaunee. Or maybe it does. Maybe she didn't like the idea of selling off to—what's the name of the company?"

"GWP, Inc."

"To GWP. Maybe she didn't trust them to give all the easements or whatever to the conservancy."

Russ rolled his eyes. "Maybe she's being held prisoner by the president of GWP, who's planning on selling her into white slavery after the signing ceremony tonight. Have you seen that picture of her in the hall? She's quite a babe."

Clare made a face. "You're impossible."

"That's what Linda says."

There was a pause. When Clare spoke again, her voice was quiet. "It could be nothing. But someone ought to be aware of it."

He kept his eyes on the letter as he carefully folded it into thirds. "And now I am." He held it up. "Mind if I keep it?"

She shook her head. He unsnapped a pocket on the outside of his camo pants and stuffed the papers inside. She tossed open the door to the pantry and snapped the light on. Surprise, surprise, there was an unopened jar of marmalade sitting next to a tin of tea and a box of farina. She turned back to Russ and set the jar next to his blackberry jam, thinking, *Why am I bothering with this?* A loaded question.

"I'm sure the team will appreciate your search efforts," he said.

She snorted. "This is the problem with letting people know you can cook. I'll probably be relegated to chef and bottle washer for every rescue they call me in on, for ever and ever, amen."

He grinned. "C'mon, Julia Child. I promise I won't stick you in a kitchen. Let's ask Eugene if there's anything else he can tell us about his sister's disappearance."

9:30 A.M.

Randy didn't set out from his house intending to drive to the Reid-Gruyn mill. He had woken at nine fresh and clear and full of energy, despite his heavy drinking the night before. His dad had been the same way. He used to tell Randy the secret was to eat lots of protein all the time. He had lived on eggs, chicken, and venison, and if he hadn't fallen to lung cancer after forty years of a two-pack-a-day habit, he'd probably be partying still.

Randy rolled out of bed, scrubbed the stale smoke and alcohol smell off in the shower, and ate six eggs scrambled for breakfast, accompanied by the frenetic blare of a morning game show. He was going to take his bike into town and retrieve his truck from Mike Yablonski's. That thought, combined with the noise from the television and the simple necessity of washing, dressing, and making breakfast, all kept the great dark heavy truth of being laid off at bay. It broke through in flashes—when he reached for his motorcycle boots and saw the steel-toed boots he wore lumbering, or when the bills piled on the corner of the kitchen counter caught his eye—but for the most part he moved in a state of deliberate unawareness.

Oddly enough, it was on his bike, headed into town, that he started to come to grips with it. The wind was whipping around him, the sun shining through the bare branches, swirling trails of fallen leaves marking where he passed. He felt good, and when he felt good, he thought of Lisa, and when he thought of Lisa, he heard her sweet voice, so full of confidence in him. "He'll find another job. He always does."

Shit. He couldn't let her down.

It was bad enough she was wasting herself, scrubbing other people's toilets. He knew she was thinking about a baby. She was nuts about her niece, Maddy—always offering to have the kid over, spending money on cute little dresses for her. Lisa deserved a kid of her own, and she shouldn't have to leave it at home to go out to work. He wanted to support her, to give her the freedom that his brother-in-law, with his polished shoes and his creases in his pants, couldn't give his wife.

God *damn,* but he had counted on that logging money. He supposed he could try for a team working farther up north, but that would mean moving out for the winter, getting home a few weekends every month if the roads were passable and he wasn't too exhausted to drive. He couldn't do that to her. She needed him. And as the new man on the team, he'd get the shit jobs and the shit hours. With no guarantee that he could come back the next year.

No, what he needed was a real job again. Regular hours, benefits, something he and Lisa could rely on. And with this thought, his Indian Chief Springfield seemed to turn, of its own accord, onto Route 57, leading him along the river, toward the Reid-Gruyn Pulp and Paper mill.

He dismounted in the employee lot and hung his helmet over the back of his seat. Just looking at the place depressed him. Red brick, with high narrow windows, it squatted in its own chemical stink like an animal too sick to move. Past the "new" building—which had been completed the year his grandfather was born—the "old" wooden mill moldered into the river, surrounded by weeds and discarded machinery. He and Mike used to sneak over there on break and smoke joints until the big Mohawk foreman had caught them and knocked them both to the floor, screaming that the place was a freaking firetrap, for chrissakes, and didn't they have the sense God gave geese?

That hadn't been the last straw, but it was near enough, and the next time Randy got into trouble, fighting in the break room with an asshole who tried to stiff him on a bet on a Giants game, he had quit before he could get fired. That had been three years ago. Now he was back, tail between his legs, asking for a chance to close himself inside with the foul air and the fluorescent lights and the foreman chewing his ass if he missed two minutes on the clock.

He closed his eyes against the cold fresh air and the sunshine and went in.

The Saturday morning shift was light, and nobody was in the break room yet. Randy walked past the scrubbed pine tables and the scarred door to the men's room, past the battered green lockers, lifted the heavy latch, and walked out onto the mill floor.

The sickly sweet smell of fermenting pulp hit him like a blow to the face. His eyes watered and he sneezed. The air was hot and heavy and moist, pulsing with the sound of the pulper and the rollers and the constant boil and slosh of water. He skirted the edge of the floor. If there hadn't been a change in the past three years—and "change" wasn't usually in the Reid-Gruyn vocabulary— Lewis Johnson would be hanging out at his stand in the northeastern corner of the floor, where he updated stacks of forms and quality reports and kept an eye on the men.

Randy found the foreman where he had expected. Same hours, same spot, same dark green uniform with LEWIS in a red oval over the chest pocket. In three years, while Randy had gotten married, buried his father, moved into the old man's house, and added four tattoos to his collection, Lewis Johnson had done nothing. He looked exactly the same: solid, square-faced, his skin like badly cured deer hide that had started to crack. He still had all his hair; one of the older guys had once confided to Randy that Indians didn't have any hair below the neck, so they got to keep what they had on top.

"Randy Schoof." Johnson didn't sound thrilled to see him again.

"Hey, Lewis."

"What are you doing here? Last I saw you, you were wiping the pulp off your boots, promising we'd never have the pleasure of your company again."

"Well. You know. Times change." God, this was going to be hard. He postponed his complete humiliation for another minute. "I got married."

"I heard. One of the Bain girls, right?"

"Yeah. We got us a house up past Barkley Mountain and everything."

"Wasn't that where your dad lived?"

"Ayeah." Ayeah. Christ, he sounded like a hillbilly. An old hillbilly. "Yes," he tried. "I got it when he passed."

Johnson nodded. "I'm sure you miss him." Randy was glad Johnson didn't try to hand him a line about how sorry he was. Steve Schoof had been everything the Reid-Gruyn foreman wasn't: fun-loving, easygoing, hard-living. Randy's dad had worked so that he could afford to party. If Johnson had ever even had a beer after eight hours on the floor, Randy had never heard about it.

"So," Randy went on, "there've been a lot of changes in my life in the past three years. I been working every winter as a logger for Castle Logging."

Johnson nodded. Randy wondered if he'd show more of what he was thinking if he weren't a Mohawk.

"But, um, Ed's decided to close up shop. He's retiring to Florida. And so I'm looking for work." He blurted the last sentence toward the stained concrete floor.

Johnson sighed. "Believe it or not, Randy, I'd probably hire you back if I could."

Randy scrunched up his face. *What?*

"I know Ed Castle some. He supplies us with pulp. And if he's kept you on for the last three years, you must be settling down some. Of course, getting married does that to a man."

Randy nodded. Where was this going?

"Problem is, we've got a freeze on. No hires. No overtime. Ed Castle's getting out of the lumbering business because Haudenosaunee is going to be closed up tight, isn't he?"

"I guess so."

"Well, the same problem is affecting us at Reid-Gruyn. No local pulp means costs go up. Mr. Reid says we've got to tighten our belts." Johnson's dark eyes were—regretful? Worried? Randy couldn't tell. "Rumor has it one of the big multinationals from Malaysia has made an offer for the mill. God only knows what'll happen to our jobs then. I'm hoping to hang on until re-tirement."

Randy looked around him. The tanks were full, the rollers grinding and thumping, the stench and the noise and the movement of the men on the floor the same as it had been three years ago. "This is Millers Kill," he said, bewil-dered. "What the hell does a company from Malaysia have to do with us?" He wasn't even sure where Malaysia was.

Johnson allowed himself a ghostly smile. "You don't pay attention to the news much, do you, boy?"

Randy bristled. "Just because I didn't graduate—"

"Calm down. I'm not yanking your chain." Johnson sighed. "It doesn't matter anyway. No jobs here. And if you're looking for another logging job, you'd better get to it, because a lot of the big outfits are bringing up Mexicans to do the work now. Cheaper than a white man, you know." He grinned out-right.

"Yeah. Thanks for the tip." Randy spun on his heel and marched away be-fore he could say something to get himself into trouble. It wasn't Johnson's fault there was no work to be had.

No work. A cold wind blew up inside him, and despite the heat on the pulp-ing floor, he shivered. He had always thought of the mill as the workplace of last resort. A place he might not choose to go but that would always be there. Stupid. Stupid.

What was he gonna do? Trucking? Work at the Kmart? Clean up after tourists at a ski lodge? None of that would cover the bills sitting on the kitchen counter right now, let alone support his family if a baby came along.

He emerged into the same cold, bright air. What was he going to do? What?

9:35 A.M.

R uss watched Eugene's face as he read the letter and examined the brochure from the Planetary Liberation Army. In the dining room, breakfast was winding down to the last few scrapes across syrup-coated plates and the dregs from the coffeepot. Russ had asked their host quietly if he and Clare might have a word. Eugene had led them into the living room. Leather and wool-blanketed chairs sprawled invitingly around them, but no one sat.

Van der Hoeven looked up at him. "I've heard of the group." He frowned at the letter. "She's always been a bit of a nut about her causes, but I can't believe Millie would get involved with extremists like this."

"How long has your sister been living with you?" Russ asked.

"Since late August." He turned the brochure over. "There's no date on either of these. Perhaps she brought them with her?"

"They were in the kitchen," Clare said. "Is that likely to be where she would store papers she brought from—where's her home?"

"Montana." He was standing near the enormous riverstone fireplace, in such a way that his scarred flesh was partially in shadow. Russ wondered how much of his positioning was deliberate and how much an old habit. "No, I have to confess it's more likely any mail in the kitchen arrived here. I pick things up from the box at the end of the road, and I tend to dump it on the kitchen desk. It's where I do the bills."

Russ glanced at Clare, and he swore he could read her mind. *Maybe the rich aren't that much different from you and me.* Of course, when he wrote out checks in his kitchen, it wasn't next to crates of wine from his own vineyard.

He focused in on Eugene. If his sister was mixed up in a piece of nasty work, he might be genuinely ignorant. Or he might be protecting her. "Mr. van der Hoeven, I know you're worried about your sister." Russ dropped his voice. He was concerned. Eugene could confide in him. "I'm starting to be worried, too. You say she's good in these woods, that she's known them all her life. Does it make sense that she'd wander off at night and get herself lost?" Toward the other end of the great room was a glassed-in case of hunting rifles and a table, next to the window seat, made from what looked to be elk antlers. It didn't take much detective work to figure out where van der Hoeven's sympathies lay. "Or could it be that she's been sucked in by some radical environmentalists? Gotten in over her head? Could that have anything to do with her disappearance?"

Eugene nodded thoughtfully. "I did hear a car, early this morning. Before I discovered Millie wasn't in the house."

Russ smoothed the surprise off his face. He hadn't expected to get anything from his fishing expedition. He just liked to tie off any loose ends.

"You didn't mention a car to the search team," Clare said.

Their host quarter-turned to her, just enough to be polite, still keeping his good side toward her. He did it more with Clare than with the men in his house, Russ noticed. He wanted to say, *Don't worry about it, buddy. She'll take you as she finds you.*

"I didn't think it signified." Eugene gestured toward Russ's camo and blaze orange. "On a Saturday in hunting season, it's not unusual to have cars or trucks drive in here by mistake. Hunters looking for one of the access roads."

"Do you have any reason to think Millie might have been involved with the PLA?" Russ asked.

"If she was, she certainly didn't tell me. She's hooked up with the local chapter of this Adirondack Conservancy Corporation." Eugene's face was still expressive enough to register what he thought of them. "A bunch of old ladies and newcomers from New York City. She had them up here just this past week. Do you think they . . . ?"

"Are a front for the PLA? No. I, um, know the president of that group pretty well. They're more into . . . passive resistance."

Clare looked at him, one eyebrow quirked. *Mom,* he mouthed. "Any other organizations she's gotten involved with?" he asked van der Hoeven. "Meetings she didn't tell you about? Absences she didn't explain?"

"She is seeing someone from town," van der Hoeven said slowly. "Romantically, I mean. At least, that's what she told me. I have to say, that's unusual for her. She doesn't have much of a track record with men."

"Maybe she prefers women," Clare said, her face bland.

Eugene dropped the coy sideways glance and stared her straight in the face. "Certainly not." Russ could see him reassessing the priest in light of her scandalous statement.

"What made you think she didn't go with her boyfriend last night?" Russ asked.

"She's always told me before. That she'd be away."

"How long has she been seeing this guy?"

"Almost since she got here. At least since early September."

"That's fast work for someone who doesn't have much of a track record with men."

"She's twenty-six," Clare pointed out. "You fall madly in love overnight when you're that age."

"That's true," Russ said. "It's also true that the presence of a boyfriend, real or not, can cover up all sorts of activities." He turned to van der Hoeven. "Have you met this guy? Has she had him over to the house here?"

"No." He said it slowly, as if considering for the first time that there might be more to his sister's nocturnal activities than young love's first bloom. He looked down at the letter in his hand. "Do you really think—is there a chance she might really be in danger?"

Russ made a noncommittal noise. "We might all be blowing smoke at this point, but I think it'll be worthwhile to track down this friend of hers. What's his name?"

"Um . . ." Van der Hoeven tilted his head back, thinking. "Michael. Michael McWhorter."

"And when did you hear the car in the drive?"

"Before I was up. So it must have been around four, four-thirty."

"You told us her bed hadn't been slept in," Clare said, "but she could have made it up before leaving."

"Of course. I just never considered Millie might be . . . sneaking off without telling me."

Russ raised his hands. "Let's not get ahead of ourselves here. The first assumption has to be the original one. That she got lost while walking last night and needs help finding her way back." He nodded toward Clare. "The second assumption I'm going to work on is that she decided, for whatever reason, to meet up with this Michael McWhorter in the wee hours, and the car you heard in the drive was him picking her up." He nodded toward van der Hoeven. "The search team will work on the first assumption. I'll take care of the second."

Eugene was clearly worried now, his shoulders hunching, his hands clenching and unclenching. Russ gentled his voice. "Chances are, if she's not out in the woods, she's holed up with her boyfriend. Clare's right, at twenty-six, you don't always think about notifying other people before you dash off to do something stupid and romantic." He glanced toward the dining room, where the other members of the search team were clearing away the dishes. "Why don't you go talk to John Huggins and let him know the police will be following up on this possible boyfriend thing."

"Right. Of course. I . . ." Van der Hoeven scrubbed his hands across his shirt. "I just don't ever want anything to happen to her." He took a deep breath and straightened, his hands falling to his side, his shoulders squaring. Becoming— what was the old word? The patroon. The master of the estate. "Right," he said, more confidently, and left to join Huggins, who was now spreading maps over the table again.

"I have to join them, too," Clare said. She lowered her voice. "What do you think?"

"I think if I were trying to come up with a hard-to-verify name for someone, I'd pick Michael McWhorter. There are hundreds of McWhorters in Millers Kill, Fort Henry, and Cossayuharie. Thousands, if you include the area be- tween Lake George and Saratoga. The business with the car—I don't like that, either."

"You don't think it could have been an assignation?"

He looked at her skeptically. "Twenty-six-year-old women may do a lot for love, but in my experience, they want to look good while they're doing it. Would you haul yourself out of bed to rendezvous with your lover at 4:00 A.M.?"

"With messy hair and morning breath and my face all creased from my pil- low?" She grinned. "Probably not." Her smile faded away. "But I'd haul myself out of bed at 4:00 A.M. to do something I didn't want anyone to know about."

"Maybe she was counting on getting home before her brother woke up."

"Eugene told us he had planned to go hunting. He would have been up and out before dawn."

"Even better. He's out of the house until ten, eleven o'clock. That gives her six hours or so to do what she needs to do and get back into the house undetected."

"If he hadn't happened to peek in on her before he left this morning, he never would have known she was gone at all."

"What about the cleaning lady?"

Clare glanced around. "I can't imagine she'd go in Millie's bedroom unless she was sure it was empty. And if Millie bumped into her walking in, so what? She says she got up and took a little stroll before breakfast. This house is so big, two people could spend all day in it and never see each other."

Over her head, Russ could see Huggins staring at them. "Unless the two are you and John Huggins. Better get back to business, darlin'."

He loved watching her cheeks go pink. Her voice was as steady as ever, though. "He'll only keep us at it for another hour or two before we get relieved. I'll be at home after. Give me a call. I want to know what you find out about Michael McWhorter."

"Ma'am, yes, ma'am."

Her mouth twitched in a half smile before she spun and walked away. He shook himself. He dug his hand into his pocket and pulled out the keys to his truck. He'd drive over to the department and assign this to someone and then hightail it out of there. It was his day off, after all. Although, they might be stretched thin, what with it being a hunting Saturday and Duane unavailable and Pete on leave. Maybe he'd take care of it himself. Linda's words came back to him: *Is this the man who can't take a vacation because the police department might fall apart without him?* Maybe she had a point. His gaze settled on Clare, bending over the table, tucking a falling strand of hair behind her ear. Maybe.

10:00 A.M.

Driving up the main road to Haudenosaunee—if two dirt ruts and some gravel could be called a road—felt odd to Becky. It wasn't that she hadn't been on the property many times before. As a kid, she would visit her dad as he hauled logs out of the Haudenosaunee woods, sometimes riding behind him in the seat of the skidder, her breath clouding the air, sometimes bouncing in the front seat of the truck as it crunched over the frozen trails toward the main road. Then, as a college student, she had visited the great camp itself as Millie's guest. They would hike to the waterfall for a swim and then smoke pot in the ruins of the first great camp, the only spot where Millie's dad was guaranteed not to stumble over them. Summer's green or winter's snow, that was her experience of Haudenosaunee, not this gray, splay-limbed November landscape, and never alone.

Around a gentle curve, and she stepped on her brakes, seeing a big red pickup headed straight for her. The truck, driven by an equally big man in hunting camouflage, slowed to a crawl, then nosed its way as far off the road as possible. The driver gestured her to proceed. As she crept past him, he rolled his window down. She stopped and did the same.

"You're not Millie van der Hoeven, are you?"

One of the search team, then. "I'm afraid not. I'm a friend of hers. She's still missing?"

He nodded. "Hopefully not for long, though. You say you're her friend? Has she ever mentioned someone she's seeing in the area? A boyfriend?"

Becky propped her arm over the edge of the window. "No, she hasn't." What a weird thing to ask. Unless— "Does she have one? Do you think she might be with some guy instead of lost in the forest?"

The man nodded. "Maybe. It's something I'm following up on." He leaned forward and fired up his truck. "Sorry to bother you. You looked sort of like her picture."

"No problem. Sorry I couldn't help." She raised her hand and shifted into gear again. When she was past the truck, she rolled her window up. Looked like Millie. She wished. She supposed that to a guy as old as her dad, any two girls with long blond hair looked alike.

She hoped Millie had an unknown, undisclosed boyfriend. It made more sense than getting lost at Haudenosaunee. *And,* that selfish voice in the back of her brain said, *it would mean she'd still show up on time for the ceremony tonight.* Becky shoved the thought away. The ceremony was going forward. Everyone would be there to sign papers and shake hands and smile for the cameras. She couldn't, wouldn't, consider the alternative.

Even this trip to Haudenosaunee was going on faith. If she had had any real doubts about the sale going through, she could have called the contractor and told him to dismiss the crew that would be meeting her at the great camp within the next half hour. She glanced at her car's clock. Make that twenty minutes. She hadn't canceled. The planning walk-through would go on as scheduled. She and the crew would discuss the most economical and efficient way to dismantle all the modern Haudenosaunee buildings.

Then came the hard part of the day. She had to tell her father, as the owner of Castle Logging, that his equipment, which he had garaged over the summer at his most recent cutting site, had to go. The conservancy's lawyer had asked her to get a detailed inventory, because they would be responsible for any buildings and machinery on the property after the title changed hands. She wasn't looking forward to getting the document from her dad. As much as she loved Bonnie, she really preferred to stay with her parents when she visited. She wasn't sure her dad would want to have her in his house after she had hit him up for his inventory and proof of insurance.

But whether or not Dad tossed her out on her ear, by 7:00 P.M. she was headed for the Algonquin Waters Spa and Resort in her party dress and new shoes. And if Millie van der Hoeven hadn't shown by then, Becky would by-God go out and find her herself. A fierce smile snapped across her face. Her dad always said she was as hard to budge as an old oak tree. It was time to prove him right.

10:05 A.M.

She considered the blankets. Could they be used to attack somehow? To defend? They were too tough to tear. One was heavy wool, almost a horse blanket, the kind you'd use as a topmost layer on a bed because it would make you itch if it was sandwiched between the sheet and the quilt. The other two were more modern, lofty fake-fiber things, soft and warm. They had satin edging. Now those, they might be useful. If she could figure out a way to rip them from the rest of the blanket.

It was funny, really. All those years of trying to shuck off her belongings, trying to find out what was intrinsic to herself instead of what was bought and paid for with her family's money. As an adult, she had tried to live simply, first from conviction and then from necessity, as her funds dwindled and her support of various organizations grew. If she ignored the fact that she didn't have to work for a living, that she could stay at her father's Park Avenue apartment in New York City and at her mother's Palm Beach cottage in Florida, she could pretend she had the same sort of life as most of her friends.

Standing in the chill of her cell, she could see how badly she had been fooling herself. Take away her parents' homes and the great camp and the private schools and trips abroad. She was still rich. She had a home and a car and a thousand objects filling them both: furniture and clothing and camping gear and books and CDs and pots and pans and sharp, long knives that rested in their own square of cherrywood. What she wouldn't give to have those knives. Now. Now that all her earthly goods had been reduced to the clothes on her back, an iron hinge pin, and three blankets.

And a plastic five-gallon bucket. When whoever imprisoned her here came back, maybe she could spill pee on their shoes.

When whoever imprisoned her here came back. She had been concentrating so hard on what she could do to get away, she had overlooked the fact that she was missing. Not where she should be. People would be looking for her. Wouldn't they?

She looked at the blankets. At the arrow slits. At the blankets again. She shuffled to the pile. *The heaviest one,* she thought. She teased it out with one boot-clad foot, balancing carefully to avoid knocking herself over. Once she had a sizable piece separated from the rest of the pile, she hobbled toward the nearest window, dragging the blanket beneath her boot tread. It was as tedious as positioning the bucket had been—step, scrape, step, scrape—although at least now her full bladder wasn't making it hard to think. Instead, she was charged with the idea that her unknown captors could return at any moment.

The dense wool blanket unfurled from the pile. She scuttled back, positioned herself at the trailing edge, and booted it across the floor. When she had it bunched beneath the arrow slit, she considered a moment, then dropped to her knees on top of it. Shuffling slowly off the fabric, she bent over like a supplicant before an almighty god and worked her head as far under the blanket's heavy folds as she could. Butted hard against the stone wall, she pressed upward. The blanket rose. She inched it higher and higher, until her kneeling form made an acutely uncomfortable triangle with the curved wall.

This would be the hardest part. Leaning into the stones until she thought the top of her head would split open, she curled her toes underneath her and pushed with all the strength in her thighs. Her legs straightened, her neck trembled, and, greased by the blanket's smooth surface, her head skidded upward. She was standing. She shuffled close to the wall. The pinned blanket rose until she could feel a change in the angle of the stone beneath her head. The wide embrasure. She pushed, rolling her head up until her face was buried in the scratchy wool. Desperate for extra height, she went on tiptoe. She felt the blanket slide upward, then catch. Pressing her chest against the stone to stop the blanket from backsliding, she risked raising her head.

The blanket was stuck in the middle of the arrow slit. She bent again, rolling her head up against the dangling edge, forcing more material into the opening. It bunched fast. Half of it must be dangling from the outside right now. For a moment, she considered letting it stay like that, but then she realized people might walk by without ever lifting their eyes to see her banner. She pressed her face against the wool and sprang up as best she could, making an awkward *en pointe* in her boots.

It worked. The blanket slithered through the window and was gone. She heard nothing except a brief *crack* where it caught and broke a brittle branch. Was it spread out like a picnic cloth on the ground? Draped over a bramble bush? Hanging from a branch? It didn't matter. It was large, it was white and red and yellow and green, it didn't belong out there. Anyone who came by would notice it.

She thought of the way it had bunched in the opening, half in and half out. She looked at one of the remaining blankets, a fluffy, fuzzy lavender. She imagined a searcher spotting the wool blanket on the ground, glancing around, seeing another blanket flapping from an arrow slit high above the ground. Imagined friendly feet pounding up the stairs. Imagined someone saying, *Hang on, I'll have you out of here in a moment.*

She shuffled over to the blanket pile and began kicking.

10:30 A.M.

Clare was in the middle of listening to Courtney Reid's litany of complaints when she heard a woman shout from the drive. The search and rescue team had completed their huddle, gone over the topo maps, and accepted assignments in different parts of the wood. The possibility that Millie had simply debunked to her boyfriend's house had acted as a sort of antienergizer, making it that much more difficult to whip up the necessary enthusiasm for hours of careful searching through cold, bare woods. Even though she was privy to Russ's doubts about the existence of the alleged boyfriend, Clare's zeal was starting to flag as well. She kept thinking about the whirlwind of activity that must be going on at St. Alban's. Next to Christmas and Easter, the bishop's annual visit was the most important Sunday of the year, at least in terms of polishing silver and waxing wood and laying out the fatted calf. Or the individual puff-pastry quiches, in this case.

"She was supposed to pick up individual pastry shells from the bakery," Courtney was saying. "Instead, she got phyllo dough. We now have phyllo dough for two hundred and no quiche pastries. What am I supposed to do with that?"

"Hang on just a second," Clare said. "Someone's hollering out in the drive." When she had asked Eugene if she could use his phone, he had escorted her to a small den on the opposite side of the foyer from the living room. He had shut the door to give her privacy, but John Huggins, whose ideas of delicacy were somewhat different from van der Hoeven's, had stuck his head in the door and reminded Clare in no uncertain terms that she'd better not sit yapping on the phone all morning. When he left, the door was still ajar. If she stretched to the length of the cord, she could see out the wide window to the drive. Her view of the porch was restricted; she couldn't see Eugene, but she could hear him. He must have left the front door open.

"What are you doing here?" he asked.

So the young blonde in barn coat and jeans walking toward the porch wasn't Millie. Clare sighed. It would have been too much to ask, she supposed.

"Reverend Fergusson?" Courtney Reid demanded from the vicinity of Clare's chest.

Clare brought the phone back to her ear, keeping her eye on the people outside her window. "I'm here."

"Okay, so my problem is, what am I going to do? Serve baklava? I could send one of the other volunteers to the baker's for the puff pastries, but I don't think our budget will stretch that far."

Eugene had stepped off the porch. The young woman approached him. She said something Clare couldn't make out, then gestured to the two—no, three men clustered behind her. Like the blonde, they were dressed in sturdy coats and jeans. One of them carried a clipboard. One had a camera looped around his neck. All of them had metal measuring tapes hanging off their belt loops.

"You can use the phyllo dough to make the shells," she said into the phone. The unheard conversation continued. The woman's body language said, *I'm being polite, but I'm in charge here.* Eugene was stiff, as he had been when Clare met him. A shy man shielding himself with an aristocrat's hauteur. "You'll have to separate the dough and bake them before you fill them, of course."

"I thought of that," Courtney said impatiently. "We don't have any individual-sized tins to bake them in."

Clare couldn't remember why full-sized quiches, sliced up, were unacceptable. She suspected raising the issue would be a lost cause at this point. "There's a great kitchen supply store in Saratoga. Send someone down to pick up a couple stacks of disposable baking tins."

"To Saratoga?" Courtney screeched.

The woman handed van der Hoeven several sheets of paper. Clare could spot a letterhead but couldn't make it out. Eugene bent his head over the documents.

"It's a forty-five-minute drive," Clare said, in as reasonable a tone as possible. "Surely you can find someone willing—" Courtney cut her off with a wail of reasons why it would be impossible, impossible, to spare one of the already-too-few volunteers for a daylong trip to Saratoga. Clare let her rattle on. *It never ceases to amaze me, how many folks jump straight over 'I'll try' to 'I can't,'* Master Sergeant Ashley "Hardball" Wright drawled.

Eugene turned and disappeared into the house. No farewell, no acknowledgement that the blond woman still stood there. Clare blinked. Not that she was an expert on Eugene van der Hoeven, but that seemed out of character. She heard his footsteps ringing over the floorboards, headed away from her into the living room.

"... and Judy Morrison hasn't even shown up like she promised...," Courtney was saying.

The young woman turned to the men gathered behind her and began speaking. She motioned toward the house, the garage, the utility shed. One of the men snapped the measuring tape off his belt, and another produced a fat, dog-eared notebook from the depths of his jacket. Surveyors? Tax assessors? They couldn't be painters—it was far too late in the season to paint outdoors.

She heard van der Hoeven's tread returning through the foyer and out onto the porch. Through the front door, she heard his voice. "Hey. You."

The young woman and the men looked up. The woman's eyes and mouth widened. Everyone froze in position, except the man holding the notebook, who dropped it, bent over, scrabbled it off the ground, then hotfooted back several paces.

"Get off my property," van der Hoeven yelled. He descended from the porch into Clare's view. She nearly let go of the phone. Eugene was carrying a rifle. Not carrying it, aiming it, stock up and butted against his shoulder, sights pointed toward the pale-faced, motionless group in his drive. "Get off my property, I said." He was shouting; Clare could hear every word.

"Courtney." She cut off the banquet preparation committee chair ruthlessly. "Find someone to go to Saratoga." She let her command voice out, the one that crackled with authority. The one that brooked no disagreement. "I don't care who, just do it. Something's come up. I'll call you back as soon as I can." She stalked to the phone, replaced the receiver, and hurried back to the window.

The young woman, with more guts than sense, had stepped forward. Clare couldn't make out what she was saying, but whatever it was, it didn't have the effect of calming van der Hoeven.

"I said *now*," he said, chambering a round.

Oh, no. Clare was out of the den, hurtling down the hall toward the front door, when she heard the shot go off. *Oh, God, no.* She lunged for the handle, flung the door open, and stumbled onto the porch.

The three men were fleeing to their cars and trucks, parked on the far edge of the drive. The young woman teetered on the toes of her boots, two bright pink spots burning high on her cheekbones. "I'll be back!" she screamed. "You can't stop this, Eugene! I'll be back!"

Eugene chambered another round and sighted the rifle at the infuriated woman.

"Stop!" Clare yelled. Eugene whipped toward her. She ducked out of the line of fire, but as soon as van der Hoeven saw who she was, he lowered his weapon. Clare sagged with relief.

Behind her, she heard the clatter of feet down the stairs. "What the hell was that?" Lisa said. Eugene turned back toward the drive, but the woman had finally come to her senses and fled. She dove into a green Toyota Prius as the three men's trucks roared to life. They spun out on the drive and disappeared down the road, gravel spitting in their wake.

Eugene mounted the porch steps slowly, his rifle uncocked, held loosely in his hand. He looked at Clare, clutching the edge of the door, then at Lisa, poised halfway down the stairs. "I open my land to hunters," he said. "That doesn't mean I allow anybody and everybody on my property." His voice was calm, but his hand was shaking.

He trudged past them, down the hall, into the living room. Clare heard the *clunk* of the gun case opening. She looked up at the housekeeper. "Do you think I should . . ." What? Report the incident? Ask if Eugene needed help? Get herself and Lisa out of the house?

Eugene returned. He stopped in front of them. "Reverend Fergusson, have you finished with your phone call?"

She nodded, speechless.

"Good. I'm going to retire to my den. Lisa, you'll find your envelope on the kitchen desk in the usual spot. Please don't disturb me."

He continued on toward the room Clare had recently vacated. She looked at Lisa, who shrugged. "Mr. van der Hoeven? Eugene?" He paused in the doorway. Half-turned toward her. "Do you need any . . . can I help you?"

"I believe, Reverend Fergusson, that the Lord helps those who help themselves." The den door clicked behind him, closing the world out.

10:35 A.M.

Shaun Reid ran his thumb and index finger over the crease in his navy serge pants, then glanced up quickly to see if Terry McKellan had noticed. He hadn't. Eyes on the proposal Shaun had brought to the meeting, reading glasses slipping down his nose, Terry was abstracted, rolling his cigar-brown mustache between his fingers, occasionally tapping out the beat of some song only he could hear against the spreadsheets scattered across his messy conference table.

Shaun congratulated himself on choosing just the right look for this meeting—country club casual. He had bought the pants and shirt in the Bahamas during his honeymoon with Courtney, from an exclusive shop with a PATRONIZED BY THE PRINCE OF WALES sign by the door. They had cost more than he usually spent on a suit, tie, and shoes combined, but Courtney had said they made him look young and fit and successful.

Terry, on the other hand, with his round moon face and vanishing hair, looked like what he was, a guy rapidly headed north of middle age, who had given up the fight to stay fit and any hopes of rising past senior vice president long ago. With his shapeless sweater stretched over his belly and his shiny-kneed corduroys, he resembled an untenured academic more than a commercial loan officer.

Looking the part wouldn't win Shaun his loan, but it couldn't hurt. In truth, he was feeling more relaxed than he had all week. He had good numbers on the past three years' profit-and-loss statements. He had a great proposal, laying out all the ways in which Reid-Gruyn could expand and grow with the future. He had highly favorable estimates of the value of his personal property. And he had a relationship with the man across the table from him. For God's sake, he and Courtney had had the McKellans to their house for dinner.

Terry propped his chin in his hand and removed his reading glasses. Shaun knew speaking first would betray his weakness, his eagerness, but he couldn't help himself.

"What do you think?"

Terry rolled one end of his mustache thoughtfully. "I gotta ask you, Shaun . . . why?"

"Why what?"

"Why are you twisting yourself into financial knots like this? You know that as a creditor, AllBanc has already seen the preliminary proposal from GWP. You stand to make a bundle if the mill sells. Certainly more than you'd realize in ten years if you went on as you have been, taking the same level of salary out of the business."

He could feel sweat starting in his armpits, damp and sour. McKellan didn't get it. He didn't see it. "That's one of the points of my proposal," he said, forcing strength and confidence into his voice. "That we don't go on as we have been. That we make a concerted effort to grow and develop the specialty paper market."

"But the capital costs of retooling the mill—"

"Are accounted for in the third section of my proposal."

"Shaun, I won't argue that those figures show a sufficient amount to upgrade the plant and still maintain operations. But you haven't taken into account any market variables. If the economy takes a downturn, if the state raises the workers' comp rates, if you can't get the union to fall into line with you, you'll be screwed. There just isn't enough of a safety net."

The sweat was creeping down the middle of Shaun's back now. His expensive Bahamian shirt clung to his spine.

"You'll be putting yourself personally in debt—deep in debt," McKellan went on. "And if it doesn't work out a few years down the road, GWP has moved on to bigger and better things. You'll have a business weighed down with excess obligations and no white knight on the horizon to bail you out. So I ask you, why?"

Shaun leaned forward, hands curling around the table's edge. "Terry, my great-grandfather founded that mill. I'm the fourth-generation Reid to run the business. I've got a son who'll be stepping into my shoes someday, just like I did with my dad and he did with his dad before him." That was not, strictly speaking, the truth. Jeremy had shown no signs of interest in his family's generations-old trade. As far as he was concerned, the money to be made in the Adirondacks was in tourism, not in timber. But the kid was young yet, still in love with his first job. Shaun would bring him around. If there was a Reid-Gruyn Pulp and Paper to bring him around to.

"If GWP buys the plant, they'll still need your expertise to run it. They'll be able to make the upgrades you'd like." Terry tapped the proposal. His cheery, pep-up tone scraped Shaun's nerves like nails on chalkboard. "Reid-Gruyn could become a name in specialty papers. There's a legacy to hand on to Jeremy."

"But I'd be working for someone else! It wouldn't be mine!" Shaun clamped his mouth shut. God almighty, he sounded like a whiny three-year-old.

Terry raised his eyebrows. They looked like two woolly caterpillars climbing Mount Baldy. "You're already working for someone else," he said. He used the mild and reasonable tone appropriate to a fussy preschooler. Shaun's face grew hot. "The Reid family owns forty-nine percent of the company. The rest of the shares are held by individual and corporate investors."

Some of which, he didn't have to say, were AllBanc's own trust accounts.

"Right. I misspoke." Shaun leaned back, propping his arm over the back of his chair in what he desperately hoped was a casual gesture. "What I meant to say was, we'll lose our local control. Decisions about the mill, the employees, the dividend payouts—everything will be coming from Malaysia. You and I have seen too many Washington County businesses get bought out and then abandoned. With me at the helm, you know the needs of our community will be at the forefront. Money is not the most important thing to me, you know that."

"I do." Terry gazed at him with his big brown eyes. Brown, brown, brown—Shaun had never realized how much like a seal the loan officer looked. A mournful seal. "And I respect that. Unfortunately, as an officer of the bank, I have to put money first. I'm afraid I won't authorize additional capital loans to Reid-Gruyn."

"Then give me the personal loan. You and I both know I have enough collateral. I can buy back enough stock to tip the family holdings to fifty-one percent. With that, I can stave off takeover attempts till doomsday."

Terry recoiled. "That's insider trading, Shaun. When GWP announces their bid publicly, there's no way the share value isn't going to shoot up. For you to buy in advance, knowing the offer will be made within days—"

"So give me a loan for home improvements, then. I don't care what it says on the paperwork. I just need the money, and I need it by Monday."

Terry's seal-like eyes looked harder now. "No. The SEC would be all over your buy. They'd look at the loan, and the first thing they'd see would be the bank's notice of inquiry from GWP. You may be fine with doing three-to-five in the federal pen, but I'm sure as hell not."

"But—" The phone rang. Terry held up a finger as he snatched the receiver off the hook.

"Terry McKellan here," he said. His caterpillar brows went up, and he looked at Shaun. "Hi. Were you trying to reach your husband?" Shaun tensed.

He hadn't told Courtney about this appointment. How had she tracked him down? "I can see where that would be a problem," Terry said. Shaun locked his hands over one knee. Casual. Casual. "Saratoga? I guess I could. What's the name of the place?" Terry jotted down something on a notepad. "Sure. Glad to be of help. I should be able to have them there in about two hours. Would that work for you?" He looked at Shaun again. "Okay. I'll see you then." He hung up.

"That was Courtney," he said. "She's at St. Alban's. There was a mix-up, and they didn't get the little pie tins for the quiches they're making for the reception tomorrow." He ripped the note off its pad. "So I'm detailed to go to the kitchen store in Saratoga and buy two hundred of the things." He stood up.

"But . . . the loan?" Shaun remained seated. He didn't want to acknowledge the meeting was over. Over, and a complete failure.

"I'm sorry, Shaun." Terry shook his head. "There isn't going to be a loan. I know it's hard, but maybe the best thing is to acknowledge that times change and businesses, like people, have a natural life span. Maybe you need to stop the extraordinary life support and let Reid-Gruyn go."

10:35 A.M.

Clare found the documents tossed on a table near the gun cabinet. She debated with herself less than five seconds before picking them up.

The uppermost letter was from the Adirondack Conservancy Corporation. It was addressed to Louisa van der Hoeven, Eugene van der Hoeven, and Millicent van der Hoeven. She shook her head. Let no one say the van der Hoevens went in for trendy names. *Dear dat-da-dat-da-da . . .* She skimmed the first paragraph, which was an effusive thank-you for the family's agreeing to the buyout. Clare wondered for a moment if they were letting Haudenosaunee go at a reduced rate. That might be behind Eugene's anger. Perhaps he felt he was getting stiffed?

The second paragraph held the meat of the matter. *Under the terms of the preliminary agreement, the ACC has consulted with the New York State Parks, Recreation and Historic Preservation's Bureau of Historic Sites, which has rendered up its opinions on the various buildings now located on Haudenosaunee land (see attached).* Clare pulled the papers apart. Sure enough, there was a letter from the Bureau, stapled to documents that presumably held its opinions in greater detail.

First, to address issues related to the original "great camp" built in 1867:
The BHS has examined the historical record of this building and its current
physical condition. Although the original Adirondack Gothic construction would
have been deserving of landmark status, the decay following the van der Ho-
even family's move into the modern house in the years following World War II
and the subsequent fire have left the building damaged past restoration. The
ACC has accepted the Bureau's recommendations that the building shell remain
in situ, in part because of the historical value of the ruins and in part due to the
difficulty and cost of removing the extensive stone structure.

Clare translated the bureaucracy-speak in her head: Tearing down old walls
into heaps of stone isn't worth the time and effort.

Secondly, as to the modern house and dependencies: The conclusion of
the BHS is that the current habitation, also known as "Haudenosaunee," is
historically unremarkable, being constructed in no particular architectural
style in the 1940s and added on to from time to time in the 1960s and 1980s.
The loss of integrity suggests no reason to include the house and its outbuild-
ings on the state list of protected properties. Therefore, in line with the ACC's
mandate to keep the protected area of the Adirondack State Park "forever
wild," the ACC has developed a plan to dismantle the currently existing
"improvements" to the property and to replace alien plantings with native
species.

Clare frowned at the letter. Did the mean what she thought it meant?

The plan is an follows: Within one week of the land transfer scheduled for
November 14 (please see the Preliminary Deed of Transfer and Grant of Ease-
ments Agreement, dated August 14 of this year), all family members and per-
sonal property shall remove from the buildings of Haudenosaunee, including
the main house, garage, gardening shed, storage shed, and boathouse.

Clare hadn't seen a boathouse. Must be by the waterfall-slash-swimming-
hole. She flipped to the letter's second page.

The ACC will engage a construction crew to dismantle the existing build-
ings. To whatever extent it is possible, the materials will be removed from the
site and reused. Unless specific exemptions are requested by the family mem-
bers, all architectural items including doors, windows, wood stock, trim, light
fixtures, hardware, etc., will become property of the ACC and may be sold or
auctioned by it to defray any costs associated with returning Haudenosaunee to
its natural state.

She looked toward the dining room, with its gleaming wood floors and its antler chandelier. Historically unimportant or not, she suspected the ACC could defray a whole lot of costs if they dismantled the place carefully enough. It would take advance planning and a skilled work team—the image of the men standing by the young blond woman popped into her head. Clipboard, measuring tape, camera. Exactly what you would bring along if you were planning the step-by-step deconstruction of the house.

The next two paragraphs were given over to plants. The plan was to rip as much out of the gardens and borders as possible before snow started to fly, then to resume in the spring by "reintroducing native plant life as horticulturally advisable." Apparently rosebushes weren't as valuable as doorknobs and countertops, and removing them was not as expensive. The letter referred to "local ACC volunteers" who would tackle the project using a checklist of approved planting materials, which was, like the reports from the Bureau of Historic Sites, attached.

Given the narrow window of time afforded by the November weather, and the inadvisability of leaving the buildings uninhabited and untended throughout the winter, the ACC would like to proceed as quickly as possible post the transfer of land rights. If you have any objections to the proposed plan, including of timeline, please notify project director Becky Castle as soon as possible. If you assent to the above-mentioned plan, as detailed here and in the accompanying documents, please sign below and return to the ACC . . . it wound up with an Albany address and an injunction to the recipients to keep a copy for their records. Beneath Becky Castle's signature, there were places for all three van der Hoevens to sign. All three lines were blank. Clare flipped back to the first page and looked at the date. August 30.

Who had signed off on the plan to demolish their family's summer home? Louisa, in far-off San Francisco, was a cipher; the only thing Clare could deduce about her was that her use of the Haudenosaunee house—if any—was restricted to occasional visits. Millie had been living here since August; surely if she had agreed to the plans she wouldn't have been whiling away her time? Anyone expecting to move in a week should be hip deep in boxes by this date. At least she knew where Eugene stood. Or did she? Maybe he was all for selling off the land but was holding out for the right to remain in his home. Maybe Millie didn't want to let go of either the land or the house and was hiding herself away in passive protest against her siblings' decision.

It all hinged on a question that sounded like a bad lightbulb joke: How many van der Hoevens does it take to transfer 250,000 acres?

She looked toward the kitchen. There was a phone in there, hanging above the desk, next to the tower of wine crates Russ had joked about. Russ. She should call him. She should— The crackle of her radio snapped her to the awareness that there was something she definitely was supposed to be doing. And it wasn't standing around speculating on the van der Hoevens or making phone calls.

"Fergusson? What the hell happened? You fall into the toilet or something?"

She bounded toward the front door and managed to make it off the porch before keying her response, so that she could honestly tell John Huggins, "I'm on my way."

10:35 A.M.

The only thing that would have made Randy Schoof feel better as he entered the post office would be a notice from the state saying he and Lisa had won the lottery. Except he didn't think they mailed those out. Weren't you supposed to call them when you saw the numbers on TV?

Lewis Johnson's words ringing in his ears, he had gone from the mill to the county employment office. The prospects were as bad as Johnson had painted them. A well-meaning girl who looked to be barely out of high school had shown him how to search the database for the help-wanted listings and told him he was free to use the computer to update his résumé and the phone to call prospective employers. But he had found that anything offering a decent amount of money required at least a high school diploma, and most wanted people with college degrees and related work experience. There was one trucking company looking for drivers, but it was based in Plattsburgh and ran mostly into Canada, which would mean days, if not weeks, away from home. There was a shipping company in Saratoga looking for loading-dock workers, but when he called, the position had been filled.

No logging companies were listed. He figured he could get some names and numbers from Mr. Castle and call them himself. For the money he could earn in a season of cutting, maybe he and Lisa would just have to suck it up and live apart for a few months. Discouraged, he logged off the employment office computer and left, giving Miss Helpful a flop of a wave as she caroled, "Have a nice day!" at his back.

There was a Certified Mail postcard in his postal box. He took it to the front desk. "Hey, Randy." Geraldine Bain, the elderly postal worker holding down the desk, was his wife's second cousin. "How's it going?"

Randy almost snarled, *It sucks*, but the sight of a poster—ASK ABOUT OPEN-INGS FOR RURAL DELIVERY ROUTES!—shut him up. "Good," he answered. "It's going good. What's this about needing deliverymen?"

She glanced at the sign. "You interested? I can give you the form for the test."

"There's a test?"

"Yep. And they've just started this new thing where you got to have a security check. But once you get those under your belt, we can put you on the list."

"The list?"

"Ayeah. We start you out as a substitute. If you work out good, you can become a regular as soon as there's need of one."

"How long's all this take?"

"We can have you up and running come early summer." She grinned. "That's less'n you've ever made anthrax, of course. Then all bets are off." She laughed.

He slid the Certified Mail postcard across the counter toward her. "I'll think about it."

Geraldine picked up the card and went hunting for the corresponding piece of mail. She emerged from the back holding up an envelope. "From the town." She pointed to where he had to sign it. "You two aren't adding on up there, are you? Sumpin' you need a building permit for? Like a nursery?"

Nosy old bitch. "Nope. Nothing to report." Geraldine ripped off the confirmation tag and handed Randy the envelope, which he tucked beneath his arm along with the three bills, grocery store circular, and *Motorcycle* magazine he had already retrieved from the postal box. "Have a nice day, hon," Geraldine said as he retreated outside the post office to check out his letter in peace.

One of the town benches, set out a century before, had been placed in front of the post office. Randy had sometimes wondered why whoever had laid out the benches had picked this spot, with no tree or view or any other reason to settle, as a likely place to sit. He supposed now it was for just this purpose, to let a man open a certified letter without having any gossipy relations check it out.

He ripped open the envelope and pulled out a lengthy letter on the town's letterhead. The tiny print and legal language swam before his eyes. *Third notice . . . significant unpaid taxes . . . interest and penalties . . . lien on the property . . .*

The town had put a lien on his land. For $5,693.47 in back taxes. Randy dropped the letter in his lap and stared across the street at the Millers Kill Free Library. Someone had taped pictures of fat-faced Pilgrim children in the windows on either side of the door. The girl was leaning against a shock of corn, and the boy had his arm around a happy turkey's neck. Randy picked up the letter and reread the notice of lien. $5,693.47. Where was he going to find that kind of money? He and Lisa were up to their necks in debt as it was.

Lisa. He had to call Lisa. He was off the bench and had taken three steps down the sidewalk toward the pay phone in front of the IGA when he stopped himself. She didn't like to get called when she was at a client's house. He sank back onto the bench, braced his elbows on denim worn to white over his knees, and hid his face like a little kid. This was going to be a nasty surprise to Lisa. It drove her nuts, the way he dealt with difficult news by putting it off. If he didn't see bills and demands for back taxes, he could ignore them. If Lisa saw them, she'd storm at him, demanding that he take care of this or make a phone call to that. So, and this was the part that was going to kill him when she got home, sometimes he made certain bills and demands and notices disappear.

He had shrugged off the letters from the town looking for payment of his property taxes. What could they do to him? His parents had paid off the mortgage in 1985. When they divorced, his dad had swapped his mom's half of the house for half his pension, the RV, and her name on his life insurance policy. His mom had come out the better in that deal two years ago, when his dad, sick of getting yelled at by his girlfriend for his hacking cough, went to the doctor's for an antibiotic to clear it up and walked out with a diagnosis of metastasized lung cancer. He died five months later. He had been fifty-six. Randy had inherited the house and land, free and clear.

What did they mean, a lien? He envisioned the cops coming to his door, turning him and Lisa out, the house foreclosed on and auctioned off. Where would they go then? Homeless, jobless, the credit cards maxed out. He winced, envisioning asking for a loan from Lisa's parents. Or worse, having to move in with them. He could just imagine what his disapproving sister-in-law and her prick of a husband would make of that.

He needed his job back. That one thing, Ed Castle not closing up shop, would make the difference between Randy and Lisa having a life or going straight down the toilet. Maybe Castle could be persuaded to hand over the machinery to Randy and the rest of the crew. They could keep the operation going, even send a little money to Ed down in Florida. Surely that would set him up better than just tossing in the towel and living on Social Security.

The blinding rightness of this idea was like hot, strong coffee on a cold morning, filling him up, warming his fingers and toes. He stood up, excited to talk with Ed, to point out retiring didn't have to mean the end of the business. Then he'd get hold of the other guys. He was sure they'd want to continue logging if they could. They would all toss in together. One of those—whaddya call it?—collectives. Boot heels ringing on the sidewalk, Randy made for his motorcycle. Lisa was right. He always managed to come out on top.

10:45 A.M.

There were blood smears on her father's SUV. The Explorer was blocking the driveway, an anodized rack mounted over its back door. It looked like any other bike carrier, except that this rack was stained with red and crusting blotches that spattered a trail up the drive toward the detached garage. Looked like he got his buck this year. Becky stepped carefully as she crossed to the front steps. Her mother would have her hide if she tracked blood onto the floor. She checked the bottom of her boots and scraped them hard on the brushy doormat before opening the door.

"Hey," she called. "Anybody home? Mom?"

The small downstairs was deserted. She walked through the kitchen and out onto the back porch. She could hear an electric whine. "Dad?" she shouted.

"Around here," came an answering yell.

Becky clattered down the back steps and followed the sound around the edge of the garage. The coppery smell of blood nearly overwhelmed her. Her father had the deer hanging upside down from a metal bar chained to a rough wooden frame. Its gut was slit stem to stern, and its hind legs, which were spread wide and clamped to the bar, glistened in the cold sunlight. They had been skinned and cut off below the joint.

"Eugh! Dad, what are you doing?"

Her father paused from sawing straight into the buck's crotch. "I'm skinning out my deer." He was wearing baggy coveralls that looked like the aftermath of a terrible fight—all bruise-yellow, greasy grime, and blood. "Then, after he's hung for a few days, I'm gonna butcher him."

Becky winced. "Can't you get someone to do that for you?"

Her father turned, the hacksaw in his hand. He had that look on his face, the one that said, *Goes off to a fancy college and she loses all common sense.* "Sure I could. But I'm not about to spend good money paying someone to do what any fool with a knife and a saw can do." He replaced the hacksaw on a strip of cardboard that was laid out like a serial killer's surgical set, with two wicked knives and a pair of long-handled pruning shears.

"I expected to see you on your last legs, the way Bonnie was talking this morning. Shows what she knows."

Ed worked his hands well into the hide near the deer's hindquarters and began to peel the skin off the body. "Bonnie's just worried about your mother and me."

"And I'm not."

"Didn't say that, did I?"

"You don't say a lot of things. You've barely spoken to me since I started working on the Haudenosaunee project."

"That what you call it? A project?" The hide stuck. Ed tugged it, then reached for one of the knives. "So what are you doing here? I mean, besides giving me grief. Weren't you supposed to be over to Haudenosaunee puttin' chains across the roads so's no one could get in tomorrow?"

"Nobody's chaining up the roads, Dad. I was visiting the great camp with a contractor. I'm trying to get things in order, so that after GWP buys the land and signs it over to us tonight, the ACC will be ready to implement its vision as soon as possible."

The words were barely out of her mouth before she wished them back. Sure enough, her father's eyebrows rose, in an exaggeratedly impressed expression.

"Implement your vision. 'S that what you people at the Adirondack Conservancy Corporation call shutting down the timber harvest and throwing folks out of work?"

Becky felt her face flushing hot. "No, that's what we call returning the land to its natural state."

"This land's been occupied three hundred years. More, if you count the Iroquois. What's this natural state you think you can get it back to?"

She knew she wasn't going to win this, but she wanted her dad, for once, to get at least part of what she was trying to do. "We'll be taking down all the buildings. Volunteers will remove the alien plants and replace them with native species. The forest will have a chance to resume its natural life cycle, unmanaged by harvesting or planting."

"Firetrap, that's what you'll get with no harvesting. Just like you get diseased herds if you don't hunt the deer." He sawed in and out with his knife. The hide sagged away from the raw flesh beneath it. "Your group really tearing down the Haudenosaunee buildings? I was up there this morning, you know. Didn't look as if anyone was getting ready to move. What does Eugene van der Hoeven think about you putting the wrecking ball to his home?"

For a moment, Becky considered telling her father the whole story of this morning's disastrous visit to Haudenosaunee. If she did, though, God alone knew how her dad would react. He might be mad at her for her role in closing off the land to logging, but that didn't mean he'd take kindly to a nutcase threatening her with a gun. Her dad had always been overly protective of his girls.

"He's not happy about it," she said, truthfully enough. "But it's not as if the ACC is tossing him out into the snow. Millie has arranged for him to move in with her, when she returns to Montana. He'll be set for life with what he'll make from GWP."

Her dad circled the deer, his knife lolling in his hand. "It ain't always about the money, Becks. I don't know as Eugene van der Hoeven has left Haudenosaunee since he came back from the hospital, after the fire. That was, what, seventeen, eighteen years ago?" He grabbed the flopping white-and-brown tail, pulled it away from the body, and began hacking it off. "So you're all done with your work for today, and the only thing left to do is go swanning off to the ball tonight, huh?"

"It's a signing ceremony, Dad, not a ball. And no, I'm not done with my work today. That's why I'm here." She folded her arms across her chest and took a slow breath. She wanted to sound relaxed and authoritative, not like a girl asking to borrow the family car. "As you may know, after GWP transfers the rights to Haudenosaunee to the ACC, we'll have the landowner's responsibility for all preexisting conditions on the property."

Ed's knife cut more delicately now, as he teased the tail off. "You mean if one of them contractors of yours trips over a sticking-up board, he can sue you?" He tossed the tail onto the frost-scarred grass.

"Basically, yeah. But we're thinking here of a particular liability. Your machinery."

Her father straightened. "Whaddya mean, my machinery?"

"Didn't you leave Castle Logging's machinery near your cutting site when you shut down last spring?"

"Course I did. You know that. Why the hell should I pay a couple thousand to garage the skidders and pickers in some truck depot when I can keep 'em for free on the van der Hoevens' land? They're on one of the access roads. They're not in anybody's way—any hikers come through, they can waltz right past 'em."

"That's just it, Dad. Anybody can reach them. And as of tomorrow, if your equipment is stolen or vandalized, you could conceivably hold the Adirondack Conservancy Corporation liable as landholder."

He flung the knife into the earth. It stuck deep in the ground, quivering with a violence to match his voice.

"I could 'conceivably hold' you liable? What the hell kind of man do you think I am? I've stored my machines on Haudenosaunee land for more'n a decade without a single problem or a complaint from the van der Hoevens! I suppose you want me to move 'em all off the sacred property before sundown."

"You may never have had a problem, and I hope you never do! But that won't let us off the hook with our insurer if we don't take care of the details. I'm not asking you to move the skidders. I just want an inventory of what's on the land and some proof of your insurance."

"To save your butts if somebody decides to blow up one of my trucks."

"Cut me a break, Dad. This is for your protection as well as for the ACC's. What if something did happen to one of the pickers or skidders or trucks before you could sell them? Would you really want to be stuck in court, your insurance company fighting ours?"

He looked at her suspiciously. "Why'd you say I'd be selling the machinery? Who told you that?"

Becky blew out an exasperated breath. "Bonnie, of course. You are planning to sell, right? She said you didn't want to try to keep the business going if you had to travel up north for the timber."

"I'll be selling, all right. You've seen to that."

"Oh, for God's sakes!" She actually stamped her foot, a gesture she thought she had left behind with her childhood. "Just give me an inventory!"

"You want to count my machines and find out if there're any dings in 'em, missy, you can go out in the woods and do it yourself! They're on fire road number 52. Have a good time communing with nature while you're there."

"And the insurance?" she gritted out.

"Eugene van der Hoeven has a copy of the current policy. I'm sure he'll be happy to hand it over to you, since he won't need it come tomorrow."

"Van der Hoeven has a copy!" She pointed a finger at him. "You've got a lot of nerve, giving me that 'what kind of man do you think I am' line. The ACC isn't asking anything more from you than what you were already giving the van der Hoevens."

"There's one difference, missy." He leaned in so close she could smell the iron-and-earth scent of raw meat and blood. "With the van der Hoevens, it was give-and-take. With your crew, I'm bending over and taking it. And I don't like it."

11:00 A.M.

There was no place for Randy to park at the Castles'. The old man's SUV was pulled up by the barnlike garage, and the rest of the short driveway was occupied by one of those experimental gas-electric hybrids Randy had read about but never seen. He looked around. Technically, there wasn't any on-street parking allowed on Sherman Street, but he figured no one would complain if he pulled his bike up close enough to the Castles' drive.

He dismounted and hung his helmet on the back. He walked up the drive and was about to mount the stairs to the house when he heard the faint sounds of voices coming from behind the garage. He headed past Ed's SUV toward the noise.

"Fine!" A woman shouted. "Fine! I'll go get it myself!"

"Good!" That was Ed; Randy had heard him roaring too often before not to know his voice. "Maybe if you actually have to work for something instead of gettin' it out of a book, you'll appreciate it more!"

Randy rounded the corner of the garage. The first thing he saw was the bloody skinned deer dangling from a homemade frame. The next thing that caught his eye was his employer—his former employer—nose to nose with a fine-boned blonde who looked like Ed with all the ugly and old squeezed out of him.

"I am not staying here with a man who can't respect my choices!" She whirled away from the old man. The fact that Randy was in her way didn't even slow her down. He jumped to one side, and she glared at him as she swept past.

"Nobody's holding you here at gunpoint!" Ed yelled after her. Randy doubted she heard; the thunder of her boots as she stomped up the back stairs drowned out any other sound.

Ed made a noise in the back of his throat. He glared at Randy in exactly the same way the girl had. "Don't ever have daughters," he snarled.

"Okay." Whatever. Randy was prepared to agree to almost anything if the old man'd give him a listen.

Ed bent over and wrenched a knife out of the ground. He wiped it against his leg, then laid it neatly next to several other knives and saws on a piece of cardboard. He picked up a hacksaw. "What are you doing here?"

"I was thinking about this plan of yours, selling off the business."

Ed took one of the deer's front legs and drew it up, resting the hoof and first joint against his coverall-clad thigh. He raised the hacksaw. "Look. Like I told you when I called you yesterday, I'm sorry to have to pull the rug out from underneath you. As soon as you talk to someone else about a job, you have 'em call me. I'll give you a good recommendation." Ed began sawing off the deer's leg above the knee joint.

"No, that's not it. I was thinking, what if, like, the guys and I took over the business from you?" Randy spoke loudly, over the wet grinding sound of the hacksaw blade chewing through bone. "I know you're tired of the work and all, but me and the other guys on the crew, we're still young enough to make it work."

Ed laughed shortly. "You're a good logger, Randy, but you're a long way from being a businessman. Take my advice. Head up north and find an outfit that needs extra hands for the winter."

"I don't wanna go up north. I wanna work near home. C'mon, Ed, give me a chance."

"You think you can run a timber operation, fine. You come up with two hundred thousand and I'll sell you the business, lock, stock, and skidder." With a wrenching *crack*, the deer's lower leg snapped. Ed sliced through the remaining string of tendon and hide and tossed the mutilated limb next to the hide and tail piled on the ground. He stretched, cracking his back, and looked at the corpse with satisfaction.

"Two hundred *thousand?*" Randy could barely get the sum out.

"That's what my trucks and skidders are worth, fair market value." Ed grabbed the deer's last remaining leg and slapped it against his thigh. "And that's just the start of what you'll have to lay out. There's money to insure your equipment, and money for fuel, and money for the men, and money for the licenses."

Randy was still getting his brain around the cost of Ed's beat-up old machines. "Maybe we could work something out," he said. "Like, I could have the use of the machines and pay you back out of what I earn."

Ed sawed into the long, thin leg. Randy watched as hair, skin, meat, and muscle severed and the blade bit into bone. "Kid, cutting a deal like that would be robbing both of us. I'd wind up with no money for my retirement, and you'd wind up broke and in the hole." Ed shook his head, his eyes on the steady back-and-forth of his saw. "Even if you could run a timber business, getting hold of my machines wouldn't help you out if you want to stay put in Millers Kill. I know I seem like Methuselah to you, but I'm not selling up 'cause I'm too old. I'm selling out because there ain't any more logging in this area." The second foreleg broke away. Ed stood and tossed it into the growing pile of body parts.

"Once Haudenosaunee's gone, that's it. Next available woodlot's another fifty miles to the north, if you can get a license. And that'll be closed to logging as soon as the landowners get a big enough offer from the developers." He wiped the saw on his coveralls and laid it on the cardboard. "Pretty soon, the only outfits making money off the woods'll be the big guys. You want a job? Go on over to the new resort and talk to the big shots from GWP. They're gonna be the only game in town."

"But if I just had the equipment, just, like, one skidder and a truck, I could—"

Ed unfolded a length of rough sacking and draped it over the frame, enclosing the deer. "Randy. You're not listening to what I been saying. A skidder and a truck isn't going to get you anywheres." He unspooled twine from a ball and, gathering the bottom of the fabric together, looped it several times around, a makeshift body bag. He straightened, groaning, and tossed the twine ball onto the cardboard. "Now if you don't mind, I got a date with a couple ibuprophen and a long, hot shower."

Randy tagged after him as he crossed the yard to the back steps. Ed paused. "Look, kid. I was born and raised in Washington County. I never wanted to leave it. So I've outlived all the decent jobs—that's not a tragedy for me. I'm old enough to retire and spend the rest of my years hunting and hanging out with my grandsons." He settled his hand on Randy's shoulder, as weighty as time itself. "Don't make the mistake of thinking this is the only place in the world you can be happy. Huh? Okay?" He vanished into the house.

Randy stood for a moment, the cold November sunshine bright on his face. Ed didn't sound like he was retiring. He sounded like he was getting ready to slit his throat.

From the front of the house, he heard a door slam. Ed had some nerve, telling Randy to move away for work, when it was him who was throwing in the towel. There were always good-paying jobs, if you were willing to hustle. Guys got old, they forgot that. He looked at where Ed's hand had curled over his shoulder. A bloody smear blotched the denim.

From the front of the house he heard a car starting up, the squeal of tires laying down rubber, and then the unmistakable sound of something big and heavy crunching into his bike.

11:15 A.M.

Becky tumbled out of her Prius and stared in horror at the motorcycle lying in the street. She wasn't sure what had happened; she had felt the bone-shuddering impact and then heard a sound like a dumpster full of recycled cans dropping onto the asphalt.

"Holy shit! What did you do to my bike?" The guy who had come to see her dad ran past her. He skidded to a stop in front of the motorcycle. "Oh, man, you've torn up my fuel line!"

"I'm so sorry." Becky glanced over her shoulder to see if her dad had heard anything. That would really be the icing on the cake—to have him charge out of the house and find her here like a sixteen-year-old screwing up on her learner's permit. "Look, let me pay for the damage, please."

His back was still toward her. He held his hands out over the machine as if he were commanding it to rise from the dead. His voice held the disbelief of a child faced with an inexplicable loss. "How the hell am I going to get it to the garage?"

He seemed to be talking to himself, but Becky answered him. "I've got Triple A. I can call them. They'll pick it up for you."

He turned toward her. He was a few years younger than she was, attractive in a farm-boy-meets-skinhead kind of way, dressed in JC Penney hip-hop, the look of someone whose only inner-city experience has been downtown Schenectady. "It'll need to go to Jimino's, out to Fort Henry."

"Wherever you like." She smiled apologetically but couldn't stop herself from looking over her shoulder again.

"What is it?"

She snapped around. "What do you mean?"

"I'm not going to, you know, tell your dad on you." He bent and lifted the bike by its handles. The arms and back of his jacket bulged with the strength of a man who makes his living by his muscles instead of his brain.

"You can park it in the neighbor's driveway until the tow truck comes." She pointed toward the Bells' next door. "They've already left for Florida for the winter." He shot her a suspicious look. "It's closer than our—my parents' driveway," she added helpfully.

He grunted but rolled the bike up the driveway next door. Becky retreated to her car, grabbed her wallet, and unplugged her cell phone from its charger. She dashed over to the Bells' driveway. "Look, I can call Triple A right now." She juggled the wallet and the phone until she wiggled her membership card out of the billfold.

He held up his hands. "Calm down, will ya? You're acting like you think I'm gonna call the cops." He squinted at her. "You carrying or something?"

She didn't have to worry about the police finding drugs in her possession, but he looked as if he might. "No," she said. She glanced back toward her house. "I just had a big fight with my dad—well, you heard the end of it—and I'll never live it down if he finds out I wrecked somebody's bike backing out of the damn driveway."

"Ahhh." He nodded, satisfied. "Now I get it." He looked at his bike, at her car, at her. "I got my truck over to a friend's house. He's out by Glens Falls. Could you give me a lift? I'm gonna be late picking my wife up from her job."

Glens Falls. Exactly the opposite direction from where she needed to go. "Where's she work?" Becky asked, mentally crossing her fingers. If it was right here in town . . .

"Haudenosaunee. It's a camp up past—"

"I know where it is! I'm headed there now to pick up some papers. Why don't you come with me, we'll pick up your wife, and then I'll take both of you to your truck."

"Uh." He swayed back and forth indecisively.

"Please? It's the least I can do."

He shrugged. "Okay. I'm Randy Schoof, by the way."

"Becky Castle." She led the way back to her car. "Go ahead, it's open," she said, as he stood by the passenger door. "You can see how I managed to run into your bike," she explained, sliding behind the wheel. "I hung my dress on the hook in the back, and it completely obscured my view." She stretched her arm over the seat, unhooked the dry cleaner's bag, and tossed it on the backseat. "I should have just settled for a few wrinkles." She looked pointedly at the seatbelt strap. "You all set?" He buckled up.

Randy Schoof sat silently as she pulled away from her parents' house, stayed silent as she put in her call to Triple A to ask for a motorcycle tow to Jimino's, and remained silent while she returned her phone to the charger. It was weird. She couldn't tell if he was thinking, or sulking, or shy. It put her on edge, and she found herself rattling on to compensate, telling him about her friend Millie going missing, railing against Eugene van der Hoeven's parochial frontier macho mentality, complaining about how utterly unreasonable her father was. He just sat there, looking out the window, making the occasional noise of acknowledgment.

"I'm sorry," she said, as they turned onto Route 53 and headed up the mountain toward Haudenosaunee. "I don't usually hijack people with nonstop talking. It's just that I woke up this morning expecting everything to be great, and so far it's been an incredibly crappy day."

"You don't need to apologize," he said. "It's been a pretty shitty day for me, too."

She opened her mouth to ask him why he had been to see her father, but the sight of the access road wiped the question from her mind. "Fire Road 52!" She slowed her car down. "Would you mind terribly if we made a stop here before we hit Haudenosaunee?"

Randy Schoof glanced at her assessingly. "I'm not late to pick Lisa up yet." He looked out the window. "Why here?" he asked, his head turned away.

"This is where my dad has his logging equipment. I need to inventory it for insurance purposes." She turned into the road.

"Come again?"

"The trucks and feller-bunchers and all are insured against damage or loss. Like your motorcycle and your truck." It occurred to her that maybe it wasn't like his motorcycle and truck. It wasn't hard picturing him as the sort who maintained his insurance just long enough to register his vehicles, then let it lapse.

"Oh," he said. Then, "Okay."

She swung her car onto the dirt road. It was wide and hard-packed, a road meant for log-heavy trailers and dump trucks full of pulpwood, navigating through the icy depths of winter. It was made wider by the dead zones on either side, gullies wiped bare of life by the heavy concentration of salt washed off the road. Another damning aspect of logging her father would not allow.

She bumped maybe a half mile uphill and then shut down her car.

"What's up?" Randy said. "We're not nearly there yet."

A childhood of traveling into the woods with her father had taught her that you never drive up an unmarked Adirondack road unless you have four-wheel drive and a winch chain. "I didn't want to get stuck in a boggy spot or burn out my bushings trying to climb the mountain," she said, grabbing her purse before getting out of the car. "You can wait here for me. I won't be long."

She started the long uphill slog. She had friends in Albany who would be aghast at her leaving her car and keys in possession of a man she had just met, but this was Millers Kill. In twenty minutes, without his even saying much, she knew his name, his wife's name and where she worked, and where he had his motorcycle fixed. They probably had a dozen acquaintances in common. Not to mention her father.

At the thought of her father, her stomach clenched. She had sworn to herself she was going to act like, and be treated as, an adult this visit. Instead, she had been reduced to a level of discourse with her father no better than "You can't make me!" "Oh, yeah? So there!" Punctuated by storming out of the yard without saying good-bye.

The echo of a slam cut off her self-recrimination. Must be Randy, bored with the view through the windshield. She didn't wait for him, pressing upward against the bright cold sunlight, looking past the tenacious brown weeds, clinging to the poisoned soil, to the forest vaulting up on either side: heavy, dark hemlocks, the ghostly remains of birch trees, mummified blackberries caged inside their briar tombs.

She could hear the clearing site before she could see it. There was something about a large open space amidst all the trees—a nonsound, a negative space in the thick mass of the forest, a pause in the breath of the woods. The road curved, leveled, and opened up into the expanse of a battlefield. She winced at the enormous gash in the forest's face, the battlement of stumps that had been chained out of the ground and discarded, the crackle-dry heaps of brush and junk wood piled like funeral pyres to the sky. The place, even abandoned, pulsed with a kind of energy, lingering ghosts of men ready to muscle miles of board feet and tons of pulp out of the raw wilderness. Machines waiting only for the overnight frosts to become a good hard freeze before tearing into the barricade of trees all around them.

They were all here, just as she remembered them from her childhood: the crawler tractor, the skidders, the bulldozer, the loader, the trucks. Back when she was a kid, her dad had tied and staked tarps over the equipment, protecting the heavy machinery from rain and leaf fall. Now he used pop-up portable shelters, which gave the machines the appearance of a herd of dinosaurs on a camping trip.

Becky sighed and dug into her purse for her portable camera and notepad. She flipped the notepad open and wrote *No. 1: bulldozer.* She walked around the dozer, snapping pictures from the front and back and sides, trying not to envision riding on her dad's lap on the thing as he leveled out a new access road.

Will you name the road for me, Daddy?

I sure will, sweet pea.

Sure enough, he had bought one of those sign kits at the hardware store, and the access road for that winter's cut was Becky Avenue—"avenue" because she thought her dad's suggestion, Becky Lane, sounded like an actress's name. That had been when she thought making her mark on the forest was the way to show how much she loved it.

She hissed, impatient with her own sentimentality, and moved on to the next vehicle. *No. 2: skidder.*

Randy Schoof appeared over the rise where the road met the clearing. He waved, and she waved back before raising the camera and capturing a side view of the skidder for posterity. Randy strolled past her as she jotted down a description of the skidder's condition, glancing at the feller-buncher and the dump trucks, resembling nothing so much as a Sunday shopper on a car lot.

We're not nearly there yet. He had said that, when she parked the Prius. She went around to the other side of the skidder. "Have you been here before?" she called out.

He stopped. "Uh. Yeah." He took a few steps toward her. "Actually, I work for your dad. I mean, I did. Before he decided to pull the plug."

Great. She was up here with a disgruntled former employee. What if he decided to goof up one of the engines to get back at her dad? "It's not really his decision," she said in a loud voice. "Once the Adirondack Conservancy Corporation takes control, logging's going to be forbidden on this land."

He looked at the slumbering giants all around them. "There's still work if you're willing to go for it. Travel farther up north for the cutting. Or harvest small private woodlots. You know, fifteen acres here, fifteen acres there."

She crossed to the feller-buncher and started taking pictures. The sooner she finished up, the sooner she—they—could get out of here. "Fifteen acres here and there won't pay my dad's costs."

"Yeah, but what about just a few guys, throwing in together?"

She looked at him sharply. "What were you seeing my father about earlier?"

"I wanted to work something out to, you know, keep the business going. Like, pay him over time for the equipment."

"It's pretty valuable." Becky tried to keep the skepticism from her voice. "I don't know if he can afford to take back a note on it." The young man's blank face indicated he had no idea what taking back a note was. "Sell the equipment to you on credit and let you pay the loan back on time," she explained.

"So he's going to sell all this." He shoved his hands into his jacket pockets and rocked back and forth on his boot heels.

"Yeah." She moved to the front of the crawler tractor and took another picture.

"Man, all I need is one break. I know I could make a go of it."

She forced herself to keep her eyes on her notebook as she wrote down the condition and VIN of the crawler tractor.

"I mean, what if a couple machines went missing? Your dad wouldn't be hurting. He'd get the insurance money."

Was he suggesting what she thought he was? She lifted her head. Randy was staring past her, past the crawler tractor, into some limitless future that existed only in his mind.

She brought the camera back up and snapped off a shot of him.

"Hey," he said.

She took another. Then another. Stepped to one side so she could center him in front of the feller-buncher.

"Quit it. What are you doing?" He took a step toward her.

"I'm taking your picture." She looked at him over the top of the camera. "I'm not sure if you got this when I was talking about my work earlier, but I work for the ACC. If you're thinking about sneaking back here and making off with some of this equipment—which is a pretty damn stupid idea all around, since you can't even move half this stuff without a flatbed—I think you ought to know you won't just be ripping off my dad, you'll be ripping off my employer."

She snapped off another picture.

"Cut it out!" He lunged toward her.

She danced back out of his way. "You really are that stupid, aren't you?" she said. "Jesus! You're actually thinking about making off with a skidder!"

"Gimme that! You can't take my picture!" He swiped one long hand toward the camera. She held it back and over her head, out of reach. "Give it to me!" he repeated.

He charged at her. At the last moment, she dropped her notebook and purse and grabbed one of the aluminum poles holding the canopy over the tractor. She swung herself around it, flying free. Her boxed and bound rage tipped over and shook loose, burning out of her skin, rendering her weightless, invincible. She touched ground, light as a feather, her eyes fierce and her chest full of a triumphant crow. To hell with Eugene van der Hoeven. To hell with Millie. To hell with her father. She could outmaneuver this idiot forever. She bared her teeth at him.

"Bitch!" He lunged for her again. This time she leaped onto the tractor itself, one foot on the tread, the other on the seat, and then over the side.

He surprised her then. She thought he would follow her route, a filing to the magnet, but instead he circled the tractor so fast she had to scramble back across the seat to the other side. She barely avoided his reach, and she nearly fell off the tread getting back to the ground. A cold bucket of reality upended over her. She was alone in the forest with a guy built like a jackhammer. He came around the back of the crawler, his body much faster than his brain, and this time she neither crowed nor grinned, just tucked her chin down and ran, flat out, toward the road. Toward her car. Toward escape.

She pounded through the clearing, eyes fixed on the ground, leaping over a wind-scattered branch, dodging a rut gouged by a massive truck tire. She was deafened by her thudding feet, her sawing breath, the blood pistoning through her, so she was caught off guard when the blow came out of nowhere, snapping her head sideways, reeling her around, filling her skull with a terrible pain that was a sound, impossible to separate from the sound he was making, rage and pain twisted together.

She staggered, tripped, caught herself, and ran again, tears blurring her vision. She got three steps away before he tackled her, sending her head snapping against the ground and all the breath jarring out of her so she couldn't make a sound when he slapped her, hard, and clawed at the camera still clutched in her hand.

"Gimme . . . the fuckin' . . . camera!" As he reached, he stretched, and from some well of self-preservation she saw her opportunity and took it, punching him in the throat.

He gargled horribly, like a drowning victim, and she shoved him off her and staggered to her feet. He was clutching his neck. It sounded as if he couldn't breathe. She stood, tiptoe, suspended between flight and responsibility. *Oh, God! What if I've killed him?* She, who had never hit or been hit before this.

Then he sucked in a rattling, tubercular breath and lurched toward her. She ran again, for the first time knowing the wild, muscle-bunching, adrenaline-spiked velocity that means *run for your life,* commonplace words she had said herself, never imagining the terror behind them. The road her father had plowed through the forest flew beneath her, tree and rock and green and gray flashing by, her heart beating *Daddy, Daddy, Daddy*—another blow, tumbling her, rolling her in the dirt—*save me,* and he was on her, punching, kicking, crying, and the pain took away every memory, every thought, took away who she was, so that there was nothing left of her but arms folding over her head and legs curling up over her belly, and the pain . . .

. . . and there was a terrific crunch to her head, and then nothing.

11:30 A.M.

Randy rolled away from the woman and lay in the dirt, his hands clenched, his breath sobbing in and out. He thought he was going to retch. He was trembling uncontrollably. His chest felt tight and hot, his heart trip-hammering as it never had before. He was having a heart attack. That must be it. He lay in the dirt and waited to die.

After a while, his heart slowed. He looked at the blue November sky, running like a river between the trees that enclosed his line of sight. His breathing came easier. His trembling slowed to twitches. He still felt feverish and sick, as if his skin were too small for his body, but he had to accept that he wasn't going to drop dead on the spot. Which meant he had to face the crumpled, unmoving heap beside him. The woman. He turned his head, his throat aching. She was still, too still, and there was blood all over her white face. He rolled his head back. Looked at the river-sky. Oh, God. He was going to die. Not right now, not here in the dirt in the middle of the woods, no. He was going to die strapped to a gurney in a clean room with bright lights in Clinton. Because he had finally, irrevocably lost his temper.

He started crying again, tears spilling hot over his cheeks and running into his ears. His nose clogged and mucus clotted his throat, until he couldn't breathe and he had to heave himself into a sitting position and hack.

He looked at her again. Should he go to the cops and turn himself in? Did he need to get a lawyer first? How was he going to afford a lawyer? Oh, God, what about Lisa? This would kill her. He had just wanted to stay with her, and now he was a murderer and he was going to be locked up for the rest of his life and die. He rocked back and forth, clamped in place by misery.

What should he do? What should he do? His whole life ruined because he hadn't been able to keep a lid on it when that teasing bitch taunted him and took his picture. He looked at the disposable camera, abandoned in the dirt. That was it. That was what he was going to the death house for.

Unless he wasn't.

The thought seemed to settle over him from the cold blue sky, to creep up on him through the gray and groaning trees. What if—he didn't turn himself in? What if he wasn't caught? What if he walked—no, ran down the hill and took her car and drove away? Was there any way to connect him to—he didn't want to name her, but he gave her a wary glance. To *her?*

He thought about his day, about the trail he had left behind him. As far as Lisa and his brother-in-law were concerned, he was still at home. Lewis Johnson had seen him at the mill this morning, and Geraldine Bain at the post office at maybe ten o'clock. He hadn't said anything about his plans to Ed Castle. So he was good there.

It broke down with his bike, though. Triple A would have a record. They had picked up his bike on her card, and he hadn't even been there. Any cop asked, it'd be pretty damn obvious he had gone with her.

He had figured, when she offered him a ride, to have her drop him off at Mike Yablonski's. He could pick up his truck there and take Lisa home.

Mike Yablonski's. What if he had asked her to take him there first? That would have made good sense. If anybody asked, Yabbo'd say Randy had been with him the whole time, no sweat.

He didn't waste any more time thinking. He snatched up the camera and rolled to his knees. Avoiding looking at *her,* he rose unsteadily to his feet. After a few tentative steps, he walked, then jogged, then ran the last of the way to her car. His throat ached with every breath. He flung open the door and bounced into the driver's seat.

The sound of the engine was like the blast of doom. He froze in his seat, waiting for the fury of the law to hear and overtake him, but nothing stirred. He drove forward. His hands were shaking so, he had to clamp them tight on the wheel. He reached the surfaced road. Stopped. The worn and rutted edge where the dirt road bled onto asphalt stretched before him like some vast gorge. If he crossed over, he was out there, in public, where anyone could see, driving the car that belonged to the woman he had—he shook his head. Took a deep breath. The only thing more stupid than going was staying.

He swung out onto the two-laner, trading the grind of tires over packed dirt for the smooth hum of macadam. The shake became a shiver running down his spine. He had gotten away with murder. Now he had to figure out how to keep getting away with it.

11:35 A.M.

R uss shoved his chair back from his desk, frustration a bitter taste in the back of his throat. He had been tracking down McWhorters for an hour, looking for a Michael who might be Millie van der Hoeven's lover, without success.

Harlene Lendrum shouldered aside his office door, which he had left half open to let the warm air circulate. She clutched a coffeepot in one hand. "Well, its no birthday cake and champagne, but you can have the rest if you want it."

"Now that's an invitation I'm hard-pressed to pass up. Three-hour-old coffee dregs. Yum."

Harlene skewered him with a glance. "Nobody made you come in here on your birthday, mister, so don't get all snippy with me." The dispatcher, who had outlasted two prior police chiefs and was bidding fair to outlast him, didn't put much stock in rank or deference.

"Sorry." He slapped his pencil against one of a sheaf of papers he was working from. "This search is ticking me off. Finding the right guy is like looking for a needle in a haystack. I ran a printout of Michael McWhorters and M. McWhorters and split it with Noble." Noble Entwhistle, a fifteen-year veteran of the Millers Kill Police Department, was Russ's first choice for jobs like this. Noble didn't have an original idea in his head, but he was dogged, organized, and content to ring doorbells all day, meeting people and checking names off lists. Work that would drive a brighter guy, like his up-and-comer, Mark Durkee, nuts.

"I take it you haven't rustled up a likely suspect over the phone," Harlene said.

He grunted. "I eliminated the ones I knew who were too old or too married for the girl, but there are still a lot of names on the list."

"Being older and being married's not necessarily going to stop a girl."

He looked at her sharply. Her face was bland. "I had to do something to whittle the size of the pool down, or I'll be here all day. There are just too damn many McWhorters."

"Before you start in on the McWhorters, I'll remind you my mother was a McWhorter before she wed."

"So was my maternal grandmother. I'm sure you and I are related somehow." Harlene patted her springy gray curls. "You can tell by our resemblance." Harlene was a good ten years older and a head shorter than he, as straight and square as a weathered wooden plank.

"We-e-ell," he temporized. "I'll ask my mom. You know how she is. Loves all that genealogy stuff." The idea waltzed in on the heels of his statement. "My mother."

"What about her?"

"You know how she is," he repeated. "What does she love even more than genealogy?"

"All her causes. Save the whales and get out the vote and all that."

"Exactly. She's president of the local branch of the Adirondack Conservancy Corporation. And I'll bet five bucks for the doughnut kitty that she knows a thing or two about our missing girl. Eugene van der Hoeven said his sister had met with the local ACC members." He stood. "I'm going to my mother's house. I'll keep my truck radio on in case anyone needs to reach me."

His dispatcher eyeballed his baggy camos and long-sleeved thermal T-shirt. "If you're going to go on duty, you ought to check out a squad car and get changed. You still keep the spare uniform down in the evidence locker, don't you?"

He waved her suggestion away. "As soon as I get a lead on this Michael McWhorter, I'm out of here. I plan to spend the afternoon reading a good thriller."

She snorted. "Now I know you're over the hill. Taking the day off when there's a live case to work? I'll believe it when I see it."

11:45 A.M.

There was cold air. The smell of earth. And blood. Where was she? The pain made it hard to think. Becky tried to take a deep breath to clear her head, but the movement jolted her sides as if someone had touched her with a live wire. Little, shallow breaths, then. Dog-panting.

She opened her eyes. Her face was half in the dirt. She could see the road, and beyond that, tree trunks, bracken, and dead leaves. The angle was wrong. It made her feel queasy. She shut her eyes. She pressed against the ground, trying to shift her weight. Her arms shook. With a stabbing pain, she rolled onto her back.

She didn't want to move; she didn't want to think; she didn't want to be in her body right now. She stared into the sky. Why was the November sky, even on a sunny day, so much less blue than in October? In October, it always felt like she could reach up and touch the sky. Now, high and pale, it had retreated to the edge of the world. Soon it would snow.

The noontime sun shone straight overhead, warming her and the rocks and the dirt indiscriminately. But this was mid-November, and the sun was like a ball tossed in the sky, quick up and quick down. Within a few hours, it would be growing dark. And cold. When the sun set, the temperatures would sink below freezing. She ached so badly, she wanted to lie in the dirt and the sunshine and pretend that her dad would discover her at any moment. But she couldn't count on that.

She rolled over again. Palms flat against the ground, she pushed herself, shoulders up, rump up, until she was on her hands and knees. She would get herself to her car. She wasn't too far, maybe a hundred yards, maybe two hundred. If she could make it to her car, she could roll it down to the county highway. There would be traffic there, people that would stop at the sight of a woman with a bloody head. She could use the cell phone hanging off its charger.

She crawled downhill. Small rocks bit through the knees of her jeans, adding an undercurrent of teeth-gritting pain to the constant, throbbing ache that was her head and the sharp electrical jolts whenever she breathed too deeply or moved the wrong way. She inched forward, and forward, and forward, in a haze of pain and sweat and dirt and sunshine, and when she paused to see how far she had come she almost wept.

She wasn't more than fifteen feet from where she started.

Think. What if she tried to walk? It would hurt, sure, with her broken ribs, but it already hurt crawling. At least she'd get to her car before sunset. Recalling that ribs were supposed to remain stable, she sat back on her heels and wrapped her arms around herself. Then slowly, ponderously, she staggered to her feet. *Yes. Yes, yes, yes.* She bared her teeth in a half smile, half grimace. Took a step. Took another. Her mind supplied her with an inane song from one of those Christmas shows that ran every year. *Put one foot in front of the other.* Down the road. Around the bend.

Where her car should have been, there was nothing.

A part of her mind that was well away from the pain noted that her Albany friends were right. She shouldn't have left her keys in the car.

She wrapped her arms more tightly around her. She was cold, cold from the inside out, her feet and fingers almost numb. Okay. She was headed for the county highway. She'd just have to walk, that's all.

So she walked. *Put one foot in front of the other.* She walked a yard, two yards, three. Made it past another bend in the road. Her head swam, and for a moment everything darkened, but she breathed, and the world came back into view. She was tired. So tired. She had to sit and rest. For just a moment. She sank onto the road, bracing herself with one hand. "Help," she called tentatively. She took a deeper breath. "Help!" Noticeably louder. "Help!" she screamed, causing a group of crows to burst out of the trees and wheel through the clear sky above the road before disappearing up the mountain. "Help! Help! Help!" she howled, until the woods around her echoed with the sound.

Enough. Get to the road. She rolled to her knees and pushed against the dirt, trying to leverage herself up again. She felt a hot pain, biting and chewing at her guts. Deep inside her, something tore loose—*oh, that's not good, that's not good,* she thought and then everything tilted and a stream of dark bubbles roared up around her head and she was gone.

AN ORDER OF SERVICE FOR NOONDAY

Officiant: O God, make speed to save us.

People: O Lord, make haste to help us.

12:00 P.M.

Shaun Reid stood in his office, considering the rest of his life. He had driven all the way home from his AllBanc meeting only to idle in the driveway, staring at his garage door, wondering what was the matter with him. Why the hell couldn't he take the money and run? Terry McKellan was right: He'd have enough bucks to retire and live in style with his gorgeous young wife. Hell, he was still young himself, by today's standards. Fifty was just breaking middle age. He had thirty, thirty-five years ahead of him if he watched his cholesterol and kept active.

That prospect was like looking into a puzzle box picture, where an endless series of boxes opened before him, and each box was a gray and empty room. He reversed out of his driveway and drove to the mill, down streets he had driven for thirty years. More, if you counted the times he had been sitting in the seat next to his dad.

He had loved coming to work with the old man. When he was too small to go onto the floor, his dad had given him the run of the administrative offices. He would ride round and round in the secretary's chair that spun and rolled, and she would let him crank the mimeograph machine and swipe candy from the bowl on her desk. When he got older, he loved the way his dad would talk to him as if he were another adult, laying out facts and figures, asking for his opinion. At home, he wasn't supposed to pester his dad, who would stretch out in his chair, tired from a hard day's work, reading a magazine and drinking the Tom Collins Mom always served him. But at the mill it was a different story. Dad was alert, energetic, attentive. They were a team.

He had never wanted to kick loose, to move away or strike out on his own. In college, when his classmates were studying Marxist literature and marching against the war, he had lied about being a business major, because that was almost as uncool as being in the ROTC. But he never questioned that he was going back to Millers Kill, where an office next to his father's waited for him.

He stood there now. It was small, tucked between the reception area and what used to be the payroll accountant's office, until they outsourced payroll to a big firm that cut the checks and handled the taxes and Social Security for them. He had hoped Jeremy would one day work there, within earshot of his father, but—he shook that thought off. Entered the office that had been his father's and his grandfather's.

Most of the old pictures, from the first days of the company, were in the reception area now, impressing anyone who got off on the quaint idea that a business might run for over a century without changing hands. The pictures and plaques in his office were personal, and looking at them, he realized how much his life had been shaped by the presence of the mill and his role in its continuity.

There were his mom and dad, and him in bibbed shorts and curly hair, squinting into the sunlight at the ribbon-cutting ceremony for the "new" dam and causeway, now forty-seven years old and aging fast. There were his high school and college graduation pictures. No honors. He had never pushed himself. Never had to. The picture of Jeremy in cap and gown, though, showed loops of gold braid and an Honor Society tassel. Even then, his son had been planning ahead for his getaway.

By his son's graduation picture was a framed newspaper clipping with a picture of Shaun and Russ Van Alstyne at the 1968 trout tourney, showing off their winning fish, their arms around each other's shoulders. Russ had left the year after that and not returned for a quarter century. Shaun had seen him a few times since he had become chief of police, at Rotary dinners and town meetings. They had nothing in common anymore. It wasn't Russ personally. Shaun didn't have much in common with many of the people he had called friends back in high school. They had aged into grocery clerks and dairy farmers, or they had left town and not come back. There weren't many success stories in Millers Kill, not for the class of '69.

He flopped onto the sofa Courtney had picked out for him. Soft leather as comfortable as an old glove. He had kicked and screamed, but once the old couch—picked out by his mother, circa 1964—had been carted away and the new one installed, he wondered why he had put up with the hard seat and scratchy upholstery for so long. Maybe selling the company would be the same. After it was swallowed up by the GWP empire, he'd wonder why he had ever fussed.

Sure. Just like the victims of the Borg never fussed on *Star Trek*. Prepare to be assimilated.

A knock on the door. He rolled off the couch as the door opened and Jeremy stuck his head in. "Hey. Am I interrupting?"

"What are you doing here?" Shaun's tone was harsher than he intended.

Jeremy entered the office. "I'm looking for you. You weren't home, and the Trophy Wife is at church, so where else could you be but at the Holy of Holies, the office."

Shaun was willing to let the crack about Courtney pass. Once. "If you ever want to rise above the level of gofer, you might try a little work ethic, too. It was putting in lots of hours in this office that paid for your college and B-school."

"And my year in London and my car. Don't forget those, Dad." Jeremy smiled insincerely.

Shaun jammed his hands into his pants pockets to avoid clenching his fists. It was always like this with them. Gretchen, Jeremy's mother, liked to say they were too much alike. Shaun didn't see it. At twenty-five, he had been a husband and father, putting in fifty or sixty hours a week at Reid-Gruyn. Jeremy was a glorified concierge who spent every minute out of the office partying. The only thing they had in common was their looks: both tall and rawboned, Shaun's faded sandy hair the remains of Jeremy's aggressive auburn.

"I repeat, what are you doing here?"

"I wanted to see if you needed me to smooth your path tonight. I can wrangle you seats at the GWP table, if you want."

"No, thanks."

Jeremy rolled his eyes. "Dad, it's in your best interest to talk with these guys. If they make a bid for the company, your future is going to depend on them. I keep telling you, you can't make it today just by keeping your nose to the grindstone. You have to be out there, networking. Schmoozing. Personal relationships are important."

"I know that! Why do you think I've been going to those damn Rotary and Chamber of Commerce meetings all these years."

"Oooo, the Rotary Club." Jeremy dropped his voice from a falsetto to his normal range. "Dad, if they like your stuff, you have a chance to be a mover and shaker within the GWP structure. You know the Trophy Wife would love that."

Shaun glared at his son. "Don't call your stepmother that."

"She's five years older than I am, Dad. I'm not going to call her Mom." Jeremy threw himself onto the couch in exactly the same position Shaun had flung himself into earlier.

"We've had this talk before. Call her Courtney."

"Is she going to wear that slinky black dress tonight? The one that shows off her . . ." Jeremy made the universal male gesture for breasts.

"Goddammit! Show my wife some respect."

"Sorry, sorry. I got carried away. Really, I came to offer help. Let me get you up at the head table. Courtney, too."

Shaun sat heavily in his chair. "Listen to you. Making table arrangements. I can't believe you got an MBA for this."

"I'm getting the ground-floor view of a growing business. This year, I'm in charge of visitor satisfaction. Two years from now, I'll be the assistant manager. Two years from that, I plan on being the manager, and from there, who knows? BWI/Opperman has resorts all over the country."

"The hospitality industry." Shaun spat the words out. It always sounded like a fancy term for prostitution to him.

Jeremy ignored his sour tone. "The future of the Adirondacks, and of the country, isn't in manufacturing, Dad. It's in experiences. Tourism, hospitality, entertainment, games—that's where the money is." He waved a languid hand at the office around them. "Unionized labor, taxes, high transportation costs—Reid-Gruyn's cost per ream of paper produced is almost twice that of GWP's."

"How the hell do you know that?"

Jeremy lifted his head. "I pay attention, Dad. I'm a shareholder, remember? I stand to make a lot of money if GWP tenders a good offer."

Shaun felt as if a live wire had just made contact with his spine. "You can't be serious. You wouldn't vote for selling the company."

"GWP could be the best thing to happen to Reid-Gruyn. They can afford to update the specialty milling presses, they can funnel cheap pulp our way . . . hell, they can even bring in workers if the union threatens to get out of hand."

Shaun circled his desk. "This mill has been in our family since 1872! I can't— that you would even think of throwing it away to those . . . those . . . Malaysians!"

Jeremy sat up. "Dad?"

Shaun could only gape at him, his mouth working, trying to find words for the perfidy.

Jeremy stood up and gripped Shaun's arm. "Dad. Serious. I don't really want to see the old place get sold. But once that Haudenosaunee timber is taken off the market, our production costs are going to rise. With everything that's going on in the Middle East, fuel prices aren't going anywhere but up. Even if you can float the costs for a year or two, eventually they'll slice so far into the profit margin, Reid-Gruyn will start bleeding red ink."

"You talk just like my banker." His voice sounded sulky, even to his own ears.

Jeremy shook him slightly, and Shaun had the inverted sense that he was the child and Jeremy the adult. "This day has been coming ever since you and Grandpa sold off the last of the Reid-Gruyn timberlands in the eighties. You left yourself at the mercy of the landholders, and sooner or later, all land goes for its best and highest use."

Was this what B-school had done to his son? Bled off all his sentiment and turned him into a living economics textbook? It made him glad he had never gotten an MBA. The import of what Jeremy said sank in slowly.

"Maybe that's it," Shaun said, twitching his shoulder enough to break his son's hold. "Maybe we ought to buy back our own timberland."

Jeremy's laugh was abrupt. "You've got to be kidding. The tax burden alone would sink your profits. I wasn't criticizing what you and Grandpa did. It was the right move. Staying in your core business."

Shaun returned to his desk and began sweeping the papers and spread-sheets and P and L statements into a folder. "I'm not kidding. Haven't you ever heard of vertical integration? Owning the raw material, the manufacturing plant, and the means to transport it to the market. It could work."

Jeremy shook his head. "You've lost it. The board would never vote to ac-quire forest land. And anyway, there isn't timberland anywhere near Washing-ton County that's for sale."

Shaun grinned at his son. "Oh, yes, there is. Haudenosaunee."

12:10 P.M.

itch the car. Ditch the car. But where? Randy's mind ran round and round like a gerbil on a wheel. The sound of the tires on pavement thrumming the question *What to do? What to do? What to do?*

At one point, he realized it was the car, and not him, shaking. He checked the speedometer. He was doing seventy, twenty miles over the limit. His heart flipped over and he slammed on the brakes, a cold sweat shocking the back of his neck and his underarms. Jesus. A cop could have been hiding in a speed trap and he would have blown right by. Wouldn't have even noticed until he was pulled over. After that, he kept his eyes on the gauges.

That didn't solve his problem, though. He needed to dump the car. Someplace where it wouldn't get found for a while. Someplace that wouldn't lead the cops to him when they found it. Someplace where he could walk to Mike's.

The sign for Lick Springs Road gave him the idea. It ran from the mountains down through rolling pastures and teed at Route 57. Route 57 rambled alongside the river that gave Millers Kill its name, through the town and east toward Glens Falls.

And the Reid-Gruyn mill was right off it.

He didn't stop to ponder the idea. He spun the wheel and heeled the little car onto Lick Springs Road. He wouldn't leave the car at the plant; that would be stupid. But he could pull in behind the old part of the mill, where nobody ever went, and where no one would see him. He could hike to Mike's from there.

The only traffic on Lick Springs Road was a minivan with Vermont plates and a tractor hauling a boxy load of hay at the far edge of the breakdown lane. Good. The fewer people who saw him driving this car, the better. Traffic along Route 57 was similarly quiet. His racing heart slowed down. He stopped sweating. No one should be entering or leaving the mill's parking lot at this time of day. He was in the clear. He slowed as the gate came into sight.

And slowed even further when he saw two cars approaching it from the parking lot. He grunted. How could anyone have such shit luck? He braked hard, yanking the little Prius to the side of the road. There were several maps in the driver's-door pocket, and he yanked one out, snapping it open in front of his face. *I'm a tourist,* he thought, *just an out-of-towner checking out my map before I get back on the road. I'm a tourist, don't notice me . . .*

He peeked out behind one edge of the map. A little BMW coupe was easing through the gate. He recognized the driver. Jeremy Reid, the boss's son. Jeremy had been in his class at Millers Kill High School. Look at the redheaded sonofabitch, driving a car that cost as much as Randy and Lisa made in a year combined. Jeremy accelerated up the road without so much as glancing in Randy's direction. That was good, that was what he wanted, but it pissed him off anyway.

Randy recognized the next car before he could make out the driver. Mr. Reid's Mercedes. Oh, he remembered that car. The Joes that made Reid's money for him would be stumbling across the employee parking lot, clutching their lunches in paper bags, and Mr. Reid would be getting out of that big German car, his cashmere coat sliding off of the leather seat. There may have been some serious belt-tightening at the mill, like Lewis Johnson said, but it sure as hell wasn't pinching Reid.

As the Mercedes swept past him, Shaun Reid barely visible through the tinted windows, Randy spotted an Adirondack Conservancy Corporation bumper sticker and a Sierra Club decal on the rear.

Guys like Reid didn't have to worry about losing their jobs, losing their houses. He could just picture the man, writing out checks to the ACC at some fancy fund-raiser. So what if guys like Randy were left with nothing to do but flip burgers. Reid was still going to get his. Reid, and Ed Castle, and the town, they would all get theirs. And what was Randy gonna get? Screwed.

Goddam Adirondack Conservancy Corporation. Goddam better-than-thou tree huggers. *Her,* too, Becky Castle, laughing at him for wanting to do something with his life instead of rolling over and giving it up to the man.

Becky Castle. Shaun Reid. The Adirondack Conservancy Corporation. It was like one of those cartoons, a big lightbulb going off in his head. He had been thinking small, thinking of stashing her car out of sight somewhere. But that was just getting some space between him and her. What he really needed to do was throw the blame on someone else, so the cops would be so busy looking at this guy they'd never go any farther.

His hands shook as he flicked on the turn signal and steered the Prius back onto the road. He drove through the gates and guided the car, not toward the old mill, as he had thought to do before, but to the administrative offices parking. There was a fancy sign fronting one spot: RESERVED FOR MR. REID. Randy pulled the Prius into the next space.

He turned the engine off and sat huddled in thought. Okay, let's say he wanted the cops to think Mr. Reid was banging Becky Castle. She was—she had been—a pretty hot babe, in an outdoorsy way. Mr. Reid had already dumped one old wife for a younger model. Who's to say he wasn't looking to do it again?

He closed his eyes and pictured getting into the offices. The admin building door was sure to be shut up tight, but the plant door was never locked. From the break room, past the entrance to the mill floor, there was a dark little hall that ran all the way alongside the floor until it reached the ladies' john. There had been three women working the floor when he was there, and that's where they went to do their business. The trick was, the bathroom opened from both ends. It had originally been built for the reception area, and when Reid-Gruyn started hiring women at the mill, they just punched a door into the wall to give the ladies their own place to go.

Even if the door was locked on the reception side, it didn't have anything better than one of those little punch-in buttons. He could pop that in five seconds with a credit card, plant a few things from Becky Castle's overnight bag in the reception area, and be out again within a minute.

He grinned. And if Mr. Reid's office had one of those feeble locks . . . he could really go to town.

12:15 P.M.

His mother's cousin Nane's car in the driveway should have tipped Russ off to the chemical stench he discovered when he opened the kitchen door.

"Good Lord." He waved his hand, trying to clear some breathing room. "What is that?"

"Happy Birthday, sweetie." His mother sat in one of her kitchen chairs, pulled next to the sink. She was swathed in what looked like a pink plastic tablecloth. Her cousin was rolling a section of her silver hair onto a tiny pink roller.

He bent down to kiss her cheek, his eyes watering. "Hi." He retreated as far as he could, to the edge of the washer and dryer. "Hi, Nane."

"Hello, Russell. Aren't you looking well? We were just talking about you, weren't we, Margy? About the day you were born." Nane was older than his seventy-four-year-old mom, but, unlike Russ and his maybe-relation Harlene, the two cousins bore a strong resemblance to each other. Both ladies were short and cylindrical, with plump cheeks that narrowed into pointy chins. They looked like the sort of sweet little old ladies who spent their days tatting doilies. It was a clever disguise.

"I swear," his mother said, picking up from their earlier conversation, "I didn't think I was going to be able to push him out."

"You were almost ten pounds," Nane said to him, clipping the roller into place on his mother's head and reaching for a plastic bottle. She squirted something that smelled like chemical solvent on the new curl.

"I had an episiotomy scar you could see from the moon. They cut me from stem to stern." She chuckled. "The first time Walter saw it he said—"

"Mom! Mom!" Russ clamped his hands over his ears. "Too much information!"

She pursed her mouth. "Really, Russell. You're a little old to be thinking we found you in the cabbage patch, aren't you?"

"Can you just wait till I leave before you stroll down that particular memory lane?"

"Well, what did you come for? Are you hungry? I've got some sandwich fixings in the icebox. Help yourself, sweetie."

Lunch had definitely been on his mind on the drive up here, but he didn't think he could manage eating with poisonous fumes wafting through the air. "What is that smell?" he repeated.

"I'm giving your mother a permanent wave," Nane said. "She's going to look like she just stepped out of a New York salon for the party tonight."

Russ, who had been reading a new bumper sticker—THERE'S A VILLAGE IN TEXAS MISSING AN IDIOT—on his mother's already plastered-over refrigerator, straightened. "You're going to the dinner dance tonight? The one at the Algonquin Waters?"

"All the active members of the local ACC chapter have been invited. I told you that, Russell."

"No, you didn't."

"Well, I left a message with Linda."

He shut up. His mother and his wife had a relationship best described as an armed truce. He wouldn't put it past Linda to "forget" to tell him about his mother coming, just to make sure they weren't all roped into sharing a table together. His mother must have had a similar thought, because she said, "I'm sitting with other folks from the ACC."

"And she's going to look just wonderful, aren't you, Margy?" Nane smiled proudly at Russ. "We went into Saratoga and she bought a new dress."

He raised his eyebrows. "Gee, Mom."

Her cheeks pinked up. "Just 'cause I'm an old lady doesn't mean I don't like to look nice now and again."

"I better get my reservation in for a dance right now. You'll probably be so swamped with men I won't be able to get near you otherwise."

"Oh, go on. You didn't drive up here to pitch woo at me. What's up?"

He decided that he'd be able to stomach a sandwich in his truck. He opened the fridge and dug inside. "Do you know Millie van der Hoeven?"

"Of course. I've met her several times since she came back east. She's been one of the driving forces behind this Haudenosaunee land deal, more power to her."

He pulled out ham slices, cheese, and a jar of mayonnaise. "When was the last time you saw her?"

"The week before last. The ACC is interested in reclaiming the gardens and the cultivated areas of Haudenosaunee. Replacing the imported plants with native species. They asked for a group of volunteers, and I signed up."

"You do love to garden, don't you, Margy?" Nane snapped another roller into her cousin's hair. Russ's mother's head was beginning to resemble a pink-and-white Wiffle Ball.

He opened the bread tin on the counter and pulled out a loaf of pumpernickel.

"We took a little tour of the grounds, made lists of what we saw, and did some brainstorming about plants and a schedule," his mother said.

"Do you know anything about Millie's personal life?"

"Like what, sweetie?"

"Like why did she come east, anyway?"

"Well, after her father died last year, she wanted to see Haudenosaunee in public hands. She said she thought that would be the best memorial for him, to have the land he had loved preserved forever wild."

"Was that an issue? Developing the land?"

His mother pursed her mouth again, this time in thought. "I got the impression that money was the thing that mattered to the older sister. She may have been pushing to use some of the land to turn a profit."

Russ plucked a bread knife from the drain board and unscrewed the mayonnaise. He looked at the unfamiliar label more closely. It was made from soy.

"Go ahead, sweetie, try it. It's good for you."

"Your mother and I are on the Atkins diet. Lots and lots of good protein. You should think about it, too, shouldn't he, Margy? You're not getting any younger, Russell. Once you reach that half-century mark, your metabolism slows right down."

He slathered the soy spread on the pumpernickel. Suspicious, he checked the wrapper. Yep. Low-carb bread. "What about her boyfriend?" he went on.

"What boyfriend?"

"Millie's. Her brother told me she was seeing some guy from around here. Michael McWhorter."

Nane squirted another glob of unbelievably foul-smelling liquid onto his mother's hair. "We know a few Michael McWhorters, don't we, Margy?"

"Mmm-hmm. But I don't know as Millie van der Hoeven was seeing any of them. She certainly never mentioned anyone where I could hear her."

"You haven't heard any talk around town? Maybe about one of the McWhorters dating a new girl?"

His mother started to shake her head and was caught short by Nane's iron grip on a strip of hair. "Ow," she said. "No, I haven't heard tell of anything like that. Have you, Nane?"

"Not me. But I'm not one to listen to gossip, am I, Margy?"

"I have to say, I'd be very surprised if Millie van der Hoeven was to keep company with any of the local boys. She struck me as too much of a high flyer."

Russ finished laying out the ham and cheese on his sandwich. Both had proudly proclaimed themselves "low fat" on their wrappers. "What do you mean?"

"She's a nice girl, don't get me wrong. And very, very dedicated to preserving the environment. But she doesn't understand why the rest of us can't simply hop on a plane and fly to wherever urgent action is needed. She wears all-natural cotton clothing and never eats anything that's not free-range and organic. I'd like to do the same, I'm sure, but I'm on a fixed income." She rustled beneath her pink plastic shroud. "I just can't see her taking up with a boy who has to work for a living. At least, not the sort of work boys do around these parts."

"Hmm." He slapped the sandwich together and turned to her cupboards. "Any chips?"

"No chips. Nuts."

He made a face. "What about her relationship with her brother?"

"They seem very close. She's sounded a bit exasperated with him at times—"

"And who wouldn't," Nane broke in, "having a brother who lives like a hermit all alone up there, never going anywhere or seeing anyone?"

"Well, yes. But she always speaks of him with great affection."

"Any sign of trouble between them? Him disapproving of her environmental work or anything?"

"Far from it. I believe she was fixing to have him move in with her after the estate sold."

He picked up the sandwich. "Okay, ladies. Thanks for the lunch. Mom, I'll see you tonight."

"Bye-bye, sweetie. Drive careful."

"I always do. Nane, be good."

The elderly lady giggled. "I always am," she said. "Except when I'm not, right, Margy?"

He blew a kiss to both women before escaping to the sweet, fresh air outside. He climbed into his truck, thinking. The boyfriend story was looking increasingly like just that, a story. The question was, had Eugene been lying to him when he brought it up? Or had his sister been lying to Eugene, to cover up absences she didn't want to have to explain?

He took a big bite of his sandwich and almost spit it out. He stared accusingly at the low-fat, low-carb, soy-enriched crap. Maybe he could stop by the KreemyKakes Diner before he hit the station.

12:15 P.M.

Clare was tromping her assigned pattern with more doggedness than enthusiasm, checking her map, crossing off the ground she unsuccessfully covered. Every step seemed to indict her for not calling Russ about Eugene van der Hoeven's gun-waving, and every passing minute left her less and less hopeful that they would find Millie van der Hoeven on her family's land.

When her radio crackled, she had thought it must be the usual half-hour check-in. Instead, Huggins's voice said, "Fergusson? We've got a couple of replacements in from the Albany team. Hand in your map and GPS and go home."

Always the tactful spokesman, John Huggins. She keyed her radio. "I'm not that tired," she lied. Her overdeveloped sense of duty forced her to add, "I can keep on going," even though she had instantly started thinking about how fast she could get to St. Alban's to help out with the preparations.

"Don't worry about it," Huggins said. "These guys have years of experience on you. Of course, they weren't in the army, but they'll do." She thought she could hear laughter in the background before he keyed off. She gritted her teeth. She suspected that along with experience, the relief searchers had the equipment that seemed most important to Huggins: a penis.

She waited until she was sure her voice was civil before answering. "Give me your coordinates, and I'll drop my stuff off with you."

Huggins gave her his location, and within twenty minutes she was handing over her topo map and GPS to a pleasant young man with a serious case of labelmania on his outdoor gear. "Thanks," Huggins said. "I'll give you a call next time we need you."

"Give me a call next time you schedule a training," she said, her tone even but emphatic. "I won't be much use unless I get better as I go along."

Huggins grunted.

"No dogs yet?" she asked.

"They're still up chasing the old lady near Plattsburgh. That search has priority. Can't disagree with them. Young girl in warm clothing and boots has a hell of a lot better chance out here than a confused old lady in pajamas."

Clare shivered, then said her good-byes and struck off for Haudenosaunee. She wondered if she was ever going to get used to living in a place where wandering past your backyard could get you killed. Funny. She had studied at Virginia Episcopal Seminary, living in the dense suburban corridor of Arlington County, working at times in Washington, D.C., a city known for, among other things, its crime rate. Yet she had never felt menaced by her surroundings, maybe because ultimately she figured she could always deal with other human beings, reason with them—or, as had happened when she was mugged once, simply surrender her bag. But there was no reasoning with the Adirondack Mountains, nothing you could hand over to ransom your life from six million acres of trackless forest, wild rivers, and hidden lakes. Not to mention arctic air flowing south from Canada and blinding snowstorms blowing east from Lake Ontario.

The woods gave way to a blaze-marked trail, which gave way in turn to a path through the trees. When she reached the stone wall dividing Haudenosaunee's cultivated garden from the wilderness, she was torn between knocking at the door and seeing if she could talk with van der Hoeven or beating a retreat to Millers Kill, where her church, her volunteers, and a hot shower awaited her. Her grandmother Fergusson prodded her. *A lady never leaves without thanking her host.* The excuse that she was one of the search team, she knew, wouldn't cut any ice with her grandmother.

Van der Hoeven was nowhere in sight when she let herself in the front door. The den was open again, but there was no sound or movement indicating anyone was inside. As she walked toward the kitchen, she felt herself quieting her steps, as if she were walking through a museum gallery. The comparison fit. Haudenosaunee, for all its beautiful furniture and rich rugs, had a curiously empty feel to it, as if it had already been closed up for the winter, the family dispersed to their real lives.

She opened the kitchen door. The housekeeper, who was just hanging up the phone, jumped and clutched her heart.

"Sorry!" Clare held up both hands in the universal "I'm harmless" signal. "I didn't mean to scare you. I'm leaving, and I wanted to pay my respects to Mr. van der Hoeven before I go."

Lisa smiled wanly. "I guess I'm not used to other folks being around while I'm cleaning." She stepped closer, her expression thoughtful. "Are you headed into town? Can I ask you a favor?"

"Sure. What?"

"My car's in the shop, and my husband was supposed to come get me, but he hasn't shown, and nobody answers the phone when I call. Could you gimme a lift into town? I'd ask Mr. van der Hoeven, but he has a thing about going off Haudenosaunee." She glanced toward the small nook at the back of the kitchen, where, Clare saw, the cellar door stood open. Lisa looked back to Clare. "I can stay with a friend in town until I can get ahold of Randy."

"You don't live in Millers Kill?"

Lisa shook her head.

"Not that I don't want to drive you, but wouldn't you be better off staying put?"

"Um . . . it's a little awkward, hanging around once the job's done."

Clare thought of the curiously empty feel to the house. She couldn't blame the woman. She probably wouldn't want to spend all afternoon waiting for a ride here. "I'll give you a lift home. Tell me where you live, and I'll drop you on my way."

The housekeeper flashed her a relieved smile before bounding over to the open cellar door. "Mr. van der Hoeven? I got a ride! The, um . . ." She looked at Clare.

"Clare Fergusson."

"Clare Fergusson's gonna take me. One of the searchers."

Clare could hear the groaning of old wooden steps. The housekeeper backed away from the door. It reminded Clare of a scene from one of those old Hammer horror flicks, but instead of pressing her fist against her mouth and screaming, Lisa stepped forward again and asked, "Can I help with that?"

Eugene van der Hoeven—or his hands and legs, all that could be seen behind another two wine crates—appeared at the top of the stairs. "No, thank you," he wheezed, staggering toward the back door. Clare leapt out of his path. He set the crates down as gently as he could, the bottles inside clinking lightly before settling into place.

He leaned back, cracking his spine, and spotted Clare. "Reverend Fergusson. Are you sure it won't be an imposition for you to accommodate Lisa? I'm prepared to deliver her home myself." His face twitched faintly to the right as he spoke.

"There's no need," Clare said. "John Huggins has relieved me of duty, so I'm leaving anyway. And you should stay here and wait for word of your sister, not be driving all over town."

The undamaged corner of his mouth lifted, as if thanking her for that ego-saving excuse.

"I wanted to say good-bye before I left," Clare went on. She held her hand out. Eugene took it in his. "There are a lot of fine people looking and praying for Millie's return. I'm sure she'll be home soon." She squeezed his hand, then released him. "I'm hoping I get the chance to meet her at the dinner dance tonight."

Eugene's eyes warmed with interest. "You're going to the dance tonight? With the conservancy and the GWP people?"

"Yep." It suddenly struck her that that might not be a recommendation to a man who held a gun on the ACC's project director an hour and a half ago. But van der Hoeven surprised her by smiling.

"Could I then ask you to do a favor for me?"

"What sort of favor?"

He indicated the two wine crate towers, each one tastefully stenciled with the van der Hoeven Vineyards mark. "These are promised for the dance tonight. I thought I had hired Randy Schoof to deliver them, but he, for reasons unknown, has failed to arrive."

No wonder Lisa felt awkward about hanging around van der Hoeven's house. Clare glanced toward the housekeeper. Her expressionless features contrasted painfully with the pink flush of her cheeks.

"I could take them myself . . . but as you say, I ought to stay here until I learn something about where Millie is."

Now van der Hoeven was pinking up. It was the Saturday afternoon embarrassment club. Clare sighed. "I'll take what I can, but I have a tiny car. I'm afraid I can't fit in more than four crates."

Both van der Hoeven and his housekeeper beamed at her. "That would be fine," Eugene said. He turned to Lisa. "If you do see your husband, you can tell him to come here and pick up the rest. Otherwise," he waved one hand in a careless arc, "I'm sure the fates will provide a substitute."

It had better be the fates, Clare thought, leading Lisa and Eugene across the gravel drive, *because it wasn't going to be the Episcopal church.* She and Lisa were each lugging one crate, with Eugene staggering beneath the weight of another two. Reaching the Shelby Cobra, she set her crate down and opened the trunk.

"We're not going to be able to fit four crates into that," Lisa said.

"I know. Two have to go in back." She reached for Eugene's top crate.

Lisa opened the passenger door. "*This* backseat? Are you sure?"

"Yes, I'm sure. Oof." She braced the crate against her chest before lowering it into the trunk. Eugene wedged the other one he carried in and turned to the front of the car. Flipping the seats forward and sliding them as far toward the dash as they could go, he and Clare were able to shove the wine into the back, although, like Lisa, he made skeptical noises as he wrestled the crates into place. When they finished, Eugene and his housekeeper stood back and stared at the tiny sports car.

"I wouldn't have believed it," Lisa said.

"Nor I." Eugene gave Clare one of the three-quarters looks she had noticed earlier, his eyes on hers, his face sidling away. "Thank you, Reverend." He shoved his hands into his pockets. "I'd like to let you in on a secret. At nine o'clock, when the deed is scheduled to be signed, I'm setting off fireworks from here." He dragged his toe across the gravel. "It's, ah, not exactly legal in New York State, so I'd appreciate it if you didn't mention it to anyone. But I've been assured that if you come out to the terrace next to the ballroom at the resort, you'll be able to see the display." He dragged his toe the other way, sifting the gravel. "Bring your friends."

Clare wondered for a moment at his parents, who evidently had never brought their son in for the sort of postinjury counseling that would have strengthened him and made him able to face the world from behind his skin. She wondered who that boy might have grown up to be, instead of a painfully shy recluse. She thought of him, all alone in the dark, sending up brilliant fountains of fire into the sky. Cries for help that would never be answered.

"I will," she said. "I'll look for your light."

12:25 P.M.

Y ou sure you heard it this way?" Billy Ellis looked doubtfully at his hunting companion.

"As sure as I can be. Gimme a break, Bill. Sound travels funny in the mountains, you know that. But trying to find it's the least we can do."

Billy sighed as loudly as he could, signaling he'd play the part of responsible citizen, but he didn't have to like it. Chuck high-stepped over a tangle of briars and held back a handful of whiplike forsythia so Billy could follow him. Normally, he liked hunting with Chuck. They both had the same attitude: namely, that deer season was an excuse to get away from the wife and kids for a few Saturdays in a row, to eat huge, heart-attack-inducing breakfasts in a greasy spoon, and to partake liberally from their flasks of coffee brandy.

This Saturday had been all set to pleasantly repeat their usual pattern, up to the moment when they heard a faint, faraway cry for help shivering through the empty branches. Billy argued it was probably some damn fool who sat in poison oak taking a dump and who now needed help wiping his ass. Chuck didn't buy it. A born crusader, if ever there was one, he had been dragging them over brush and briar for the last half hour. At this point, a twelve-point buck could have jumped up and offered Chuck a drink and he wouldn't have noticed.

"Chuck," Billy said, trying again.

"Dammit, Billy. That was a call for help. What if somebody's seriously hurt? Maybe got himself shot?"

"Then it's like to be some idiot flatlander on his first trip into the woods who saw a doe and shot his foot off in the excitement. If you help 'em, you know, you're only encouraging 'em to come back."

Chuck looked back and glared at him.

"I'm coming, I'm coming," Billy said. It was hard going. This part of the forest must have been logged or burned over sometime in the past decade; the trees were slim and close-set, still competing with each other for the space and light that only a few mature trees would eventually share. Brambles were everywhere, and Billy kept his gloves cinched tight around his cuffs for protection. They broke through a final screen of bittersweet and sumac and stumbled onto a wide dirt road.

"Where the hell are we?" Billy asked.

Chuck unbuttoned his coat pocket and pulled out his map and compass. He folded the map and held both it and the compass in front of him, squinting in the strong sunshine after the fitful shade of the woods. He turned himself right, then left, then completely around.

"What are you doing?" Billy was losing his patience. "Are we anywhere near the car? Because there's no way I'm going through that piece of woods again."

"I think we're on one of these lumbering roads." Chuck pointed out a dotted red line on the map. "If we go downhill"—he pointed right—"we'll come to Route 117. Could be whoever yelled for help is along here someplace. I don't think we woulda heard it so well if it was on the next access road marked." He pointed to another dotted red line farther west.

"If whoever yelled is still here—and that's a big if—he better be downhill. 'Cause I'm damned if I'm hiking uphill for some flatlander." Billy took off without waiting to see if Chuck followed him. He didn't have to. He had their car keys.

"We ought to go uphill first." Chuck ran to catch up with him. "What if we don't find him downslope?"

"Chuck, I hate to burst your balloon and all, but I gotta tell you this, as a friend. I've seen you lose keys and coats and your glasses, and once at the Washington County Fair you lost your kid."

"I found her again!"

"She turned herself in at the office. What I'm trying to say is, and don't take this the wrong way, you couldn't find your ass with both hands."

That was when they rounded the bend and saw the girl sprawled in the road. Billy was frozen in place by the surprise for several seconds while Chuck pelted forward, laid down his rifle, and knelt beside her. He turned toward Billy. "C'mere, dammit. You're the one who took the Red Cross course."

That broke the spell. Billy ran downslope and skidded to a stop next to them. The girl's head was bloody; her hand, when he took it into his own, cold. He pinched his fingers over her wrist.

"Is she . . . ?" Chuck looked like he was going to puke.

Billy shook his head. "Get down to the road, see if you can raise some help. She's alive."

12:30 P.M.

Sitting felt good. Too good. The tiny, enclosed area inside her Shelby made Clare forcefully aware that she had stepped in and splattered through some unpleasantly decayed substances and that, in her haste to make it out to the search zone on time, she had forgotten to apply her deodorant before she dressed. She stank.

She unrolled her window, then glanced toward Lisa. "Do you mind?"

"Oh, no. Not at all." Wonderful. Her passenger could smell her, too. She threw the car into gear, said a brief prayer that nothing would break or fall off on the Haudenosaunee drive, and left the great camp behind.

"Where do you live?"

"You go left on Highway 53, then cross Muddy Brook Road, and it's down Route 127 a ways." She looked sideways at Clare. "So, I gotta ask, what was in those papers you were reading?"

Clare, startled, took her eyes off the road. That was when she heard it. Two shotgun blasts, one right after another, the sound so close through her open window that she instinctively flinched in her seat.

"What the hell?" Lisa whipped her head around, looking for the source of the shots.

"That's an alarm signal." Clare glanced in the rearview mirror. "For hunters. If there's trouble, they fire twice." The road was empty in both directions. She stepped on her brakes. She leaned out into the cool air. "Hallo the alarm!" she yelled. "Where are you?"

A garble of voices resolved into a single "Here!" Close.

Lisa pointed down the road. "There's a dirt road that leads onto the Haudenosaunee land down thataway."

Clare shifted the car into neutral and let it coast down the county road's gentle incline. "Keep yelling!" she shouted.

A sound like an underpopulated pep rally swelled up from the woods in front of her. In front and to the left. It grew louder and louder as she rolled down the two-lane highway, until she reached another barely-there dirt road.

"That's it," Lisa said. "The lumbering company my husband works for kept its machines there over the summer. Jeez, I hope it wasn't some kids fooling around got hurt."

A lone hunter stood at the entrance of the road. He waved his gun in the air and hotfooted it out of the way as Clare turned off of the surfaced road.

"Thank God you heard us," the hunter said. "There's a girl unconscious about a half mile up the road. My buddy Billy's staying with her. We didn't want to move her. There's lots of blood, and I think she's hurt bad."

Clare and Lisa looked at one another. "A girl?" Clare asked. "A little girl? Or a woman?"

"What does she look like?" Lisa asked, leaning past Clare toward the open window.

The man frowned. "She's—I dunno, a young woman. Younger 'n you." he nodded at Clare. "She's got long blond hair. That's about all we could tell. I didn't want to move her any in case she's hurt her back."

"Do you think . . . ?" Clare asked Lisa.

The housekeeper nodded. "It sounds like her."

"Who?" The hunter shifted his gun into his other hand and wiped his face.

"A young woman's been missing from the van der Hoeven estate. There's a search team out for her now." She glanced over at Lisa. "You did say this is Haudenosaunee land, right?" Lisa nodded.

The hunter looked back up the dirt road. "I can tell you at this point, the girl doesn't need a search team, she needs an ambulance. Do you have a phone? A cell phone?"

Of course. She was an idiot. She reached into her minuscule backseat, tugged her knapsack into her lap, and reached inside for her phone. She turned it on and was greeted by a blank "no signal." She hissed in frustration. Typical of the moun-tains. "Look," she said to the man, "we'll drive back to Haudenosaunee and use the phone there. That way, we can tell the young woman's brother she's been found. Will you stay here to meet the ambulance?"

"Course I will. Hurry," the hunter said, unnecessarily.

"Hang on," Clare told Lisa. She reversed the Shelby and tromped on the gas pedal, fishtailing out of the dirt access road. She zoomed back up the mountain highway. Swinging past the stone pillars marking Haudenosaunee's entrance, she accelerated up the dirt road, her small car jouncing and shuddering. She roared into the gravel drive, skidding to a stop in a shower of small stones and clearly alarming Eugene van der Hoeven, who was crossing from the house to the pathway that led into the woods. He had on a coat, with a small day pack slung over his shoulder. Joining the searchers after the tumultuous events of the morning.

"Reverend Fergusson?" He strode across the drive.

"Some hunters have found your sister," she said, tumbling out of the Shelby. "I need to use your phone."

"What?" He paled, his scarred face half-twisting in concern. "Is she . . . ?"

She shook her head, her hair flying out of its knot at the back of her head. "She's not dead, but she's been hurt. The hunters who found her are afraid to move her. We need to get an ambulance."

Eugene stared at her. "Where was she? How did they find her?"

"She's on one of the access roads, not far from here." She jerked her thumb to where Lisa was sitting white-faced in the car. "Your housekeeper says it's where her husband's timber company keeps its machines."

"Good God." Van der Hoeven turned to look at the trailhead that opened be-tween the house and the garage. He turned back to Clare. "Is she . . . conscious?"

"The phone?"

He shook himself. "Of course. God, what am I thinking?" He bounded toward the porch, took the steps two at a time, and threw open the door. He pointed to-ward the den. "Will you call it in? Since you know exactly where she is?"

Clare dialed 911 and described the location and what little she had heard of the young woman's injuries. She hung up, turned, and nearly collided with van der Hoeven.

"You didn't—you didn't see her yourself?" His face had regained its control, but he still sounded like a man in shock.

"I didn't. I'm sorry."

"So you don't know what happened to her? Was it an accident? Was she attacked?"

"I'm sorry. I don't know." She laid her hand on his arm. "Look, I need to take your housekeeper home. Why don't I meet you in the hospital afterward?" She hoped his agoraphobia wasn't going to prevent him from going to his sister's bedside.

"The hospital," he said.

"I could . . ." Clare searched for a way to make her offer tactful. "I could come back and drive you. Bad news has a way of scattering your concentration. It makes it hard to do ordinary tasks, like making phone calls or driving. I'd be happy to help."

His eyes snapped into focus. "No," he said. "Thank you. I can make it to the hospital. I was just thinking that I need to contact the search team first and let them know." He shouldered the day pack he had slipped to the floor while she was on the phone. "Let's go."

Outside, she paused at the foot of the porch stairs. "I'll meet you at the hospital as soon as I can."

"Yes."

Eugene trotted around the house and was out of sight before Clare made it back to her car. "He's going to tell the search and rescue team Millie's been found," she said to Lisa, buckling her seat belt. "Let's go tell that hunter help is on the way." Clare careened down the Haudenosaunee drive with Lisa bracing herself against the door and dashboard. The Shelby bumped up and down so violently during the brief trip, it probably shortened its life span by at least a year. Even so, it still felt like too long by the time she pulled up next to the hunter guarding the dirt roadway.

"The ambulance is on its way," Clare said through her open window. "Do you need any help?"

"No, thanks," he said. "My friend Billy's kind of a pain in the ass, but he's good at first aid. We'll keep a watch on her until the paramedics get here. There's no need for you to stay."

"Her name's Millie van der Hoeven."

"You mean, like *the* van der Hoevens?" He looked around him, as if more members of the Social Register might charge out of the woods. "Geez, this whole place belongs to them." He returned his gaze to Clare, looking somewhat embarrassed at his starstruck moment. "Don't you worry. Billy and I'd take good care of her no matter who she was."

12:40 P.M.

The ambulance siren startled Shaun Reid. He slowed, coasting to the side of the otherwise deserted county road. The ambulance swung round the bend ahead and flew past in a whirl of lights and sound. Heading away from the mountains, toward Millers Kill and the Washington County Hospital. He pulled back onto the highway for the last mile or so to his destination. He was just about to turn into the private road leading to Haudenosaunee when a rusting Jeep Cherokee bounced into view. Shaun once more steered his car to the side of the road; the last thing he wanted was to tangle with a driver that wouldn't care if his vehicle gave the Mercedes tetanus. After the jeep rattled down the mountain highway, Shaun pulled into Haudenosaunee's road, only to come head to head with another truck, this one a pickup that evidently needed more than the usual number of tires.

Both drivers edged as close to the enclosing screen of trees as possible and proceeded at a crawl. Shaun powered down his window and gestured to the other driver, a youngish man whose hair, cropped like a marine's, contrasted with his earring.

"What's going on?" Shaun asked. "This place is supposed to be as isolated as a monastery, but today there's more traffic than on the Northway."

"We're part of the search and rescue team," the man said. "Are you a family friend?"

"Business acquaintance." That was true. He had occasionally dealt with the late Mr. van der Hoeven over the years. "I'm here to see Eugene van der Hoeven."

"Mr. Van der Hoeven's sister Millie went missing last night. We've had a team here since dawn, looking for her."

Shit. It would fit in with his current run of luck, wouldn't it. Van der Hoeven probably wouldn't even be able to see him. "That's terrible," he said with feeling.

"No, she's been found, which is good, but she's been hurt. Mr. van der Hoeven was still at home when we left, but he'll probably be taking off for the hospital any minute now."

Shaun, digesting the news, barely managed to thank the other driver as he rolled up his window and continued up the road. If that had been van der Hoeven's sister in the ambulance, as seemed likely, he didn't have much time to meet the man and make his pitch. Unfortunately, a succession of hulking SUVs and pickups retreating down the road required him to keep wedging his car between their mud-spattered sides and the trees. By the time he reached the gravel expanse of Haudenosaunee's drive, his hands were clenched and his head pounding. His mood wasn't improved any when, after parking, he circled his Mercedes and found several fresh scrapes on the passenger side.

Shaun stomped across the gravel and up the porch steps. He paused before ringing the bell, giving himself a moment to get into the right frame of mind. Cheerful. Upbeat. This would only take a moment. He had something to offer that was going to make Mr. van der Hoeven a very happy man. He leaned into the doorbell, then rocked back on his heels. Cheerful. Upbeat.

He glanced around while he was waiting. The so-called great camp wasn't very impressive. Oh, it was sizable, all right, but if he had had the van der Hoeven money, he'd have put in one of those big, two-story-high windows and decorated the porch with brass lights and done some first-class landscaping. Look at the door, for chrissakes. It was right out of *Little House on the Prairie*.

The plain door swung open so suddenly he forgot to be Cheerful and Upbeat. "Uh," he said.

Eugene van der Hoeven stood precisely halfway in and halfway out. He was dressed for the outdoors, in a dark sweater and pants topped by a blaze-orange hunting jacket. His face was tilted, so that one side was less visible than the other, but what Shaun could see was enough. He had heard about van der Hoeven's boyhood accident, but Christ, he hadn't expected it to be so . . .

"May I help you?" Van der Hoeven's voice was chilly.

Shaun pasted on a smile and stuck out his hand. "Mr. van der Hoeven? I'm Shaun Reid, president and CEO of Reid-Gruyn Pulp and Paper."

"Mr. Reid," Eugene said sharply. He closed his mouth and started again, his voice softer, his irritation controlled. "Mr. Reid. I'm sorry, but you've caught me at a bad time."

"I understand," Shaun said. "I heard about your sister. I'm so sorry she's been hurt. I certainly don't want to keep you. However, if you could spare me just a few minutes of your time, you won't regret it. I have a business proposal for you that will benefit us both."

Van der Hoeven managed to peer at Shaun without turning his head and revealing his scars straight on. "Are you sure you're the president? Of Reid-Gruyn? The same company that owns the mill?"

Shaun raised his hand. "I swear. I'm not trying to sell you vacuum cleaners or life insurance."

Eugene stepped into the house. Shaun stood, paralyzed. What had just happened? Was he supposed to come in? He took a step forward and then scrambled backward as van der Hoeven surged out of the door, a backpack over his shoulder.

"I'm on my way out," van der Hoeven said. "You have five minutes." He continued past Shaun and down the steps. Shaun clattered after him.

"You and your siblings are selling off the Haudenosaunee lands. I'm guessing there was a problem with your father's estate planning and that you all owed a lot more in taxes than you expected."

Eugene's step faltered. He shot a look at Shaun.

"You may have thought only a large operation like GWP could afford to make an offer on your property. Not true. I'm here to propose Reid-Gruyn Pulp and Paper as your partner."

They came to a stop in front of the three-bay garage. "Reid-Gruyn can afford to purchase a quarter of a million acres?" Eugene said. "I'm impressed." He bent to lift the garage door.

Shaun wondered if the lack of an electric door opener indicated the van der Hoevens were worse off than he suspected, or if it was more of that old-money-cheaper-than-thou act.

"I was thinking more of fifty thousand acres," Shaun said, grabbing the edge of the door as it rose and helping it up. "That would still leave two hundred thousand to be preserved in their natural state," he added, in case van der Hoeven was more of a tree hugger than he thought.

"GWP and the Adirondack Conservancy Corporation want to preserve the whole parcel." Poised once more between the sunshine outside and the shadow within, van der Hoeven's face twisted in an expression of disgust. "My family has managed and protected this land for a century and a half, and a fifteen-year-old organization staffed by out-of-state do-gooders and underemployed biologists believes it can do a better job." He snorted. "I'd like to see the nonprofit that can hang together for as long as the van der Hoevens have."

Yes. This was it, this was what Shaun had been looking for. A kindred soul, who understood that it wasn't about the business. It wasn't about the money. It was about stewardship. Accepting the responsibility from the previous generation, holding it for the next.

Unwarmed by the day's sunshine, the interior of the garage was dank and cold. The first two bays held a Land Cruiser and a Volkswagen Beetle and smelled of oil and old packed earth. The third bay stored wicker lawn furniture, a garden cart, a folded canvas sun umbrella, and an ancient lawn mower. It smelled faintly of Shaun's eighteenth summer.

Eugene fished a single key from his pocket. Shaun darted past him to the side of the Land Cruiser. "You and I are in the same situation," he said, hurrying to make the sale before van der Hoeven got into his vehicle and drove away. "We both head family concerns. And both of us are being pushed by people who think GWP will do a better job than we can. I don't want to take Haudenosaunee land away from your family. I want to go into partnership. Reid-Gruyn will manage the timber harvest, and the van der Hoevens will continue to protect the land as they see fit."

Eugene sidled past him and opened the driver's door.

"Except unlike a onetime payment that you'll receive from GWP, our partnership will provide a steady stream of income."

One foot in the truck, van der Hoeven paused. "How's that?"

"The sale will be in cash and stock. The van der Hoevens will become part owners in Reid-Gruyn. Hell, between our two families, we could take the company private again."

"I'm not a businessman, Mr. Reid. I have no interest in running a company. And our family investments are very well managed by A. G. Edwards and Sons."

"You don't have to be a businessman. You have the natural resource. I have the experience." Shaun inched closer. "Do you really want to sign over all control of your land to the Adirondack Conservancy Corporation? Those people will micromanage your home so thoroughly you won't be able to plant a tulip or burn off a caterpillar nest."

Eugene opened his mouth, then snapped it shut. "It doesn't matter. The land isn't going to be sold."

Shaun felt his jaw hanging open. He scrambled for solid footing. "What do you mean?"

"Just what I said. We won't be signing over any control to anyone."

Shaun was baffled. "But a representative of GWP spoke with my board members just two days ago. He was confident the deal was going through." It had been the man's assurance that had scuttled his remaining support on the board.

He gathered his proof. "And my son works for the Algonquin Waters. He just stopped by this morning to talk to me about the banquet tonight. My wife and I are attending."

"You are? Excellent." Van der Hoeven leaned into the backseat and tugged out a crate. Shaun could hear bottles clinking inside. "I'm trying to make sure this gets to the hotel in time for the ceremony tonight. If you'd deliver it, I'd be grateful."

I'd be grateful. Shaun put on his best smile. "Be happy to help." He accepted the crate from van der Hoeven's hands and turned toward his Mercedes. He was surprised to hear more clinking. He swung around. Van der Hoeven had another crate of wine out of the Land Cruiser. The younger man nodded at Shaun to lead the way.

Now this is surreal. The dazzle of sunshine, after the darkness of the garage, made his eyes water. He had left his keys in the ignition, so rather than retrieving them to pop the trunk, Shaun opened the rear passenger door and slid his crate onto the backseat. Van der Hoeven nestled the second crate next to the first.

"So you're supplying Château van der Hoeven for the party, but you say there's not going to be a deal."

The younger man flushed, on one side of his face only, and twitched his head to the right. "They're getting our wine. They're not getting our land." He stepped backward. "I thank you. And now, I have to bid you good day." He turned and strode toward the garage, leaving Shaun standing there like a delivery boy who's just gotten his order form signed.

"But—" Shaun said.

"Thank you," van der Hoeven tossed over his shoulder.

Shaun shut the rear door, crossed around the back of the car, and opened the driver's door like a man in a dream. He keyed the ignition and looked one more time toward the cold darkness of the garage. He couldn't see van der Hoeven. He shifted and looped around the drive, heading for the private road. What the hell had just happened? Could van der Hoeven have been telling the truth? Was that it, all his worries about losing their source of pulpwood, gone in an instant? It didn't seem believable. And why would the van der Hoevens just pass up the millions they stood to gain on the deal? It sure as hell wasn't because the stock market's performance had wiped away all their money worries.

Unless . . . his foot eased off the gas as the thought formed itself. Unless the van der Hoevens and GWP had decided to cut the Adirondack Conservancy Corporation out of the deal. The price to be paid to the family was based on the value of the land, but that value must have been adjusted downward to compensate GWP for turning all the easements over to the ACC. GWP would be the landholder in name only. All the potential economic value from the property—money from natural resources, money from development—would belong to the Adirondack Conservancy Corporation. And the ACC wasn't going to use it. They would never realize one red cent from Haudenosaunee. But what if GWP had decided to keep all the property rights? With their money and lobbying power down in Albany, they could buy approval of any number of "ecologically sensitive" developments around the lakes and mountains encompassed in Haudenosaunee's vast acreage.

Christ. The money from timber was nothing. Hell, a year's—*five* years' profits at Reid-Gruyn were change from a lemonade stand compared to the money that could be made developing real estate at that scale.

Shaun had reached the county highway. He looked left, then right. The coast was clear. Was he going to slink back home with nothing more to show for his efforts than a few bottles of wine?

He rammed the Mercedes forward, backward, forward, in a tight three-point turn that put him nose up on the Haudenosaunee road again. He stomped on the gas. He considered the chance he might crunch into van der Hoeven's Land Cruiser, heading down the drive, Eugene hurrying to his sister's side. *Bring it on.* A collision would hang up the bastard for as long as it took a tow truck to come up from town and clear the narrow road. And if Shaun couldn't get the whole story out of him by then, he'd follow van der Hoeven to the hospital and hang around the waiting room.

12:40 P.M.

Randy had walked out of the Reid-Gruyn parking lot without running into another soul. He headed down the side of the road toward Glens Falls, but when, after fifteen minutes, he came to a Stewart's convenience store, he figured he'd give it a shot and see if Mike was already home.

Mike picked up on the third ring. "Hey, man," Randy said. "Can I ask you a favor? Can you meet me at the gas station just down from the mill?"

"What are you doing there?"

"Long story. I'll tell you later. Can you come get me?"

"Sure. You got good timing—I just got back from hunting. I got my buck this morning, isn't that cool?"

Mike was at the Stewart's in ten minutes. Everything was humming along, right like it ought to. Randy thought of all those times he had heard somebody say, *He's getting away with murder.* And now he was.

Randy hadn't realized that "just back from hunting" translated to a freaking big bloody deer corpse tied to the hood of Mike's car. He couldn't stop staring at the thing, its head lolling and bouncing with every pothole they hit, its big brown eyes staring sightlessly at him through the windshield.

"So my brothers were totally whipped when I bagged him," Mike was saying, the glow from his victory in the sibling wars still shining from his face. "Two years in a row, I got my buck first. Two years! Yeah!" He raised a clenched fist in salute.

"That's great, man." They bumped over a frost heave in the road, and the deer nodded in agreement. *You bet!* "They still out there looking to get theirs?"

"Nah. By this time of day, the deer are all bedded down. They'll be back out there tomorrow at dawn, I bet. While I'm sleeping in, dreaming of venison steak."

Randy wondered if anyone had found Becky Castle yet. Should he drive by later to see? What if somebody saw him? He glanced out the side window at the clear sky. No cloud cover. Cold tonight. Below freezing and then some. He and Lisa would roll tight together under their quilts, keeping each other warm. And Becky Castle?

It might be better if nobody finds her. The idea scared him. The idea of going back there scared him. But it wouldn't go away, the dark thought, like a long afternoon shadow seen out of the corner of his eye. If she wasn't found, there would be no need for him to sweat and worry and wait to see cops at his door, looking for him.

After all, he hadn't meant to kill her. He hadn't even meant to hurt her, just to get the damn camera back. If she . . . disappeared . . . there wouldn't be anything pointing to murder. Just another person who went into the mountains unprepared and never came out again. It happened every year.

A bad pothole jolted them down and up. The deer's head thumped and nodded on the hood, its dry eyes on Randy. *Life's hard out in the mountains. It's easy to die.*

He didn't have to make up his mind. He could just go over there. See if she'd been found. He'd just check. He turned to Mike. "I gotta go pick up Lisa from her cleaning gig. You mind if I don't help you get the deer off when we get back to your place?"

Mike shrugged. "I can handle it."

"Look, would you do me a favor? If it comes up, I been with you the last hour and a half."

Mike took his eyes off the road to glance at Randy. "An hour and a half ago I was humping the deer outta the woods."

"There wasn't anybody with you, was there?"

"No."

"Did you stop to register the deer at a station?"

"Nah. I figured I'd call it in."

"Well, there you go. Nobody can say that we weren't together."

Mike looked suspicious. "What's up?"

Randy hesitated. "I don't want to tell you. But it's nothing that'll come back and bite you in the ass, if you're worried."

"You ain't screwing around on Lisa, are you?"

Randy's jaw dropped. "No! I'd never do that." He shook his head and folded his arms across his chest. "It's got nothing to do with her."

"Okay, then." Mike nodded, satisfied. "You were with me."

This would be perfect. On his way to pick up Lisa, he would cruise past the logging road where he'd left Becky Castle. See what was going on. If anyone was there—he had a vague image of a scene from *CSI,* with a fire truck and an ambulance and cops—he'd just keep on going. If she was still there . . . no one would be surprised at the sight of a hunter coming back out of the woods empty-handed.

They pulled into Mike's driveway and stopped. The stiffening deer sagged in its ropes, as if relieved to have reached its final destination at last.

"Hey. Can I borrow that extra orange vest you got? And your orange gloves?"

Mike looked surprised. "You going into the woods?"

"Lisa's working way up in the mountains. I figure it can't hurt to be careful."

Mike opened his door and unfolded himself from the tiny seat. He stretched and thumped the buck's rump affectionately. "You got that right. Some of the guys wandering around up there? You can't be too careful."

12:50 P.M.

To his surprise, Shaun didn't meet Eugene van der Hoeven on his precarious ride back up the Haudenosaunee road. He roared onto the gravel drive and parked. Getting out of his car, he could see that the garage door was now shut. What the hell? There was no way the man could have left without passing Shaun.

Was there another way to the county road? Shaun studied the open space between the garage and the house. Framed by stalks and stakes from now-dead flower beds, there was enough room to drive a vehicle through, a path leading past the house and gardens into the woods. He glanced back at his Mercedes and amended that to a four-wheel-drive vehicle.

He rattled across the gravel drive and peered through the streaky, cobwebbed window at the side of the garage. The Land Cruiser was still there. He glanced at the porch. There was something about the blankness of the windows that made him think, *There's no one home.* In an instant, he abandoned the garage and headed up the path. If he were a scientist, he'd examine every location, in order, to determine van der Hoeven's whereabouts. But Shaun was a businessman and experienced, he could say without bragging, in making decisions based on a handful of facts and a gut feeling. Right now, his gut was telling him that if he wanted to buttonhole Eugene, he was going to have to find him in the woods.

Ten yards or so past Haudenosaunee's stone-fenced backyard, the trail split. He stood, indecisive, reaching for a spark of intuition, when a faint noise to his right made clairvoyance unnecessary. He went as quickly as he could without kicking up the leaves drifted over the path. He couldn't have said why, but silence seemed like a good idea.

The way was broad and easy. Shaun wasn't one for botany—he left the flowers to Courtney—but even he could recognize that this branch of the trail wound through overgrown apple trees and berry bushes run wild. Cultivated land, then, or at least it had been a few decades ago. It wasn't until he saw gray stone and charred timber through the gnarled branches that he realized where he was headed. The old Haudenosaunee. The first great camp.

He stood stock still and stared. It was like stumbling over the corpse of a dragon, its massive ribs burnt and broken, its stone skin tumbled in or scattered piecemeal on the ground. Holly and boxwood advanced across what must once have been a lawn, their hard-edged, dark green foliage an impenetrable wall. Feral rose vines clawed up the remaining walls, and through the outlines of windows and over the jagged fence of scorched timber, young hemlocks bristled out at him like adolescent giants.

It was a scene out of a fairy tale, complete with a single intact tower rising out of the forest at the far edge of the ruined house. What were buildings like that called? He had seen some on a historic-houses tour in England.

A folly. That's what it was. This one must have been meant for viewing the scenery; he could see two wide, Roman-arched openings, each tall enough to accommodate a small cluster of sightseers, the lower one facing due west, the next a quarter turn round to the south and a floor higher. The airy effect was spoiled, though, by the blank stones and arrow slits piercing the other parts of the tower. It looked as if the architect and the owner had disagreed about whether they wanted an Italian duomo or a battlement, and each had gotten half his own way.

As he marveled at the architectural oddity, a man passed through the southern gallery and disappeared.

Shaun blinked. Had that been Eugene? He had only glimpsed the figure from the waist up, wearing blaze orange over something dark. Shaun walked a few steps toward the tower, then faltered. He wasn't a superstitious man, but wrecked mansions and vanishing figures were out of his usual arena. Maybe . . . maybe coming out here wasn't such a good idea. Maybe he had better go back down the path, get into his car, and drive away. He could catch van der Hoeven another time. If it was van der Hoeven he had seen.

But who else could it be?

He took another few steps. Then another.

One part of his head was already gone, down the path and in the Mercedes. Picking out a CD. Going home.

The other part of his head was whirling with opportunities, with advantages, with unanswered questions about the GWP deal, about Haudenosaunee, about this place, which everybody knew had been the site of van der Hoeven's great tragedy.

Then he saw the blanket. Heavy wool, brightly striped, dangling off the upper branches of a birch tree growing hard by the edge of the tower. Clean of bird droppings and dried leaves. Unstreaked by rain, unfaded by sun. That blanket hadn't been outdoors very long. And it hadn't gotten into the tree by someone throwing it up from the ground. He glanced up at the dark rectangular openings at the top of the tower. Despite the brilliant sunshine, he felt a shiver go through him.

What the hell was Eugene van der Hoeven doing?

He ran for the tower door.

12:55 P.M.

Clare had wanted to wait until the ambulance arrived. It seemed wrong somehow, driving on while a young woman was bleeding on a dirt road a half mile away. But the hunter had pointed out she would have to move her car anyway, in order for the ambulance to get in, so she and Lisa, who clearly just wanted to get home, took off.

"I'll swing by the hospital after I drop you," Clare was saying. "Poor woman. God, who would do something like that?"

"That boyfriend they were talking about? Maybe someone from that group that sent her the brochures?" Lisa shuddered in her seat. "I just hope her brother's not around when they catch the guy."

"Mr. van der Hoeven? Why?"

Lisa's eyes widened. "You saw him this morning, didn't you? With the rifle? I swear, I think if you hadn't yelled, he would have shot that girl. If he was willing to do that to someone delivering bad news, just think what he'd do to someone who hurt his sister. He really loves her."

"He's never been violent before, has he?"

Lisa shook her head.

"Then it was probably a onetime thing. His sister was missing, he was stressing about the land sale, and he acted irresponsibly with a firearm." Lisa gave her a jaundiced look. "Okay, very irresponsibly. I don't condone it, but that doesn't mean he's about to go out and act like Dirty Harry."

"Who?"

And Russ thought he was getting old. "It means to be a vigilante."

"Whatever. I'm just saying. He looked like he was ready to get medieval all over that woman. If he hadn't had that shotgun, he would have been all over her anyway." Lisa pointed to where a sign announced the intersection of Muddy Brook Road with Highway 53. "Turn right there."

"From what I've seen of him, Eugene doesn't seem like the type of man who'd let himself get physically close enough to anyone to assault them." Clare signaled and turned onto the road. "He's carrying around a load of baggage from that fire he was in."

"No lie. You know, his mother died in that fire."

"Good God, really?" Clare slowed down as Muddy Brook Road approached another narrow blacktop.

"Go left here. Yeah. I guess she and his father had been divorced for a while, but she was up at the camp visiting. From what I heard, she was looking for stuff to take from the old building, you know, to use in her new home? Mr. van der Hoeven—well, he was Eugene then, wasn't he? Only, like, fourteen years old. He was helping her."

"How did the fire start?"

"I dunno. I wouldn't have known all that about his mother, except the lady who used to clean for them, she filled me in when I took over for her."

"Had they had a bad divorce? Eugene's mother and father?"

"According to her, it was all smiles and roses. Whatever fucked him up, you can't blame it on a bad childhood." There was a beat. Clare waited for it, and wasn't disappointed. "Sh—" Lisa clapped both hands over her mouth before she could swear again. She looked at Clare with enormous eyes. "I forgot you're a minister. I'm so sorry."

"Don't sweat it. I've heard the word before. Even said it a time or two."

"Really?" Lisa jerked her gaze away from Clare. "There. There's our drive."

Clare turned into a rutted dirt road remarkably like the one to Haudenosaunee, complete with kidney-jarring bumps and exhaust-scraping potholes. It never ceased to amaze her, the number of country residents in the Adirondacks who had driveways longer than the average suburban street.

There were several cars in the side yard, none of them looking remotely drivable. She pulled in close to the forlorn steps leading up to an unadorned front door. The house, set in the middle of a bare expanse of dying grass and dirt, seemed unspeakably lonely. No flowers, no bushes, nothing but the limitless forest stretching away in all directions. Lisa climbed out of the car.

"Are you sure you'll be okay all by yourself?" Clare asked.

"Sure." She smiled crookedly. "I don't know who did it, but I can guarantee you whoever worked over Millie van der Hoeven isn't coming after me."

1:00 P.M.

Millie never would have guessed fear for her life could be washed away by sheer boredom. At first she had waited, her heart pounding with a combination of fear and rage, next to the door. Later, she hobbled around and around the circumference of the walls, peering as best she could out of the arrow slits, going over and over her plan in her mind. As time slipped past and the sunshine disappeared from the wooden floor, she found it harder and harder to focus—on her planned attack, on her anger, even on her fear of what was to come.

The adrenaline that had spurred her to action earlier burned away, leaving her cold and shaky and tired. She had used the bucket twice more, each time successfully. She tried to ease the cramping pain in her shoulders by leaning into the stones, by sitting, finally by lying on her side on her remaining blanket. She came close to drifting off, only to be snapped awake by the distant cawing of a raven.

The boredom was as painful as her shoulders and wrists—nothing to do, nothing to look at, not even her own voice to keep her company. She began to yearn for her captor to come back, not so much so she could escape but so the endless, monotonous waiting would be over.

Plus, she was hungry. And thirsty. Her stomach had started rumbling at least an hour ago, and beneath her duct-tape gag, her mouth was tissue-paper dry.

What if no one came?

What if she wasn't being held for ransom but had been snatched by someone who wanted revenge? Although it was difficult to imagine who, or who the target of the revenge might be. Once in a while her mother offended some other Palm Beach matron with whom she played bridge, but those ladies were more likely to spike her mother by tittle-tattling on her face-lift than by kidnapping her daughter. Eugene's poor mother, who might have held a grudge against the woman who stole her husband, was dead. And Louisa's mother didn't give a damn about anything except her horses.

Millie rolled from her side to her back, wincing, and rocked herself into a seated position. Her lower back twinged, and her stomach growled. Stones, bucket, blanket, floor. Nope, nothing had changed. The thinnest line of sunlight striped the floor beneath the western window. Must be past the noon hour.

What if no one came?

There was a scrape at the door. A bolt drawn back. A shock of amazement surged through her, and for a split second all she could do was stare. Then her head caught up with the rest of her senses, and she kicked against the floor furiously. She scooted across the planks, desperate to reach the wall and get on her feet. The door swung open.

It was a man. The brilliant blue sky framed in the open gallery arches behind him cast him into shadow, making him hard to see. Boots, dark pants, a dark sweater, and a blaze-orange jacket. Face hidden by an olive green balaclava. All of it straight off the floor of an army-navy surplus or hunting supply store. In his hand, a dark backpack, just large enough to hold a lethal explosive. Weapons. Surgical tools. A video camera.

He stooped over to set it on the floor. She thrust against the wooden planks once, twice, and fetched up hard against the solid stone. She raised her knees, planting her boots on the floor. With aching thighs, she heaved herself into a standing position.

Her captor stood as well. He held up his hand, one finger raised, as if to ask, *Can you wait just a moment?* He reached into his pants pocket, pulled out a horn-handled knife, and unfolded it.

Some remote part of her stood apart, amazed that she didn't fall on the floor in a dead faint. Instead, Millie braced herself against the wall and let the iron hinge pin slide from between her wrists into her palm. She felt clearheaded, weirdly calm, like a shock victim before the pain sets in. She prepared to fight for her life with both hands tied beneath her back.

The man paused. Looked behind him. Then she could hear it, too, a rhythmic creaking noise. She was utterly incapable of placing the sound until the man flipped his knife shut and ducked back out the door, closing it. Of course. The stairs. The winding stairs between the galleys were wooden, and old, and a memory fell into her head, entirely complete, of climbing them, her father's big hand holding hers, letting her peep over the railing at the mountains rolling away on every side. Her father's step made the stairs creak just like that.

The man had gone. He had shut the door.

But not locked it.

Was it a trick? Was there a whole gang of them out there? Maybe arguing over what to do with her? She gripped the pin, her only weapon, more tightly. Swaying forward, she hobbled toward her cell's single flat wall. Not toward the door itself. Next to the door. Where someone whose eyes were filled with the bright November sky would find it hard to see her, if only for a moment. She knew what she had to do.

1:05 P.M.

Shaun didn't like the stairs. They were lit only by the residual light from the galleries, so that in the very middle of their wall-hugging curve, he climbed in darkness. The stone walls pressed suffocatingly close on either side, and decades of raw weather blowing in from the open arches had left far too many steps half rotten, the tread sagging beneath his weight.

It was hard maintaining forward momentum under circumstances like that. The higher he got, the slower he climbed, at every turn wondering who—what—awaited him at the top. His head and shoulders felt hideously vulnerable. Every instinct for self-preservation shrieked at him to turn around and go home and never look back, but an imperfect, unarticulated thought kept him climbing. He couldn't put it into words; it was more of an equation. Secret + van der Hoeven = leverage. Or perhaps IF van der Hoeven's actions = illegal, THEN opportunity. Whatever it was, it was enough to spur him slowly upward, despite his skin shrieking that something bad was about to happen.

"What the hell are you doing here?" The shape looming over him was much too big to be van der Hoeven, and Shaun knew a strangled instant of panic. Then the man yanked his balaclava over his head, and Shaun realized it was van der Hoeven's angle, above him on the stairs, and his oversized sweatshirt that had made him appear larger than life.

"This is private property," Eugene hissed. "Get out now, before I call the police and have you arrested for trespassing."

Why was he whispering? Shaun's glance flicked past van der Hoeven to the gallery just visible beyond his shoulder. What was he hiding? "This is a very interesting place you've got here," Shaun said loudly.

Eugene's head whipped around to look behind him. That was all Shaun needed. He charged up the stairs, slamming bodily into van der Hoeven, and kept going.

The younger man let out an outraged cry and grabbed him by the shoulders. Shaun bent forward, breaking van der Hoeven's grasp, and stumbled up another step. "What do you have up there?" he asked. "What's going on, Eugene?"

"Get out! Get out!" van der Hoeven's voice was almost shrill. He lunged at Shaun, but the heavier man squared his shoulder and absorbed the blow before knocking van der Hoeven back. The younger man stumbled, caught himself, but retreated a step.

Shaun almost smiled. Lightweight. This was what not having to work did to a man. "C'mon, Eugene," he said, lowering his voice. "I want to be your friend. Just tell me. I won't blab it around."

Eugene's face was a stark divide: the unscarred half bright red, the scarred half ice white. He lunged for Shaun, who danced up three steps and avoided him. Eugene's outstretched hands slapped against the wooden tread.

"What's going on, Eugene?" Shaun glanced over his shoulder. He was almost at the gallery. The light from the open arches showed, instead of the wide and empty circular rooms of the first and second floors, a wall. And a door. With a keyhole. "Is there something in there? Shall I take a peek?"

"It's my sister."

The voice was so low Shaun wasn't sure he had heard what he thought he heard. "Your sister?"

Eugene bent over, hands on his knees, nodding.

"Bullshit," Shaun said. "I spoke with one of the search and rescue team. Your sister's been found."

Eugene shook his head. "No. That's what I told him. To get rid of them."

"The ambulance passed me on the road! Don't tell me the paramedics were hauling ass to the hospital because you told them to."

"I don't know who they actually found! Somebody they mistook for my sister!"

"There was another woman, hurt and unable to tell anybody who she is, who just happened to be found on your property. And you've got your sister, who everybody thinks is this injured woman, locked up in a tower." Shaun stared at van der Hoeven, amazed that he had sweated bullets over pitching a partnership deal to this guy. "You are one sick freak," he said, and strode up to the gallery.

"Wait!" Eugene scrambled after him. "Goddammit, wait!"

Shaun reached for the iron door handle. Eugene knocked him out of the way. Shaun stumbled back. The door swung open, and a blond battering ram exploded from out of nowhere, head-butting van der Hoeven in the gut, sending him flying into the next level of stairs.

Shaun caught a glimpse of wild, panicked eyes and a mass of hair before the woman's unchecked momentum sent her sprawling on the floor. Her hands and feet were bound, and she was squalling loudly, in a horrifyingly voiceless way that made him wonder if she was a deaf mute—or worse, if her tongue had been cut out.

"Christ," he said. "Holy Christ." He turned, ready to hammer van der Hoeven into the floor. The younger man's blow caught him by surprise and sent him reeling. He clawed at thin air, desperate for a purchase to stop him from a fatal tumble backward down the stairs. He twisted, grabbed the edge of the archway, and stumbled forward.

Eugene pounced on the woman, seizing her ankles and dragging her back into the room. Shaun lurched toward them, knocking into van der Hoeven, but the other man was ready for him this time and rolled back with the blow, sending Shaun sprawling onto the floor inside the room. Eugene tried to grab the woman's ankles again, but she twisted and kicked so violently that he gave up and shoved his hands beneath her torso instead, shoving her with enough force to flip her over.

Shaun staggered to his hands and knees, shaking his head to clear it. The woman—the girl, she looked young enough to be his daughters—grunted and groaned as van der Hoeven shoved her even farther away from the door, but he could see the gag preventing her voice from spilling out. She was still fully dressed, so the bastard hadn't molested her yet—

Van der Hoeven straightened. Dug a long iron key out of his pocket. Sprang for the door. The door with the decorative lock that must, Shaun realized, be fully functional. The bastard was going to lock him in.

It had been over thirty years, but by God he still remembered how to tackle. Eugene went down, half in and half out of the doorway. The key thunked on wood somewhere beyond his head, but as soon as Shaun loosened his hold to climb off the floor, van der Hoeven kicked him in the face. Shaun howled, clutching at his nose, blood spurting from between his fingers. Eugene was all over him, punching, clawing, shrieking, "Leave her alone! I'm protecting her! Leave her alone!"

Roaring, Shaun surged to his feet, using his weight to slam van der Hoeven backward. "Give me the goddam key!" he snarled.

Van der Hoeven rolled, faster than Shaun would have thought possible, his hand closing over the key. He continued to roll, evading Shaun's lunge, scrambling to his feet. He kicked up, like a kid playing soccer, and connected with Shaun's breastbone. His air rushed out so fast Shaun thought a lung was collapsing, and his heart—he clutched at his chest. Jesus Christ, was he having a heart attack?

"I told you to leave!" Eugene rushed him. Shaun, still flailing and airless, feebly warded off the blow. "I told you!" He slammed into Shaun again, sending him tottering through the open door.

Shaun tried to demand van der Hoeven let the girl go, but he was wheezing so hard, what emerged was "Let . . . girl . . ." and a series of gasps.

"She's here for her own protection," Eugene said, and his hand closed over the edge of the door, and Shaun saw what was going to happen, saw himself imprisoned by this lunatic, this fucking rich man's son who hid out in the woods so no one knew he had gone insane, and his rage and fear filled him up until it stretched his skin and then even the bounds of his body couldn't hold it back and he was surging, up, forward, plowing into van der Hoeven with all the force his seventeen-year-old self had used plowing into a row of defensive linebackers and the key arched out of van der Hoeven's hand and Shaun roared and they thudded against something hard and unyielding and van der Hoeven tilted—

—and there was a moment, before gravity caught him, his eyes wild with fear, looking at Shaun, begging him, begging him—

Shaun slammed forward. Eugene fell over the gallery rail, screaming, screaming until there was a wet thud and the scream cut short.

1:15 P.M.

Shaun stared at the unmoving figure that used to be Eugene van der Hoeven. There was noise around him: the rattle and rustle of the wind in the November trees, the cawing of crows, a rhythmic muffled whine behind him. But he was staring down into a well of silence, into a place where noise and movement and life were swallowed and went still.

He stared and stared, waiting for an arm to twitch, for a chest to heave upward, knowing as he did so that it wasn't going to happen. The rhythmic noise wormed its way into his frozen brain, first as a whine, then as an annoyance, and then, as his brain unfroze and the living world closed over the well, as a fear.

He whirled. The blonde in the room had squirmed across the floor and was inching her way into a standing position against the far wall. She met his eyes, and he could see she was terrified.

"It's okay," he said, approaching her. She shrank against the wall in a way that made him feel like a loathsome worm. "Really. It's okay. He can't hurt you." He reached for her duct-tape gag. She flinched away, her eyes flooding with tears. "I'm going to take this off. I'm sorry, but it's going to hurt." He pried off a tiny edge while she stood, trembling, and then yanked as hard as he could.

She made a noise he would never forget as long as he lived—half scream, half wail. "You killed my brother," she said, her heart breaking in her voice. "You killed my brother. I saw you."

Shaun stood there, the duct tape dangling stupidly from his fingers, while the young woman sobbed. "Your . . . brother."

She nodded.

"You're Millie van der Hoeven?"

She nodded.

He was utterly lost. What was going on? Were they into some sick bondage fantasy? "What the hell was he doing with you up here?" he asked.

Her lunge took him by surprise. He fell heavily backward, Millie thudding on top of him. With her hands held behind her back, she tried to hit him with her head. He shoved her away roughly and scrambled to his feet.

"He was trying to rescue me," she said, her voice twisted by grief and rage.

"What the hell are you talking about?" Shaun's confusion was settling into his stomach as an ache and an anger. *He* had rescued this girl, goddammit. She should at least show him some gratitude. Not try to club him unconscious with her skull. "You were the one who knocked him on his ass when he came through the door! Don't tell me that's how you get rescued."

She pressed her cheek flat on the floor. Tears ran over her nose and dripped onto the wood. "He hid his face," she said more quietly. "He hid his face and he had a knife and I didn't recognize him."

"Yeah? Well, when a masked man with a knife comes after you, it doesn't commonly mean that he's here to save you." He strode to the backpack lying near the door. It was the same one van der Hoeven had been carrying earlier. "Let's just see what he had in store for you, shall we?" He unzipped the bag and upended it.

A Thermos fell out, clanging dully on the wooden floor. Two sandwiches followed. An apple rolled out, landing on the sandwiches. He shook it again, numbly, and a roll of toilet paper bounced to the floor. A slim thermal blanket slithered out after it.

Shaun stared at the young woman sprawled on the floor. She looked at the food and supplies, then at him. "You killed my brother," she said.

He backed out of the room and slammed the door. The key. The key. He scrabbled around the base of the stairs where he had seen the thing fall. When his hand closed over it, he sagged with relief before turning to the door and locking it. He pocketed the key, and then, without being conscious of descending, he was outside the tower.

It was the same day it had been when he went inside. The sun had hardly budged in the sky. The trees, the ruined house, the forest closing in all around—it was all the same as when he set foot in the tower.

Except that he had killed a man.

Okay. He wasn't going to panic.

He was a smart man. He was going to figure out what to do, and in what order to do it. He tried on the idea of heading for his house and calling the police. Who would then arrive and take Millie van der Hoeven's statement that he had killed her brother before locking her in a tower room. No.

He considered calling his lawyer first. No, calling his lawyer and getting her to give him the name of a good criminal attorney. Who would stand beside him when the police asked him how Eugene van der Hoeven had toppled from the tower. And why he had shut the man's sister up instead of freeing her, as any innocent person would have done. Oh, yes, having an attorney there would certainly reassure the police that Eugene's death had been an accident.

Hadn't it?

He thought about that moment, about van der Hoeven's expression, about the rage and frustration that had been coursing through his body, pounding in his head. He sucked in a breath. Of course it had been an accident. He had no motive to wish van der Hoeven dead. Not one.

Of course, now he knew for sure that one of the three owners of Haudenosaunee wasn't going to be signing anything over to GWP tonight.

And the second of the three owners was trapped in a tower. No one knew she was there. Except Shaun.

What if Millie van der Hoeven didn't show up for the ceremony tonight? The sale of the land would be, if not voided, at least delayed. Eugene's estate would have to be settled. There would be time for Shaun to unearth alternate financing. Buy back-stock. Maybe tender his offer of partnership to Louisa van der Hoeven.

Admittedly, she wouldn't be likely to be receptive if he had been arrested for her brother's death in the interim. But he could cross that bridge when he came to it.

Meanwhile, his thoughts circled around to tonight's ceremony. To Millie van der Hoeven. The person who had walked into the tower, the man who hadn't ever caused anyone's death, was horrified. *What are you thinking of? Just keeping her?*

The old nursery rhyme sang in his head. *Peter, Peter, pumpkin eater. Had a wife and couldn't keep her. Put her in a pumpkin shell.* He looked up at the tower. *And there he kept her very well.*

He was thinking what to do with the body as he walked around the tower. He wasn't cocky, but he was rather pleased by his composure and rationality—until he stepped around a birch tree and finally saw Eugene van der Hoeven up close. There was something *wrong* about the way Eugene's limbs lay. As if he were a mannequin put together in a hurry. Or a marionette doll flung aside by a careless child. Shaun started shaking. His breath sawed in and out, too fast, until black spots swam in front of his eyes. Eugene wasn't a person anymore; he was a broken *thing*. And Shaun had done it to him.

He bent over and lost his lunch.

He staggered back around the base of the tower until the corpse was out of sight. He bent over, breathing deeply, willing the light-headed, spots-in-front-of-his-eyes feeling to go away. *Okay*, he thought. *Okay. Eugene is dead.* He was not going to touch Eugene. But he had Millie. He had to see the opportunity in it. Everything was an opportunity, if you were gutsy enough to take it. He would get Millie out of the tower, take her . . . someplace. A motel. The van der Hoevens don't show at the signing ceremony tonight. Haudenosaunee keeps producing cheap pulpwood for Reid-Gruyn.

And what do you do with her after? the old Shaun asked. But the new Shaun, the one who was going to come out a winner in this debacle, was already figuring how he could get a vengeful, uncooperative Rapunzel out of her tower.

He would need something to carry her in. He flashed back to the garage, talking with Eugene, the garden cart in the third bay. Perfect.

The walk back to the drive passed in a blur. There were the trees, the still-green grass, the dead hydrangeas, and then he was standing in front of the garage, thankful, now, for van der Hoeven's out-of-date, manually opened doors. He hauled up the far door. There it was, the garden cart, stored against the coming winter. Rectangular, with metal-bound wooden sides, it was big enough to hold a grown woman, if she curled up.

He rolled it over the gravel, past the edge of the house, along the broad part of the trail. He could see the stone wall enclosing the back lawn and the mellow, peeled logs of the house's rear facade. He was just swinging the cart onto the edge of the trail to the old camp when he heard it. The crunch of tires on gravel. He shoved the cart ahead hurriedly, only to stumble in its wake and nearly fall.

A door slammed. He froze in place. He heard the sound of footsteps, gritting over the gravel, thumping on the wooden porch. There was a pause, as if the unseen visitor had rung the bell and was waiting.

Shaun took a deep, silent breath.

"Hello!" a voice called. "Anyone home?"

1:20 P.M.

R andy had his excuse for being on Fire Road 52 all ready. The Haudenosaunee entrance was marked only by stone pillars and was easy to miss if you weren't paying attention. He was on his way to pick up his wife. He was absentminded. He thought this was the road. Who could argue with that?

Of course, he hoped there wouldn't be anyone to argue with at all. He slowed as he approached the entrance to the logging road. No sign of any activity. He signaled, then turned in. Was she there? Undiscovered? Should he risk going on? He accelerated gently, rolling uphill. Just a guy out to pick up his wife. That's all. He rounded a bend.

He almost hit the red pickup parked in the middle of the road. He jammed on his brakes, the slight shuddering stop making his stomach swoop as if he were on a roller coaster. Past the truck, he could see—oh, shit—a cop car. No ambulance, no hearse, no sign of *her.* He didn't see anybody. He worried his lip. Should he back out? Would that look more or less suspicious than getting out and taking a look-see? He sat in the driver's seat, paralyzed by his options, until a man in hunter's camos and a blaze-orange vest wrenched through the thicket of brush lining the road and walked toward him.

A hunter. He started to smile in relief, until the man looked at Mike's license plate. Looked at the tires. As he approached Randy, the man ambled wide of the car, in a path that might have been dictated by a rut in the dirt road but that also placed him in a position where he could see what was coming at him if Randy opened the door. He took off his cap, and that was when Randy saw it was the chief of police.

Russ Van Alstyne smiled and motioned for him to crank down his window. The handle stuck at each rotation, and the resulting squeak of glass on rubber sounded like a chorus in Randy's ears: *You're screwed, you're screwed, you're screwed.*

"Hey, son," the chief said. "What're you doing out here?"

Randy blanked. What was he doing out here? He was . . . he was . . . "Looking for my wife," he said.

Van Alstyne's blue eyes sharpened. "When was the last time you saw her?"

Oh, shit. The chief thought he meant Becky Castle. Probably had him tagged as a wife beater. Randy shook his head. "She works up to Haudenosaunee. Cleans house for them. Our car's in the shop, so I had to come get her."

"Cleans house for Eugene van der Hoeven? I think I met her this morning." Van Alstyne stepped closer and peered into the window. "I know you," he said. "You're Mark Durkee's brother-in-law, right? Schoof? Randy Schoof?"

Randy nodded. If being Mark's relation by marriage saved him, he would hug the self-righteous prick the next time he saw him.

"So you're looking for your wife, Randy?" The chief's voice was relaxed, friendly. His eyes, however, were as bright as ever, his glance flickering from the backseat to the passenger side to the well beside the door to Randy's clothes. "What's that on your pants, there?"

Randy looked at his lap. To his horror, a smear of blood stained his jeans. His mouth worked soundlessly, searching for some explanation. Why was there blood on his pants? He cut himself shaving? Jesus, that was ridiculous. He looked up at the chief, caught like a deer in the headlights. A deer. Mike's deer. "I went hunting this morning. My friend took a buck. I helped him with it." His relief at coming up with a good answer made his smile genuine. He gestured toward the chief's hunting gear. "How did you do? Got yours yet?"

Van Alstyne shook his head. "I have lousy luck." He grinned. "But I'm persistent. So, you're out here looking for your wife?"

"At Haudenosaunee," Randy repeated. "Isn't this the road to the house?" He slapped at his jacket pockets, as if searching for a telltale crinkle of paper. "I have the directions written down here somewhere."

"Have you been out here before?"

Randy froze. "Before?" Shit. If he told the chief he'd never been here before, he could easily get caught in the lie. His brother-in-law could tell them Randy used to work for Ed Castle.

"Yeah. Were you and your friend hunting out here or anything?"

Randy tried to sound relaxed. "Nope. Why?"

"A couple hunters found a young woman on the road here. She'd been hurt real bad."

Hurt? Hurt? What did that mean? Randy stopped himself from blurting out *You mean she isn't dead?* Instead, he pursed his lips in a look of concern and said, "I hope she's all right."

"Maybe. She's been taken to the hospital. She was in pretty bad shape. Unconscious. Internal injuries."

He wasn't a murderer. He wasn't a murderer. He wanted to kiss the cop standing by his window. "That's terrible," he said, trying not to beam his relief.

"It is. What makes it worse is that another young woman is missing."

"Huh?"

"Millie van der Hoeven. I'm sure your wife will tell you all about it. The hunters who ran across this girl thought they had found Miss van der Hoeven, but now it seems she's still out there somewhere." The chief's unshaven face settled into hard lines.

Randy searched for something, anything, to say that would make him sound like an innocent bystander. "Uh . . . any idea where?"

The chief shook his head. "No." He pierced Randy with a look. "I think your wife must be around the same age as these two girls. Keep an eye on her. Don't let her hang around outside on her own."

"I won't."

"To get to Haudenosaunee, you want to get back on the county road and turn right. The road is about a mile up. It's marked by two stone pillars."

Randy shifted the car into reverse. "Good luck in finding the missing girl!" He cranked the window up as he backed out of sight. The chief watched him the whole way.

Randy cursed himself as he drove up the county road. He had to get Lisa, drop her off home, and talk to Mike Yablonski. He needed his friend to say that he picked Randy up after his bike got wrecked. Randy didn't want Russ Van Alstyne even thinking about him in Becky Castle's car. The man saw way too much for comfort. Christ, why had he insisted on taking the bike to Jimino's? Frank Jimino would know it was his. If he had let it go to whatever the nearest garage was, he could, if he had to, abandon it. Now there was a clear trail: him to Ed Castle's, then Becky taking responsibility for his bike.

He was so distracted by his thoughts he nearly plowed into the black Mercedes at the top of the Haudenosaunee drive.

"What the hell?" He parked his truck near the front door and got out. There was nobody in the car. He walked closer. Except for a fresh scratch on the passenger side, it was an exact duplicate of Shaun Reid's car. He walked to the rear. Yep. There they were. Sierra Club and Adirondack Conservancy Corporation stickers. What the hell?

He circled the Mercedes before heading toward the front porch. He climbed the steps and knocked on the door. No one answered. He knocked again. Then he opened the door and took a single step inside. "Hello? Anybody home?" he shouted. The echo of his own voice convinced him of what he had already felt. The house was deserted. He closed the door and wandered out onto the gravel drive. Where was his wife? Could van der Hoeven have given her a ride home? From what Lisa told him, her employer never left Haudenosaunee if he could help it. That was why—oh, hell. He slapped one hand over his face. Lisa had told Mr. van der Hoeven that Randy would deliver some boxes of wine for him. If van der Hoeven had to take Lisa home and make the delivery himself, Randy would never hear the end of it. Never.

But if Lisa and van der Hoeven were gone, what was Shaun Reid doing here? Hiking by himself in the woods?

"Hello," Randy shouted, crossing the drive toward the back of the house. "Anyone home?" He listened as he walked to the head of a well-marked trail into the forest. "Is anybody here?"

He heard nothing except the dry rustle of wind through dead leaves. The place gave him the creeps. *The hell with it,* he thought. His life had been unfolding like a bunch of horror movies today. He didn't want to add *The Blair Witch Project* to the playlist.

He made a beeline for the back door. Inside the kitchen, he was relieved to find two crates of wine stacked by the cellar door. He had thought it was supposed to be more—that was the whole point, that he could bring his pickup and take a bunch—but at this stage, he wasn't arguing. He picked up both crates at once and walked back to his truck, staggering slightly under the load.

He'd make the actual delivery later. Right now he would go to ground at Mike's—hang out and help him cut up his deer and polish up his alibi. In the back of his head, the flip side of his not being a murderer loomed: Becky Castle, alive, could identify him. He didn't know what to do about that. He didn't even know how to think about it, other than by denial. He needed time. He needed a few minutes of normality in the midst of this crazy-ass day to catch his breath and get his feet under him. But he couldn't take too much time. He thought of the deer waiting for him back at Mike's. Just like him, that buck had been in the gunsights. And it had waited a fraction of a second too long before making its move. Now it was brisket and ground venison. He shook his head. He wasn't going to make the same mistake.

1:35 P.M.

The name tag on the nurse across the admissions desk from Clare read HOLLI MURRAY, LPN, CMA, but it might as well have been HOLLI MURRAY, LPN, PIA for all the help she was. *Pain in the ass, indeed,* Clare thought, giving it one more try. "Just look her up. Millie van der Hoeven."

"I've told you already, ma'am, we don't have any Millie van der Hoeven registered."

"I think her full first name is Millicent. Maybe they dropped part of her last name when she was admitted. Can you try Van Hoeven or just Hoeven?"

"Ma'am, we don't have her."

"Oh, for heaven's sakes!" Clare dropped her hands heavily on the admissions desk to avoid clutching at her hair. "Could you check and see if she was admitted at Glens Falls, then?"

Holli Murray, LPN, CMA, gave Clare a condescending look. She was a tall, stick-thin woman, with peroxide-brittle hair and a heavy hand with makeup.

She looked like she was auditioning for the run-down-and-tired "before" spot in an ad for iron supplements. "Ma'am," she said, "are you a family member?"

"No, but I'm a priest."

Murray's overplucked eyebrows rose as she very visibly gave Clare the once-over, taking in her baggy, stained pants, her aged thermal shirt, and her hair, flattened by her hat and escaping in straggly pieces from the knot at the back of her head.

"Really!" Clare protested. "I'm one of the hospital chaplains!"

The Washington County Hospital was too small to have its own social worker, pathologist, and chaplain. The first two it shared with Glens Falls and the county medical examiner's office. The latter post was filled on a rotating basis by Millers Kill's Baptist, Methodist, and Presbyterian ministers—and by its Episcopal priest.

"Uh-huh," Holli Murray, LPN, CMA, said. "And I'm Clara Barton."

The elevator chimed, and Clare caught sight of a familiar face getting out. Alta Brewer, the senior emergency department nurse.

"Alta!" Clare called. "Can you vouch for me?"

"Hey, Reverend Fergusson." The nurse switched directions, bearing down on the admissions desk. A head shorter than Clare, Alta was built like a miniature Humvee and had the same approach to obstacles in her way. She glanced up at Murray. "The reverend's on the roster. Give her what she wants."

"But she was asking for confidential patient information," Murray whined.

"Oh, for crying out loud." Alta bumped Murray away from the computer screen. "Go get yourself something to eat, will ya? Before you keel over and give us all more work to do." She punched her password on the keyboard as Holli Murray, LPN, CMA, huffed away into the back office. "Fuggun' stick women. Can't stand 'em." Alta glanced up at Clare. "Whatcha looking for, Reverend?"

"Millie van der Hoeven. She should have come in on an ambulance within the last half hour. She had been injured up in the—"

"I know who you're talking about." Alta keystroked furiously. "Holli couldn't find her because she's not Millie van der Hoeven."

"What?"

"The cops went out to where she was found to have a look-see, and they got her purse. Her name's Becky Castle."

Clare felt her jaw drop like a character's in a Warner Brothers cartoon.

"The name Millie van der Hoeven never even made it into the computer, because Chief Van Alstyne called with the update right after she arrived."

"I saw her today! Becky Castle! At Haudenosaunee!"

Alta looked at her sharply. "Yeah?" She trundled around the desk and took Clare's elbow. "Come with me. Holli!" she yelled toward the office. "Get back out here! You're on duty!" She steered Clare toward the elevator.

"Why am I coming with you?" Clare asked, as the elevator doors opened, then closed behind her.

"The patient's parents just got here. The mom asked for a minister."

"It's Dr. Feely's week."

"He hasn't answered his page yet. You're here." The elevator chimed. Alta pushed her out onto the third floor.

"But . . ." Clare plucked at her grubby clothes. Alta looked at her unsympathetically. "I thought I was meeting Eugene van der Hoeven. Millie's brother. He's already seen me like this."

"They asked for a minister, not a model." She recaptured Clare's elbow and led her to the surgery waiting room. "There they are. Go on."

"What's going on with their daughter?" Clare hissed.

"She's in surgery now. Internal bleeding." Alta gave her a little shove. "She'll probably live," she added, with the bluntness of a twenty-five-year veteran on the front lines.

Clare instantly recognized Ed Castle from their earlier meeting, and she kicked herself for not putting the two names together. She kept forgetting one of the primary rules of Millers Kill: Any two people who share a last name are related in some degree.

When Russ had introduced them, Ed Castle had been bundled up in a Day-Glo vest and camouflage jacket. Now he looked softer and infinitely more vulnerable in a flannel shirt and padded windcheater. Most of his hair was gone, and he had the pale line of a farmer's tan high across his forehead. He was sitting with his head in his hands, and she could see his neck, cracked and lined from decades of exposure to the elements.

The woman next to him was, like Ed, in her early sixties. Her pastel makeup was marred by streaky shadows of mascara, and her mouth was wiped clean of lipstick. Despite her too-good-to-be-true blond hair, she looked old, stitched and seamed by a lifetime of hard work or the strain of the recent news.

"Excuse me," Clare said, her voice low. "Mr. Castle? I'm Clare Fergusson.

We met this morning at Haudenosaunee. I was one of the team searching for Millie van der Hoeven."

He looked up at her blankly. "Oh," he said. "The lady minister. Sorry, I didn't recognize you." He waved a hand at the woman sitting next to him. "This is my wife, Suzanne."

The woman's good manners kicked in and she automatically smiled at Clare, as if she really were glad to meet her, here in the hospital where they waited on word of their daughter. *When she isn't ravaged by grief,* Clare thought, *she must have a soft, sweet face.*

"What did you say your name was, dear?"

"Clare Fergusson. I'm the priest at St. Alban's Episcopal Church. I understand you asked for a minister. Is there anything I can do to help you? Anyone I can call?"

The older woman looked vaguely across the waiting room. "My younger grandson is already here. I let him go to the gift shop, poor thing. It's hard for him to sit around waiting."

"Hard for me to listen to that damn Game Boy of his," his grandfather grumbled.

"Our other girl, Bonnie, is working up at the new hotel today. I've left a message there and on her answering machine at home. I'm sure as soon as she gets word, she'll be here." She smiled again, but the effort seemed too much for her, and the expression slid off her face into oblivion.

At that moment, a woman with dark blond hair and reddened eyes appeared in the waiting room entrance. "Mom? Dad?" She hurried toward her parents, her arms open.

"How is she? Have you seen the doctor yet?"

"Just for a moment," Suzanne said. "She's in surgery now. She was bleeding internally." Her soft features crumpled. She leaned her head on her daughter's shoulder and began to cry.

The woman—Bonnie, Clare guessed—looked over her mother's head to her father. "What happened?"

"Internal injuries consistent with assault," Ed said, his voice low and hard. "You know what that means? Some bastard beat the crap out of her. Broke her ribs and busted her up inside and left her on one of my logging roads up to Haudenosaunee. One of my roads." Ed Castle bowed his head again, exposing his shiny skull and thread-fine silver hair. A penitent, hopelessly seeking forgiveness.

"It was my fault." His voice broke. "I should never have sent her up to Hau-denosaunee alone. I knew that other girl was missing. But I was too damn full of myself to give her the lousy damn insurance papers."

His wife, still weeping, broke free of her daughter and laid her hands over his shoulders. "It wasn't your fault, Ed. It wasn't your fault."

"It was!" Ed Castle stood abruptly, walking around them in short, jerky steps, propelled by the galvanic force of his pain. "Who told her she had to see Eugene van der Hoeven? Me!"

Okay. At least this thorn she could pull. "Becky wasn't hurt when she went to see Eugene van der Hoeven," Clare said, projecting her voice just enough to arrest Ed Castle's attention.

"What?" He turned to her.

"I was there. I saw the confrontation. Things got very tense, yes, but Becky walked away unhurt. In fact," Clare smiled crookedly, "she was full of what my grandmother would have called 'spit and vinegar.' Yelling at Eugene that she would be coming back and he couldn't stop her."

Bonnie and Suzanne bumped together and wrapped their arms around each other. Ed Castle squinted at Clare. "What do you mean, things got tense?"

Clare hesitated, uneasy. She hadn't even had a chance to tell Russ about Eugene's behavior that morning. "You know. Some conflict. Some shouting. Eugene wouldn't let her into the house."

"Did he . . . did he lay hands on her?"

"Good Lord, no. He did . . . okay, he did point a rifle at her. Ordered her off his land. But I swear, nothing happened. He was overwrought, she was over-wrought. She left, he put the gun back in its case, that was the end of it."

"When was this?"

"Midmorning. About an hour after you left, I guess."

Ed's bald head flushed red. Bright spots appeared high on his cheekbones. "I sent her to get insurance papers from Eugene this afternoon. At lunchtime."

A ghastly silence filled the waiting room. No one moved. Ed stared sight-lessly into nothing. "Eugene van der Hoeven," he whispered. He blinked. A tear spilled over his cheek. Clare thought, *It'll be all right, it's grief, it's just grief,* but then Ed's face crumpled into a tinfoil ball of rage.

"Eugene van der Hoeven!" he snarled. "I'll kill the bastard! I'll kill him!" Then he was gone, pounding down the hallway.

Suzanne Castle screamed. Clare turned toward her. She was crumpled in Bonnie's arms, wailing. Her daughter looked at Clare through a swamp of disbelief. "I'll get him," Clare said.

She sprinted toward the elevator, but it had closed and was already descending by the time she skidded to a stop in front of it. "Stairs?" she shouted to an unnerved technician. He pointed toward the end of the hall. She thundered past him, dodged an elderly lady in a walker, and whipped the heavy door open. Down the stairs she thunked, two at a time, until she reached the first floor. She flung the door open, spotted Ed crossing the lobby, charged toward him, and slipped and fell on a sopping-wet piece of tile flooring. She hit with enough force to knock the breath from her body. The first thing she saw, when she levered herself up on one elbow, was a bright yellow plastic floor sign. PISO MOJADO, it warned her.

"Holy cow, I'm sorry!" A young man in janitorial green sloshed his mop into a bucket and reached to help her to her feet. He had the wide-spaced eyes and curving cheeks of Down's syndrome, knit into a look of fierce remorse. "I shoulda put the sign closer to the elevator before I started cleaning the mess. Are you okay?"

Clare squeezed his hand. "It's my fault. I was running not looking where I was going." Her backside was damp and smelled—she sniffed—bad.

"A little kid threw up," he confided. "It's still pretty stinky."

She squeezed his hand again. "Gotta go." She took off, his warning trailing after her: "Don't run!"

She dodged past visitors and patients being discharged, shoving against the automatic-opening doors in a hurry to get outside, but once she had stumbled out of the lobby foyer and into the cool sunlight, she couldn't catch a glimpse of Ed Castle.

She mentally reeled off a string of curses. She abandoned the idea of racing to the visitor parking lot in the hopes of spotting his SUV. It wasn't as if she could stop him once he was behind the wheel. Call the police. That was the best thing she could do.

She slapped her pockets. She had left her cell phone in the car. She loped to the admissions desk, leaving a trail of wrinkled noses behind her. Holli Murray, LPN, CMA, looked at her with unconcealed dismay.

"Can I use your phone?"

"Pay phones are over there." Murray pointed across the lobby.

"I don't have any change on me. It's an emergency."

Murray opened her mouth, then paused. Her lip curled. "What is that smell?"

"The phone?"

"The admissions phone is not for the use of hospital visitors or patients."

"Look." Clare leaned over the desk. "Here's the deal. You let me use the phone, and I won't hang around you smelling like baby barf for the rest of your shift."

Murray hooked the phone in her fingers and slid it across the desk.

Clare dialed Russ's cell number. It rang once.

"Hello."

She closed her eyes at the sound of his voice. "It's me," she said.

She could hear him smile. "Hey, you."

"Are you anywhere near Haudenosaunee?"

"No, I'm at the Washington County Hospital."

She stared at the phone. "Are you here to talk to the Castles?"

"How do you know about the Castles? Where are you?" he asked.

"In the lobby of the Washington County Hospital."

He made a noise that might have been a snort. "I'm headed that way from the ER. I'll be there in thirty seconds. I take it I'll recognize you by your all-black outfit accessorized by a classic white collar?"

"No, but don't worry. Unless you have a head cold, you won't be able to miss me. Bye." She hung up.

Murray pounced on the phone. "That didn't sound like any emergency to me."

Only the sight of Russ emerging from the hallway stopped Clare from telling Holli Murray, LPN, CMA, what she thought of her little admissions Nazi routine. She left the woman wiping down the receiver and crossed the lobby to his side.

"Cell phones. You gotta love 'em." He grinned at her. "You look like you came straight from the search party. How did you know about—" He paused. Sniffed. "What in God's name is that smell?"

"Don't ask." She sketched in her involvement with the young woman she had thought was Millie van der Hoeven and with the Castles. When she got to the part where she spilled the beans about Eugene and Becky's confrontation, Russ frowned.

"How come I haven't heard this before?"

"I was going to call you. It's been kind of a crazy day."

"Jesus, you can say that again." He winced. "Sorry."

She flipped the blasphemy away. "This is why I was calling you. When Ed heard about what happened, he just about bust his gut. He ran out looking like the wrath of God, swearing he was going to kill Eugene van der Hoeven. Eugene might not even be at Haudenosaunee—I told him the injured girl was his sister, and I doubt anyone called him from the hospital to tell him otherwise. Did you?"

Russ shook his head.

"I was worried Ed might be a threat to Eugene. Was I overreacting?"

Russ looked down at her. "No. Ed Castle's been known to have a temper. You don't run a successful logging business for forty years by always being Mr. Nice Guy." He glanced at his watch. "Tell Suzanne there'll be an officer in to speak with her and to gather as much information as possible about Becky."

She nodded. "I'll stay with them until Becky's out of surgery."

"Okay. I better head out and stop Ed before he does something stupid."

"I'm going to get my phone from my car. Will you call me? Let me know what's happening?"

His weight already shifting away from her, ready to go, he paused. He looked at her, looked into her, his blue eyes full of words he wouldn't say. He nodded.

Then he was gone, leaving her with the work she had to do.

1:35 P.M.

Shaun Reid crouched, frozen, next to the garden cart, as the footsteps crunched closer and closer.

"Is anybody home?" a man called. Shaun ducked his head, as if averting his eyes could keep him invisible. The footsteps paused. Shaun held his breath. Then he heard the man walking away. He listened as the sound of stones scattering beneath his shoes grew fainter and fainter. There was another noise, he thought—a door opening? He pushed the cart silently forward, one foot, two feet, four. Then he heard the footsteps again, not moving toward him, but heavier somehow, as if the walking man were carrying a load. Shaun waited, unmoving, until he heard the distant noise of a car engine firing up.

He stood and stretched, and when he was limber again, he trundled the cart swiftly through the forest, its hard rubber wheels rolling over root and stone effortlessly. By the time he reached the old camp, he was overheated, sweating, and anxious to be done with the job.

He left the cart at the tower door, stripping off his jacket and tossing it inside before climbing up the stairs. They seemed even narrower and darker than they had the first time. If he had to spend much more time here, his touch of claustrophobia would flare into a full-blown panic. But not yet. He still had to get the girl out of the tower.

He was smiling grimly at that turn of phrase when he reached the wooden door to her cell. He dug the oversized key from his pocket and, mindful of how she had knocked her brother ass-end over teakettle, he turned the key, kicked the door open, and stepped back into the gallery landing.

Nothing. He walked into the room. Millie van der Hoeven sat Japanese style against the far wall. She had somehow moved the contents of the backpack, the empty sandwich wrappers and apple core testifying to her ability to eat while her hands were tied behind her back.

She stared at him. He could see a resemblance to the unscarred half of her older brother—the pale skin, the fair hair. Her eyes, swollen and rimmed with red, were the same cool blue-gray. She said nothing. She stared at him.

"I'm taking you out of here," he said, his voice loud in the silence. "I'm not going to hurt you." She didn't react. "I'm going to move you to someplace where you'll be safe."

Her face shifted minutely, from blankly hostile to scornful. Shaun spoke more loudly, as if volume could convince her of his sincerity. "I'm going to keep you overnight. That's all. I don't know what your brother was up to or what he thought he was protecting you from, but I promise you, no harm will come to you. You'll be free to go in the morning."

He wasn't sure if this was a lie or not.

He crossed the floor cautiously. He had already seen she could move, despite being bound. There was a lavender blanket crumpled beneath one of the arrow-slit windows, and he picked it up. He shook it out so it trailed across the floor.

"I'm going to roll you in this so it's easier to get you down the stairs. I don't want to hurt you, so let's make this easy on both of us."

She sat. Stared.

He approached her in a defensive posture, low, arms out, blanket clutched between his hands. Her head turned to follow him as he enclosed her in the blanket, but she remained as she had been, silent. Motionless. He wrapped both ends around her in a gesture that reminded him uncomfortably of a lover helping his beloved into her coat, or a father wrapping his child in a towel.

She sank her teeth into his arm.

"Jesus Christ!" he screamed. She wouldn't let go. The pain was blinding. He smacked her head almost by accident, trying something, anything, to make the hurt go away. He jarred her, but she bit deeper, so he balled his free hand into a fist and slammed it into her temple, once, twice, three times.

She pitched to the floor. Blood poured from his upper bicep, staining his expensive shirt and dropping on his made-in-Bermuda pants. He staggered to his feet, pressing his other hand against the wound, blood smearing his fingers. "God Damn!" he spat out. He had never hit a woman in his life, but right now he could cheerfully kick the shit out of the blonde crumpled over the blanket. Instead, he took advantage of her temporary acquiescence and, grabbing her shoulder, hauled her onto the blanket.

She moaned and stirred feebly. He let go of his arm and tossed the edge of the blanket over her, wedging it under her body before rolling her up tight. In a moment, she was trussed like Cleopatra in the fabled rug.

"Let me go," she said, her voice raspy.

"So you can snack on my other limbs? Fat chance." He bent to her and heaved her over his shoulder in a firefighter's carry. The exertion caused a fresh gout of blood to swell out of his arm. Balancing her with both hands, he could feel drops running into his armpit. He walked, stiff-legged, to the door.

She grunted and writhed inside the blanket, thrashing her legs in an attempt to hit some part of him. He slapped her butt through the layers of fabric. "I'm going to tell you this once," he said, "so listen up. We're going down the stairs. They're steep and twisty, and some of them are in none too good condition. If you try to escape or hurt me, I'm dropping you. I want you alive and whole, but I'm not going to risk my neck to keep you that way."

She stilled. "I'll get you, you bastard," she hissed. Carefully, slowly, he began his descent. The treads creaked and complained beneath the double weight. Millie's body remained still, but her mouth ran at full speed, growling out a series of threats and warnings and accusations. His arm throbbed and his legs shook and he had shooting pains from his lower back.

Trembling, he emerged from the tower. He stumbled to the garden cart and dumped the woman in, ignoring her shriek and the thump as her head hit the wooden side. He shoved her into a rough fetal position.

"Stay there," he ordered.

"Fuck you!"

"Christ," he muttered, picking up the handle and setting off toward the woods. "Haven't you ever heard of the Stockholm syndrome? Don't you know enough to ingratiate yourself with someone who has the power of life and death over you?" The weird thing was, when he said it, he realized he meant it. Not that he would kill her, of course—he wasn't a monster—but that really, truly, he had the power. "I could do anything to you," he said, trying out the idea. "And nobody would know."

She shut up after that.

He bumped her along the now-familiar trail. When he got near the house, he paused and listened for any signs that they weren't alone. He was too tired and wrung out to remain at the peak of alertness, though, and after a few seconds of silence, he rolled the cart onto the gravel drive, heading for his Mercedes.

His Mercedes. Crap. Whoever had been up here earlier must have seen his car. He shut his eyes, his temples pounding. Okay. Some variables were out of his control. He would have to accept that and move on.

He retrieved his car keys—smearing more blood on his pants—and popped the trunk. "I'm putting you into the trunk of my car," he said to the girl. "I'm going to drive you to a secure location. I expect it will be uncomfortable, but there's nothing I can do about that."

"You can let me go," she said, her voice bitter.

Shaun ignored her. He slid her tightly wrapped form forward until he could hoist her over his shoulder. As he heaved her into place, he heard her whimper, an admission of fear too great to be contained. "I'm not going to hurt you," he said, angry that she kept misinterpreting his actions, that she had put him in this position by refusing to believe that her brother had been the villain here, not him.

He dumped her into the trunk. He had time to notice her eyes, wide with terror, before he slammed the lid down. He pushed the cart into the garage, retrieved his jacket—the only item of clothing he had not fouled with his own blood—and made his way back to the car. His legs were shaking as he lowered himself into the driver's seat. He started the ignition, and k.d. lang began

singing, *"Black coffee . . ."* He glanced at the clock. He had arrived at Haudenosaunee an hour ago. An hour. For a moment, he could almost believe he
had gone back in time. There was his water bottle in the cup holder. There was
his phone plugged into the recharger, and his CD case on the passenger seat. As
if nothing had ever happened.

Then he heard a thump from the trunk, and his arm throbbed in response.
He pulled on his jacket, covering most of the bloody marks, and started down
the long dirt road. The wine bottles in the backseat clunked against each other,
k.d. lang kept on singing about walking the floor at 3:00 A.M., and he nearly
wept with relief when he pulled out onto the highway blacktop.

Glancing into his rearview mirror as he drove down the highway, he glimpsed
a brutish SUV with a bike rack muzzling its grill turning into the entrance to
Haudenosaunee. He lifted his foot off the gas, staring into the mirror. No mistake. Someone else was headed for Haudenosaunee. He caught his breath.
That was the margin that separated success from failure. A minute. Maybe
less.

He accelerated. He planned to be far away from Haudenosaunee when the
cops showed up.

2:00 P.M.

R uss had left the siren screaming all the way up the dirt road, wanting anyone up at the camp to know the police were on the way. In his experience,
unless two guys were already way into it, incipient fights usually dissolved as
soon as a cop car made its appearance. He hoped the sight of his red truck
would have the same effect.

Ed's SUV was in the middle of the gravel drive, not so much parked as abandoned. The driver's door was still open. Russ pulled in behind his friend's vehicle, switching off the siren and toggling the light. He slid from his seat with the
sound still echoing in the air.

"Ed!" he shouted. "Eugene?" He took a few steps toward the open garage,
close enough to see that Eugene's and Millie's cars were still parked inside. He
tipped his head back and filled his lungs with air. "It's Russ Van Alstyne! I want
to talk with you!"

You, you, you, you, the blue hills sang back.

The door to the house swung open, and Ed Castle stumbled onto the porch.

"Jesus Christ," he said. "Thank God it's you. He's dead. Van der Hoeven. He's dead."

Russ felt the weight of dread settle over his shoulders. God, he hated this. He was getting too damn old to play this scene one more time. And he liked Ed Castle. He liked him a lot. "What happened?" he asked dully.

"I don't know." Ed clunked down the porch steps. "I got up here, and he wasn't in the house. So I was looking around, thinking he was maybe hiding out, and I saw the trail."

"What trail?"

"Come take a look." Ed beckoned Russ toward the wide, hydrangea-framed trailhead that lay between the house and the garage.

Past the low stone wall marking the edge of civilization at Haudenosaunee, the trail split off in three directions. "I was walking along here, see." He could tell Ed was rattled. "I could see where the search and rescue team blaze-marked their trail this morning." Ed pointed to a tree on the edge of the wider middle path, sprayed with a single orange stripe. "Then I noticed the trail on the left." Ed pointed.

The long, thick grass growing between the trees had been recently trampled and torn. A single rut, the width of a bicycle tire, had dug into the earth in spots, leaving a crumbling of rich brown loam in its wake.

Russ's mind supplied a picture of the open garage he had scanned a few minutes ago. Land Cruiser. VW Bug. And in the last bay, a garden cart, carelessly shoved inside, its handles almost protruding out into the drive.

"So I took off this way. C'mon, he's up here."

They both struck out along the trail. Russ kept his eyes moving, scanning the grass, the dead leaves drifting among the trees, the gray-limbed distances closing all around them.

He knew what the ruined buildings were as soon as he saw them. He could compare them, in his mind's eye, to the black-and-white photos he had seen in the historical society archives. Saturated in the honey tones of the afternoon sun, even the subdued November colors were beautiful: granite and lichen, oak and boxwood, grass green and blaze orange.

"That's where I found him."

Russ swore under his breath. He headed toward the still figure in the grass, Ed at his side. "I touched his neck, you know, to see if I felt a pulse," Ed said. "There wasn't nothing."

Russ slowed as he got close to Eugene's body. "Oh, Christ, Ed. Jesus Christ."

"What?" Ed drew himself up, outraged. "You don't think I had anything to do with this, do you?"

"Ed. You heard this guy pulled a gun on your daughter. You ran out on your family at the hospital screaming that you were going to kill him." Ed looked down. His face flushed. "I get here, you're holed up in the house, and Eugene van der Hoeven's dead." Russ bent over the body. No gunshot wounds. No knife wounds visible. The angle of van der Hoeven's head looked wrong. "What did you do?" Russ barely got the question out. He took a breath and said more loudly, "Hit him with your car?"

"T'hell with you! I got here, I followed the trail, I found him! Period!"

"What's he doing way out here?"

"How the hell should I know?"

Russ dropped his hand on Ed's shoulder. "Come on back to the house."

Ed shrugged him off. "What for? You gonna arrest me?"

"I'm going to call in the crime scene unit. Then I'm going to ask you to come to the station and answer a few questions."

"The hell you are! I'm not the bad guy here!"

Russ put his hand more firmly on Ed's shoulder and turned him toward the trail. The older man jumped, spinning around to face Russ, his fists up.

Russ was six inches taller and twenty pounds heavier than Ed, and he loomed over his hunting partner now, letting his size remind Ed what a bad idea this was. He had no gun, no cuffs or stick or radio. If Ed attacked him, he was going to have to hurt the man in order to control him, and he didn't want to do that. God almighty, he didn't want to do that.

"I'm not arresting you," Russ said quietly. "I'm asking you to come in for questioning." He stepped forward, toward the trail.

Ed stepped back. "I'm not saying one word without a lawyer."

"You have the right to retain an attorney." Russ took another step. Ed retreated back. "I hope it doesn't have to come to that." Another step forward. Another step back. "It's just questioning. You're not being charged with anything."

"Yet." Ed turned away from Russ and marched ahead of him into the forest.

When they reached the great camp, Russ asked Ed to turn over his car keys.

"What?" Ed dug into his jacket pocket. "No. Never mind. I know." He pulled out the keys and bombed them onto the gravel. "There. Now I can't escape. Are you sure you don't want to tie me up, too? In case I knock you out and steal your truck? 'Cause you never know what I might do, do ya?"

Russ bent and picked up the keys without comment. "You can wait in the house," he said.

"I'm gonna use the phone," Ed announced, stomping up the porch steps.

"There's one in the kitchen," Russ said. Ed, slamming through the door, ignored him. Russ tipped his head back and closed his eyes. He hated this. He absolutely hated it. He lived in the town he was born and raised in, but he could count the number of people he called "friend" on one hand. And he had just lost one. He fished his phone out of his pocket. No signal, of course. He sighed and crunched across the driveway to the radio in his truck. He had thought no birthday could ever be as bad as his twentieth. He and his platoon had spent the day pinned down under heavy fire. He watched Gary Weyer, the radio guy, bleed to death over the course of the afternoon, and when they finally got air support in, the freaking flyboys nearly blew up their LZ. His buddy Mac kept saying, "At least it's not raining! At least it's not raining!"

He opened the door and reached for the mike. "At least it's not raining," he reminded himself.

2:00 P.M.

Shaun heard the siren before he saw the car. He had gotten into town a few minutes before and was looping around, Main to Church to Elm to Washington, facing up to the flaw in his plan to scuttle the sale of Haudenosaunee land tonight.

He didn't have any idea where to stash the girl.

At first he had thought a motel, but the more he considered it, the more dangerous it seemed. Unless he was willing to stand over her all day and all night—and he could just imagine trying to explain that to Courtney—there was no way he could guarantee she wouldn't be able to attract attention, by banging on the door or blasting the television or even breaking a window.

He had a friend with a camp up past Lake George, but Davis liked to hunt, and Shaun wasn't going to gamble that he'd stay away this weekend. His son's apartment? He could say he wanted Jeremy to spend the night at home. But then, even if he could con his son, which he doubted, he faced the same breaking-the-window problem. The basement in his house? Forget it. Maybe he could drive into the country and find an old hay barn in someone's back field. There was one they used to use for making out when he was a teenager. If he could remember where it was.

Then he heard the siren. He took his foot off the gas and craned his neck, trying to spot from which direction the sound was coming. It grew louder. Louder.

Shit, it was right behind him. He felt as if all the blood in his body had drained away, to be replaced by ice water. He glanced down at himself. The jacket covered most of the blood on his shirt, but the smears on his pants would be visible to any cop looking through the driver's window. The siren was shrieking in his ears. The cars ahead of him were pulling over. Hands shaking, he steered the Mercedes to the side of the street. He had nothing to cover his pants with. Nothing to disguise the telltale stains. Nothing—he registered the water bottle in the cup holder. He yanked it up, unscrewed the top, and dumped it over the bloody spots on his pants.

A red pickup truck with a whirling light clamped over its driver's side hurtled past him. Dumbly, he watched it go, the plastic bottle still upended in his hand. Beneath him, water squished and puddled, soaking his pants and boxers, ruining the SL-7's leather seat.

He hurled the empty plastic bottle to the passenger-side floor, where it ricocheted and rattled before rocking to a halt. Gritting his teeth against the exquisitely uncomfortable feel of wet fabric clinging to his thighs, he merged back into traffic. People like to say, "It was the worst day of my life," but Shaun realized the cliché was literally true for him. He had broken his leg on a ski slope once and had to wait over an hour for the ski patrol to rescue him. He had sat through a counseling session where his soon-to-be ex-wife told him everything he ever did wrong in twenty years of marriage. He had buried his parents. But this, today, was the worst day of his life. Sitting in wet shorts, every muscle aching, a woman in his trunk and a dead man on his conscience, he wished, as he had never wished for anything, that he had never set foot out of his office this morning.

His office. He blinked. Up ahead, a red light slowed the line of traffic, and he braked. His office. No, the mill. The old part of the mill. The original building, now half-crumbling into the river, unused for the past twenty years except to store machine parts too valuable to junk. No one went there. The doors locked securely, to prevent vandals from getting in and trashing the place.

There were windows, but they overlooked the Millers Kill, the river that gave the town its name. No one could get close enough to hear a single voice over the rush and fall of water over the dam and into the millrace.

It was perfect. And it was his.

For the first time on the worst day of his life, Shaun Reid grinned.

2:25 P.M.

Suzanne Castle stumbled back into the waiting room from the nurses' station, where she had been called to the phone several minutes ago. She stared at Clare and her daughter, slack-jawed and blank-eyed. "That was Ed. He's been . . ." She paused. "Your father's been arrested."

Bonnie Liddle straightened in her seat. "What? Arrested? What on earth for?"

Suzanne shook her head. "Not arrested. I'm sorry. He said they're taking him in for questioning. That's what it was. Questioning."

Clare's stomach clenched. "Questioning him on what, Mrs. Castle?"

Suzanne turned toward Clare, although Clare wouldn't have bet the older woman was actually seeing her. "Eugene van der Hoeven's death. Ed says he found his body. But the police are taking him in for questioning."

Bonnie rose and put her arm over her mother's shoulders, hugging her. "It's a mistake, Mom. It has to be."

"He asked me to get him a lawyer as soon as possible. To meet him at the police station." She turned to her daughter. "Should I call Woodrow Durkee?" Suzanne's voice was detached. Floating somewhere above reality. "He's handled some things that have cropped up over the years. With your dad's business."

"I think we need to contact a criminal lawyer, Mom."

Suzanne frowned. "Your father is not a criminal. He's not. He's not." She burst into tears.

Bonnie looked at Clare. "What are we going to do about a lawyer? How are we going to find one on a Saturday afternoon?" Suzanne Castle wept, rocking into her daughter's shoulder. Bonnie held her mother more tightly and spoke over her head. "I don't even know what questions to ask. No one in our family has ever been arrested." For a moment her face wavered, and behind the competent, take-charge woman Clare could glimpse the scared eyes of a child lost in the woods. Then she blinked, and the child was gone. "Do you know anybody?"

Clare hesitated. "I don't think I ought to be recommending a lawyer for your dad. That's a huge decision."

"It doesn't have to be permanent. All we need right now is someone who'll be with Dad when he's questioned. Someone who will know what to do if Dad . . . if the police decide to charge him. So Dad doesn't have to stay in jail."

Suzanne Castle wiped her eyes with the heels of her hands. "No," she agreed, her voice shaky. "He doesn't go to jail. Whatever it takes. We'll mortgage the house if we have to."

Bonnie bent down toward an end table and tugged several tissues out of a waiting box. She handed them to her mother. "I don't think it'll come to that, Mom."

Clare blew out a resigned breath. "The junior warden at my church does criminal defense work. His name's Geoffrey Burns. I can call him for you."

"Mrs. Castle?" A well-built man in scrubs stood in the entrance to the waiting room.

Suzanne nodded, snuffling wetly into a sodden Kleenex. "It's Dr. Gupta, Becky's surgeon." Dr. Gupta crossed the room to them. Up close, he looked more like a dashing Bollywood star playing a part than a real physician. Clare half expected him to launch into song.

He smiled, displaying perfect white teeth. "I have good news. Becky is out of surgery and doing well. We've caught all the bleeding. I want to keep a close eye on her kidneys for the next few days, but she's young and strong, and I think there's an excellent chance she'll pull through with no permanent damage at all."

Suzanne Castle burst into tears.

Dr. Gupta smiled understandingly. "She's in recovery right now," he told Bonnie. "After she wakes up, you and your mother may go in and speak with her."

"Thank you," Bonnie said. "Thank you so much."

"Do you have any questions?"

Clare waved a brief "excuse me" and retreated to the other end of the waiting room, out of earshot. She fished her cell phone from her pocket. Fortunately, she had her junior warden's home and office numbers saved in her phone's address book. Unfortunately, no one answered at either location. She left messages for the lawyer to call her as soon as he could. He was probably, she realized, at St. Alban's, helping to set up for the bishop's visitation. She should head over there herself—catch Geoff Burns in person and spend at least some time aiding the volunteers.

She was about to return to Suzanne and Bonnie and make her farewells when her phone began playing "Joyful, Joyful, We Adore Thee."

"Hello?" she said.

"It's me," Russ said.

"I thought you might be Geoff Burns."

"What a horrible thought. Why?"

She glanced at the Castles and sat down, turning away from them. "I'm here at the hospital with Suzanne Castle and her other daughter. They asked me to help them find a lawyer for Ed."

"Ah." There was a pause. "You heard, then."

"Are you going to arrest him?"

"I don't know. A lot's going to depend on the autopsy. We're still not sure how he died."

"Why do you think Ed did it?"

"I'm not sure he did. He was in the house when I got here. Said he followed one of the trails back to the old part of the camp—the burned-out buildings I told you about?"

"Uh-huh."

"He said he found Eugene there. Lying in the grass."

"What do you think?"

"Somebody used the garden cart to move something heavy from the house to the old buildings this afternoon. There's a raw track cutting through the trail and dirt stuck in the cart's tread."

"You think Ed killed Eugene and tried to hide his body?"

"Maybe. We're waiting for the crime scene team to arrive. They'll set up for prints and pictures and tracks. We'll see what they say."

"Are you going to be questioning Ed yourself?"

He sighed heavily. "I can't see handing the job off to anyone else."

"I can. Ask Lyle to do it." Russ's deputy chief was the most experienced man on the force. "You shouldn't have to do it yourself. Ed's a friend of yours."

"I don't think so. Not anymore."

Her heart ached for him. "Oh, Russ."

"I'll be okay."

"Stop it." She curled her feet up under her in the squishy seat, tuning out the rest of the world. "Do you want to talk about it?"

There was a pause, and she could picture Russ pinching the bridge of his nose beneath his glasses. "Not right now. Kevin's taking Ed to the station, and I need to be here while the team works up the crime scene."

"Later."

"Where will you be?"

"If the Castles don't need me, at St. Alban's. Or the rectory. I haven't done anything to prepare for the bishop's visit tomorrow." She brushed a clot of dried leaf rot off her pants. "Or to get ready for this dinner dance tonight. God knows I need a shower."

"You're going to be at the new resort tonight?"

"Yeah. My friend Hugh Parteger was invited. He works for an investment bank in New York City. You met him at Paul and Emil's last year."

"Oh, yeah." Russ's voice was devastatingly unenthusiastic.

"His firm wound up investing in the resort, so Hugh's driving up this afternoon for the grand-opening celebration." She tried to keep her voice neutral. "I'm going as his date."

There was a long pause. Somehow, she didn't think he was rubbing the bridge of his nose this time. "Nobody drives up from the city for a party and then turns around and goes home," he said. "Where's he spending the night?"

She blinked. "Excuse me?"

"I'm just thinking of your reputation."

"Do you mean to sound like a pompous hypocrite, or was that accidental?"

"I worry about what people might say about you!"

"You're jealous."

"I'm not going to get into this right now."

"Hypocrite." She knew she sounded childish and spiteful, but she couldn't stop herself.

"I'm not the one who has to set a good example for my flock. What is it your church teaches? Sex should be reserved for marriage?"

"For a committed, monogamous relationship," she said snottily. "Since I haven't dated anyone other than Hugh for the past two years, I think we qualify."

"A high roller from New York is only interested in one thing, and it's not the Book of Common Prayer."

Suddenly she deflated. "I kind of wish that was true," she said quietly. "But it's not. He likes me. A lot."

There was a long pause. When he finally spoke, Russ's voice was scarcely more than a whisper. "I'm sorry. I have no business sticking my nose into your relationship with him. Forget I said anything." He paused, then went on with badly faked cheer. "If you two are, you know, moving ahead . . . that's great. I mean it."

"Well, there's your trouble, as the song says. He's moving ahead. I'm not." She stared at the stains on her pants as if the secrets of the universe were written there. "I can't give him something that already belongs to someone else." She gave herself a shake. "And you know what? You're right, this is the wrong time to talk about this. Compared to the Castles and the van der Hoevens, I have no troubles." She smiled brightly. "Time to go where I can be useful. Don't worry about trying to catch me later. You're going to have your hands full."

"I'll see you tonight," he said.

She paused. "No, I'll be at the—"

"We're going, too. Linda and me." She could hear his humorless smile. "We'll see you and Hugh there."

2:30 P.M.

She was going to die. She realized, now it was too late, that her panic at waking up in the tower room of the old house had been more like playacting than the real thing. She raged and shook and whimpered out of the unknown, the faceless whoevers who had put her there. But she had been on Haudenosaunee land, at home, in a way, and some part of her must have been soothed and strengthened by that realization. She prepared to be the heroine in her own action film, counting on a lucky break like the ones that heroines always catch by the end of the third reel.

Shut in the stifling trunk of a car, she lost any illusions she had left. There was only the darkness, and the noise, and the continuous rolling and thumping and jolting, leaving her bruised and breathless and unable to think. She was in the hands of the man who had killed her brother, and she was so afraid she couldn't even grieve for him.

The car stopped. She heard the driver's door open, then one of the back doors. There was a clinking sound and then footsteps going away. After a while, they came back. She braced herself, but once again she heard the clinking in the backseat and then the footsteps disappearing. The next time they returned, though, there was an electronic *click,* the trunk sprang open, and she was blinking in the light, unable to make out anything other than a blurred black silhouette. He tangled his hands in the blanket that was still wrapped loosely around her and was hoisting her out before she could collect herself enough to protest.

She opened her mouth to scream, but he slung her over his shoulder, knocking the wind out of her. He climbed a short set of stairs, teetering under her weight, and she had the stomach-jolting sensation that she was about to fall. The steps were old, massive stone slabs instead of concrete, and there was a cold, fresh wind and the sound of water. That was all she absorbed before he passed into a dim, still place. He swung around, and she glimpsed a whirl of worn wooden floor and two small wooden crates, and then he flexed beneath her, straining, and she heard the squeak of unused wheels on a metal track.

"Nooo!"

The rumble of the door rolling shut cut off her despairing cry.

He didn't bother to tell her to shut up. That, more than the cavernous, disused space around her, convinced her she was well out of earshot. Whatever happened here, no one would hear.

He humped her across the floor, between tarp-covered lumps and pallets of old-fashioned wooden crates, much larger than the ones he had stepped around at the door. Despite the golden afternoon sun outside, the huge space languished in twilight.

Facedown, she had no idea how high the vast room was, but overhead she thought she heard the sound of wings. The place reeked of machine oil and damp wood and mouse droppings. As her captor crossed the floor, the dust-flecked air grew lighter and the shadows clouding the machinery and the crates grew more defined. She noticed another thing: The sound of water, faint at first, was increasing steadily.

He stopped, leaned forward, unseated her from his shoulder, and thumped her onto a crate like a sack of grain. She tilted her head back. Above her, I-bars and rafters glinted in the pale light streaming from lozenge-shaped windows set high in the wall behind her. She looked at the man who was going to kill her. She had always thought of herself as a fighter, as a leading-the-charge-from-the-deck-of-the-*Rainbow-Warrior* sort. Now she discovered it was possible to be so tired, so hurt and sad and scared, that the *Rainbow Warrior* sank beneath a black sea, leaving her adrift, no surface under her feet. "What are you going to do to me?" she asked, her voice bleached of emotion.

"For chrissakes." The man wrapped his hand around his upper arm, where she had bitten him. "I told you before, I'm not doing anything to you. You're going to stay put for tonight. I'll let you go tomorrow." He paused. "Or Monday, at the latest."

"You're going to let me go."

"I'm not the bad guy here. Christ! All I wanted to do was talk with your brother about buying some of the Haudenosaunee land. I didn't know he had his own sister locked up in some kinky game of hide-and-seek."

"That's not what was going on!" She was grateful for the tears rising in her eyes. It meant she could still feel grief and outrage. "My brother was protecting me." At some point between seeing her brother's face in the tower and facing his murderer here, she had come to accept that Eugene hadn't discovered she was missing and come creeping in to rescue her. He had put her in the tower, given her a bucket and blankets and food, and if she couldn't imagine the reason right now, it didn't mean there wasn't one.

"Okay, then I'm protecting you, too. In better style, I might add. I'm leaving your gag off, for one."

He didn't have any duct tape. Not that she was about to point that out to him.

"There's a washroom over there." He pointed toward a dark shaft of a doorway at the far edge of the room. "It's not in great condition, but it works. And I'll bring you something to eat and a sleeping bag later. There's even two cases of your family wine by the door. Be good, and you can have some later on."

Along with grief and outrage, she could still feel amazement. His tone of voice clearly invited her to admire his generosity. To thank him. He stared at her, expecting some reaction. She didn't know what to give him. He huffed and turned away. "You're next to the kill," he said over his shoulder, and for a moment she had an image of a serial killer's dumping ground, before common sense reasserted itself. The kill. The river. "You can't be heard, so don't bother to wear your voice out yelling." His figure blurred into the darkness at the other end of the building. "I'll be back later." His voice floated through the dusty air.

She expected to see a blaze of light as the wide door—a type of loading dock, she recognized now—slid open. Instead, she heard a muffled *thunk* and *click* from another, smaller, unseen door. She was alone.

She waited, unmoving. Was it a trick? Did he want to toy with her before doing whatever it was he was going to do with her? Her proximity to the river suggested several unpleasant possibilities. She could hear it more clearly, now she wasn't focusing all her attention on her captor. Water gurgled and swished directly below the wooden floor, and to her left she heard a steady rumble and hiss, water falling, fast, over an obstacle.

She waited some more. Minutes passed. More wings overhead. Birds. She hoped they were birds. The idea of sitting in this echoing space as the sun went down, surrounded by flying creatures that weren't birds . . . she shivered. Then caught herself. She was thinking of the future, wasn't she? At least, a future a few hours from now.

Her heart, painful, tender, hopeful, resurrected itself in her chest. He had really gone. She had time. She had an entire warehouse of possibilities. And tucked inside her sleeve, she still had the sharpened iron rod from the door hinge. She stood, a movement that was much easier from a crate than a floor. Better get started.

2:35 P.M.

John Huggins was ticked off. "You mean it wasn't Millie van der Hoeven?"

"No," Russ said for the third time. He was in van der Hoeven's study, sitting in the dead man's chair, using the dead man's phone. He was not a happy man at the moment.

"Well, I'll be damned." There was a pause. "I didn't just decide to call off the search, you know. Mr. van der Hoeven told me his sister had been found. If anybody's screwed up here, it's him."

Russ pinched the bridge of his nose beneath his glasses. "Eugene was . . . mistaken. Did your searchers leave all together? Or did they straggle out one by one?"

"No, we always do a head count and equipment check before we break a search. We all left together."

"What time was this?"

"Half past twelve or thereabouts."

Right around the time when Becky Castle was being taken to town in the ambulance. "Did any of you see Eugene van der Hoeven?"

"Sure. He came out and thanked us all for our help."

"Was he inside or outside when you left?"

"Inside. He went inside after he spoke with us. I figured he was fixing to head out to the hospital to be with his sister."

"Did any of your team go inside the house before they left?"

There was a stack of catalogs by the phone. Russ picked up the top one. Hunting gear. He flipped through a few more. L.L.Bean, Eddie Bauer, army-navy surplus. It made sense. A man like Eugene van der Hoeven, phobic about leaving his house and grounds, probably did all his shopping over the phone.

"No. What the hell's going on?"

Russ uncovered another catalog. "I can't say right now. Did you notice anything odd or unusual, anything at all, in the time between breaking the search and leaving?"

"No." Huggins paused, then said, "Yes. Sort of. When I was driving down the road to the county highway, I passed a car coming up. It wasn't actually coming up right then. It had pulled off as far as it could to let us through. We make quite a wagon train when everybody's truck starts rolling."

"What sort of car?"

"It was a black Mercedes. Looked kind of new, but you know how they are. Hard to tell."

"Do you know the model?"

Huggins laughed. "Do I strike you as a guy who spends a lot of time around Mercedeses? Ask me about Chevys, then I can help you out. It was a four-door hardtop, New York plates, that's all I can tell you."

"Did you see who was in it?"

"Some guy. I couldn't make out any details from my angle. I ride a lot higher up than that Mercedes." His voice turned serious. "Look, if Millie van der Hoeven is still missing, do you want me to reassemble the team?"

"You got your dog handler back?"

"She's on her way down from Plattsburgh right now."

Russ thought for a moment. "We're in the middle of an investigation, so I can't have your people up here until we've cleared the scene. But put everyone on hold. Especially the dog handler."

"Okay." Huggins was clearly consumed with curiosity, and only his image of himself as a hard-bitten professional was keeping him from breaking down and begging Russ to tell him what was going on.

Russ said his good-bye and got off the phone. Outside, Lyle MacAuley was squatting in front of the third bay of the garage, squinting at the garden cart stowed there.

"What do you think?" Russ asked.

"It's been used. Today. Look." He pointed to where a torn blade of grass, still green, clung to a dab of dark soil. "That's fresh." He stood, stretching. "I don't need some fancy-pants statie technician to tell me that. And take a look at the handle." He pointed. "Smear of blood."

"Yeah, I noticed that as well." Russ pinched the bridge of his nose. "I didn't see any open injuries on Ed when I took him into custody."

"What about van der Hoeven's body?"

Russ shook his head. "I asked Emil Dvorak to get the preliminary results to us as quickly as possible. There's something about this whole situation"—he waved, indicating the cart, the house, and the wide woods beyond—"that sticks in my craw."

"I dunno. I like Ed Castle as a suspect. He gets here, smashes into van der Hoeven with his SUV, and then dumps the body in the back of beyond." Lyle spread his hands as if presenting a fait accompli. "We're back home in time for the evening news."

"Somebody else was here."

Both of Lyle's overgrown eyebrows rose.

"John Huggins saw a black Mercedes driving up the road to Haudenosaunee when the entire search team was making their way down."

"Tight fit."

"Huggins couldn't identify the year or model, just that it was a sedan with New York plates."

"Great. I'm sure there aren't more than two, three hundred thousand Mercedeses in New York. Saratoga alone probably has more'n a hundred. I'll get right on it."

"We have a blank spot in van der Hoeven's timeline as well," Russ said. "An hour, an hour and a half between the time the search team left and you found him here with Ed."

"Any possible witnesses?"

"He had a part-time housekeeper. I can't remember her first name, but the last name's Schoof. She's Mark Durkee's sister-in-law."

"Lisa."

"Good memory."

Lyle leered. "You may be getting too old to notice, but the day I forget a good-looking woman's name is the day you can haul me away in the garden cart."

"I'm going to radio Kevin Flynn. Have him question her. Her husband came by to pick her up, so he may have seen something as well."

"Kevin?" Lyle looked skeptical. "You sure about that?"

"He needs to start somewhere."

"What about me?"

Russ grinned. "You've not only started, I think you've damn near finished as well."

"Smart-ass. What do you want me to do?"

The *whoop-whoop-whoop* of a siren stopped Russ before he could answer. He watched as a paneled van emblazoned with NYSP CRIME SCENE INVESTIGATION UNIT pulled up between Lyle's and Noble Entwhistle's squad cars. Russ let himself feel relieved when Sergeant Jordan Hayes stepped down from the driver's side. Hayes had worked scenes for the Millers Kill PD before, and he was close to local law enforcement's ideal of a trooper—smart, willing to take direction, and not likely to push for jurisdiction.

"You were going to tell me where you wanted me," Lyle reminded Russ.

"Yeah. Get over to the hospital and take Becky Castle's statement. She's out of surgery."

Lyle looked surprised. "The hospital called you?"

"Uh." Russ forced himself not to look away from his deputy chief. "No. I was talking to Reverend Fergusson. She told me."

"Ah." Lyle paused. "You know, at fifty you're supposed to be too old and too smart to be messing up your life."

Don't go there. Just don't go there. Russ strode across the gravel toward the van, where another technician had joined Hayes in unloading the gear.

"Sergeant Hayes," he said, his hand outstretched.

The trooper shook his hand briefly. "Chief Van Alstyne."

"Ready to help us make a quick close on this one?"

"You bet. Show us the way."

Russ pivoted toward one of the squad cars. "Noble," he shouted.

Noble Entwhistle popped up from his slouched position against the side of his car.

"You're with me." Russ pointed a finger toward Lyle, who had drifted up beside him. "You. To the hospital." He lowered his voice. "Be good."

"Funny," Lyle said. "I was going to tell you the same thing."

2:40 P.M.

Clare had always considered the narrow brick stairs leading from St. Alban's semibasement kitchen to street level her own private escape hatch. The great double door of the church was for Sundays and weddings and inconveniently faced Church Street's public square, in the opposite direction from the rectory. The doorway out of the upper parish hall, opening onto Elm Street and the large parking space the church rented, was much more frequently used, like the driveway-side entrance in a house where the front door is too grand and inaccessible. As a result, the chances of Clare slipping in and out unobserved were slim to none. But few people used the kitchen stairs, which scuttled steeply up to St. Alban's own minuscule parking lot and from there to a tall boxwood hedge dividing the rectory from the church grounds.

Her plan had been to sneak down the stairs, find Geoff Burns, and then hightail it out of there to her own house. She needed food and a shower. Or a shower and food. Maybe a sandwich in the tub.

The presence of an unheard-of three cars squeezed onto the postage-stamp-sized asphalt square was a tip-off that her plan was about to require some modifications. She nosed her Shelby against a plastic garbage bin and opened the door gingerly, so as not to smack into the neighboring Volvo.

She could see a sliver of the top of the door. Open. The sound of cascading silverware and voices conferring was almost drowned out by an enthusiastic rendition of "A Mighty Fortress Is Our God." That would be Judy Morrison, former Lutheran. Since her interpretation of gourmet cooking was crushing Pringles over her casseroles, Clare hoped she was on cleanup rather than the food prep crew.

Then she caught a whiff of something buttery and delicious. Her stomach lurched forward, and her feet followed. She pattered down the stairs, salivating.

Courtney Reid and Sabrina Campbell were talking, heads bent together, stirring pots on the eight-burner stove. Judy Morrison was elbows-deep in sudsy water, pans and canisters of silverware piled on the counters around her.

All three women wore the HAVE YOU HUGGED AN EPISCOPALIAN TODAY? aprons that had been such a hit at the springtime fund-raiser.

"*A bulwark never failing,*" Judy sang. "*Our helper he amidst the flood—*" Courtney shot her a glance, rolling her eyes, and spotted Clare.

"Reverend!"

Clare smiled to keep from wincing. She never heard the word without hearing her grandmother Fergusson sniffing, *Reverend. Why, you might as well start calling priests 'Holy.' It's just as grammatically incorrect.* Although Clare accepted "Reverend Clare" as a compromise—since she manifestly wasn't a "Father," and "Mother" made her think of aged Armenian nuns—she much preferred to be addressed by her first name than by a naked "Reverend."

"Hey, everyone. How's it going?" The source of the mouthwatering odor was a huge baking tin crammed with tiny quiches. "This smells amazing. Can I have one?" Her hand was almost on one of the miniature tins when Courtney pinned her with a coolly arched brow.

"Only if you want to risk running out at the reception tomorrow." Courtney's nose wrinkled. "What is that smell?" She peered into the sink. "Judy, did you put something rotten down the drain?"

Clare made a tactical retreat. "Anything in the fridge?" She wrenched open the professional-sized refrigerator. "Holy cow, you've been busy." Crustless, quartered bread towered next to mixing bowls filled with tuna salad and thinly sliced ham. Scallops enveloped in bacon strips awaited the broiler. Tiny, perfect strawberry cheesecakes bumped into miniature shish kebabs ready for reheating. And in pride of place, Clare's own suggestion for the lunch: deviled eggs. Her favorite. Could she appropriate one or two? To taste-test? She glanced over her shoulder. Courtney was watching her.

"Uh-uh-uh," the woman singsonged. Clare shut the door with a sigh.

Sabrina Campbell stuck a spoon into the pot she had been stirring and lifted it to her mouth, blowing on it. It was, Clare saw with a dizzy yearning, chocolate. "Where have you been?" Courtney asked. "We expected you hours ago."

"I thought you'd be done by now. I mean, I'm really headed home to take a shower." Clare realized that this statement didn't cast her in the best light. She hesitated, not wanting to go into too much detail. "I got an early morning call from the search and rescue team. There's been a young woman lost in the woods. I filled in until one of their more experienced volunteers replaced me."

"Well, I won't even begin to tell you what a nightmare it's been here," Courtney said. Judy Morrison, her face hidden from the younger woman's view, grimaced; whether in exasperation or solidarity, Clare couldn't tell. "First there was this awful mix-up with the crusts for the individual quiches. Then we had to go back to the store because the kiwi and the strawberries weren't fresh."

"There weren't that many that had gone bad," Judy said under her breath.

Courtney rolled on as if she hadn't heard her. "And then we had a terrible time making the crème fraîche. I suspect the fat content wasn't all it could have been."

Judy mumbled something that sounded like ". . . if we had settled for whipped cream . . ."

"Anyway, we're well sorted out now. D'you want to come upstairs and see how the setup is going? I was just headed up." Courtney whipped off her apron. "Sabrina, you can keep an eye on my rémoulade, can't you?"

"Mmm-hmm," Sabrina said, tucking a strand of silvered blond hair behind her ear and tasting the now-cooled chocolate.

"Reverend?" Courtney was holding the kitchen door open. Clare tore her eyes away from Sabrina Campbell's now-clean spoon and trotted after the fast-moving brunette.

Courtney strode down the dank hallway, passing the boiler room, the sexton's supply closet, smelling of disinfectant, and the shuttered doors to the undercroft, the church's subterranean attic. She pounded up the narrow steps, Clare following on her heels, and burst through into the sunlit parish hall.

Noise assailed them. Three women and two men snipped stems and chattered loudly across the room. A tropical forest of blooms and branches was spread out on a plastic-sheeted table. Terry McKellan and Tim Garretson wrestled folding round tables off an enormous dolly and rolled them into place, rumbling like Ezekiel's chariot wheels. A phone was ringing in the office. From the church, Clare could hear the music director and the choir, going over a particularly difficult section of the choral evensong they'd be singing tomorrow at four.

"*God of love and God of power, Make us worthy of this hour,*" the basses thundered down, only to be cut off by a shrill "No! No!"

The members of the floral guild spotted Clare first. "Thank heavens you're here," Laurie Mairs said, dropping her intertwined stems of roses and stephanotis and hurrying toward Clare. "The silver vases are all locked away, and

Delia's lost her spare key!" She shot a glance at the guilty woman, who shrugged her shoulders, smiling sheepishly.

"Delia, you have to let me or Mr. Hadley know if you lose one of the keys," Clare said, raising her voice to be heard across the room. "That silver is irreplaceable. We can't allow—"

"Clare!" Mae Bristol cut off what was threatening to become a rant with the authority only a forty-year career as an elementary school teacher can bestow. "Where have you been?" She bore down on Clare from the upper hallway, stopping only when she got within sniffing distance. "And what have you gotten into?"

"Miss Bristol." Laurie Mairs, like many of the other parishioners aged forty-seven and under, seemed to find it impossible to address Mae Bristol by her first name. "I was just about to have Reverend Clare open the—"

"This will only take a moment, Laurie." Mae peered up at Clare with her black-currant eyes. "Mr. Hadley has brought every banner ever sewn up from the undercroft. We need you to help us select which ones to hang. Some of the older ones are quite lovely, but I'm not sure they'll take the strain of being hoisted up to the ceiling."

"Reverend Clare!" Clare swiveled, following the alto voice to the hallway, where Karen Burns was waving a sheaf of pink message slips. Clare stared at Geoffrey Burns's wife.

The Castles. "Excuse me for just a sec," she said, shouldering her way past Miss Bristol, Laurie Mairs, another member of the floral guild who had arrived to press their claim against Mae Bristol's, and a miffed-looking Courtney Reid. Courtney, lovely, chestnut-haired, perfectly shaped, should have resembled Karen Burns, who was also all these things, but Karen wore her self-confidence and her simple, expensive clothes with an effortless style, while Courtney always seemed to be trying too hard. There was no love lost between the women.

"Have I rescued you?" Karen said, baring her perfectly white teeth. "Has Courtney spoken to you about making her the events coordinator at St. Alban's?"

"What on earth do we need an events coordinator for?"

Karen shrugged. "Well, you know, she *was* the cruise director aboard one of those ships before she snagged Shaun Reid." Her eyes glittered. "I understand she was 'Kourtnee' before the marriage."

Clare tried to smother her smile. "That's not very nice, Karen."

"We first wives have to have some fun at the expense of these youngsters stealing away husbands twenty years older than themselves."

"Somehow, I can't imagine any twenty-four-year-old stealing Geoff away."

"He knows what would happen." She held up one hand and made a snipping motion.

Clare quickly stifled her laughter. No need to give the cluster of ladies glaring at Karen any ammunition. "Speaking of your husband, where is he?"

"He should be here any minute with the booze for the postevensong reception."

"Oh, God, I'd forgotten about that."

"How on earth could you forget the fifty biggest donors to the church meeting the bishop for an intimate cocktail party?"

"Do we have to serve drinks?"

"If you want to hit people up for money, believe me, it helps to liquor them up first." She rustled the pink slips in her hand. "I've been calling everyone who's RSVP'd to the evening reception. I'm reminding them that we're asking everyone to bring a nonchurchgoing friend to enjoy the beautiful music in our stunning Gothic Revival sacred space."

Clare could never figure out if Karen was serious or being ironic when she spoke as if she were reading out of a guidebook.

"After all," Karen went on, "it's all about bringing new members into the fold. New pledging members."

Clare groaned. "I used to believe the three legs supporting the Episcopal Church were scripture, reason, and tradition. That was before I became a priest. Now I know the three legs are really get 'em in, get 'em back, and get their pledges."

"He may already be down in the kitchen," Karen said. "Let's go see." Clare trailed her down the stairs, through the hall, and into the kitchen. "Aha." She pointed to a cardboard box containing several fifths on the counter.

Clare heard the sound of feet clattering down the stairs, and here came a small, sandy-haired man in a leather bomber jacket, arms wrapped around another box.

"Hi, sweetheart." Geoff leaned back and pecked Karen on the cheek before depositing the second box on the counter. He sniffed. "What's that smell?" He checked his pants. "Is it me? I was carrying Cody earlier—"

"It's not you." Clare stepped forward. "I was looking for you. I have a favor to ask." She cocked her head toward the kitchen stairs. "How 'bout we go outside and I stand downwind?"

Squeezed in behind the Burnses' Land Rover, Clare told Geoff about Becky and the hospital and Ed and the arrest. Burns didn't say anything while she rattled out all the details she could remember, just *hmm* and *go on* and *I see*. When she finished, he folded his arms and frowned.

"Can you take his case? Even though he might not need to keep you on?" Clare asked.

Geoff nodded. "I'll charge him a flat fee for advising him during questioning and arranging bail, if it becomes necessary. He can apply that toward my retainer if he decides he needs my services further."

Clare blew out a breath in relief. "Thanks, Geoff. When can you get to the station?"

"I'll go now if you help me hand Cody off to Karen."

"You've got a deal."

Geoff opened the back door and handed Clare a diaper bag disguised as an expensive tote. She slung it over her arm while Geoff eased the sleeping toddler out of his car seat. Cody Burns had dark hair pasted to his sweaty temples and was clutching a rubber squirrel scored by dozens of teeth marks. He let out a protesting whine and dug his face into his father's shoulder. Burns shushed him and carefully transferred him to Clare's arms. She buried her face in his fat neck and breathed in his sweet and pungent baby-boy smell. Still sleeping, he clutched at her. The squirrel fell, squeaked once, and bounced under the Land Rover.

"For God's sake, get Mr. Squeaky," Clare whispered. Burns dropped to his hands and knees, groping beneath his vehicle for the toy. Mr. Squeaky was vital to Cody's happiness. The two-year-old came to church every Sunday with his parents, who did not like to leave him in the nursery, and Clare had grown almost used to the rhythmic squeaking that accompanied her sermons.

Geoff clambered up from the pavement and handed her the toy. "Don't you need to give Karen the car seat?" Clare asked.

Geoff looked at her as if she had suggested he strap the kid to the running board. "We have car seats in all our cars," he said. "But thanks."

"Okay. Bye." She turned and stepped slowly down the stairs, keeping a tight hold on the sleeping toddler and the toy.

Judy Morrison let Clare know Karen had returned to the office. Clare followed, Cody heavy and warm in her arms. When Karen spotted them, she crossed from the secretary's desk and met them in the office doorway. She raised one perfectly groomed brow. "I take it my husband agreed to do that favor for you?"

"Yep. I'm sorry, I didn't think of Cody. Is this going to be a problem for you?"

"Not if I can use your office instead of Lois's," Karen said, glancing behind her at the church secretary's desk. "I just need a telephone."

"You've got it." They retreated to Clare's office, which was warm for a change and filled with liquid afternoon light. Karen retrieved a baby blanket from the diaper bag and, easing Cody away from Clare, nested the sleeping toddler on Clare's aged and saggy sofa.

"He can finish out his nap there," Karen said.

"Great." Clare bent over and kissed Cody on one rosy cheek. "I'd better get back to the others."

"Oh!" Karen ducked out into the hall and reappeared a moment later, waving another stack of pink phone message slips. "I almost forgot. These are for you." She laid them in Clare's hand.

"All of them?" Clare couldn't keep a note of horror out of her voice.

"Most of them are from Willard Aberforth. Diocesan Deacon Willard Aberforth." Her exaggerated baritone gave Clare the feeling that Karen had spoken with the deacon herself—and had not been impressed.

"Yeah, he contacted me earlier this week. He said he wants to have a meeting with me."

"He's the bishop's hatchet man, you know."

"Karen!"

"I'm serious. One of the duties he performs for the bishop is making sure everything is ready for the annual visit. Another thing he does is make sure priests and congregations are toeing the line." She leaned forward, her face grave. "Watch yourself with him. You've already had more controversy and publicity in two years than Father Hames had in twenty. I doubt the bishop looks favorably on that."

"I didn't expect the Spanish Inquisition," Clare said weakly.

Karen's mouth curved. "Nobody expects the Spanish Inquisition," she said, completing the quote. "Don't let Aberforth get you in his sights. I think he's got a lot more up his sleeve than the comfy chair."

2:55 P.M.

Surgical recovery was an open room, with six beds widely spaced to admit crash carts and a team, if the worst happened. Not that it was going to be necessary for today's solitary patient. She had been stirring fitfully for several minutes, her arrhythmic breathing and occasional moans a good sign that she was surfacing from anesthesia normally.

Since she was the only one in the room, the recovery nurse was ready when the young woman's eyes cracked open. She laid her clipboard down and dropped her pen into her tunic pocket.

"Wha . . ." her patient croaked.

"Hello, Becky." The nurse leaned over, not close enough to disorient the girl, but near enough so she could see and hear her. "You're in the hospital. You were brought in with internal bleeding. You've had an operation, a splenectomy."

"Hurts."

"I bet it does." The girl's face was pale, throwing the rapidly purpling bruises on her jaw and temple into stark relief. Somebody sure did a number on her. "Dr. Gupta's prescribed Percocet for you. Do you think you could swallow a pill if I helped you?"

"Mouth . . . dry."

"That's a normal effect of the anesthesia. Do you feel at all nauseous?" She reached toward the stainless steel bedside cart, where she had put a large plastic cup of crushed ice and water.

"No. Thirsty."

"Okay. I'm going to press the button and raise the head of your bed . . . okay? Not too much?"

"My shoulder hurts."

"That's the gas left inside during the operation. It's going to make you a little uncomfortable for the next few days." She shook the Percocet out of its small paper cup.

"Ha . . . uncomfortable."

"Yeah, I know. Medical terminology. We're afraid if we tell you it's going to hurt like a bear, you'll get discouraged."

Becky swallowed the pill. The nurse held the ice water upright for her while she drank it through a bendy straw.

"Not too much, now. Dr. Gupta will be in to see you soon, and when he gives the go-ahead, we'll move you to your room. Then you can see your family. If you want to." She had dealt with enough domestics, as the staff called them, to know that sometimes family members were the last people a battered woman wanted to see.

Becky closed her eyes. Opened them. "Police," she said. Her face twisted. She tried to sit up.

"Ssh." The nurse laid a hand firmly on the young woman's shoulder. "We've already informed the police that you're out of surgery. As soon as you're strong enough to talk, an officer will be in to interview you. You can talk to him alone or have one of the nurses with you—whatever you feel comfortable with. In the meantime, you're safe here. I promise you. No one can harm you."

"Randy Schoof."

The nurse paused, one hand on the bed's controls. "What?"

"Randy. Schoof. Hit me." She sank back with the bed, trembling with exhaustion.

"Take it easy," the nurse said automatically.

"Randy Schoof," Becky said. Her eyes slid shut. "Hurts."

"The medication will take effect soon." The nurse looked up at the wall clock. Dr. Gupta wouldn't be back for another check until she called him. She looked at the phone hanging from the wall behind her station. Internal line only. "You rest," she said. "I'll let Dr. Gupta know you're awake. Don't try to talk."

She crossed the white room. The doors hissed open as she approached and hissed shut behind her. She turned right down the hallway, where the floor station gleamed ahead of her like the light at the end of a darkened tunnel.

"Stacy?" The charge nurse glanced up, startled. "Can you take recovery for five minutes? The patient's still resting. You don't need to do anything."

Stacy frowned. "It's not your break time."

"Please? I need to call home. You know how it is."

Stacy groaned exaggeratedly, getting up from her chair. "You gals with young kids. I swear, it really does take a village to raise a child. A village of coworkers."

"Thanks." She swung behind the counter and had her hand on the phone when Stacy called to her from halfway down the hall.

"Rachel? You owe me one."

"I do." Rachel Durkee forced a smile before picking up the receiver. She had to call her sister. Fast.

3:00 P.M.

Shaun pulled into his garage and waited until the door shut behind him and the fluorescent lights popped on before getting out of the car. He stared in dismay at the caramel-colored leather seat, which now looked as if a big baby had wet all over it. God only knew if it was salvageable or not.

Slamming the door shut, he dug out his garage door key and let himself into the breezeway. He eased off his shoes, crusted with mud and leaf rot, and went on stocking feet through the kitchen and up the stairs. Jeremy was certainly at work, and the cleaning woman didn't come on Saturday, but he was worried Courtney might be home already from her church thing.

He slipped into the guest bathroom and locked the door, stripped off his bloody shirt and trousers, and tossed them into the bathtub. His arm was a mess—a deep row of bite marks clotted with drying blood, surrounded by plum and indigo bruises. The skin around the bite already looked inflamed. He remembered, from the days when Jeremy was in preschool and biting was part of his peers' social coin, that the human mouth was worse than any animal's for germs and infections. Could you get tetanus from a human bite? It didn't matter, he supposed—he wasn't going to the doctor's for any treatment, that was for damn sure. He reached for the medicine cabinet and froze as his face came into view.

He was a mess. His nose was puffy, the flesh beneath his eyes purpling. His skin had split over his chin, and a goose egg was hatching on his forehead. He looked like someone who had been in a knock-down, drag-out fight. Courtney was going to freak.

Shaun flipped the door open and grabbed the hydrogen peroxide. He unscrewed the top and, holding his arm over the bathtub, poured half the contents onto his wound.

He bit down on his yell. Holy *God,* did that sting. The peroxide bubbled furiously in the bite marks. He turned on the tap, and when the antiseptic had done its job, he used a washcloth to sluice away the dried blood. He let the tub keep filling, soaking his clothes, while he bandaged the bite. He scrubbed off his face and dabbed antibiotic cream on his cut. Short of breaking into Courtney's cosmetics, there wasn't anything he could do for his black eyes.

He leaned in closer to the mirror. Behind the bruising, his eyes looked the same as they always had, pale blue and preoccupied. He marveled that he didn't look any different. That his eyes didn't show he had killed a man.

He blinked. Of course, technically, he hadn't killed van der Hoeven. He had simply . . . let him fall. They had been struggling, and perhaps he had pushed him harder than necessary. But still, he knew now. What it felt like.

He remembered a conversation with Russ Van Alstyne. He had been in college, and Russ had been home on leave. It was before they had given up on their awkward attempts at rejoining the severed ends of their friendship. *What does it feel like?* he had asked. *Killing someone?*

It doesn't feel like anything, Russ said.

C'mon. You have to feel something.

Russ had taken a long pull on his bottle of Jack Daniel's. *When you're doing it,* he said, *you feel hot. And fast. Like doing speed in a sweatbox.*

And after?

Russ's eyes looked a long, long way off, into a place Shaun couldn't go. *After,* he said. *After, you feel cold.*

Shaun looked into his own fifty-year-old eyes and felt something Russ had left out. Or maybe, being a nineteen-year-old grunt, he hadn't known the feeling for what it was. Exultation. And power. Let Terry McKellan sit behind a desk and say yes or no. Let the Reid-Gruyn board cluster around a table voting up and down. He had exercised real power, the ultimate power. He was taking his destiny into his own hands.

Don't get cocky, he thought. Events were still too fluid, too slippery. Squeeze too tightly or hold too loosely and he could be right back where he had been, waiting for the ax to fall on Reid-Gruyn. Except this time he'd be waiting inside a jail cell. But if he were smart, and daring and, most important, willing to use the power he had taken into his hands . . . he looked down at them. Flexed his fingers. Let himself think, for the first time since he had hauled Millie van der Hoeven out of that tower, that maybe there could be another accident.

3:05 P.M.

Lisa Schoof held the telephone tightly, as if loosing her hold, even for a moment, would let the malevolent black thing fly apart, its shrapnel embedding in her flesh, her blood seeping around the plastic wounds, her life dripping away from a hundred openings that could have no healing.

"Say something," her sister hissed over the line. "For God's sake."

The thing that came to mind, *I wish you had never called me, I wish I didn't know, I wish it were still ten minutes ago,* was useless. Lisa didn't bother to ask for reassurance—*Are you sure? Couldn't there be a mistake?*—because Rachel, smart, precise Rachel, didn't make mistakes like this.

She cleared her throat. "How long?" she asked.

"How long what?"

"Until it's out."

Rachel clicked her teeth. A habit she had had since girlhood. "I can justify not calling the doctor in to see her for another half hour or so. She's still sleepy and just had her medication. After that . . ."

She didn't have to finish. Lisa could guess. The patient tells the doctor. The doctor tells the police. The police arrest her husband. It reminded her of the circle game they played as kids. *The cheese stands alone, the cheese stands alone . . .*

"Thank you," she said.

"I'm doing this for you, not for him," Rachel went on. "If anyone finds out, it'll mean my job. Not to mention what it'll do to my marriage. Be smart. Take care of yourself for a change."

"Thank you," Lisa repeated.

"I love you," her sister said.

"I love you, too."

Rachel's voice was replaced by a toneless buzz. Carefully, carefully, Lisa replaced the receiver in the cradle. She caught a glimpse of her blurred reflection in the microwave door. *I'm happy,* she thought. She pinched her cheeks for color, ruffled her hair jauntily. *It's just another Saturday afternoon.* She strolled back into the living room.

Kevin Flynn, who had been examining the photos hanging on the wall, turned. "Everything okay?" he asked brightly.

"Yep." She settled herself in the middle of the sofa, tucking one leg under her. She wasn't up to controlling her face, voice, hands, and legs all at the same time. She grabbed a pillow, a souvenir from their honeymoon in Aruba with scenes from the island stitched on the cover. She wrapped her arms around it, one hand on a conch shell, one on a palm tree. "Just my friend Denise. Denise Hammond, you remember her."

It helped if she thought of him as little Kevin Flynn, who had been a painfully thin freshman during her senior year at Millers Kill High. Skinny Flynnie, that had been his nickname. She did her best to ignore his uniform, the belt strapped around his waist like Batman's utility belt, for chrissakes, his gun.

She wouldn't think about his gun.

Kevin lowered himself into the only other seat in the room, the wooden rocking chair. "Yeah, I remember her. Whatever happened to her?"

"She moved to Glens Falls. Got a job at the *Post-Star*." She put on a teasing voice, one part of her marveling that she sounded so natural. "You should look her up. She's still single, and she says a good man is hard to find."

Kevin blushed. "She's older than me."

"That only matters in high school. Once you're both out, who cares?"

He shook his head. Evidently she wasn't the only one who remembered Skinny Flynnie.

What would I be saying if I didn't know what I know now? What would she have done if the phone hadn't rung a minute after Kevin knocked on her door, asking to come in? She'd ask him why he was here. Innocent people did that.

"You didn't come all the way out here for dating advice," she said, still using that *where did it come from?* teasing tone. "What brings you to my door?"

"Uh, is Randy at home?"

She concentrated on keeping her voice even, her hands relaxed. "No, he's been gone all day. Running errands. You know. Typical Saturday stuff."

"He didn't bring you home? From your job at Haudenosaunee?"

"No."

"Oh. See, the chief bumped into him while he was on his way up there— Randy, I mean, not the chief. I wanted to ask him if he had seen anything while he was up there. And you, too, of course, I want to ask you."

She was lost. Did Kevin have a coldheartedly clever way of befuddling suspects until they spilled everything? What the hell did anything up at Haudenosaunee have to do with Randy and . . . and . . . Her mind slid over the rest of that sentence. "I don't understand," she said honestly.

He sighed. "Sorry. I'm still getting the hang of questioning people." He drew himself up straight and tilted forward, stopping the gentle rocking he had slipped into. "I'm sorry to have to tell you this, but your employer, Eugene van der Hoeven, is dead."

What he said was so far from what she had expected, it took her several minutes to decipher his meaning.

"Lisa? Are you okay?"

She stared at him. "Mr. van der Hoeven's dead?"

"Yeah."

"How? What happened to him?" She hoped her voice wasn't as light and bubbly as she felt. Poor Mr. van der Hoeven. She tried not to smile. Poor, poor Mr. van der Hoeven.

"Uh, I don't think I can give you any details yet. We do know he was killed sometime between twelve-thirty and two o'clock. I was hoping you could give me some details."

"I don't know what I can tell you. He was alive and well when I left at noon."

"Did you drive yourself home? Is that why Randy didn't pick you up after all?"

Careful. "No, I got a ride with a woman named Clare Fergusson. I knew Randy was going to be running around town, so I told him I'd find my own way home. He must have forgotten."

"Reverend Fergusson?" Kevin glanced up from the small wire-bound notebook where he was writing down her words. "Do you think she might have gone back up to Haudenosaunee after she dropped you home?"

"I don't think so. She was done with the search team for the day."

"Do you know if Eugene van der Hoeven had any enemies? Had he fought with anyone?"

She made a face. "I cleaned up after him for four years, but I don't know much about the man. He was neat, polite, and always gave me a good Christmas bonus. He never had anybody to stay at Haudenosaunee except family—his sisters and his dad, while he was alive." She hesitated. "I was worried that Millie van der Hoeven was getting into something not so good."

Kevin looked up from his notebook.

"But your chief probably knows about it. I told it to Ms. Fergusson this morning, and she said she was friends with the chief and she would tell him." She untwisted her leg and tucked the other one up. "Starting from when Millie got here at the end of the summer, I've been finding these pamphlets and letters from the Planetary Liberation Army."

Kevin looked impressed.

"You've heard of them? Yeah, they're a nasty bunch. Anyhow, it worried me. Millie is one hardcore earth mama. And it always struck me as strange, the way she just up and left her own home in Montana to move in with her brother."

"Did she ever mention leaving?"

"Nope. Isn't that weird? Makes me wonder if she maybe *had* to leave her other home."

"Huh." He riffled through his notes. "Anything else you want to tell me?"

The innocent question punched her in her gut. She shook her head.

"Okay." He flapped the notebook closed. "It looks like Randy was one of the last people up there before Mr. van der Hoeven was killed, so we'll want to talk with him as soon as we can. Let him know when he gets home, okay?"

She nodded. "Let me walk you out," she said, unfolding herself from the couch, pleased to find her legs didn't wobble at all. At the front door, she blocked his way with her arm on the doorknob, smiling up at him. He blushed again. "Give some thought to what I said about Denise, hmm?"

He mumbled something, and she opened the door.

Just in time to hear tires crunching down the drive. She and Kevin both looked out as her husband's pickup rolled to a stop next to where Officer Flynn's squad car was parked.

Kevin turned to her.

Skinny Flynnie, she reminded herself. *Skinny Flynnie*.

"Hey," he said happily. "Randy's home."

3:10 P.M.

W̲e are not the first to be, Banished by our fears from Thee; Give us courage, let us hear, Heaven's trumpets ringing clear."

"No! No! Tenors—you're supposed to be trumpets! Not kazoos!"

Clare, unfolding a chair, paused. "They sounded pretty good to me," she said to Terry McKellan.

He opened another chair and drew it up to one of the round tables. "Me, too. But then again, I have lousy taste in music."

"Nonsense," Courtney Reid said, snapping a tablecloth between them. Settling in generous folds, it transformed the battle-scarred folding table into white linen elegance. "I'm sure you have very nice taste in music. Who's your favorite group?"

"Herman's Hermits."

Clare and Courtney looked at each other. "You're right," Clare said. "You do have terrible taste in music." She wrenched open a final chair and slid it beneath the snowy waves. All around her, tables and chairs waited for linen and china and silver to work their magic. "Courtney," she said, eyeing the large stack of tablecloths and napkins heaped on a still-bare table, "do you want me to help with those?"

She could see Courtney catalog the mud splatters and stains on her clothing. She resisted the urge to curl up her hands. Lord knows what her nails looked like right now.

"No-o-o," Courtney said, giving a credible imitation of someone who was sorely tempted to say yes. "I think I can handle it. And Sabrina's finishing up in the kitchen. She can help me. I'm sure you want to . . ." She gestured with her hand, a neutral movement that might have indicated "read a book on theology" or "scrub yourself with Lysol."

"Okay. Thanks. I really need to get things ready for tonight."

"What's tonight?" Terry asked.

"A friend from New York City's arriving this afternoon. We're going to the dinner dance at the new resort tonight."

Courtney brightened. "Are you really? Shaun and I are going too! I got a fabulous dress on a shopping trip to Manhattan." She dropped her voice, despite the fact that only Clare and Terry were there to listen. "We're going to be at the VIP table, so I wanted to make a good impression."

Clare smiled wanly. She would be wearing a dress she had snapped up on sale in Germany during a three-day layover waiting for her unit's helicopters to be loaded into a C-141 and flown to Saudi Arabia. It had been cutting-edge European designer chic—in 1991.

"One of the sponsors of the evening, GWP, is ferociously courting Reid-Gruyn." At Clare's blank look, she explained, "Shaun's business. Pulp and paper. They want it bad." Courtney glowed at the prospect. "I can't wait. With the buyout, Shaun won't ever have to work again. We can spend our time traveling and having fun—" She caught sight of Terry McKellan's astonished expression. "Oh, and work for the causes we hold dear, of course. Like St. Alban's."

"That sounds wonderful." Clare tried to inject some enthusiasm into her voice. Coming to rest after a half hour of nonstop activity brought the hunger and the icky-sticky feeling roaring back. She could swear she was hallucinating a hamburger floating in front of Courtney's face.

"You look done in," Terry said. "Let me walk you to the rectory."

She straightened. "I'm fine." The last thing she wanted was for one of the old-guard vestry members to think she didn't have the stamina to set up a few folding chairs.

"Humor me," he said. "I want to catch you up on some vestry issues."

Surprised, Clare nodded. "I guess I'll see you tonight," she said to Courtney.

"Well . . . during the dancing. We'll be up at the VIP table during the dinner, remember."

"Mmm." This smile was even less convincing than the last. Terry McKellan tucked her hand under his arm and shambled out the back door. "What's all this about vestry issues?" she asked as soon as they were out of earshot.

"Nothing. I just wanted to get you alone without having to explain everything to Courtney Reid." He angled across the withered grass toward the sidewalk. "This may not fall under the rubric of 'need to know,' but I'm aware you like to keep your finger on the congregation's pulse." His big, round face fell into serious lines. Clare had long ago pegged Terry as "the jovial one" in her vestry lineup, and it was disconcerting to see him so grave.

"What is it?"

"It's what Courtney Reid was saying. About her husband selling out and retiring."

They reached the sidewalk. "Yes," Clare said, giving him permission to continue.

"It's not going to happen. Well, it is, but not the way she describes it."

They walked past the hedge dividing the church from the rectory. "Uh-huh," she said. What did Courtney Reid's husband's business plans have to do with her? She wondered if too many years in the corporate loan department had slanted Terry's view of life.

"As far as Shaun Reid is concerned, any move by GWP will be a hostile takeover. I believe he'll do anything, including putting his house, his savings, and his family's stock holdings on the line, to stop it." He shook his head. "He's not going to succeed. And when he loses control of his family's company, he's going to lose everything, as far as he's concerned."

They had gone down the driveway and reached Clare's kitchen door while

Terry was speaking. She rested her hand on the railing and turned to him. "So the happy retirement and the traveling and all that?"

"That's Courtney's fantasy." Terry sighed, puffing out his great brown mustache, increasing his resemblance to a walrus. "I feel a little . . . guilty, because I turned him down for a loan today. It was the right decision to make, but . . ."

She smiled. "You have a good heart, Terry."

His face reddened. "That makes me sounds like a character out of a Dickens novel."

"Okay, then, despite your razor-sharp business acumen, you have a good heart."

"Better." He smoothed his hairy brown wool sweater over his expansive stomach. "Will you . . . I don't know, keep an eye on Courtney Reid?"

"I will. Thanks for letting me know." She climbed the two steps to her kitchen door. "I'm going to go off duty for a bit. I'll see you later."

Terry waved good-bye and shambled back down the driveway. Clare slipped inside, closing the door with a careless kick and sinking into one of the old wooden chairs she had purchased in an attempt to warm up her all-white, straight-out-of-the-box kitchen. She sat for a moment, listening to the silence. Blissful silence.

This, she thought, *is the real reason for celibacy.* She had no husband, no children, not even a dog or a tropical fish relying on her, yet she still felt as if she had half the weight of the world sitting on her lap. She tried to imagine what it would be like, dragging home all the concerns and issues of people who needed her as a priest, only to deal with the people who needed her as a spouse and parent. She could remember how exhausted her mother had always looked at the end of the day, riding herd over two high-energy girls and twin boys. And she didn't have an outside job. How had she done it? How did any woman do it?

Groaning, she pushed herself up from her chair. Time to shower. Then she'd raid the fridge and pour herself a glass of wine. She crossed through her living room, taking a moment to look over the framed photographs clustered on the sofa table. Come to think of it, that had been her mother's method, too: a long, hot bath and a martini.

She had one hand on the banister when she heard the knock at her front door. For a split second she debated ignoring it, but even as her head urged her to stay still and be silent, her feet were crossing the foyer.

She opened the door to a looming crow of a man. "Ms. Fergusson?" he said. "I'm Deacon Willard Aberforth."

3:15 P.M.

They walked slowly down the path, single file, Sergeant Hayes and the assisting technician in the lead, then Noble Entwhistle, then Eric McCrea, who had been called on-shift early and had made it to Haudenosaunee just in time to join the trek to Eugene van der Hoeven's last resting place. Russ brought up the rear. He and his two men carried Maglites, long flashlights that were heavy enough to be potentially lethal and could light up an entire grove in this forest if they had to.

They might. Twilight came early in the mountains, and the sun already sat on the high horizon like a campfire burning out. Orange light stretched in long, dying streamers through the trees, stitching a shadow forest across the landscape.

Hayes paused every now and then to take a picture of the trampled grass or the single rutted track of the garden cart. There was no other evidence as to who or what had been down the track.

The forest opened up onto the red-washed remains of the old Haundenosaunee. Russ heard someone whistle. "Watch out for Count Dracula," Eric said.

"Is this it?" Hayes asked.

"Yeah," Russ said. "This is it." They skirted the blank-faced wall of boxwood and approached the place where Eugene's body had been found. Hayes and the technician began to set up a lamp on a tripod for photographs. Russ glanced up at the tower. When he had been here with Ed Castle, he had looked briefly for a sign that Eugene's death might have been a cruel accident, but from the ground, the stone balustrades that bound the galleries and circled the top of the tower were aggressively intact.

"Noble. I want you to circle the base of this thing, see if you find anything. Eric, you're with me. Let's take a look inside."

The men split apart, Russ and Eric going along a rough path toward the open tower door, Noble into the deep grass. Russ took the corroded handle and opened the tower door, creaking the hinges. He switched on his flashlight, throwing a bright circle on a bare flagstone floor, and moved from that to a flight of wooden stairs running up the inner wall. "Up we go," he said. "Watch your step."

The treads creaked and groaned. Russ tensed with every step, ready to leap to the next step if the wood beneath his boot gave way. When they reached the first open landing, he leaned over the carved stone banister. Sergeant Hayes and the technician were hard to his right, just visible beyond the edge of the gallery.

They mounted the next flight of stairs. They were circling around the tower, corkscrewing higher and higher. At the next balcony, they could see Noble below, methodically sweeping through the shaggy grass. Russ squatted down and examined the edge of the balcony and the floor in front of it. "Nothing," he said.

"It's all stone," Eric said. "You could go over it without a snag. Hell, those balcony rails are so low you could fall over just by leaning out too far."

Russ looked at him sharply. "You okay? With the height, I mean?"

Eric jerked his chin up and down. "It's not my favorite thing. I'll be okay."

The third level held the surprise. Instead of the open interior of the first two stories, this one was bisected by a sturdy wall with a thick door, standing just ajar.

"Jeez," Eric said, reaching for the handle. "It looks like something out of *Young Frankenstein*."

Russ grabbed his wrist. "Don't touch it. Prints."

Eric's face flushed red. "Sorry. I wasn't thinking."

"'Sokay." Russ dug into his pocket for the pair of latex gloves Hayes had handed him and wrestled them on before tugging the door wide.

"Holy shit," Eric breathed. He paused for a moment before fumbling to switch on his flashlight.

Russ's first thought was *Everything's empty*. The crumpled blanket, the husk of a backpack, the plastic sandwich wrappers littered across the floor. The smell of urine made him realize that not everything had been turned out and abandoned.

He and Eric circled the floor, cataloging the apple core—"May be DNA on that," he said—and the Thermos, which Eric unscrewed after putting his own gloves on.

"Chicken soup," he said, sniffing. "Cold."

Russ spotted the olive green balaclava, tossed near the door, and was about to bag it when Eric whistled.

"What?"

The younger man was on his hands and knees at the opposite side of the tower. "I think I've got some blood on the floor. A few drops." He sat back on his calves and looked up at Russ. "What the hell was going on here, Chief?"

Several possibilities came to mind. All of them were bad.

He crossed to the stone banister outside the door and leaned over. "Hey!" He called. He was, he saw, directly over Jordan Hayes. The state trooper looked up, his face blurring in the swift-moving shadow. "We've hit the jackpot. Get your stuff up here."

He stepped back and beckoned to Eric. "Let me have your radio."

The officer unhooked his radio and passed it to Russ. Russ keyed the mike. "Dispatch? This is the chief."

A squeal of interference and a swish of static. He glanced at the stone walls around him and moved to the edge of the banister. Beneath him, the evidence technicians were packing up. "Dispatch," he said again. "This is the chief."

Harlene's voice was faint but recognizable. "Go ahead, Chief."

"Who's on duty at the station?"

Static.

"Come back?"

"Tim Foster."

"Okay. I want him to take Ed Castle's statement on the events this afternoon at Haudenosaunee. And then tell Castle he's free to go. With our thanks and apologies." He thought for a moment. No, any apology from the department was as likely to land them a lawsuit as anything else. Better he apologize to Ed in person. "Cancel that last."

"No apology. Got it."

"I want you to call everybody in. Mark, Duane, everybody."

Even with the bad reception, he could hear the surprise in her voice. "What's up?"

He glanced toward the room behind him. Food. A toilet. Blood. "Damned if I know."

"Come back?"

"I'll tell you later."

I have—" The last word was swallowed in static.

"Come back?"

"I have a message from your wife. 'Don't forget you promised—' " A squeal of static wiped Harlene's words away.

He didn't ask her to repeat. He knew what the message was. He stared down at Hayes, lifting his collection box on his shoulder as his tech tagged along with the light. This place would be dark within the hour. They had an unaccounted-for death in the morgue, an unaccounted-for woman somewhere out there, and an unaccounted-for assault suspect on the loose. If ever he should be on the job, it was tonight.

He thought about what Linda had said, about her work. *It's my turn now.*

"Tell my wife I'll be there as promised. Chief out."

He stood for a moment in the freshening breeze, the last of the sun-warmed air flowing toward the cold dark. At the mountains' edge, the sky was enough to make a man believe in glory, red-orange and pink and lavender. It was going to be cold and beautiful tonight, no clouds, the moon one day from full.

Too bad Eugene van der Hoeven and Millie van der Hoeven and Becky Castle couldn't enjoy it. He closed his eyes briefly before turning from the beauty. Back to work.

3:20 P.M.

Once, Lisa Schoof had driven home drunk. She hadn't been Lisa Schoof then but Lisa Bain, nineteen, partying all afternoon at Lake George and then setting off home because she had to work early the next morning. She had been muzzy-headed, happy, sailing along, until she saw the state trooper in her rearview mirror.

Oh, God, oh, God, oh, God, she had thought. She was going to get arrested. She was going to be disgraced, fined, lose her license, which would mean losing her job. The world narrowed around her. Some things faded away—the green of the trees, the other cars, the music on the radio. Other things sprang into terrible clarity—the lines painted on the road, the odometer, her rearview mirror. She drove for miles and miles, her heart pounding, all the time intensely aware of the lines, the speed, the cop car relentlessly behind her.

She felt that way now, standing at the door with Kevin Flynn, watching her husband sitting in the front seat. Why wasn't he getting out? Any moment now, Kevin was going to ask her what was taking so long, and then he'd walk over there and pull Randy from the truck, and then—

Randy opened the door. He sauntered toward them, smiling, but Lisa knew it was a fake smile, knew this was a Randy she had never seen. His teeth glared in the sunlight, like the headlights of the state trooper in her rearview mirror, and as she looked away from his face, unable to bear the sight, she saw he had blood on his clothes.

Blood. On his clothes. And he was walking toward her, saying, "Hey, honey," walking toward her, and Lisa thought her driveway was stretching down one of those optical illusion tunnels in the Washington County Fair funhouse, stretching out forever.

She heard Kevin Flynn breathe in, saw the rise of his starched tan uniform shirt, and between then and the moment he opened his mouth, she had time to think, *Should I yell, 'Run?' If I knock Kevin to one side, will Randy have time to get away?* But instead of ordering her husband to stop, Kevin said, "Hey, Randy. How you been?"

"Been good," Randy said, and he marched up the front steps one, two, three with his big fake smile and grabbed her hand, grabbed it. There was the real Randy, his hand shaking, holding on to her tight enough to break bones. He kissed her cheek casually. "Good hunting weather, I can't complain. My buddy Mike took a buck."

"Good on you," Kevin said, his voice betraying no suspicion, no reservations, no coolness.

"I've been helping him dress it out," Randy said. "He's giving us some choice cuts, babe. Get out the grill, 'cause I have a hankering for Bambi burgers."

The men laughed. Lisa, squeezing against the pressure of her husband's hand, was focusing too hard to join in. Was that a bruise on Randy's face? A scratch on the back of his hand?

"Hey," Kevin said, "I stopped by because I wanted to ask you and Lisa if you saw anything suspicious when you were at Haudenosaunee."

Something flickered over Randy's face, and for the first time, it struck Lisa that there might be a connection between Eugene van der Hoeven's death and his presence there. She looked at him, this man she had known since she was in sixth grade, and wondered what he was capable of. If he could beat a woman into unconsciousness . . .

"What do you mean, suspicious?" Randy asked.

"Out of the ordinary."

"Nope. Nothing. Except that Lisa wasn't there."

She squeezed his hand. "You forgot I told you you didn't need to pick me up today, didn't you?" she said, her teasing voice as fake as his smile.

"Uh, yeah."

"You didn't see any other vehicles?"

His hand went still in hers. "What's this all about?"

"Did you see any other vehicles? Any sign that anyone else was there?"

Time slowed down again. She could see Randy's mind working furiously, wondering which was the right answer. Kevin had said Randy was one of the last people to see Mr. van der Hoeven alive. The important thing was that he not be *the* last person to have seen him alive.

"Oh, honey, it's terrible," she burst out. "Mr. van der Hoeven's been killed!"

Randy's jaw dropped. He pulled his hand from hers and stared at her as if she had spoken Swahili. "He's what?"

At that moment, Lisa had never been happier. Whatever else he had done, Randy had nothing to do with Mr. van der Hoeven's death. Suppressing her giddy relief made her voice shake, so it sounded as if she were trying to keep from falling apart when she said, "The police think it happened sometime after all the search and rescue team folks left. Were you there after everybody else was gone? If you know anything, it may help them find whoever did this to . . ." Her voice broke, of its own accord.

"Oh. Wow." Randy turned to Kevin Flynn, who had flipped open his little notebook again.

"Did you see any other vehicles?" Kevin asked for the third time.

"Yes," Randy said. "They must have belonged to the search and rescue guys. I ran into Chief Van Alstyne, and he told me about van der Hoeven's sister being missing."

Kevin went on with "Did you see Eugene van der Hoeven while you were there?"

"I didn't see anybody. I wandered around a bit, looking for Lisa. I yelled for her a few times, but nobody answered me."

"Randy!" Her indignation popped out, as if there were still a need to worry about what Mr. van der Hoeven would think.

"Sorry, honey." He shrugged at Kevin. "If there was anybody in there, they were keeping quiet."

"Okay." Kevin shut the notebook. "Thanks for your time." He took a step toward his cruiser. Stopped. As if he had thought of something else. He turned to Randy. "Do you know a Becky Castle?"

Randy was silent. He had recaptured Lisa's hand and was squeezing it harder than ever.

"There was a Becky Castle a few years ahead of us in school." Lisa was amazed at how normal her voice sounded. If she lived through this, she was going to Hollywood, because she was one hell of an actress.

"Castle," Randy said. "Is she related to Ed Castle? I used to work for him. Last year."

Lisa cast about for a plausible question. "Is she a suspect?"

"Oh. No. Just a thought I had." Kevin's eyes had gone unfocused. "Thanks," he said vaguely.

"Don't forget to call Denise," Lisa said.

With a flush of red beneath his freckles, Kevin came back to earth. He mumbled something under his breath and waved before trotting to his car.

Lisa waited until he had pulled up the drive and out of sight before she turned to Randy. "Inside. Now," she hissed. "We have to talk."

3:25 P.M.

Clare was trying to decide who Willard Aberforth reminded her of. He was tall, several inches taller than Russ, which put him in the six-and-a-half-feet and up camp. However, his bones and flesh were afraid of heights; he stooped forward, arms dangling, while his jowls and eyelids and earlobes sagged toward the safety of the ground.

His face was all she could see, because Father Aberforth was in full clericals, black-swathed and white-collared, black shoes polished to a high shine, black jacket and black coat. He gave her a long once-over as she stood at the door, taking in her bean-sprout hairdo, her ratty thermal shirt, her stained pants, and her grimy sweat socks.

"You are the Reverend Clare Fergusson?" he asked doubtfully.

Sometimes, Hardball Wright drawled in her ear, *the only option you have is to go straight ahead through the firefight.* "Yes," she said in her most chipper tone. "I am. Would you like to come in?" She stood to one side and opened her front door wider.

"Thank you." He stepped past her.

"May I take your coat?"

He handed her his overcoat, his gaze traveling across her living room. The coffee table was entirely hidden by old copies of the *Post-Star* and stacks of books. Her running shoes and socks lay abandoned in front of the sofa, and one of the club chairs was occupied by a sweater and a bag of overdue videos.

"I'm afraid I wasn't expecting you." The words were out before she could stop them. Damn. She hated apologizing for the state of her house. "Can I get you a cup of coffee?"

He coughed, a strangled sound that made her think of tubercular wards. "No, thank you. I trust this won't take long."

She had the same sinking sensation she used to get when her CO called her into his office. She indicated the chairs and sofa, darting forward to kick her shoes out of sight and remove the video bag from the chair.

She sat. He sat opposite her.

"The bishop asked me to speak with you, before his visit, on a serious matter. He didn't feel he could give it the attention it deserves during his visit tomorrow." He smiled thinly. "Between the Eucharist, the luncheon, the evensong, and the reception afterward, you've got him quite swept off his feet."

"I'm sorry," she began automatically. *A serious matter.* Her heart sank. There were almost too many possibilities. In the two years she had been at St. Alban's, she had wound up in the newspaper or on television far too many times. She viewed it as an unfortunate consequence of her work as a minister. Russ, on the other hand, referred to it as hanging around with losers and butting into police business. Perhaps the bishop agreed.

Aberforth waved off her apology. "The bishop would rather this not get around any more than it has. It's better for all concerned if we deal with the situation quietly." He leaned forward. "I'm sure you'll appreciate that we don't want to be giving any of the other clergy in the diocese any ideas."

There was another possibility, of course. She didn't want to imagine it; the thought skittered around like a mouse trying to hide in the dark. What if gossip had reached the bishop's ears? Gossip about her and Russ.

Oh, God, she thought. *Oh God, oh God, oh God.* She tried to settle her churning stomach with the thought that the bishop couldn't know anything, that he couldn't have anything other than rumors and innuendo.

"This bishop understands that a new priest, untested and untried, can make mistakes."

Who told him? One of the vestry? One of her congregation? She felt another nauseating lurch. What if it were Linda Van Alstyne? Oh, God, what if she'd been followed around by a private investigator and there were photos of Russ coming in and out of the rectory, of them lunching together, of her walking at his side along dark streets?

"It's easy, without proper guidance, to believe you're making decisions out of compassion. Or that your decisions only affect the people involved. But," he smiled his thin smile again, "as you can see, nothing stays secret in a small town. And every individual congregation, whether in Millers Kill or in Manhattan, is a small town."

But still. There was nothing to prove that they had slept together, because they hadn't. The times they had touched, over the past two years, she could name, date, describe, because they were so very rare. And precious. She could bull her way through this, because she had done . . . nothing . . . wrong.

Aberforth's black eyes searched hers. "I can see you're troubled. Please. I'm not here to punish. I'm here as the shepherd, seeking the straying lamb."

She flashed on a picture of Aberforth scooping her up in his scarecrow arms, carrying her bleating back to the fold.

"So, I'd like to hear in your own words why you broke your vows of obedience to your bishop and performed a"—his mouth worked as if the words inside had a bad taste—"ceremony of union between two homosexuals."

Clare stared at him. "What?"

"Why you gave the church's blessing to an invalid union."

She knew she must look poleaxed, but she couldn't help it. "What are you talking about?"

His face collapsed into deep folds as he frowned. "Ms. Fergusson, feigning ignorance is unbecoming. The bishop has received reliable information that this past January, you celebrated a public ceremony wherein two men exchanged vows with one another. Whether you call it a blessing or a ceremony of union, it—"

"You mean Emil and Paul's service? That's what this is all about?" She started laughing in relief.

"Ms. Fergusson! This is hardly the response I was hoping for!"

She bent over, laughing and gasping for breath. "I'm . . . I'm sorry," she managed. "It's just . . . I thought . . ." She pulled herself together, sniffing and wiping her eyes. Father Aberforth was looking at her as if she were the scriptural woman possessed by unclean spirits. "I apologize," she said, under control now. "I . . . when . . . it was the stress."

"Ms. Fergusson, are you aware that the bishop has stated explicitly that no such ceremonies will be performed in his diocese?"

She folded her hands. "Yes, I am."

"And you did, in your ordination, promise to, and I quote, 'obey your bishop and other ministers who may have authority over you and your work'?"

"Yes, I did."

He sat back and let the words hang in the air. "Well?" he said finally.

"When I performed the ceremony of union, it was at a local inn, not at St. Alban's. I didn't mark down the union in our church register, and I made sure both of them knew I was there as a friend, not as a representative of the Episcopal Church."

"Were you wearing your stole?"

The long, scarflike symbol of her priesthood. "Yes," she said.

"Did you pronounce God's blessing over them?"

"Yes. But you don't have to be ordained to bless—"

"Don't equivocate with me, Ms. Fergusson. You were acting as a priest of the diocese of Albany."

"Father Aberforth, I interviewed both the men involved, as I would any candidates for marriage. They had been together ten years. No one could claim they were rushing into it 'unadvisedly or lightly,' to use the words from the marriage ceremony. They satisfied me that it was their desire to formalize, as best they could, a loving and monogamous relationship."

Aberforth crossed one long black-clad leg over the other. "I'm willing to accept that you mistakenly thought you were not acting as a priest and that your inexperience clouded your judgment. Are you willing to confess that you were wrong in what you did?"

She phrased her answer carefully. "I felt that they were reaching out to God. I wanted to reach back, to help them connect."

"Then you should have done so by gently correcting their sin, not by encouraging it."

"I cannot believe that two adults in a faithful and self-sacrificing relationship are sinning."

"Ms. Fergusson." Aberforth speared her with his black eyes. "You have been ordained a scant two years. Bishops and learned theologians have been debating these issues in our church for longer than you've been alive. Do you really think you are the best judge of what is a sin or not?"

She kept silent.

"Are you willing to confess and repent?"

Are you now, or have you ever been . . . Ridiculous, the way her mind ping-ponged sometimes. She took a deep breath. "I confess my disobedience. And I'm sorry to have caused the bishop any distress by failing to follow his guidance on these issues."

"You're equivocating again."

"Father, I cannot repent of what I did. I don't think I was wrong."

He sat in silence. What happened next? Was the bishop going to issue a commination against her in the pulpit, denouncing her? Was she going to be kicked out of St. Alban's and bounced to another diocese?

And even now, the treacherous thought: *If I leave Millers Kill, I'll never see Russ again.*

"The bishop asked me to call him after I spoke with you. I will lay this information before him."

She nodded.

Aberforth stood. "If you have anything further you wish to add, or if, upon prayerful consideration, you change your stance, you can reach me at the Algonquin Waters."

She stood as well. *Great. Let's meet up tonight after the dinner dance. You and me and Hugh and Russ. We'll all have a drink together.*

"One more question, before I go."

"Yes, Father?" She sounded as if she were being catechized.

"At the start of our conversation, you were listening closely to what I was saying, and you were obviously concerned. Yet when I mentioned performing the illegal ceremony, you were"—he twisted the word—"surprised. To say the least."

"I am sorry about laughing. I didn't mean to offend or belittle—"

He cut her off. "What I want to know, Ms. Fergusson, is why you were so distressed." From his stoop-shouldered height, he examined her. "What did you think I was going to say?"

3:50 P.M.

L isa shut the door, locked it, and barred it with her body, facing her husband.
  "What's the matter, babe?" he said.

She had heard naughty six-year-olds fake innocence better. "You beat up Becky Castle."

His face went white. His eyes bugged out. "N-no," he stammered.

"You worked her over so bad she wound up in the hospital getting surgery to stop her internal bleeding!"

He shook his head, his mouth working.

"I know you did, you shit!" She started to cry. "My sister was her postop nurse! She called to warn me."

In the middle of the living room, he fell to his knees. "Oh, babe." He reached for her. "I'm sorry, I'm so sorry, I didn't mean to do it, I was just trying to get a break, to save my job, and Ed Castle turned me down flat and she laughed at me and said she was going to spread my picture around and have me arrested, and I got so mad, so out-of-my-skull mad, and she was such a smug-faced bitch, one of those people who get everything handed to them and can't understand what it's like to try so hard, and then she was so still, and I thought she was dead, I really thought I had killed her . . ."

Lisa wiped her arm across her eyes. Randy's agonized expression, his plead-ing confession, steadied her. "For God's sake, Randy. Get up." She reached down a hand. He staggered to his feet. He looked as if he wanted to hug her but was afraid to move closer. "How could you think she was dead? Didn't you feel for a pulse? See if she was breathing?"

His face sagged. "I didn't think of that."

She sighed. "That's because you're not the detail person. I am." She rubbed her hands over her eyes and looked at him wearily. "So did you think of what you could do to not get your butt hauled into jail?"

He stared at the wall-to-wall carpet. "I . . . I didn't think . . ." He looked up at her hopefully. "Maybe she won't remember?"

She opened her mouth. Closed it. Shook her head as if to dislodge some-thing from her ear. "For God's sake, Randy, she already told Rachel. Any minute now she'll be speaking with her doctor, and as soon as she points to you, he'll have the cops on you. We've got maybe thirty minutes before Kevin comes back. If we're lucky. And he won't be smiling and all 'Hey, Randy, how's it go-ing?' this time."

"I never meant to hurt her in the first place!" Randy looked as if he were going to cry.

"Baby, that's not going to stop them from putting you in Clinton for the next ten years."

"Look. There's no evidence. It'll be my word against hers if she tells the cops."

"Oh, Randy." She couldn't help it. She wrapped her arms around him. "You spilled your guts to me in fifteen seconds. How much longer do you think you could hold out to the police?"

He buried his face in the crook of her neck. "What should I do?"

That was the question. She hadn't had a chance to gather her thoughts since Rachel's call. "Did you leave anything behind? Any evidence?"

She felt him shake his head. "I drove her car to the Reid-Gruyn plant."

"The mill? Why on earth did you dump her car there?"

He leaned back so she could see him. "I was thinking, there should be another story, right? Another version of how it happened. So I parked it in Mr. Reid's space. Then I left some of her personal stuff in the office." He held his hands out. *Don't you get it?* "Reid belongs to some of those environmental groups. And he likes young babes—look at who he dumped his first wife for. I figured, if worse came to worse, I could argue that they were getting it on, and he hurt her, and she didn't want to turn him in."

She squeezed him. "That was smart. But what about fingerprints and bloodstains and stuff like that?"

"I wore my gloves."

She chewed the inside of her cheek, staring into the middle distance. He waited. Finally she said, "I think you need to disappear for a while." He opened his mouth to protest, and she went on. "Just for a while. You made a good start, making it look like Mr. Reid was involved. If we have a little time, I can think of a way to back that up, so the cops will seriously look at him instead of you. If it comes down to a trial"—he made a whimpering sound, and she gripped his shoulders—"if it comes down to a trial, all we'll have to do is cast a reasonable doubt that you did it."

She wasn't sure if he followed her reasoning, but he grasped the essential thing. "Where do I go? And how long do I have to stay away?"

"Go to one of your buddies' hunting cabins. Or, here." She broke away and hurried into the kitchen, where she kept cash payments in the cookie jar until she could deposit them. "Head up north and stay in one of those no-tell motels." She handed him the cash. "Wherever you go, you need to stick to the back roads, because they'll probably be looking for your truck."

He had been thumbing through the bills, impressed, but mentioning the police tracking him brought his head up. "That's right," she confirmed. "Whatever you do, don't let anybody see that license plate." She turned him toward the stairs. "Grab one of the duffle bags and throw in enough clothes for a few days. I'll pack you some food. It'd be better if you stayed out of stores. Especially convenience stores. Those places have security cameras every two feet."

He stopped, his hand on the banister. "You really do think of everything." His voice was threaded with awe.

"Go on, you don't have much time."

Lisa unhooked one of the plastic IGA shopping sacks from behind the pantry door and began emptying out the refrigerator. A loaf of bread, a jar of mayo, an unopened package of bologna. Hard cheese and applesauce in a jar and Randy's favorite pickles. Stuff that could fill him up and last, if not in a fridge, then hanging outside a window in the cold November air. All the while, the back of her mind kept count of how many minutes it had been since Rachel called. She tossed in a bag of Chips Ahoy and a jar of instant coffee, on the chance that he'd have hot water. She threw in a couple of spoons and a knife sharp enough to slice the cheese and twisted the bag handles in her fist and lugged it to the foot of the stairs.

"Hurry!"

A moment later he appeared, a backpack slung over his shoulder and one of their sleeping bags beneath his arm.

"Good idea," she said.

He stood before her, unsure, not Jesse James making a break for the border but a kid heading out to summer camp for the first time. She hooked him around the neck with her arm and pulled his face close to hers. "First thing," she said quietly, "is that I love you. Second thing is, if you ever, ever lift your hand to me, I'll cut off your balls and feed 'em to the fishes. And then I'll move out west and you'll never see me again. Got it?" She pulled him tighter into the crook of her arm.

"Yeah," he breathed.

She released him. "When it's safe, give me a call." She handed him the bag of groceries.

At the door, he hesitated. "Maybe I—"

"Go on," she said, cutting him off. He nodded. Stepped outside and closed the door behind him. She didn't stand at the window to see him pulling out. Randy could talk of omens and foretelling, of bad luck and good luck. She knew it was thinking and planning that made the difference between success and failure. She flung herself onto the sofa and picked up the Aruba pillow. She had a lot of thinking to do if she was going to save them from disaster.

3:55 P.M.

K evin bounded up the granite steps to the Millers Kill Police Department. He knew Mark Durkee thought it was an old dump, the brick-and-stone exterior unchanged since it was built over a hundred years ago, but it still pumped Kevin up every time he passed beneath the carved sign. Knowing that he belonged here. He had wanted to be a cop since he was six years old, and how many other people could say they were living out their dreams?

He yanked his cap from his head and struggled out of his jacket as he headed up the hallway to the squad room.

"Hey! Kevin!" Harlene's voice. He swerved into the dispatcher's office, where she was enthroned on her swiveling, adjustable, ergonomically correct Aeron chair in front of a bank of phone lines. He had asked her once, on a dare, how she rated a seat that cost ten times more than any other piece of furniture in the station. She had looked up and up and up at him—like the chief, he was over a foot taller than she was—and said, "Because I'm worth ten times more than any runny-nosed police academy graduate."

"Where's the chief?" he asked, throwing himself into a chair. "Still up to Haudenosaunee?"

"The birthday boy just called in. He's en route to the ME's office. Don't you get comfortable over there," Harlene said. "Lyle's been trying to get ahold of you. He interviewed the assault victim, and she's ID'd her attacker. The deputy chief wants you to meet him and be in on the arrest."

Kevin felt a warmth, like the sun rising in his chest. "Me?"

She looked over her half-glasses at him. "It's Randy Schoof."

The sun sank. "You're kidding."

"I wish I was." She swiveled away from him, needlessly snapping one of her monitors on. "The chief asked me to call Mark in early before we heard about this latest development. God only knows who's going to tell him his brother-in-law's put a girl into the hospital."

Randy Schoof. He had stood on the man's front steps and talked with him, smiled at him, taken his information. And all the time he had been eating a bunch of lies.

"Not that any of us will have time to sit and soothe him," Harlene was saying. "Everybody's coming in, off duty or not. Part-timers, too. Chief's found something up at Haudenosaunee, mark my words."

No. Not lies. He had been asking the wrong questions. And Schoof had taken advantage of his idiocy. Thank God Harlene had caught him before he entered his report. He would have never lived it down.

"In all the years I've worked dispatch I've never seen the like. A murder, a missing person, and an assault case all in one day? It's like one of those signs of the Apocalypse, that's what it is."

Kevin jammed his hat on his head. "I'm outta here."

"You be careful." Harlene always made the words sound like a direct order.

"Don't worry," Kevin said. "If anybody's getting hurt today, it's not gonna be me."

4:05 P.M.

Randy Schoof was on the road toward Lake George when he heard the siren. He floored the gas pedal, one eye on the road and another on the rearview mirror.

When he saw an intersection ahead, he slammed on the brakes and fishtailed into a turn. He immediately stood on the gas again, sending the truck leaping forward on the deserted road, and when he spotted a farm stand whose sign read CLOSED FOR THE SEASON, he didn't hesitate. He spun into the U-shaped drive and bumped over the dying grass to pull in behind the small wooden building. He killed the engine and rolled his window down.

The siren wailed through the rapidly cooling air, faint and getting fainter. He waited, his heart pounding, until he heard nothing. Then he started up the truck and headed for Route 57.

He had had the idea in the back of his mind the whole time Lisa had been talking about hiding out at a buddy's cabin or finding a motel. The problem with both those ideas, he figured, was that wherever he was, somebody would know.

But there was a place he could go—at least for tonight—that no one would know about. He wouldn't have thought of it if it hadn't had been for his earlier visit to Reid-Gruyn.

The old mill. He could park his truck right in the regular employee parking lot. No one would think twice about it being there—there were always cars and trucks around, and if anyone realized his truck was there and he wasn't, they'd put it down to a mechanical problem. Then he could hike over to the old mill and sneak inside.

He grinned. Lisa would be pleased. It was the perfect spot. No one ever went there. No one would ever think to look.

4:30 P.M.

Despite having the bathroom door shut tight to keep the steamy warmth in, she heard the kitchen door open as she shut the shower off. The rectory was an old house, and it thumped and creaked and popped with every change of pressure, whether it was a door opening or a footstep on the floor or a stair tread swelling and shrinking as the humidity rose and fell.

Good Lord, it had better not be Deacon Aberforth, coming back for another round. She had barely escaped intact that last time, when he asked her what she had been so apprehensive about. She had stammered something about the fund-raising for the roof repairs and stuffed him out the door.

But no, she couldn't imagine Aberforth letting himself in. It had to be Hugh Parteger, stopping by on his way to the bed-and-breakfast where he would be spending the night. She had been surprised he hadn't arrived before now; although New York City was light-years away from Millers Kill in every way that counted, it was only a four-hour drive.

She grabbed a towel and bent over from the waist, flipping her hair down before wrapping it into a terrycloth turban. She lifted her robe from its hook and slipped it on, belting it firmly. She stepped out of the bathroom in an explosion of steam and checked herself out in the mirror at the top of the stairs. Swathed in white toweling from her head to her ankles, she looked like someone auditioning to be an extra in a remake of *The Mummy*. Hugh would be amused. She briskly rubbed at her hair through its wrapping, then took the towel off and tossed it over the banister.

She padded down the stairs. "Hey," she yelled. "Is that—"

Russ was standing next to her sofa table.

"—you?" she finished, her voice gone small.

"Uh," he said. "Um, I was on my way back from the ME's office . . ." His voice trailed off. He was holding a picture of her with her family, taken this past summer when she had gotten away to Virginia for two weeks. He tried to put it back, but he was watching her instead of his hand and wound up bumping the heavy silver frame against two others, knocking them down.

That got his attention. He tore his gaze from her and started propping the pictures up, nearly tipping over three more in his haste to clean up after himself. "Sorry," he said. She could have sworn he blushed.

"It's okay," she said. "I shouldn't have so many on that table anyway. They're bound to fall over." Part of her was thinking at how pleased her grandmother Fergusson would have been to hear her taking the blame on herself, like a good southern belle. Another part of her was acutely aware that under her all-enveloping robe, she was naked.

That thought must have occurred to Russ as well, because when he turned back to her, he looked not at her face but at the tie belted around her waist. Her heart was trip-hammering, blood like heated honey flowing through her veins, raising her body temperature until it seemed the cloud of steam was still with her, enveloping her in dampness and warmth.

He looked at her, his blue eyes that crackled like the glaze on a Japanese pot, and the fierceness and the ache she saw there dropped the bottom out of her stomach and made her go loose-limbed.

She stepped toward him. Something flared in his eyes. She took another step. She wasn't going to stop. She couldn't stop. She was alone with him, in her own house, on her own time, and they were both adults, and why should she stop? She *wanted,* and she realized that everything she believed in, everything she placed between this man and herself, was just another robe, and she could shrug it off and be naked. Be nothing more or less than who she was.

She took another step. It was easy. She wanted to laugh. She took another—

—and he looked away. Turned his whole body, so that he was edge on toward her, and she thought stupidly, *Oh. So that's the cold shoulder.*

"Don't," he said, his voice tight.

In an instant, every cell in her body was icebound. She had never been so mortified in her life. "I'm sorry," she managed to get out through her constricted throat. "I'm so sorry. I was—"

"For chrissakes, Clare, it's not that." He wouldn't face her. "What, do you think I don't want you?" He clenched his hands. "I can't be responsible for both of us. You sashay across the room with your eyes saying, *Take me, take me*—what do you think I'm going to do? I'm not a monk." He turned back toward her.

She stared at him. He stared at her. She felt her lips twitch. Then grin. Then she started laughing, hard, clutching her stomach through the robe.

"Okay, okay." He sounded abashed, but he was grinning, too. "The monk remark was not well thought out."

Sighing from laughter, she wiped her eyes. "I love you," she said.

She had never told him that straight out, without an apology. He looked as if he didn't know whether to laugh or cry. "I love you, too," he said.

They stood there, three feet apart, not knowing what to say. Clare glanced down to where her feet were peeking out from underneath the robe. "Well," she said finally. "Now that we've covered that, would you like some soup?"

She walked to the kitchen without waiting for his reply, knowing that doing something, keeping busy, was the safest course. And even though she wasn't the least bit hungry at the moment, she also knew she'd be starving once he left.

She had her head in the fridge when Russ pushed through the swinging doors separating the kitchen from the living room. "What kind of soup?" he asked. She could hear it in his voice, too, a deliberate attempt to be casual, as if the two of them hanging out in her house while she was practically undressed was a normal thing.

"Butternut squash. I made it yesterday. It has squash, onions, chicken broth, peanut butter." She pulled the Tupperware bowl from the bottom shelf and placed it on the counter.

"Uh . . ." He looked dubious. "I'll pass."

She shrugged. "More for me." She retrieved a pot from the dish drainer and poured the soup in.

"So," she said, opening the fridge again and bending down for the good bakery bread. "If you didn't come here to have your way with me, why did you come?"

Silence. She straightened, turning, in time to catch him staring at her rump. His eyes looked glazed. "Uh," he said.

Flustered, she nearly dropped the bread. She grabbed at the first topic to come to mind. "You said you were on your way back from the ME's office. What's happening in the van der Hoeven case?"

His eyes snapped into focus. "Ed Castle's off the hook. Dr. Dvorak confirmed that Eugene died from a fall. As in, off the tower where we found his body."

"The tower?"

"I told you about it, remember? A nineteenth-century folly." He flattened his hands on the kitchen table. "Even if I could spin a theory whereby Ed chased Eugene up to the top of the tower and threw him off, the weird setup we found would argue for something entirely different. What different thing it was, I don't know yet."

"What did you find?"

"It looks like someone was being held there. There was food, articles of clothing, blankets . . ."

"Good Lord. Millie van der Hoeven?"

"That's my thought. The crime tech guys didn't find any prints, but there were a number of long blond hairs around."

"Becky Castle has long blond hair," she reminded him.

"Yeah, but she wasn't unaccounted for for any length of time. Besides, we know who assaulted her. Lyle interviewed her when she got out of surgery."

Clare stopped, her serrated knife halfway through the loaf. "Who?"

"A guy named Randy Schoof."

"Is he related to Lisa Schoof? The woman who works at Haudenosaunee?"

"They're married. *And* he's Mark Durkee's brother-in-law. It's a small town."

She shook her head. That poor young woman. "How do you handle something like that?"

"Obviously, we keep Mark away from that investigation. Believe me, there's more than enough to keep him busy elsewhere. He's following up on a black Mercedes some of the search and rescue guys saw driving up to Haudenosaunee before Eugene died."

"You think the driver might be Eugene's killer?"

"At this point, I'm more concerned with finding Millie van der Hoeven. There's nothing I can do to help Eugene now. But Millie . . . hell, I have no idea if she's alive, if she's dead, what she was doing in that tower room, who was keeping her there."

"Sounds frustrating."

"It is." He sniffed at the soup. "Can I have a taste of that?"

She slid the bowl along the counter. He downed a spoonful. Then another. He looked at her, surprised. "Is it too late to change my mind?"

She grinned. "According to my theology, never." She fetched another bowl from the cupboard and filled it from the pot. "Let's eat in the living room," she said. "My feet are cold."

He took both bowls from her while she slapped the bread on a plate and followed him through the swinging doors. He laid the bowls carefully on the square coffee table before sinking into one of the cushy chairs facing each other across it. She settled the bread plate between the bowls, then turned on two lamps and the CD player. She glanced out the window before sitting down. "It sure gets dark early these days."

"It's November."

She tucked her feet under her and smiled. "I didn't get a chance to say this before, but happy birthday."

He looked embarrassed.

"So you're fifty now."

He leaned forward, put his face in his hands, and groaned.

"That's really, really old."

He gave her a stony look. "Brat."

She laughed. "Then don't be in such a funk about it. As my grandmother used to say, getting old isn't so bad when you consider the alternative." She picked up her soup bowl. "What do you want for your birthday?"

"To find Millie van der Hoeven alive and well and to nail Eugene van der Hoeven's killer."

"Any ideas?"

He plunked his spoon into his soup. "The guy didn't get out and about enough to make enemies. Unless he was harassing somebody through the mail for the past umpteen years, I don't see how he could have whipped anyone up enough to kill him."

"He whipped Becky Castle up when he chased her away at gunpoint."

He flipped his hand open. "I'm damn sure Becky Castle didn't kill him."

"I wasn't suggesting that. I was suggesting that the land sale itself may have stirred somebody to kill him. There's a lot of money involved."

"Yeah, but the main players are all benefiting. GWP gets glory and a big tax break, the Adirondack Conservancy Corporation gets more protected parkland, and the van der Hoevens carry home bags of cash."

"There are people who depend on access to Haudenosaunee land for all or part of their livelihood."

"Like who? Ed Castle? I told you, he simply doesn't fit as the killer."

"What about Shaun Reid?"

Russ sat back. "What about Shaun?"

"Do you know him?"

He paused for a moment, as if thinking her question over. "He was my best friend in high school." He leaned forward again and took another spoonful of soup. "We drifted apart after I went into the army. He was in college when I was in Nam, and by the time he returned to live in Millers Kill, I was long gone."

"You didn't pick things up again after you moved home for good?"

"Too many differences. Too much water under the bridge. Besides, you put on a uniform, people look at you differently."

"I've noticed that," she said dryly.

"Yeah, but at least you don't have to worry that you might wind up arresting one of your buddies." He shifted in his seat. "You start to get kind of friendly with someone, you think, here's a guy I'd like to hang out with, go fishing, and then you think, what is it gonna be like when I pull him over for DUI? Or go to his house because he's been brawling with his wife? Or surprise him at work because his boss finds he's been cooking the books?"

"You don't have a very upbeat view of human nature, do you?"

"Linda said the same thing to me this morning."

Clare smiled a little. "She knows you well."

"Yeah."

She studied him for a moment while he ate his soup.

He lifted his head. "What?"

"I didn't say anything."

"You were thinking something."

She smiled. "I wonder if one of the reasons you let yourself get close to me is because you felt, somehow, that a woman priest was less likely to fail you."

He thought about it. "Less likely to wind up in trouble, you mean?"

"Or less likely to have any human frailties."

"Well, if that was what I was thinking, the joke's on me, isn't it? I've never met anybody who attracts trouble like you."

"That's not fair! Just because I'm called to get involved—"

The smirk behind his soup spoon alerted her to the fact that her chain had been yanked. She picked up her bowl, trying to keep a scowl on her face. "You think you've got me all figured out, don't you?"

"No." His voice was low. "I think you continually surprise and delight me. And that's why I let you get close."

She stared at him, her face growing hot. He looked back at her, steadily, and it felt as if they were sinking in deep water, holding each other by their words alone. If she looked up, she would see the pale blue surface of the ocean, far, far above her.

The kitchen door crashed open.

"Vicar?" a British voice called. "Are you home?"

EVENSONG

5:00 P.M.

They looked like a hokey tableau in one of those British sex farces. There she sat in nothing but a robe, which, she discovered as she followed Hugh's eyes, had loosened up noticeably while she was bending and stretching in the kitchen and was now showing off a good deal more of her chest than she had intended. There sat Russ, superficially relaxed, tension radiating from every line, his attempt at appearing casual and friendly marred by a defensive glare that screamed guilt. And there stood Hugh, wine bottle in hand, storm clouds rumbling across his face, glancing back and forth between them as if waiting for someone to say the first line and start the scene.

Clare resisted the urge to yank her robe tightly together and insist, *It's not what you think.* Instead she smiled brightly and said, "Hugh! I was wondering where you were. I hope the drive wasn't too bad. You remember Russ Van Alstyne, don't you?"

The two men looked at each other with loathing.

"Russ dropped by as I was ladling up some soup." She felt a spark of unease at how easily the lie slipped out. "Would you like some?"

"No. Thank you." Usually, Hugh was the embodiment of Prince Charming, with twinkling eyes and dimples on both cheeks he flashed to great effect. This closed-faced, tight-mouthed man was somebody she had never met. "I find I'm not very hungry." He looked at Russ again. "I've heard of neighborhood polic-ing, but I've never seen it practiced in such an intimate way."

"I'm off duty," Russ growled.

"Ah. Yes. I take it from your costume you've been looking for animals to kill? You know what Wilde said about hunting. 'The unspeakable in pursuit of the inedible.'"

Russ rose from his seat. "Oscar Wilde was talking about hunting foxes, not deer." Clare blinked in surprise. Hugh did as well. Russ looked Hugh up and down, taking in his purple corduroy pants and floral button-down shirt. "You ought to quote him correctly if you're going to dress like him." He turned to Clare. "Thanks for the soup, Clare. I'll see you later."

He vanished between the swinging doors. A moment later, she heard the kitchen door shutting. She was alone with Hugh.

If you're trapped with no way out, you've got two options, Hardball Wright said. *Surrender or attack. Since I don't expect anybody who's gone through my course to surrender, that means you attack.*

"I'll thank you to treat my guests civilly," she said, rising from her chair and picking up the soup bowls.

"Me?" Hugh's jaw dropped. "What about him?" She swept past him toward the kitchen. "And what about you?" he continued, dogging her through the doors.

She dropped the bowls in the sink and turned on the faucet. "I think you look fine," she said, deliberately misunderstanding his question. "Very English. American men are scared of color and pattern."

"I'm not talking about my damn outfit. I don't give a rat's ass what Dick Van Dyke there thinks about my clothing. What were you doing sitting there with him practically nude?"

She considered saying, *I don't understand. He was fully dressed,* but figured one purposefully obtuse response was her daily limit. "I'm perfectly decent," she said firmly. "He happened to stop in right after I got out of the shower. I didn't think he was staying long enough for me to excuse myself and get dressed."

"Oh, but he stayed long enough for a bowl of soup and a cozy little chat."

She turned to face him, bracing her hands against the counter. In her bare feet, she was only a few inches shorter than him. "What exactly are you trying to say, Hugh?"

"I don't think you realize how much you talk about him. When you're on the phone to me." He raised his voice to imitate her. "'I was having lunch with Chief Van Alstyne the other day and . . . I asked Chief Van Alstyne about . . . Chief Van Alstyne says . . . '"

"He's my friend. I'm sure I also mention my friends Anne Vining-Ellis and Roxanne Lunt."

"But I don't find you sitting around sharing *soup* in the buff with them!" The word "soup" curled off his tongue with a salacious hiss.

She tilted her head up, searching for a ray of calm to settle her enough to talk to Hugh without tearing his head off. He was angry and troubled, and it was her job to help people who were hurting, not to exacerbate their wounds.

"I'm sorry you're upset about walking in on us like that," she said, taking a measure of pride in how even her voice was. "But I can assure you, Russ and I didn't do anything while he was here that we couldn't have done right in front of you, if you had gotten here earlier."

"Lovely. I'm assured you didn't have a before-dinner *cock*-tail."

Her mouth gaped open. "That is just plain nasty!" Her voice, no longer even, sounded distinctly screechy, even to her. "Maybe you ought to hightail it over to the hotel. I'll meet you there later when you've had a chance to rinse your mouth out."

"There's another thing. We've been dating for over a year now, and every time I visit you I have to make shift in a damn bed-and-breakfast."

"I've told you I can't have a man staying in the rectory with me. For God's sake, Hugh, my church is right next door."

"That doesn't explain why you won't stay with me in my apartment when you come to the city."

She looked down. "Is your friend Jackie complaining?" Clare had been the guest of a divorced coworker of Hugh's during the three times she had visited New York.

"Of course she's not. But even if you're paranoid enough to think it might get back to your congregation if you shack up in my apartment, there's no way you can tell me anyone would know if we spent a discreet afternoon or evening together."

"I'd know." She pushed the sleeves of her robe up. "I'm not just playing goody-goody because I'm afraid I'll get caught. I believe that sex should be reserved for a committed, monogamous relationship."

"Then how do you explain Chief Vincent Van Gogh in your living room?"

She stepped toward him. "I swear, in Jesus' holy name, that I have never, ever had sex with Russ Van Alstyne."

"Ah, but Vicar." Hugh looked at her ruefully. "Can you swear you don't want to?"

Her silence condemned her. She knew it, but she couldn't bring herself to play Peter and deny her feelings three times. Finally she managed, "What I want or don't want isn't important. It's what I do."

"He's married, isn't he?" Hugh's voice was gentle.

"Yes."

"And I suppose his wife is a real piece of work."

Clare looked at the kitchen wall. "His wife is a beautiful, dynamic woman who loves him very much. A sentiment that he returns."

"Ah." He stared at the bottle of wine he'd been holding since he walked in. "What say we crack this open and have a couple of glasses while we talk?"

5:05 P.M.

Randy Schoof was being very cautious. Thinking before acting. Lisa would be pleased. He had debated hiding his truck as best he could by the old mill but had decided parking it in plain sight in the employee lot was better. There was always a collection of vehicles there, and no one in a hurry to clock in or rushing to get home would be curious about one more. He had carried everything—his backpack, his sleeping bag, the groceries—in one big load rather than hiking back and forth from the mill to the parking lot. He stuck to the shadows next to the rotting clapboard as he worked his way through the skeletons of waist-high weeds. And he was quiet, as quiet as could be, despite the roar of water over the dam washing out the sound of his footsteps. At the small side door, sheltered by an enclosed overhang, he fished out his ATM card. The door was locked, but Mike, who had snuck into the building every once in a while for a joint before he was laid off, had told him the secret: The lock was crap. You could pop it with a card and reset it from inside.

A jiggle, a lift, and Mike was proved right. He pocketed the card, slipped inside, and shut the door behind him. He took a few steps and was reaching into his backpack for his small emergency-use flashlight when he tripped over something square and painfully solid.

"Shit!" he cried, smashing into the floor, the flashlight and the bags flying, jars and boxes thudding and clunking, his sleeping bag bouncing off into the darkness. "Shit! Shit!"

"Who's there?"

He froze.

"Who's there?"

It was a woman. Faint and seemingly far away, but a woman. How in the hell had a woman gotten in here?

"Look, whoever you are!"

Christ, they didn't have some sort of security guard now, did they?

"I don't care what you're doing here! I'm trapped, and I need help!"

He climbed to his feet. Now what was he supposed to do? Silently he bent over, feeling for his backpack. He brushed it with the back of his hand and grabbed it. The zippers jingled, a faint noise he heard as a clash of cymbals.

"I know you're here. I heard you fall over something."

Maybe he could just stand still. Stay quiet over here by the door. Maybe he could open and close the door, pretending to leave.

"Help me! Please, please, help me! Please!"

Oh, God. He was never going to be able to ignore that. "Hang on," he yelled. "I'm looking for my flashlight." He knelt carefully and began patting down the floor, feeling for the narrow cylinder.

"Thank you! Thank you!"

He got a fat bottle and a loaf of bread and something smooth and cool that he managed to identify as a knife before he sliced his palm open. He jammed everything into his backpack. Everything except his flashlight, which was nowhere within reach. "Crap," he said.

"What is it?" the woman called.

"I can't find my flashlight." He had one in the glove compartment of his truck, but he didn't want to appear out in the open again so soon. Maybe later.

"Talk to me," he said loudly. "I'll find you by sound."

"I'm over here," she said. "Near the far wall, the one closest to the river. Over here. Watch out for the stacks of pallets and the—"

"Oof!" There was a *clang* as he ran straight into something large and immovable.

"—the big machinery parts."

He groaned. "What are you doing here? What do you mean, you're trapped?" He could imagine maybe one of these machines dislodging and pinning someone. But in that case, he'd expect her to sound like she was in pain.

There was a pause. A long pause. Finally she said, "It's embarrassing."

Embarrassing? Like what? The only thing that embarrassed Lisa was stuff like other people knowing she had her period, or that time he told a couple friends about her getting the hair on her upper lip zapped. "Keep talking," he said. He meant so he could find her, but she took it as an order.

"I met up with someone here. We were going to . . . do a bondage thing. But instead, he tied me up and left me here."

Randy felt a flash of heat in his belly. Christ almighty. Maybe she was wearing some weird leather getup. Or nothing at all. Not that he'd do anything. He loved his wife. But Christ, what a story to tell the guys. Then he remembered that he wasn't going to be telling this story to anyone. Because he wasn't here.

His eyes had adjusted, and he could make out shapes in the darkness. Still, he almost stumbled across her. She was on the floor, leaning against another stack of pallets. The rectangular windows a story above them shed enough moonlight across the blackness that he could make out her legs, stretched out and covered in something pale. He dropped to his knees.

She was rolled loosely into a blanket, so he couldn't see what she had on. He couldn't make out the details of her face, but he figured that was just as well, since that meant she couldn't see him too well, either.

"Hey," he said.

"Hey." She sounded like a runner after a race, breathing hard but trying to bring herself under control. "I'm . . . my hands and ankles are bound."

He reached for the blanket covering her, not touching it. "You mind if I . . . ?"

"Please."

He could tell by the way she talked that she wasn't from here. "What's your name?" he said, still not touching the blanket.

"M-Mel. Melanie." She sounded as if she wasn't sure.

"Nice to meet ya, Melanie. I'm Mike." He had thought the fake name up while he was crossing the floor. No use hiding out if someone could identify him by name. "I'm, uh, going to take the blanket off now."

"Okay."

"I can't see you very well."

"It's fine," she said impatiently.

Maybe she wasn't the modest type. He tugged the blanket away, using both hands to unwrap it.

"Sorry," she said. "I didn't mean to snap. It's just that I've been tied up like this all day, and it feels as if my shoulders are going to break off at this point."

He wasn't interested in her explanations. He was interested in why she was trying to sell him a bullshit story about bondage gone bad. He and Lisa had married right out of high school, and he didn't have a whole lot of experience, but he knew for sure that no woman would show up for a kinky scene with her lover dressed in a flannel shirt and sweatpants. And hiking boots? He could imagine—just—some guy getting turned on enough by the idea of struggling to undress her to leave the clothes on while he trussed her up. But hiking boots?

His hand slipped down to her wrists, and he felt the unmistakable texture of duct tape. "I need to get my knife," he said.

"Of course. Thank you. Thank you."

He stood up and threaded his way back to the backpack and plastic bag. Thinking hard the whole way.

His camping kit had a utility knife, but he grabbed the kitchen knife Lisa had tossed in with the groceries instead. Its serrated edge would go through the duct tape a lot faster. If he used it. He made his way back to her, this time stopping a few feet away, when he could see her outline in the dark.

"I have the knife," he said.

"Thank God." There was a quiet *clink* as she bent forward, like an iron manacle tapping against the cement floor. "Please, undo my hands first. My arms are numb."

"Yeah. Sure." He squatted. "Just, I want to know what you're really doing here first."

She stopped moving. "I told you."

He waited, not saying anything. It was what his dad used to do whenever he thought Randy was lying. He wouldn't argue; he wouldn't explain why he thought Randy wasn't telling the truth. He'd just sit there. Quiet. Until Randy broke.

"Cut it off! I told you, I was meeting someone here and he tied me up. I thought it was for fun."

He squatted, silent. He held the knife out and tilted it until the blade caught a dull gleam of light from the faraway windows.

"Please!"

Part of him wanted to giggle. Who would have thought it, him using his dad's silent treatment instead of blowing up? He felt strange, grown-up and aware that he was feeling grown-up, all at the same time. Like the first time he and Lisa slept in his parents' house, after they'd gotten married.

"All right," she snarled, and he was jerked into the present. "All right. Cut me loose and I'll tell you."

"Tell me and I'll cut you loose."

She made a noise. "Okay." She took a breath. "I saw a man kill my brother. He put me in his car and brought me here. I think he's trying to decide if he's going to kill me or not."

His head whited out for a moment while he tried to fit that statement into the real world he lived in. The first thing he thought was *Again, my luck is lousy.* He had stumbled into a freaking *Sopranos* episode. If he let this woman go, he'd have some contract killer after him.

"What . . . what was your brother into? So that this guy killed him?"

"Into? He wasn't into anything." Her voice broke. "He was a recluse who lived in the mountains and never saw anyone except me and my sister if he could help it. I don't know why he was killed. I don't know anything about what's going on."

Recluse. Mountain. Lisa saying, *Oh, honey, it's terrible. Mr. van der Hoeven's been killed!*

"You're not Melanie. You're van der Hoeven's sister, Millie," he said.

She was silent for a moment. "Yeah," she finally said.

"You're missing!"

"If you cut me loose, believe me, I won't be."

He moved behind her and worked the tip of the knife under the fraying edge of one of her duct-tape manacles. He sawed back and forth. He had found the missing woman. Maybe she'd be so grateful, she'd give him an alibi. The duct tape parted around one of her wrists, and with a groan of pain she brought her arms around to her front.

"God." She bent over, rocking back and forth. "Oh, that hurts."

"Um." He sat down, scootching a little way from her so he was out of range, in case her arms weren't really as useless as they seemed. "Maybe since I'm helping you out, you could help me out."

She made a noise that might have been an encouragement to continue.

"I'm, um, in a bit of trouble. That's why I'm here. Maybe you could say that I was with you earlier? Like, in the middle of the day for a few hours?"

"I could," she said, her voice thin with pain, "but don't you think it would look odd that you left me tied up all day? Whatever trouble you're in, I bet kidnapping would be worse." Her voice changed. Became harder. "Besides, it's up to me to get the man who killed Gene. I was the only witness to what that bastard did."

"What happened?"

"I was . . ." She hesitated. "I was in an old observation tower. It's a good walk away from where our camp is now. This man tried to take me, and my brother was protecting me, and he—the man—threw him over the railing." She wavered for a moment before going on. "The bastard left him lying there, out in the open. Like garbage. I have to get to him, take care of his body before—" She broke off.

Randy thought of what could happen to a body left out in the woods for a few days. "I'm sorry."

"Yeah. Me, too. And so will that rat bastard be. As soon as I get out of here, I'm heading straight to the cops."

Randy twitched. It sounded too close to his own actions today. Maybe the man who killed her brother had been a cold-blooded murderer. But maybe he had been like Randy, someone who just took one more kick from life than he could take and was then left frantically pedaling to get out from under what he hadn't even meant to do in the first place. It didn't seem fair that a man could spend his whole life doing the right thing and then blow it all up in five minutes' time.

"Who was he? This guy. I mean, why was he after you?"

"I don't know. I don't know his name." He couldn't see her face at all, hunched over like she was, but he could hear the edge of satisfaction in her voice when she said, "But I got his license plate number. Right before he dumped me in the back of his Mercedes. I said it over and over to myself while I was locked in there."

Randy stared into the darkness, seeing not the cold and grimy old mill but the Haudenosaunee driveway under brilliant sunshine. The driveway that was blocked by a black Mercedes.

"This Mercedes," he said. "Did you see a bumper sticker on it? Something about the Sierra club?"

A swish of hair. She lifted her head. "Yeah."

"Shaun Reid," he said, scared and exultant. "That's who killed your brother. The guy who owns this mill. Shaun Reid."

5:10 P.M.

Lisa was expecting the two squad cars that pulled into her drive. After Randy left, she had gone about her normal routine for a Saturday afternoon, showering, a load of laundry, cooking. She had a big pot of stew simmering on the stove, figuring that if she really didn't know what her husband had done or where he had gone, she'd have dinner waiting for him. She stuck *Titanic* in the VCR and poured herself a glass of rum and Diet Coke, props to simulate a normal afternoon: hanging out, watching a chick flick, waiting for her husband to get home. She picked up the drink, thinking to calm her nerves, but decided the last thing she needed was to have any of her edges dulled by alcohol. Instead she swilled some around in her mouth and spat it into the sink, following that with half the contents of the glass. Simulation. The illusion of reality.

So she shouldn't have felt sick to her stomach when she saw the headlights swinging into her dooryard. She did take a swallow of the rum and Coke then, for real, and breathed slowly and deeply before walking to the door. No sense pretending she hadn't heard anyone driving up the road. She dropped her hand to the doorknob.

I don't know anything. I didn't do anything. I'm innocent. I know nothing.

She opened the door. Not surprisingly, it was Kevin again, and some old cop who was, with his brush-cut hair and weight-lifting body, a preview of what her sister's husband was going to look like in thirty years. She supposed she should be grateful. At least they didn't send Mark out for this.

"Lisa?" No smiles this time. "May we come in?"

She stepped back, opening the door. "What's the matter?" She had thought about this, about how she'd first react. Tossing bagged veggies into the stew pot, she'd considered what she would have thought if the police had come to her door last Saturday, a time that was forever now going to be set off as *before*. Now was *after*. And she did as she rehearsed.

"Oh, my God." A hitch of breath. "Is it Randy? Has he been in an accident?"

The old cop smiled as he walked past her, crinkling up his eyes, as if he were playing Santa Claus. "No accident." He held out his hand. "I'm Lyle MacAuley, Mrs. Schoof." She took his hand, staring mostly at Kevin the whole while.

"What is it, then? Is it Mark?"

Kevin shook his head.

"Kevin was here earlier, asking about what you might have seen at Haudenosaunee."

She nodded. Realized she was standing there with the warm air pouring out of the house. Shut the door.

"There's been another incident today. A young woman was beaten and left on one of the logging roads on Haudenosaunee. Did your husband mention it to you?"

"No," she said. *How would I react to this news?* she wondered. *I would be scared of it happening to me.* She glanced toward the window nervously.

"Why don't we sit down?" The old guy phrased it like a suggestion, but he was already crossing the room, taking in everything, the movie, the drink, the stack of bills by the phone, the water stain on the ceiling. "Is your husband home?" he asked, sitting on one end of the couch.

"No." She glanced back toward the door. "Do I need to worry about being alone out here?"

Kevin crossed his arms over his chest. "Where's Randy?"

Lyle MacAuley patted the couch next to him. "Calm down, Kevin. Let the lady have a seat."

She couldn't not sit after that. She wedged herself in the corner opposite MacAuley.

"You certainly don't have to worry right now," MacAuley said, smiling again. "And if you'd like, we'd be glad to drop you off at a friend's or neighbor's when we go. If your husband isn't home yet. Do you expect him soon?"

"By dinnertime," she said. "He didn't say he'd be gone longer than that."

"Where's he off to?"

"Errands, I guess. I was in the shower when he left."

"When was that?" Kevin said.

MacAuley shot him a look. "I'd hate to leave you alone out here if you feel uncomfortable," he said. "Do you have someone you usually stay with?"

"What do you mean?"

"Oh, you know. If things blow up and one or the other of you has to cool down."

"You mean Randy and me? We don't fight like that."

"No?" His expression invited confidence. "I've been there myself. You're young, married, money's tight, one or the other of you is always working . . . you mean to say you never fight?"

"Of course, we have fights. I mean . . . not so's one of us has to leave."

"He's never gotten a little rough?"

She was genuinely outraged. "No!"

He raised his hands in surrender. "Whatever. I don't like to interfere between husband and wife." He smiled. "Has your husband ever mentioned a woman named Becky Castle?"

Her heart jumped so hard she knew he must have seen it in her throat. She shook her head.

"I'm sorry?"

"No," she said. "Kevin asked us if we knew her. Earlier."

He leaned forward. "I don't want to upset you, here, but . . . have you ever suspected your husband might be seeing someone else?"

"No!" She glared at Kevin. "Kevin, what's this about?"

This time, he kept his mouth shut. "Becky Castle was the young woman who was assaulted today," MacAuley said. "The poor thing was beaten so badly she had to undergo surgery to stop her internal bleeding. Somebody punched her and kicked her and hit her until she was so much raw hamburger."

The words, the images, were so ugly she wanted to slap her hands over her ears and howl until they burned themselves out of her brain.

"We think your husband might be able to help us in our inquiries," MacAuley went on. "It's important we talk with him as soon as possible."

She forced herself to nod. "Of course. I'll have him call you as soon as he gets home."

"Is there anyplace he's more likely to be? At a bar, or a friend's house? Time is important. You know, we always say the first twenty-four hours of an investigation are the most important. 'The golden hours,' we call them. We want to be able to talk to anyone who may know something as quickly as possible."

"I don't know," she said. "He was at Mike's earlier. Mike Yablonski."

MacAuley glanced at Kevin, who nodded once.

MacAuley stood, startling her. "Okay, then. Thanks, Mrs. Schoof."

She unfolded herself from the couch and joined the two police officers heading for the door. She didn't understand. She had thought he would keep at her. Ask her more about her husband. "I'll be sure to have Randy call you as soon as he gets home tonight," she repeated.

MacAuley smiled at her, eyes crinkling, bushy brows rising. "We'd sure appreciate it."

"Um . . . is there anything else I can do to help?"

He smiled even more broadly, looking less like Santa and more like the cat who swallowed the canary. "Why, yes," he said. "Can we have a look around the house?"

5:15 P.M.

Clare looked into the burgundy surface of her wine. If she sat very, very still, she could see her reflection. Or rather, the reflection of her eye. *For now we see through a glass, darkly,* she thought.

Hugh thumped his glass against the table. They were sitting in the kitchen. The only other spot to sit face-to-face downstairs was in her living room, where she and Russ had been talking. By mutual, unspoken agreement, Clare and Hugh avoided that room when she returned downstairs dressed in a sweater and jeans.

"I don't think I've ever seen you at a loss for words," Hugh said.

"There's nothing to say." In a way, she was telling the truth. For close to two years now, she had kept her mouth soldered shut, refusing to even think about the unthinkable. She had cracked and admitted it to herself; eventually, she had admitted it to Russ. It terrified her to think that the truth was so close to her surface that she was on the verge of admitting it to a nice man she saw every six or seven weeks. "There's nothing to say," she repeated.

"Is he going to divorce the little woman?"

That made her look up from the depths of her glass. "No."

"Are you planning on chucking the whole priest thing and living a life of wickedness as a kept woman?"

She couldn't help it; her lips twitched. "No."

"Bit of a sticky wicket, eh?"

"You sound like someone in the 1939 version of *The Four Feathers.*" She took a sip of the Shiraz. They had discovered, on her first trip to New York, that they shared a common devotion to prewar British films.

"The fellow who went blind and gave up the girl because it was the right thing to do, no doubt."

She smiled into her wineglass.

He swallowed a gulp of wine. "Where do you think this thing is going? With you and me, I mean."

She was surprised. "I don't know. I haven't thought about it."

"Good Lord. You must be the only single woman over thirty I know who isn't thinking about how to get herself married off." He spread his arms and looked down at himself. "Am I not eligible? Not repulsive, don't drool or pick my teeth in public, ready for housetraining."

She took another sip, uncertain if he was joking or not. "Hugh, are you proposing? Or just looking for more affirmation that your shirt looks okay?"

"I'm just trying to figure out why you don't at least eyeball me as potential husband material."

She sighed. "Because for the past six or seven years, I've thought of myself as someone who is never going to get married. It's not as if I've had men throwing themselves at me. Believe me. When I realized my calling, it sort of dovetailed with my spectacular lack of a love life. I figured I was meant to be a celibate."

"Okay." He ticked off one finger. "So, aspirations to be bride of God. Anything else?"

"Hugh." She interlaced her fingers and propped her chin on the back of her hands. "Look at you. You're urban, you're trendy, your job involves travel and parties and reveling in the spoils of capitalism. I'm a priest who has settled in a little Adirondack backwater. Can you honestly see any way of me fitting into your life? Or you fitting into mine?"

He ticked off another finger. "Lifestyle differences. Anything else?"

I'm in love with somebody else. Something in her face must have given her thoughts away, because he held up a third finger. "Emotional complications." He waggled the fingers at her. "It's rather like choosing a substantial investment, isn't it?"

"Spoken like a true venture capitalist."

He took another sip of wine. "You have two candidates vying for your investment."

"I don't—"

"One is old enough to be your father, entombed in the same small town where he was born, and, oh, yes, is married."

She drained her glass and poured herself another.

"The other," he spread his arms again, showing off the floral shirt in all its splendor, "is handsome, youthful—comparatively speaking—amusing, well educated, has a healthy bank account and a career that gives him some flexibility in relocating as you climb the ladder to ecclesiastical success. Oh, and is single." He leaned back in his chair. "And," he stressed, "is Anglican."

"Your virtues are exceeded only by your modesty." She slid the bottle toward him. "You still haven't told me if you're proposing or not."

"Not. Not yet," he amended. "I'm not sure yet if you and I are suited for the long haul together." His voice sharpened. "But I'd like a chance to find out without the local law enforcement cramping my style." His chair scraped as he stood up. "I'd better get over to the hotel. I want to check in and freshen up before dinner. Do you want me to come back and pick you up?"

She shook her head automatically. "No, it doesn't make sense for you to drive in and out of town twice."

"I could wait for you to get dressed. We could lounge about the hotel together."

"No. I still have to get to the dry cleaners and pick up my dress after you go. Then I'm going to make a quick hospital visit to a family I was with this afternoon before coming back here to get ready."

"Right. I'll see you later, then."

"Wait!" She stood up. "What about—what about all this?" She waved her hand, indicating the table, the glasses, the remnants of conversation hanging in the air. "What are you going to do?"

He looked surprised. "I'm not going to do anything. We're still friends, right?"

She nodded.

"And we can keep seeing one another occasionally?"

"Of course."

"Then I don't have to do anything. Except wait." He stepped closer. "Because sooner or later, the choice you've made is going to blow up in your face. Bad investments always do. And when it does," he smiled, "I'll be here."

She was still pondering his words when she heard his car pulling out of her drive. She hadn't dated the whole time she had been at Virginia Episcopal Seminary. Now, in the space of one afternoon, she had two men in her house who wanted her. Who knew a clerical collar was such a turn-on? Of course, neither was exactly what you'd call a healthy, promising relationship. "Is this one of Your little jokes?" she asked. "Because if You're trying to give me a message about what I should do with my life, I wish You'd be more clear."

5:40 P.M.

She should have called a lawyer. She should have told them no, they couldn't look through her house, they couldn't try to find some scrap of something tying her husband to Becky Castle. But it was too late now. If she said no, if she said stop, if she made Lyle MacAuley come down from upstairs, where she could hear him lumping around in her bedroom, looking at God knows what, they'd know. They'd know she'd folded. That she knew what her husband had done, and therefore that she probably knew where he was and when he was coming back. Her supposed innocence and the fact that Randy had gotten rid of any evidence were the only cards she held now. She had to play them.

Lisa sat on her couch, facing Kevin. They had spilt up, him and MacAuley, and Kevin was sticking to her like glue, supposedly so she wouldn't feel so uncomfortable having some old cop pawing through her underwear drawer. She knew the real reason was to make sure she didn't pick up the phone and warn her husband not to come home.

"Can I get you anything? A soda? Water?"

Kevin shook his head. "No, thanks."

She stood, stretched. "I think I'll make myself some coffee."

Kevin stood as well. "I guess I will have a cup, if you're going to make one." He followed her into the kitchen.

She had just pulled the box of filters out when the phone rang. She froze. *Oh, no. Not now. Please, no.* Before she could recover and lunge for the phone, Kevin crossed the floor and snatched up the receiver. He held it out a few inches, so they could both hear, and beckoned her over. At that moment, she hated him. If she had thought she could get away with it, she would have clawed the receiver out of his hand and clubbed him to death with it.

He motioned again, fiercely. She walked over to his side. "Hello?"

"Lisa? Is that you? You sound like you're on a speakerphone." Lisa trembled with the effort of not sagging with relief. "It's my sister," she said.

"What?" Rachel said.

Kevin handed her the receiver and went back to the coffeepot as if it were perfectly normal for him to hijack someone's phone.

"Sorry, Rache." Lisa glanced toward Kevin. "Kevin Flynn is over, and he mistakenly thought you were a call he was expecting."

There was a long pause on her sister's end. "Is he alone?" Rachel eventually asked.

"Nope."

"Oh, God, they didn't send Mark over, did they? He called me just a little while ago. He has to go in to work early."

"Mark was a real sweetheart to drive me to my job this morning. Will you be sure to thank him for me when you see him?"

There was another pause as Rachel parsed Lisa's statement. "You need to be careful," she said. "Mark told me they're calling everybody in, all shifts, the part-time guys, everybody. The only time they usually do that is when things get really crazy, Christmas week, New Year's, stuff like that."

"Uh-huh," Lisa said. Across from her, Kevin was scooping coffee out of a can. "Why do you think Mom and Dad are doing that?"

"Mark didn't say, but I'm guessing they're pulling out all the stops to find your husband. Lise, you need to think about hiring a good lawyer and having Randy turn himself in. This isn't like ducking out of a traffic ticket. Mark and the rest of them will be searching for someone they think is dangerous. They have guns. People get killed evading arrest."

Lisa's throat closed up.

"Look, I'm off shift. I'm going to pick up Madeline from the neighbor's, and then we're coming over to keep you company."

"With what's going on? Mark won't like it." Her sister and Mark were both control freaks. They tended to wrangle a lot.

"He doesn't get a vote. Besides, he'll be at work. He doesn't need to know. The important thing is, will it help, me being there? Or would you rather be alone?"

"I'd love you to come over," Lisa said gratefully.

"Okay. I'll see you when I get there. Till then, keep your legs crossed and your mind on higher things, as Mom would say."

Lisa was laughing as she hung up.

Kevin looked at her. "What's up?"

Her brief bubble of good humor faded into air. She shrugged. "Our parents."

"I know how that can be. Coffee's almost ready, if you want to get the cups."

Lisa turned over possibilities as she unloaded two clean mugs from the dishwasher and took out the sugar bowl and spoons. She could do as Rachel suggested. Find a lawyer, tell Randy to turn himself in when he called. But then where would they be? If Randy was found guilty, he'd do time, no way around it. They knew a guy who got into a bar fight in Lake George with somebody who'd been messing with his girlfriend. Busted him up. Got sent to Plattsburgh for a year. How would she and Randy survive for a year without his income? They'd have the lawyer's bills to pay, on top of the loans and the credit cards and everything else.

She opened the refrigerator and removed the jug of milk. Ultimately it boiled down to the fact that prison would kill Randy. He needed to be outdoors. He hated the jobs that shut him up inside; being locked away for a year or more would gut him. Then there was his temper. He needed to have her around for ballast. On his own, bottled up and seething, he'd explode. And some drug dealer, some guy who was a *real* criminal, unlike Randy, would knife him.

The coffee ceased bubbling out of the filter. She waited a second to see if any last drips fell, then pulled out the pot and poured two cups. So. No lawyer, no surrender. Or not yet. That could always be their reserve, their fallback position.

Clumping on the stairs. MacAuley poked his head through the doorway. "Thought I smelled coffee."

Lisa forced a smile. "Can I get you a cup?"

"Sure." He sauntered in and took up a post leaning against the refrigerator. "Nice place you have."

She poured MacAuley a cup and handed it to him. "Thanks," he said. He slopped in enough milk to turn it tan and took a deep, appreciative drink. Then he looked at her over the rim of the cup. "I hate to cause you distress, ma'am, but we do have reason to believe your husband may have been seeing Becky Castle."

Lisa had split firewood before, and she knew what he was about. He was poking at the surface of the log, looking for a crack he could wedge his splitter into. It could take hours to chop apart a log with an ax. You needed an opening. It didn't matter how small: Once you worked a splitter into it, down came the maul, and that log was gone, split in two, ready for the woodstove.

She took out her own splitter. "No, he wasn't. And I know that to be true, because I know who she was seeing."

MacAuley's bushy eyebrows flicked upward. She had caught him off guard. "Who?"

"Shaun Reid."

"The guy who owns the mill?" Kevin made a face. "Get out! He's older than my father!"

MacAuley looked at him wearily. "It doesn't shrivel up and drop off when you turn fifty, Kevin." He turned to Lisa. "How do you know this?"

The first rule of lying: Keep as close to the truth as possible. "I clean for the Reids. Thursdays. And I was at Millers Kill High when she was. I know some of the same people she knows. There's always talk. It's a small town."

"She lives in Albany now."

"He never travels 'on business'? She never comes up to 'visit her folks'?" She shrugged. "Maybe I've got it wrong. But I've never heard any whispers about her and my husband."

MacAuley set down his mug. "Mrs. Schoof, what would you say if you I told you that Becky Castle has named your husband as the man who assaulted her?"

"I'd ask why on earth Randy would want to hurt a woman he can barely remember from school."

"She says he was planning on stealing her father's logging equipment. She took pictures of him, and when she wouldn't surrender the camera to him, he beat her up."

"Oh, please. Randy was going to steal a skidder? And what, escape with it down the highway at twenty-five miles an hour?" Ladling scorn kept her from wincing. She knew Randy tended to act without considering the consequences, but she hoped even he wasn't stupid enough to try to guarantee job security by ripping off heavy equipment. "Who's more likely to have a reason to try to shut her up for good? A man who wants to get a good recommendation from her father? Or a man who's already been through one expensive divorce and can't face another one?"

MacAuley and Kevin glanced at each other. She clicked her teeth together. The second rule of lying: Don't say too much.

"Miss Castle told us she ran into your husband's motorcycle at her father's house this afternoon. She called the tow truck and had it taken to Jimino's garage on her dime. We've got a confirmation on that from the tow truck dispatcher and the mechanic."

Lisa noticed MacAuley had dropped the "what would you say if I said" fig leaf. She looked him straight in the eye. "So she did meet up with him today. That explains why she used his name when she had to find someone to pin her injuries on."

"Oh, come off it," Kevin said.

Lisa put her hands on her hips. "Are you trying to tell me you've never known a battered woman to lie about what happened to her because she was afraid of the guy who hit her? Or in love with him?" She let her anger and her irritation show fully in her face, so they wouldn't see past those emotions to where she was desperate and afraid.

Lyle looked at her as if he were measuring her. Finally he swung his gaze toward Kevin. "Time to go," he said. Kevin promptly put his cup down, coffee untouched.

"When your husband comes home," MacAuley said, "have him contact us immediately. Whether he's responsible or not, things will go a lot easier for him if he does."

Thunk. Thunk. The sound she heard as she ushered them out of her house was the echo of two pieces of wood falling, neatly and sweetly cloven in two.

5:55 P.M.

Clare barely made it into the dry cleaners before they closed. She wasn't the only person to wait until the last possible moment. Ahead of her, a harried-looking woman balanced a cranky toddler on her hip while accepting a stack of shirts. Behind her, the door chimed in a good-looking young man whose suit and camel coat looked decidedly out of place on a Saturday in Millers Kill.

"Clare Fergusson," she told the attendant, after the woman had struggled away with kid and clothing. "One dress and two blouses."

The woman took her slip and nodded past her at the young man. "You?"

He reached past Clare to hand in his pink receipts. "Jeremy Reid and Shaun Reid."

Clare twisted around, interested. "Excuse me," she said as the woman bustled toward the back. "I don't mean to be nosy, but are you related to Courtney Reid?"

He raised his dark brows. "She's my stepmother." He looked at Clare. "And you'll have to excuse me, but you don't look at all like one of Courtney's usual friends."

"I'm the priest at St. Alban's. Clare Fergusson." She held out her hand.

He shook it. "I remember. One dress, two blouses. I'm Jeremy Reid." He grinned, exposing teeth so dazzlingly white they had to have been bleached.

"Are you home for a visit?" Behind the counter, she heard hangers rattling. Millers Kill boasted the last dry cleaner in America to resist automation.

"Nope. I work here. Well, not here, exactly. At the new resort."

"Oh! I'm going to be there tonight. At the grand-opening dinner dance. At least," she considered, "I think I'm going. If it's still on."

"It's still on. Why wouldn't it be?"

"Because of the van der Hoevens." A plastic *thwap-thwap* drew her around. The woman laid Clare's clothes on the counter.

"Twenty dollars," the attendant said, her impatient expression signaling that she was mentally already locked up and gone.

"What about them?"

Clare dug her wallet out of her jacket pocket. "Millie van der Hoeven is missing." She dropped her voice. "And I don't think it's made the news yet, but Eugene van der Hoeven died today."

"Holy shit!" His eyes went to her collar, which she had put on for her hospital visit, and he blushed slightly, burnishing his high cheekbones. She smiled to herself. Her sister Grace would have gone after this one with both hands. "Sorry. But no, we haven't heard anything about canceling the dinner dance. When I left, preparations were in full swing."

She handed over her twenty. "Who's sponsoring the event?"

"GWP, the Adirondack Conservancy Corporation, and the resort. It's not just for the land transaction, you know? It's also a thank-you for Mr. Opperman's investors and big donors to the ACC." He frowned. "Even without the van der Hoevens, I don't think Mr. Opperman would pull the plug. He wants to open the resort with a bang."

"Mmmm." She had met John Opperman two summers ago, when the resort was just breaking ground. He had engaged in the most cold-blooded business dealings she had ever witnessed. She had destroyed his corporate helicopter. It was safe to say neither had been left with a good feeling about the other.

The clerk hoisted a stack of suits and shirts onto the counter. "Forty-three bucks," she said. Jeremy handed her a card.

"Do you think your father will be worried? If the land deal is off?"

He looked at her sharply.

"I heard the company buying the property was on the verge of making a bid for your family's mill."

"That's not widely known."

She smiled in what she hoped was a disarming fashion. "Priests hear all sorts of stuff that's not widely known."

He bent over to sign the charge slip. "Yeah, well, Dad won't be shedding any tears if the deal doesn't come through."

"Oh? I heard he was looking forward to retirement and travel."

Jeremy stood. "Courtney told you, right? I swear, Dad could shave his head and become a Buddhist monk and she wouldn't notice if it didn't fit in with her worldview." He dragged his clothing off the counter. "He's not happy about the acquisition. I think it'll be good for the company and good for him, and I'm trying to convince him of that, but I'm not fooling myself into thinking he's all okay with it."

"Excuse me," the woman behind the counter said. "We're closed now." She stared pointedly at Clare's dress and blouses, still on the counter.

"Right. Sorry." Clare scooped up her clothing. "What do you think your dad will do? If the company gets bought out?"

Jeremy shrugged. "Join the twenty-first century? There's not much call for small manufacturers who want to pass down the business from father to son like a feudal lord. Maybe if he's forced to hand over the reins, he'll finally accept that I'm not going to be the fifth generation of Reids to spend his life chained to a paper mill."

"Excuse me," the woman said loudly. "We're. Closed. Now."

Jeremy stepped ahead of Clare and opened the door for her. "Thanks," she said.

"My pleasure. I'll see you at the dance tonight." He flapped the plastic bags. "You'll recognize me by my neatly pressed dinner jacket."

She smiled. "Nice meeting you, Jeremy." She watched him cross the street before turning and walking down the sidewalk to her car. She had parked in front of Coffee To Go and was considering getting a cup before heading over to the hospital when she became aware of a large red pickup parked behind her little Shelby.

She laid her dress and blouses in her car and crossed to the truck's passenger side. The window rolled down. Warm air and the sound of country music spilled out of the truck cab.

"Are you following me?"

Russ hooked one hand over the steering wheel. "I'm on my way from the station to the hospital. I saw your car. There was a parking space right behind it."

"That's quite a coincidence."

In the faint light from his dashboard, she thought she could see him blush. "It's not entirely coincidental. I, um, remembered you said you were going to the dry cleaners."

"And to the hospital?"

"Mmm."

She couldn't stop her mouth from curving into a smile. "Why don't you walk with me, then?"

"Walk?"

"Sure. It's only, what, five or six blocks away?"

"More like eight or nine," he said, but he was already shutting down the engine and sliding out of the truck.

"C'mon. Walking's supposed to be good for you senior citizen types."

He gave her his death-ray glare. She laughed.

"Just you wait, darlin'," he warned. "First time you jaywalk—you'll feel the long arm of the law."

6:00 P.M.

Help me get this stuff off my ankles."

"No."

"For chrissakes, then!" Millie stood up from the box where she had been sitting. "Just give me the damn knife! I'll do it myself!"

Randy backed out of reach. "No."

"I thought you were going to help me!" Anger fueled her stride, and she tried to stalk toward the man fading into the darkness. The six inches of duct tape stubbornly twined around her ankles caught her up short, and she would have plunged face forward onto the dirty floor if she hadn't flung her arms wide and dropped into a squat. Finally her yoga lessons were paying off.

"I have helped you." She couldn't see him at all now. "I cut your hands free, I gave you food, I helped you to the bathroom—"

Her face burned. "You're keeping me as much a prisoner here as Shaun Reid is." Her gratitude toward this guy for putting a name to her brother's murderer had shriveled up somewhere between the sandwich and the potty break, when she realized he was keeping her hobbled for a reason. "You're probably in it with him."

"I am not!"

She had learned a few things about Randy Schoof in the hour or so since he had stumbled into her new prison. One: He had little, if any, control over his emotions. Her father would have rolled his eyes at the way Schoof revealed his passion and his envy as he spoke about his wife, his hard luck, and Shaun Reid. He gave himself away with both hands, something van der Hoevens learned not to do by the age of four.

Two: Randy Schoof wasn't very bright. She discounted formal education—she knew several environmental activists who hadn't graduated high school and yet were razor sharp and well read—but Randy didn't fall into that class. He seemed little informed about and less interested in the world. She got the feeling that in the right circumstances he might be downright gullible.

Three: He was scared of something. And that made her scared as well, because he had all the impulse control of a fourteen-year-old with ADHD. If it was Shaun Reid who frightened him, she might be in bigger trouble than before.

She sat back down. She needed to keep him her friend. "Just tell me what it is that's keeping us here. You know, I have friends and connections all over the country. I could help you disappear."

"I don't want to disappear. I just want to stay in my house, with Lisa."

"Lisa could come with you. I have an awful lot of money, you know." Actually, compared to her parents in their heyday, she was practically a pauper. But she was pretty sure that in Randy Schoof's eyes, she was rich.

"I don't want a handout." He was only a shadowy form as he spoke. Moonlight from the window above them shafted onto the floor several feet away. "I wasn't looking for no special favors. I just want a chance to make a decent living out in the woods. That's all I want. But you know, everything's stacked against a guy like me. If you didn't get into the business forty years ago, like Ed Castle, forget it."

"Look, all I'm saying is that I can help you. But you have to help me."

"I will. But we need to stay put for a while. I'm gonna call my wife soon, and then we'll see."

Theoretically, there was nothing keeping her from getting to her feet and inching her way across the warehouse until she found the door to the outside. She had more than a hunch that he'd stop her by force if he had to, though. Her arms were untied, but she didn't have any illusions on that account. He had carried her into the ancient and odiferous water closet, and although he wasn't much taller than she was, he was built like a hunk of Adirondack granite. It was, she thought, a kind of game. If she put him into a position where he felt he had to restrain her, she would lose. In order to keep playing, she had to stay on his side.

"Why don't you go call her, then?"

She felt, rather than saw, his consideration.

"I won't try to leave," she promised. "If you want, you can even tie up my hands." She forced a chuckle. "Although I'd appreciate it if you did it in front instead of in back. My shoulders are still aching."

"Well . . ."

She crammed her fear and desperation into a tiny, tight box and pushed it to the back of her mind. She spoke to her latest captor in the jolly "we're all in it together" tones that she used to cajole agreement out of sulky activists trapped in overlong meetings. "C'mon. I'm in a jam. You're in a jam. I know you need to talk to your wife before you do anything else. The sooner you do that, the sooner we can get out of here."

"Okay."

His capitulation surprised her. "Okay," she echoed. *Stay on his side. Show him how well you cooperate.* "Um . . . do you want to tie up my hands?"

"Naw. I figure you ain't going nowhere. Even if you made it to the door, I'd be back by the time you could get outside. And outside, there isn't no place to hide." There was a scraping sound. Millie stiffened, but it was only him rising from whatever crate he had been perched on. "I'll be back."

She was alone in the darkness again.

6:05 P.M.

Millers Kill was closing down for the night. Russ walked with Clare along Main Street, hearing the door chimes jingling as shopkeepers locked up, looking into store windows where display lights simmered like fires banked to last out the night. This being one of the last dry towns in New York, there were no bars or pubs springing to life, no restaurants gearing up for an influx of customers. Except for gamers hanging out at All Techtronik or dads dashing into MacPherson's Video for the latest movies—action for him, chick flick for her, Disney for the kids—the streets emptied out. If you lived in Millers Kill, you went elsewhere on a Saturday night. To the Dew Drop Inn across the Cossayuharie line, or to the second-run cinema in Fort Henry, four screens, no waiting. If you wanted Dolby Sensurround and well-sprung seats, it was another half hour to the Aviation Mall in Glens Falls. If you wanted to drink in a place where the bartender didn't look at you funny for ordering a martini, well, Saratoga was forty minutes and a whole cultural time zone away.

"Are you having second thoughts?"

Clare's voice broke him out of his reverie. "About what?"

She jammed her hands into her bomber jacket pockets and stared straight ahead. "Walking with me. In public."

He laughed. "Are you kidding?" He looked at her more closely. Under a sodium streetlight, she was burnished orange, striped by black shadows from a leafless maple arcing over them. Like a kid wearing tiger face paint for Halloween. "No," he said more seriously. "I don't worry about stuff like that." He hesitated. "Do you? Did—has anyone said anything to you?" By anyone, he meant Hugh Parteger. He was trying, he really was, not to be unreasonably jealous, especially because he recognized that if he were a better friend to Clare, he'd be throwing her toward the rich, single guy who was obviously nuts for her, instead of snarling like a dog in the manger.

She glanced behind her. "I had a visit from the diocesan deacon this afternoon. Before you, uh, arrived."

"I hope you didn't entertain him in your bathrobe, too."

She glared at him, then blew at a strand of hair that had worked its way free of her usual knot. "It turns out the bishop sent Father Aberforth to—"

"Wait a sec. Who's Father Aberforth?"

"The diocesan deacon."

"Shouldn't he be Deacon Aberforth?"

She glanced up at him sideways, the ghost of a smile in her eyes. "Somebody hasn't been reading *The History and Customs of the Episcopal Church in America*. Career deacons are, in fact, properly designated 'Father.' Unless, of course, they're women, in which case I'm sure Aberforth refers to them as 'Ms.'" She snorted. "Anyway, he was there to call me out on a serious matter.

One that he attributed to my inexperience and to not understanding how people will talk in a small town. A matter he wanted to keep quiet so as not to give any other priests bad ideas."

His stomach sank. "Us?"

"Ha! Exactly what I thought. I was sure someone had come tattling to the bishop about seeing the two of us together."

"We're not doing anything wrong," he said automatically.

"Oh, Russ." She looked up at him ruefully. "Tell me you'd have no qualms describing our relationship to your wife. And make me believe it."

He kept his mouth shut.

"Anyway, it turned out he and the bishop are hot under the collar about Emil Dvorak's and Paul Foubert's union ceremony. I was supposed to apologize and repent, and I wouldn't—"

"What a surprise," he said under his breath.

"—so Father Aberforth is going to talk to the bishop and let me know what shape my discipline will take."

"Discipline? This isn't just them getting cranky?"

She shook her head, sending another strand of hair floating loose.

"What's the worst that could happen?"

"I could be removed. Have to try to find a position in another diocese with a disrecommendation from my bishop."

"Another diocese. In New York?" *Leave? Leave? How could you leave?*

"Maybe. I'd probably have better luck in one of the more liberal dioceses, like Maine or New Hampshire."

Okay. New Hampshire wasn't that far away. Of course, coming up with an excuse to visit there would be a challenge. And traveling to see Clare would be tantamount to acknowledging, to himself at least, that they were having an affair. Whether or not they were sleeping together. He tasted the idea: him and Clare, together, somewhere no one knew his name or marital status. How long would his self-control and fidelity to his vows, both of which he took great pride in, last under those circumstances?

About forty minutes, was his guess.

She looked up at him, her face grim, and he wondered if she was thinking the same thing. "It's not getting censured that upsets me. It's the fact that the whole time I thought Father Aberforth was talking about us, I was frantically thinking of ways to discredit what he might have heard."

"That's natural. Your bishop can't get on you for your thoughts, Clare. Only for your actions."

"Don't you see? I wasn't thinking about what was true, or what was right, or about being honest in my relationship with my church. I was thinking about covering my ass. Period."

They had come to the intersection of Main and Radcliff. A wind off the mountains skirled across the open streets, rustling dried leaves and drawing a shiver from Clare. At least, he hoped it was the wind making her cold. They turned left toward the hospital. He considered, and rejected, several variations on *Buck up! It's not so bad!* Finally he settled on "What can I do to help?"

Her lips curved. "You make me think of that *Star Trek* episode. Where Captain Kirk tells his love interest 'Can I help' is the most beautiful phrase in the universe."

"Yeah, and then she gets run over by a truck. Let's not go there."

She looked away from him. "I'm wondering if I ought to talk with someone. About"—she waved a hand, indicating him, her, the town, everything— "the situation." She glanced up at him again, and in the streetlight he could see her anxiety. "I wouldn't have to name you."

He was embarrassed. That had been his first thought, that he would be exposed. "To Father Aberforth?"

"Probably not. He hasn't struck me as the sympathetic sort so far."

He gagged the part of him that was yelling, *Tell? Are you crazy?* This was about her, not about him. "Is that what you want?" he asked carefully. "Sympathy?"

Her shoulder sagged. "I don't know what I want. Absolution, I guess. For someone to tell me that I can sustain this tightrope act with you without hopelessly compromising my standards. For someone to confirm that what I feel for you isn't wrong, that it's a gift from God."

"Some gift." They rounded the corner and saw the Washington County Hospital sign glowing white and blue in the darkness. "'Here, here's your soul mate, the person who completes you. Whoops, did I mention you can't actually be together? Have a nice day.'"

He glanced down at her. She was looking ahead, a complicated smile on her face. "That's the nature of His gifts. He wants to see what you do with them."

"Thanks, but I'll stick to stuff from stores that take a return with receipt." They had reached the walkway to the admissions lobby. Smokers clustered along the wall, the tips of their cigarettes glowing in the dark. From the parking lot, visitors drifted up in twos and threes toward the doors. A nurse and a man in a wheelchair waited for a car making its way along the circular drive.

He turned to Clare. "If you need to talk with someone, do it."

She looked at him doubtfully.

"I mean it. This"—he waved his hand in exactly the same way she had earlier, wondering why he couldn't come up with a better way to indicate an emotional tidal wave threatening to swamp his life— "shouldn't make you less of who you are. I don't want that, and if you have to go to confession or talk to the bishop or whatever, you should do it."

"And name names?"

He pinched the bridge of his nose beneath his glasses. "If you have to. Although, I gotta tell you the truth, I'd rather you fudged the identity thing if you can. But if you have to, go ahead." He settled his glasses firmly over his ears. "Just don't make yourself smaller for me."

She nodded.

"Let's get inside. Talk to people who have worse problems than we do."

6:10 P.M.

The first thing Rachel said when Lisa opened the door was "You do know your house is being watched, don't you?"

"What? Where?" Lisa stepped past her sister onto the doorstep. The automatic floodlight had come on when Rachel drove into the dooryard, and the beaten dirt and withered grass were brilliantly, if temporarily, lit. "I don't see anybody."

"Across the road from the start of your drive. I could see the squad car. I don't know who's staking you out, but it's not Mark."

Lisa stepped back inside and pulled the door shut behind her. "How do you know?"

Madeline was sound asleep on her sister's shoulder, her eyelids almost translucent to her fine blue veins, her pink mouth open. A tiny snore bubbled from her nose. "Here, take her for a moment," Rachel said, easing the five-year-old off her shoulder. Lisa took her niece, grunting slightly. Maddy's frail baby-girl look was deceiving.

Rachel stripped off her coat. "Whoever was in the squad car waved to me.

Mark would've flashed his lights." She wiggled Madeline's jacket off the little girl. "She fell asleep in the car," she explained. "Mark dropped her off with the Tuckers when he was called in. Three little girls and a hyperactive dog—she probably didn't stop running the whole time she was there."

"You want to put her down in my bed?"

"Thanks."

Lisa mounted the stairs, one hand on the banister to keep her from keeling over backward beneath the unexpected weight. Rachel slipped past her in the hall, and by the time Lisa reached her bedroom, her sister had the covers drawn back on the double bed. Lisa laid her niece down. The little girl curled like a bear cub in its den and buried her face in the pillow. Rachel tucked the bedclothes around Madeline, and the two sisters stood looking at her in the light shafting in from the hallway.

"She looks like a total angel," Lisa said quietly.

"It's an adaptive trait," her sister said in the same low voice. "The child who looks sweet and adorable while sleeping is the child whose parents forget what a pain in the butt she can be when awake."

Lisa smiled lopsidedly. Rachel could afford to be cynical about kids. She already had one. Lisa had hoped, this year, maybe . . . but if Randy went to prison, there weren't going to be any kids, not this year. Maybe not ever.

Rachel, perhaps reading her mind, wrapped an arm around Lisa's waist and hugged her. "C'mon," she said. "Let's go downstairs and have a drink."

In the kitchen, Lisa ladled out two bowls of stew to go with their rum and Cokes. Rachel dug into hers, but Lisa had no appetite. She sat and watched her sister eat and listened to her dole out sensible advice between bites.

"You have got to call an attorney. Forget the whole court-appointed thing. Believe me, when it comes to criminal trials, you get what you pay for, and you have to be willing to pay for the best."

"How are we going to afford that?"

"Mortgage your house? Sell it? You'll find a way. Mom and Dad may help out."

Lisa stared into her stew. "Great. Then we can spend the rest of our lives getting out from under a mountain of debt."

"I'm only saying. If it was Mark, that's what I'd do."

"What if they don't find Randy?"

Rachel wiped her mouth and pointed the napkin at her sister. "Lisa, you can't get on a Greyhound bus nowadays without showing some ID. Even tiny little police departments like ours have computerized records and access to national databases. How long do you think Randy could last out there under those circumstances?"

"But you're always hearing about crimes where no one was caught."

"No one was caught because no one was ever identified as the perpetrator. That's not what's happening here. The woman ID'd Randy."

"Then it's her word against his! And he has an alibi!"

Rachel put her spoon down. "And that's exactly why he needs a sharp lawyer. Somebody who can take whatever holes exist and tear 'em open enough so that the jury has a reasonable doubt about whether Randy did it."

Lisa wanted to shove her bowl and spoon out of the way, to set her forehead against the table and weep. She wanted a way out of this nightmare, and her sister, with her steady, implacable voice, was telling her there was none.

The phone rang.

"You want me to get that?" Rachel said.

"No." Lisa rose from her chair and crossed the kitchen. "Hello," she said into the receiver, already thinking about how quickly she could get off the phone and how on earth she was supposed to find a good criminal lawyer.

"Hey, honey. It's me. Can you talk?"

"Randy!" Across the kitchen, Rachel sat up straighter. "Babe, where are you? No, wait, don't tell me yet. Are you safe?"

"I'm fine. Look, I need to talk with you."

"So talk."

"In person."

Her eyes widened. "I don't think that's a good idea."

"It's really important. I think I have a way to get out of this mess. Remember how I told you I left some stuff in Mr. Reid's office? To, you know, make him look suspicious instead of me?"

"I do, babe. That was so smart of you."

"What if I told you I might have a way to get him to confess that he beat up Becky Castle?"

Lisa stared at the phone. *Now* what was he thinking? She couldn't begin to imagine, which probably meant it wasn't that good an idea. "I'd say that sounds . . . not very likely," she said.

"I don't want to get into all the details right now," he said. "Please, honey. You gotta trust me. I need you to help me pull this off."

Oh, boy, she was going to regret this. "Okay."

"Great! Come to the Reid-Gruyn mill. Park in the back of the employee parking lot. You'll see my truck. I'll meet you there."

The Reid-Gruyn mill? She had figured he would be halfway to Plattsburgh, holed up in a motel by now. "Where are you calling from?"

"The employee break room."

"That's crazy! Somebody will spot you!"

"That's why I want to get off the phone."

"I'll be there in twenty minutes," she said. "I love you. Bye." She hung up without waiting to hear his reply.

"What's going on?" Rachel's voice, behind her, startled her. While she was wrapped up in the call, Rachel had risen from the table and was now standing in the doorway.

"He wants me to meet him."

"Where is he?"

Lisa looked at her sister. Rachel's face colored. "Oh, for heaven's sake! What do you think I'm going to do?"

"Oh, Rache." Lisa opened her arms and gathered her reluctant sister into an embrace. "If you don't know anything, you won't have to choose between protecting me or lying to Mark."

Rachel took Lisa by the shoulders and held her at arm's length. "Please, please promise me you'll consider what I said. About getting a lawyer."

"I will. I am."

Lisa broke away and strode through the living room. She had opened the closet door and had her hand on her jacket when Rachel said, "Not that way. You'll be followed."

"Huh?"

Rachel pushed Lisa's jacket back into the closet. She grabbed her bright red parka from where she had tossed it over the back of a chair. "Wear this."

Lisa put it on.

"My keys are in the car," Rachel said. "Wave to the cop watching the end of your drive. If any car flashes its lights at you, flash back."

"What about Maddy's booster seat? Will he notice that it's empty?"

"I've got a tote bag full of books and Maddy's backpack in there. Stack them in the seat and drape one of her blankies over everything." She hugged her sister. "For God's sake, be careful."

The expression on Rachel's face made Lisa pause. "Are you sure?" she said. "I don't want to screw up your marriage or get you into trouble."

Rachel smiled an echo of a smile. "We're sisters. Of course I'm sure. Now go. The faster you get to wherever it is, the faster you can get back."

There was something about starting up Rachel's car, wearing Rachel's parka, that made Lisa feel less like a desperate wife out to help her fugitive husband and more like a teenager breaking curfew. Her hands shook with nervous excitement as she shifted into gear, and she held her breath as she rolled down the length of her drive.

She reached the hardtop road and put on her blinkers in the opposite direction from where she intended to go—just in case. Sure enough, parked in the darkness, sat a squad car, just as Rachel had said. Lisa hunched into the parka, and as she turned onto the road and passed the cop car, she raised her whole arm and waved, putting as much sleeve between her face and the window as possible.

She drove in a state of suspended animation for the next several minutes, her eyes on the rearview mirror instead of the road, expecting at any moment to see swirling red lights and headlights flashing her to the side of the road. But nothing happened. No one was following her. She had gotten away with it. She grinned, and the feeling of power and relief that flooded her body was almost enough to make the earlier fear and anxiety worthwhile. She switched her attention to the road in front of her. She had to find a crossroad to take her to one of the roads that would set her on the route to the Reid-Gruyn mill.

6:15 P.M.

The first thing Clare heard was raised voices. Halfway down the hall from Becky Castle's room, she stopped in her tracks as Ed Castle bellowed, "Goddammit, whyn't you stop harassing her and find the son of a bitch who put her here!"

Russ frowned and quickened his pace. In other rooms, behind half-closed doors, hushed visitors clutched bouquets and green plants and peered toward the hall. Suzanne Castle's voice fed the interest: "Will you be quiet, Ed! You're upsetting her!"

Clare broke into a jog, catching up with Russ in time to round the corner and see him plunge through the door to Becky's room.

"What the hell are you doing here?" Ed Castle snarled. She couldn't see his expression, but he didn't sound like a man ready to forgive and forget.

Clare hovered in the doorway. Russ filled the minuscule hallway between the toilet and the rest of the room, and she didn't want to squeeze past him and stick her foot through the moment.

"Why'n't you lower your voice, Ed." Russ sounded like a twenty-year sergeant reining in a frightened PFC, simultaneously nerve-settling and authoritative. "I don't think you want everyone in the hospital knowing your business." He nodded in the direction of the far bed. "Becky, I'm glad to see you feeling better. Lyle."

Clare edged along the wall behind Russ until she spotted Lyle MacAuley, propped up against the window.

"You're not welcome here." That was Ed. She still couldn't see him, but she didn't need to. The anger threading through his words spoke for itself.

"Ed, I'm sorry about what happened this afternoon. I truly regret it, and I wish I'd never been put in a position where I had to choose between a friendship and doing my job. But I wouldn't be any kind of a cop, and I wouldn't be keeping the people of this town safe, if I had done otherwise."

"Safe? Safe?" Clare heard a footfall. "Look at my little girl! You call this keeping us safe? If there weren't ladies present, I'd tell you where you can stick your apology."

"Ed," his wife soothed.

Russ stepped into the room, enabling Clare to see the Castles for the first time. Ed was standing pugnaciously beside the head of Becky's bed; Suzanne was rising from a chair, her hands stretched toward him. When Russ took one more step toward his deputy chief, she finally saw Becky Castle.

And gasped.

Lyle's gaze flicked toward her. His bushy brows raised, in surprise or salute, she couldn't tell. Suzanne caught sight of her, too; the older woman wrenched her mouth into something halfway between a grimace and a smile. Ed kept his eyes on Russ.

"I'm not just here to apologize," Russ said. "Lyle and I need to talk with Becky."

"Talk with her? What's wrong with you people? She's told you who beat her up. I gave you his address! What else do we have to do, make the arrest?"

"We've been out to Randy Schoof's place," Lyle said. "He's not home, but we have an officer staking out his drive. I've interviewed a friend he was with earlier. The friend alibis him, but he did give a list of places Schoof might be."

"Fine. Get out there and find the little bastard."

"We intend to, Ed. But we need to cover all the bases." Lyle twisted so that he was facing Becky directly. He smiled at her as if she were still a pretty girl. "Becky, do you know a man named Shaun Reid?"

"Sure." Her injured mouth slurred the word. "He owns Reid-Gruyn Pulp an' Paper."

"What's your relationship with Shaun Reid?"

Despite her stitches, Becky frowned. "Wha' d' you mean?"

"Is it professional? Personal?"

"I don' have a relationship with him. I know who he is, that's all."

Lyle glanced up at Ed and Suzanne, a protective wall of parenting. "Maybe we should talk about this without your mom and dad here."

"The hell you say." Ed bristled. "Anything you got to ask Becky, you can ask in front of us."

Lyle's cool gaze flickered toward Russ. Russ nodded, almost imperceptibly. "Becky," Lyle said, "are you involved with Shaun Reid?"

"Wha'? No!"

"For chrissakes, Reid is married. And he's practically my age! What does this have to do with Becky's assault?"

Lyle ignored Ed. "Becky, we've heard there's a rumor around town that you've been seeing Shaun Reid. We'd like to know if there's any truth to it, and if there's anything more you'd like to tell us about when you were attacked."

"Randy Schoof attacked me." Becky spoke slowly, enunciating the words carefully. "When I wouldn' give him the camera. I don' know Shaun Reid personally."

"You heard her. Now get out and arrest this Schoof before I—"

Russ raised one hand. "Ed, you really, really don't want to be making threats in front of two peace officers."

Suzanne stepped forward for the first time, laying her hand lightly on her daughter's shoulder. "Please. Find the man who did this." She looked at Russ, then Lyle. "Please."

Lyle glanced at Russ again and saw something there Clare wasn't privy to. The deputy chief nodded. "We will, Suzanne. You all take care. I'll let you know as soon as we have more information." He slipped past Russ and vanished into the hall.

"Ed," Russ said. The older man scowled at him. "I'm sorry."

Ed waved him off. "Words are cheap. Show me by bringing in that punk Randy Schoof."

She could hear Russ take a breath, as if he were going to say more. Instead, he nodded, as Lyle had done, and trudged out of the room. Clare stepped into the space he had vacated. "Hi." She put on a cheery smile. "I thought I'd stop by and see how everybody was doing."

6:25 P.M.

What do you think?" Lyle was leaning against the wall opposite the elevator bank.

"I think she's either telling the truth, and it was Schoof, or she's afraid to say anything in front of her parents, and Reid is somehow involved." Russ removed his glasses and polished them on the sleeve of his thermal shirt.

"You want me to clear the room? Question her again?"

"No. We've pissed off the family more than enough for now. Schoof is our main target. Shaun's probably a dead end. Consider the source of the information. If we uncover anything to change that, then we'll come in with the full court press."

"We've got an APB out on Schoof, and Noble's cruising the town, checking out places he's been associated with. Relatives' houses, places of employment, the works." Lyle's radio squawked for attention. He unhooked it from his belt and keyed the mike. "MacAuley here."

"Lyle, it's Noble."

Lyle looked at Russ. "Go ahead."

"I've found the Castle girl's missing car."

"Good work. Where is it?"

"In the office parking lot at the Reid-Gruyn mill."

Russ rehooked his glasses over his ears and reached for the mike. "Noble? It's Russ. I'll be there in ten minutes. Hold down the fort."

"Will do, Chief."

Lyle turned off the radio and stowed it. "So. Maybe there is something to the Reid angle after all."

"We'll see. I want you to follow up with Schoof's buddies. Lean on the guy he said he was hunting with. See if you can shake anything else loose."

"Okay. Anything new on the van der Hoevens?"

"Eric and the state lab guys were on site when I left." Russ glanced at his watch. "If Judge Ryswick has come through with a warrant, Eric should be searching the house right now. Mark's running the black Mercedes angle with the DMV. Washington County first, then surrounding counties."

"That's going to be the proverbial needle in the haystack."

"I know. I'd pay good money for a single other lead as to where Millie van der Hoeven has gone, but the Mercedes, right now, is our best bet. You wouldn't believe how many Mercedes have been registered in the tri-county area in the past two years."

"And you didn't believe 'em when they said the economy was recovering."

Russ snorted. "Wanna guess the most popular color for Mercedes sedans?"

Lyle rolled his eyes. "Black?"

"There you go. That's why you get to be the deputy."

Lyle shoved away from the wall and punched the elevator button. "Coming?"

Russ jerked his head toward the other end of the hall. "I want a word with Clare before I go."

"We should have her pry the truth out of the Castle girl."

"No lie." The elevator dinged, and the doors whooshed open. Russ slapped his hand against the edge of the door. "You know, she told me something earlier. Thinking about Shaun Reid."

"What?"

"Have you heard anything about this GWP buying the mill out from under him?"

Lyle shook his head. The door dinged impatiently.

"According to the new Mrs. Reid, it's on the table—if the Haudenosaunee land sale goes through. The question is, does Reid want to sell the place? Or would he be willing to try to throw a spanner in the works?" He let go of the door and was rewarded by the sight of Lyle's thoughtful expression as the doors slid closed.

6:40 P.M.

R uss had always liked the Reid-Gruyn mill. When he had been a high school student, he had occasionally met up with Shaun at his father's office, which even back in the late sixties had the ossified feel of a memorial to an industrial age long passed. He swung by regularly on patrol, but he hadn't been past the twin stone pillars in decades. Driving through the remains of the gates—the actual iron grills had been taken down before Russ was born—he was pleased to see nothing had changed.

The old mill, moldering into the river, was a half-hidden shadow, tucked behind the new mill and far removed from the parking lot's faded white lights. The new mill, which hadn't been new since Calvin Coolidge was president, loomed beside the black, glittering rush of water. Even from the edge of the gate, Russ could see the phosphorescent white of the dam spill and, fronting the mill, long and low, the offices. Russ wondered how many of them were still occupied in an age of downsizing and outsourcing.

Noble was parked in the row of reserved spaces in front of the offices. His squad car was angled so its headlights bounced off an apple green Prius. Russ pulled in alongside him and got out.

Noble got out of his car. "Hey, Chief."

"You got a flashlight?"

Noble handed over his Maglite. Russ shone it through the windows. The light picked out an overnight bag, a pair of sneakers, and the usual junk that collects in busy people's cars: CD cases, crumpled fast food wrappers, an empty soda bottle.

"No dress." Russ looked up at Noble. "She was supposed to be going to the big shindig at the new resort. Where's her dress?"

"In the bag?" Noble was a bachelor, which led him to misinterpret women once in a while. Like now.

Russ shook his head. "Women don't roll long dresses up in little bags. It's like a guy's suit. It has to be on a hanger."

He fished his cell phone out of his jacket pocket and dialed 411 while handing the flashlight back to Noble.

"Millers Kill. New York," he said. "Shaun Reid. Please connect me."

His phone rang once. Twice. Three times. Then a female voice: "Hello, Reid residence."

"Hi. Could I speak to Shaun, please?"

"May I ask who's calling?"

"Russ Van Alstyne. From the Millers Kill police."

There was a beat. "Has something happened to Jeremy?"

Jeremy? Was that Shaun's kid's name? "No, ma'am. Nothing like that."

"Are you fund-raising?"

Russ felt his temper turn over, like a lazy engine on a cold morning. "Ma'am, it's illegal for police to solicit funds. I need to speak to Shaun Reid on official business."

"Well." He could almost hear her unspoken rejoinder. *There's no need to get huffy about it.* "I'll get him for you."

He stared at the finish of the gas-electric hybrid while waiting for Shaun to get to the phone. It was fresh and pretty and young. Like its owner. He was 95 percent sure that she had told them the truth, and Randy Schoof was their man. But Lyle had this story about Shaun's involvement, and now here was the Castle girl's car sitting smack-dab in front of his office. Two points of contact. Could be coincidental, but Russ didn't like coincidences.

"Russ? Hey, long time no see. When was it, the Rotary Club meeting last year?" Shaun sounded upbeat, as if hearing from his old high school buddy were the highlight of his Saturday evening.

"Has it been that long? Time flies."

"It sure does. How are you doing? How's that beautiful wife of yours?"

"Linda's great. Look, I have a little situation here at your mill, and I wonder if you could come over and take a look at it with me."

The pause over the line was so long, Russ held the cell phone away from his ear to make sure he still had a signal. "Shaun?" he said.

"Sorry. A situation at the mill? What is it?"

"I'd rather explain it when you get here."

"I'm, uh, due to be at the Algonquin Waters resort by seven-thirty tonight. Courtney and I are going to a dinner dance there. Business with some overseas guys. I really can't miss it."

"Don't worry. I shouldn't keep you too long. Linda and I are going, too, and she'll have my head if I stand her up."

"Ah. Yeah? Okay, then. I'll be over as soon as I can."

"I'll be waiting right here in the parking lot." He said good-bye and switched the phone off, wondering if maybe, just maybe, there was something to Lyle's rumor after all. Shaun certainly sounded nervous about something.

7:00 P.M.

His palms were so damp the steering wheel slicked through his grip as he cornered the car. Shaun started to wipe his hands on his thighs and stopped himself at the last moment before making sweaty streaks on his tuxedo pants. Then he barked an unpleasant laugh. In a matter of minutes, he might be the best-dressed occupant of the Washington County jail.

He noticed the speedometer and eased up on the gas. He had taken Courtney's Volvo wagon, since his Mercedes still had a small fan blowing across the driver's seat. He knew his wife would want to appear at the dance in the sedan, and he had no way to explain the wet leather. It had, at the most, another thirty minutes to dry. That was if he made it to the dance, of course.

What had Russ found? What did he know? The list of possibilities was short and terrifying, so he refused to think about it. He breathed: in with the calm, out with the fear. He needed to be cool, collected, at the top of his game. Maybe this was just a fishing expedition. If it was, he had a chance to sail away unscathed—if he didn't look like Richard Nixon proclaiming he wasn't a crook. Russ had been a lifelong army guy. Narrow-minded. Unimaginative. Shaun had successfully gone toe to toe with CEOs and shareholders and bankers. He could handle Russ. Yes. In. Out.

His first surprise was seeing a squad car parked right up front, by the offices. Its headlights were trained on some little green car. Not that he was going to complain. The farther away Russ stayed from the old mill, the happier Shaun would be. He coasted to a stop a few spaces away from the mystery car and, retrieving tissues from Courtney's center compartment, hastily wiped his palms dry.

Russ and a uniformed cop were flanking the car. Shaun walked forward, arm outstretched, on the offensive. "Russ, my man. What's going on? What's this car?"

Russ shook his hand. Then his eyes widened. "What the hell happened to your face?"

Shaun was ready for this one. He touched his cheek with two fingers and laughed ruefully. "This is what happens when you try Rollerblades at our age. I flew straight off the sidewalk and ran into a tree."

"I hope the tree looks worse."

"I'm afraid it doesn't."

Russ gestured toward the green car with a solid-looking flashlight. "You recognize this car?"

"Never seen it before. It's one of those hybrids, isn't it?"

"Yep." Russ shone the flashlight into the interior. Shaun could see a cheap tapestry overnight bag.

"Is it stolen?"

"Nope. It's been missing, though."

Shaun felt an electric prod against the small of his back. Christ. What if it was Millie van der Hoeven's car? What was it doing here?

"It belongs to a young woman named Becky Castle. You know her?"

What the hell? "No."

Russ made a grunting sound. "There should be a fancy dress hanging in here. I don't see anything, do you?"

"No." What was going on? What was Russ suspicious of? Shaun felt himself stretching out, seeking balance, looking for the right path through a potential minefield. Information was power, and he had precious little of it right now.

"This is where someone would park if they came to your office, right? It doesn't look like the layout's changed since your dad's time."

"There was no need to change it."

"Were you in the office today?"

"Yes." That sounded too bald. "It's not unusual for me to come in on a Saturday for a while. I can get a lot of work done without any calls and faxes coming in."

"I bet. About what time were you here?"

Shaun calculated rapidly. "Noon until two-thirty."

Russ tipped the flashlight so the beam pointed at Shaun's starched white shirt. The edge of the light splashed across his face. "Could we take a quick look inside your office?"

"Sure." He needed to know what Russ was looking for. He had nothing to do with this car, and there wasn't anything in his office that might point toward the van der Hoevens. But why did Russ have him come out to see Becky Castle's car? Wait a second. Castle. He knew a Castle. "Is this Becky Castle related to Ed Castle? Castle Logging?"

"His daughter." Russ pointed his flashlight toward the station wagon. "Is that your car?"

Shaun's face tightened. He forced a light tone into his answer. "Sure is."

"Were you using it earlier today?"

"Yeah," he lied. He dug into his pants pocket, fumbling for the office keys. "Here we are," he said when he found them. "Let's go on in."

Inside the door, he flicked on the lights. The reception area sprang to life. Thank God, there was nothing amiss. He crossed the floor and unlocked the door to the inner offices. He flung it wide open. "Here they are. Nothing much has changed. Mine is where my dad's used to be."

Russ strolled into Shaun's office, his gaze taking in everything. "Looks like you did some redecorating."

"Courtney," Shaun said.

"Nice couch. Long enough to really stretch out on."

"Yeah, she has an eye for—" He spotted the pale pink fabric wedged in the cushions the same time Russ did.

Russ leaned forward and pulled it free. It was a pair of pink thong panties. Russ held them up on one finger. "Yours?"

"Where the hell did that come from?"

Russ bent over and pulled the leather cushions away from the couch frame. There was a scattering of coins, some crumbs, and, balled into one side, another piece of fabric. Russ lifted it, and it unfolded into filmy pale pink pantyhose. He looked at Shaun.

"I swear. I have no idea how those things got here. I never saw them before in my life."

"Where's that door lead to?" Russ nodded toward the far wall.

"It's my bathroom."

"Anybody else use it? Your secretary, maybe?" Russ opened the door and switched on the light.

"Not . . . usually."

Russ's large frame blocked Shaun's view into the bathroom. "You sure you don't want to rethink your statement about not knowing Becky Castle?"

"I've never met the woman!" Shaun struggled to keep his breathing even. In with the calm. Out with the fear. It didn't matter what Russ thought about this Castle woman. In that, Shaun was completely, utterly blameless. The important thing was to make sure they didn't link him to Eugene van der Hoeven. And that they stayed away from the old mill.

"Come on in and take a look."

Shaun squeezed into the bathroom next to Russ. There, on the vanity, was a woman's makeup bag, unzipped. Next to it was a pair of dangling chandelier-style earrings, the kind that would go with a—Shaun caught a flash of hot pink out of the corner of his eye. He turned to see a full-length strapless satin dress on the shower rod. It was dangling crookedly from its straps, as if someone had hastily looped them over the hanger and then hurried away.

"It looks to me," Russ said, "as if a woman came in here to give someone a private showing of her fancy ball gown and all its accessories. And then she let someone take them all off." He looked down at Shaun. "Or I suppose it could be that you're a transvestite."

"I am not a cross-dresser!" Shaun managed to get out.

Russ nodded. "Pink would be a lousy color for you, anyway." He moved toward the door, forcing Shaun to back out ahead of him. "We're still missing Becky's coat."

"This is ridiculous. You have no proof these are Becky Castle's."

Russ ignored Shaun's protest in favor of walking back to the reception area. "This where you hang your coats?" He rolled the closet door open.

Thank God, there weren't any strange articles of clothing hanging there. "That's my secretary's raincoat," he said, "and the other two are mine."

Russ ran his boot across the floor of the closet before patting down the coats. He dipped his hand into Shaun's jacket's pocket and came up with a shiny clutch of keys.

"Yours?"

Shaun shook his head. He was speechless.

"Let's see if the slipper fits, huh?" Russ crossed to the door and stepped outside. Shaun hurried after him. Next to the green Prius, Russ bent over and, careful not to touch the car itself, inserted one of the keys. He turned it. There was a popping sound as all the locks sprang free.

Russ straightened and spoke to the uniformed cop. "Noble, will you get on the horn and get a crime scene investigation unit over here? And since Lyle headed up Becky Castle's questioning, let's get him on the scene, too."

The cop nodded and disappeared into his squad car.

Russ turned to Shaun, a mournful expression hanging from his face. "So, old friend. Anything you want to tell me?"

7:15 P.M.

So how come you're going to let him go?" Lyle cocked an eyebrow at Shaun Reid, sitting slumped on his receptionist's desk while a state police evidence technician powdered his leather sofa for prints. Reid was staring at his fingers, smudged black with ink. He had volunteered his prints after Russ told him they needed to be able to rule out the things he had touched in the office. Russ hadn't pointed out that the prints might also rule in Shaun if he had been in Becky Castle's car.

"We've got her stuff in here," Lyle continued. "Her car parked out front. And he looks like he's gone three rounds with a baseball bat. Skating injury, my ass."

"Where's he going to go?" Russ crossed his arms. They were standing in the doorway to the office, out of earshot, able to keep an eye on the work going on inside and outside, where the second technician was going over the Prius. "He and his wife are attending a dinner dance. If he were scheduled to fly out of the country, I'd be worried. The Algonquin Waters, I think we can cover."

Lyle's expression was half in light, half in darkness. He reminded Russ of an Iroquois false face mask, lips curving, eyes piercing. "Are you sure you're not bending over backward to give an old friend the benefit of the doubt?"

"What do you mean?"

"You've been hunting with Ed Castle for the last four years. The man handed your head to you on a platter an hour ago. I'm not saying you two were best buds, but that's gotta hurt. I'm just wondering if you're not hedging your bets to keep it from happening again."

"If Shaun Reid had anything to do with Becky Castle's assault, I'll be first in line to haul him in. As far as letting him loose now, I have two good reasons. One." He held up a finger. "The simplest story is the one most likely to be true. Schoof beat up Becky Castle. In support of that theory, we have the victim's own testimony—"

"Which may be unreliable."

"Randy Schoof's disappearance," Russ continued, "and the fact that your informant on the Reid-Castle affair is none other than Mrs. Randy Schoof."

"Okay, okay. I agree, Schoof is the number one suspect. I still think there's something weird about Reid."

"Which brings me to point number two. I can keep an eye on him at the party tonight. Who he talks to, if he leaves, whatever."

"Speaking of which, aren't you supposed to be home right now? Getting all prettied up?"

Russ looked at his watch. "Crap. Yeah. Look—"

"I know. Cell phone, beeper, check-ins. We'll stay in touch."

Russ smiled. "Thanks, Lyle. The only reason I can do this for Linda is because I know you're on the job."

"You're making me blush. Get outta here."

Russ strode into the office. "Shaun!" Reid looked up quickly. "Thanks for all your help. Better hit the road. You and I are already going to be late to this thing."

Shaun blinked. "I'm free to go?"

"Course you are." Russ bared his teeth in a grin. "We can't be disappointing the ladies, can we?"

7:20 P.M.

L isa Schoof drove slowly past the gates to the Reid-Gruyn mill for the third time since seven o'clock. When she had first approached the mill, she had been ready to drive through the entrance and on to the employee parking lot but had been frozen with terror at the sight of a cop car idling outside the offices. She had slammed on the brakes, coming to a dead stop in the middle of Route 57, expecting at that moment to see her husband escorted out of the building in cuffs. It was only the honk of a driver approaching from her rear that got her moving again. She took the first cross street she could and circled back toward the mill.

The second time she slid slowly, slowly past, a panel van had joined the squad car. She couldn't make out the writing on its side, but the state seal and the lights on top made it clear it was another sort of police vehicle. Every light in the office appeared to be on, and she could make out a uniformed cop standing between the squad car and a small green car.

Now, on her third pass, the cop car, the van, and the lights were still there, but a pickup and a station wagon that had been parked next to the squad car had disappeared.

Could they have taken Randy away while she was driving in circles? Should she loop around a few more times in the hope they would all clear out? The dark pressed in all around her sister's car. She wanted to hide in it, to scurry away from the mill office, lit up like the guard tower in a prison.

She clamped her hands around the steering wheel and turned through the gates. She wanted to think of herself as brave, but she admitted to herself it was hopelessness that propelled her across the parking lot, the knowledge that if her husband had been arrested, she couldn't effect his release, and if he was still free, somewhere in the mill, she had to pass by the police. She had no choice. He was waiting for her.

She drove slowly, steadily, curving past the carnival of light that was the administration building, but not going so far out of her way that it would look suspicious. She had a cover story in her head: If she were stopped and questioned, she was delivering a meal to her husband, who worked on the floor. She knew that a lot of guys working second shift brought a big bag lunch to take the place of dinner with the family.

She was not stopped. No one emerged from the offices to wave or shout or blow a whistle. Instead, she slipped around the corner into the employee parking lot, a rectangle of asphalt running from the edge of the offices to the bank of the river. A dozen or more vehicles, almost all trucks and SUVs, clustered beneath a few fluorescent lights on aluminum poles. Three picnic tables sat near the featureless mill wall, scoured flat by cold and darkness. Cigarette butts littered the lot like spent casings.

Lisa got out of her sister's station wagon. Randy had said he would meet her, but she didn't know if he would recognize or trust the Durkees' car. She walked toward the black and rushing river, passing one truck, then another. The third one was Randy's.

"Babe?" she whispered. Nothing. She kicked the door gently. "Randy?"

His face appeared in the window. She almost screamed, clamping her hand over her mouth to still her surprise. He motioned for her to come around to the passenger side.

When she got into the cab he clutched at her, and she dug her hands into the back of his coat, and they held each other as if it had been four years instead of four hours. Lisa couldn't stop patting him. "Are you okay?" she asked, over and over. "I was so scared when I saw the cops at the office."

"I know. They were there when I tried to leave the mill. I nearly pissed my pants. I was going to go back to the old mill to wait for you, but I decided the truck was safer."

"Okay," she said. "Okay." She sat back, separating them by a few inches. "Tell me what's so important that we're both here in the parking lot where we could be spotted any minute."

Randy grinned. "I know who killed Eugene van der Hoeven."

This was so far outside anything Lisa expected, she thought she must have misheard him. "Come again?"

"I know who killed Eugene van der Hoeven. It was Shaun Reid."

"Mr. Reid? The guy who owns the mill?"

Randy nodded. She glanced out the windshield, wondering when the *Candid Camera* guy would show up and Randy would announce the whole day, everything, had been an elaborate gag. "Well," she said.

He made an impatient noise. "You know the missing woman? Millie van der Hoeven? She's in the old mill." He pointed to where the building moldered, hidden behind the faceless brick wall of the new mill. "She witnessed the whole thing. Shaun Reid killed her brother, stuck her in the trunk of his car, and stashed her there to hide her."

"You're serious."

"Of course I'm serious."

She leaned forward and rested her head on his shoulder. "Okay. So how is this going to help you?"

"We tell Mr. Reid that we have her. If he confesses to beating up Becky Castle, we'll keep her hidden away. If he doesn't confess, we bring her out and he's going down for murder."

Lisa blinked at him.

"Don't you see? He'd for sure rather be charged with assault than murder."

It was such an ambitious and, in its own weird Randy way, brilliant idea that she almost hated to point out the flaw. "What about Millie van der Hoeven?"

"What about her?"

"What do we do with her during the months it takes for Mr. Reid to come to trial? Or is she volunteering to go into hiding to save you?"

He looked abashed. "That's the fuzzy part of the plan."

"Fuzzy? Babe, that's a freaking jungle growing up around you. It'll never work."

"It could," he insisted. "Think about it. Even if we didn't make it stick, you know, with Mr. Reid, we could buy some time. We could take her home with us—"

"Take her home with us?" Lisa screeched.

"Long enough for it to set up in the cops' minds that Mr. Reid did it. Then, even if we let her go and she narcs on Reid and he says he didn't have nothing to do with Becky Castle, it'll be his word against mine. Or who knows? Maybe we could convince her to say she saw him beat up Becky *and* kill her brother."

"Like a buy-one-get-one-free."

He didn't hear the sarcasm in her voice.

"Yeah! There's nothing says we have to, you know, treat her bad while we keep her. Maybe we can make her our friend."

Lisa held up her hand for him to stop talking. There was something in what he just said—some kernel of an idea that might just possibly work. She closed her eyes so she could think better. Okay, what if Shaun Reid confessed? The cops would focus all their investigation on proving Shaun was the guy who beat up Becky Castle. Stuff that incriminated Randy would be pushed aside. Overlooked. Maybe, if they were lucky, forgotten. It wouldn't be perfect, not with the victim herself yawping on about Randy, but it would be a big old help to that smart lawyer Rachel thought they should hire.

It would be terrible for Mr. Reid, of course. Maybe even—and here she shivered, from deep inside the core of her, because she hadn't known that she was capable of thoughts like these—maybe he would even commit suicide.

Maybe it could just look like he had committed suicide.

Maybe Millie van der Hoeven, who had so mysteriously vanished without a trace or clue left behind, might never show up again.

Lisa looked into Randy's hopeful, innocent eyes. "I think it's a great idea, babe. I think we can really do something with it."

7:50 P.M.

Millers Kill, like most towns within reach of Lake George, Saratoga, and the mountains, had numerous campsites, cabins, and motels devoted to summer vacationers. Visitors arriving after leaf-peeping season was over had a far narrower range of accommodations. If the travelers didn't want to stay in one of six bedrooms divided among three bed-and-breakfasts, they had the choice of the Sleepy Hollow Motor Lodge, the Stuyvesant Inn, or the brand-new and very luxurious Algonquin Waters Spa and Resort.

After nearly two years living in the area, Clare knew this. So she shouldn't have been surprised when she entered the lounge at the Algonquin waters and found her date chatting with Deacon Willard Aberforth.

They were sitting at the long green-granite bar, identical glasses of peat-brown whiskey in front of them. From the high color on Aberforth's face, his was the latest in a line of drinks.

Hugh spotted her first, jumping off his stool and clutching his heart, staggering like a man blinded by beauty. He recovered in time to take her hand and help her onto his abandoned seat, assistance she was grateful for, given the volume of material in her skirt. "Vicar! You're absolutely stunning! You're going to be the most beautiful woman here tonight. Doesn't she look absolutely amazing?"

His last remark was directed to Deacon Aberforth, who examined Clare with a great deal more attention than he might have had he been strictly sober. "Elegant," he pronounced with a disappointed air. "Although perhaps a bit too revealing?" He waved in the direction of Clare's shoulders and chest. "I myself prefer to maintain the dignity of the church with good, classic clothing." Aberforth still wore his black wool jacket and dog collar; he had spiffed up for the evening by replacing his black blouse with a deep purple one.

Clare resisted the urge to tug her neckline higher. "I'm trying to envision the intersection between clerical clothing and ladies' evening wear. Maybe an off-the-shoulder cassock?"

Hugh laughed. "If you write up the business plan, I promise you, I'll have my firm invest." He waved the bartender over. "Do you want a Macallan?"

She nodded. After the day she'd had, she wanted several Macallans.

"You didn't tell me, Ms. Fergusson, that your friend here is the nephew of the bishop of Warwick." Aberforth leaned his elbow on the bar and toasted Hugh.

She raised an eyebrow. "That's because I didn't know."

Hugh smiled smugly. "Told you we'd make a good match. Stick with me, Vicar, and we'll have a pectoral cross on you before you can say, 'the Very Reverend Mrs. Parteger-Fergusson.'"

She stared at him.

"Fergusson-Parteger?" he suggested, handing her her glass of whiskey.

How much had he had to drink? "That's the silliest name I've ever heard," she said. "And I don't believe in this married-hyphenating business. Either keep the old name or take the new one."

"Hear, hear." Aberforth toasted both of them. From the lobby, a bell rang out, so perfect in pitch and modulation, it had to be a recording of some sort.

"I think that's the sign to head in to dinner," Hugh said. "Father Aberforth, it was great meeting you. P'raps I'll see you tomorrow."

"I'm sure of it. I will be attending the ten o'clock Eucharist at St. Alban's, with the bishop."

"Ah. Yes." Hugh's face had a trapped expression. Anglican and episcopal-nephew though he was, Clare had yet to see him inside a church. She took pity on him. "Do you need to stop off anywhere before we go in to dinner?"

Hugh's face cleared. "Yes. Yes, I do. I'll meet you outside the ballroom door." He dashed off before Aberforth could pin him down about tomorrow.

Clare collected her whiskey and carefully slipped off the bar stool. "I'll see you bright and early tomorrow morning, Father Aberforth."

He surprised her by taking her bare upper arm. "Ms. Fergusson." She frowned at his hand, but he didn't release her. "Let me give you some advice. The only female clergy who are successful at celibacy are the ones who are too old and dried up to care or the ones who are too mannish to attract members of the opposite sex."

Her fingers tightened around her glass. If she had had anything, *anything*, heavy to hand, she would have brained him.

"Any other woman, alone, attracts attention of the wrong kind. As, I hear, you may have done."

She froze.

"Find a nice young man and settle down. Your congregation and your bishop will thank you. With the help of the right sort of spouse, you may find you have a career in the church, not just a vocation."

Clare didn't trust herself to say anything. She nodded stiffly to the deacon, gripped her skirts in one hand, and stalked out of the bar. Hugh was loitering near the ballroom entrance. "What's the matter?" he said. "You're white as a sheet."

"That . . . disgusting old man." She lifted her drink and saw her hand was shaking. She knocked back half the whiskey in one swallow.

"Go easy," Hugh said. "That's too good to take as medicine. What did that disgusting old man do?"

"He told me I had three options open to me if I wanted to be a successful parish priest. Go through menopause, become a dyke, or get married."

Hugh was silent for a moment. "So," he said finally. "I guess this means you'll be wanting an introduction to Brunhilda over at the Womyn's Moon Circle Collective, then."

She laughed.

"C'mon," he said. "You can't let a relic from the nineteenth century get your goat. You'll outlive him, anyway. Someday he and all the old gents running the show will die off, and who will be left? That's right, a bunch of postmenopausal lesbian and married women."

She smiled at him gratefully. "You really are very good for me, you know?"

"Of course I do. Let's get inside and find our seats."

The Algonquin Waters ballroom elevated Adirondack haut rustic to new heights. The rosewood floor glowed in the light from a dozen antler chandeliers. Three walls of polished pine were punctuated with twenty-foot riverstone pillars, while the fourth, which faced them as they walked through the entryway, was glass, sheets and slabs of glass, providing indigo and silver views of the mountains and the nearly full moon.

"Not bad," Hugh said.

"This place is going to be wedding reception central," Clare said. "Believe me. I officiated at twenty weddings this year, and at least half the brides and their mothers would have given their right arms for a place like this."

Round tables encircled the dance floor, long white linen and low dark flowers with votives that reflected in the silver and silver that reflected in the crystal. Clare felt self-conscious suddenly, out of place amid the finery. Her grandmother Fergusson would have been thoroughly at home here, admiring the men in their dinner jackets, critiquing the women's long dresses. But every step Clare had taken in her life had brought her farther and farther away from places like this, and she found herself nervously plucking at her skirts, wondering if that off-the-shoulder cassock might not have been a better idea after all.

Then Hugh spotted someone from Saratoga that he knew, and she was swept up in introductions and chitchat. The bell rang again, and waiters began to emerge from doors on the far side of the room, carrying trays of salads and carafes of water. Clare tugged Hugh away to search among the tables for their name cards. She had just bent over to eximine a piece of pasteboard more closely—it turned out to read CHERYL ERNGARTEN—when she heard a voice behind her. "Reverend Fergusson! Over here!"

She turned and saw her senior warden, Robert Corlew, standing and waving. She wended her way past the intervening tables and took his outstretched hand. "You look terrific!" he said. "By God, say what you like about Father Hames"—Clare smiled patiently at the mention of her saintly predecessor—"he couldn't do justice to a dress like that!"

The other man sitting at the table had also risen, and Clare saw with interest it was Jim Cameron, the mayor of Millers Kill. "Reverend Fergusson," he said. "Nice to see you again."

She introduced Hugh to the mayor and to Robert, and they in turn presented the ladies at the table, Eunice Corlew, a small, wrenlike woman so self-effacing she seemed to disappear into the furniture at times, and Cameron's wife, a keen-jawed, graying blond Valkyrie named Lena Erlander.

"Sit with us!" Corlew urged. "We have two empty places. Two little old ladies came by, looked over the rest of the names at the table, and then collected their cards and went away!" He swept his hand, indicating the empty seats between him and Lena Erlander. "Guess they must have been Republicans, Jim!" He laughed at his own joke.

Clare glanced at Hugh. Corlew could be a bit of a blowhard, but she wouldn't mind having some face time with the mayor. That was the sort of relationship that could pay off when the church went looking for, say, donated space for their young mothers' child care program.

"You're a Republican, Robert," Cameron pointed out. He turned to Hugh. "Please, do join us."

"Well, I suppose if Clare doesn't—"

"Oh, yes, sit here! Sit with us!" The new voice was richly feminine, bright and breathy. "I haven't had a chance to talk with Reverend Fergusson since she saved my poor husband's leg."

Clare jerked around. A tiny blonde wrapped in pale pink satin that made her resemble a well-endowed Greek goddess stood framed between Eunice Corlew and Jim Cameron. She smiled at Hugh, and despite the fact that she was easily a decade or more his senior, Clare could feel him straighten his spine and expand his chest in response. "Hi," she said. "I'm Linda Van Alstyne."

8:05 P.M.

R uss watched across the table and counted the expressions flickering, subtle as brushstrokes, across Clare's face. Horror. Chagrin. Embarrassment. And now the dawning realization that she wasn't going to be able to get out of sitting down with them. Cataloging Clare's emotions helped him ignore his own.

Linda was chattering away. ". . . so Russ was tromping around in the woods, doing some investigation or something, and he slipped into a woodchuck hole and broke his leg! If Reverend Fergusson hadn't been there to help get him to the hospital, he would have frozen to death." She beamed up at Clare. "Sit! Sit!"

Hugh Parteger, whom Russ hadn't even registered until that moment, pulled out the seat next to Robert Corlew. Clare collapsed into it with none of her usual grace. Parteger, who looked considerably more at home in his tuxedo than Russ felt in his, sent a cool glance across the table before seating himself next to the mayor's wife.

"How brave and clever of you, Reverend Fergusson," Lena Erlander said in her Scandinavian accent. "Your name—is it Swedish?"

"Scots," Clare said. "And please, call me Clare."

Jim Cameron launched into the story of how he and Lena met on a trip to Scotland three years back, which opened the door for Parteger to make the table laugh with a description of learning the Scottish fling for a party, which got Rob Corlew onto dancing lessons he and his wife took on their last cruise, which pretty much got them through the salad. All that time, Russ watched Clare, avoided watching Clare, watched her without seeming to watch her, and felt like a complete shit.

He was the guy in the cartoon with the comic angel on one shoulder and the leering devil on the other. One of them was smacking him upside the head and saying, *Look at this gorgeous woman sitting next to you! Do you want to screw that up?* The other had eyes popping out on cartoon springs and was drooling. *Those eyes, that hair, all that skin . . .* He'd never seen Clare so undressed before. He wanted to run his hands over her pale white shoulders and down her— He forked a large and bitter piece of endive into his mouth and crunched it.

"You still working on that?" the waiter said. Russ dropped the silverware onto the plate and waved it away.

Linda started describing the frantic hours of work she put in today to get the draperies up all over the hotel. He let his gaze wander to the table next to them, and to the table next to that, automatically checking for signs of intoxication or aggression or distress. Way up at the front of the room, he saw his mom and her cousin Nane, talking and laughing with a rowdy group of women he assumed were the volunteer gardeners of the ACC. A little distance away, he spotted a table with an imbalance of seven men: four elegantly dressed Asians, three white guys in badly fitting rental tuxes, and one slim, older woman in a smoke-gray dress.

"What was the oldest van der Hoeven's name?" he asked Clare, without thinking.

"Luella? No, Louisa."

"I think that's her over there." He pointed with his chin. His wife gave him an incurious glance before returning to the mayor. She was pitching him on re-decorating his office.

Clare turned around in her seat. "It could be," she said. "I can see a family resemblance." She turned back. "Do you think she knows?"

"Knows what?" Robert Corlew looked at Clare, then Russ, then back to Clare.

"Eugene van der Hoeven was killed today," Russ answered.

"No sh——oot!" Corlew said. "Is that going to put a stop to the land sale?"

"Evidently not," Clare said. "Those Malaysians are the bigwigs from GWP." She bit her lower lip. "Oh, crud. I have two cases of wine in my car I was sup-posed to deliver for them." At Corlew's baffled look, she went on, "Eugene asked me to do it as a favor. The guy who was supposed to pick them up never showed."

"Eugene?" Corlew said. "How did you get to be on a first-name basis with the van der Hoevens?"

Clare launched into an account of her time as a search and rescue volunteer. Russ checked out the table next to the GWP brass. And whaddya know, there was his old friend Shaun Reid, with his young and lovely second wife. The ta-bles at the head of the room had already been served their entrees, and he could see Shaun eating methodically. Even from a distance, Russ could see his movements were those of someone stiff and sore.

One of the waiters came up to Shaun. Russ, expecting to see a wine bottle produced, was surprised when the uniformed man handed Shaun what looked like a piece of paper. Shaun unfolded it, read it, and looked around wildly. He sat, head bowed for a moment, then rose and followed the path the waiter had taken out of the ballroom.

That's interesting.

Russ skidded his chair back. "I think I'll excuse myself before dinner ar-rives," he said. He left through the main entrance, but instead of turning right toward the restrooms, he turned left. He walked past the length of the ball-room until he came to a door bearing a discreet brass plaque: EMPLOYEES ONLY. He pushed against the door and was disappointed to see it led into a shallow room lined with shelf upon shelf of table linens. He stepped back into the lobby. The wall continued unbroken to the corner. Somewhere behind there was the kitchen, but it obviously had an entirely separate entrance, so that unsuspecting guests couldn't stumble their way into the noisy chaos that made their dinners possible.

He reached into his jacket pocket and removed his cell phone. "Hey, Harlene," he said when his number connected. "Any news?"

"Hey, Chief. The crime scene boys just finished up at Reid-Gruyn. They said there's a load of prints off the couch, so it may take 'em a while to eliminate the duds."

"Do you know if anyone's tried to get ahold of Shaun Reid? To question him, or maybe to get him to open up a room or something?"

"Not to my knowledge. Lyle's still on the road checking out places where the Schoof boy might be. Kevin's still watching the house. He's called in a few times to complain about how bored he is."

"Tell him boredom is good. It's when things get interesting that you have to worry."

"Ain't that the truth. Eric's still up at Haudenosaunee. Mark's trying to eliminate some of the Mercedes . . . oh, wait, he wants to talk to you."

There was a pause, and then he heard Mark's voice. "Hi, Chief."

"Hi. You find something?"

"Not yet. But there was something interesting. I've been going through the names trying to see if anybody who's ever had a connection to the van der Hoevens has a black Mercedes, right? And I run across a name that doesn't have a connection to the family but may be linked to Haudenosaunee."

"Who?"

"Shaun Reid. He's a possible suspect in the Castle assault, right? And she was found on Haudenosaunee property."

Shaun Reid. Who looked for all the world as if he had been brawling today. "Good work. I think it might be time to pay Shaun a more formal visit. Pull together every thing we've got for a warrant request. If Ryswick comes through, maybe we can hit him early tomorrow morning. In the meanwhile, keep looking for any other connections for the Mercedes. This could easily be someone from the city, you know. Their father, Jan van der Hoeven, headquartered his business there."

"Yeah, I know."

From the entryway in the middle of the lobby, Russ could hear the muted clinking of forks hitting china. "Gimme back to Harlene, will you?"

Harlene came onto the line. "Yeah?"

"Tell Lyle I want him to drop by the hospital again as soon as he can. See what the reaction is when he tells Becky Castle her stuff was found in Reid's office. Have Eric call me from Haudenosaunee as soon as he can. I want to know if he's turned up anything."

"Will do, chief. How's the fancy party? Is it making up for having to work on your birthday?"

He thought about their table. Linda and Clare and Hugh and Russ. Like a bad Italian art movie. "Harlene, I can honestly say I'd rather be eating greasy takeout and waiting for an autopsy report than be here."

8:20 P.M.

Lisa Schoof tried to control her shaking. She stood in the passageway outside the Algonquin Waters kitchen, listening to pots hammering iron burners and dishes clanging against stainless steel. The door swung open, and she jerked to attention, but it was only an assistant in a grease-spattered white shirt, ducking down the hall for a quick smoke. The door, shutting, pumped a blast of steam and smell and the sound of harsh voices jabbering in a language Lisa couldn't even recognize.

She had found her way to the kitchen door easily enough: In her sweater and padded motorcycle jacket she looked nothing like the guests she had seen in her brief flight through the lobby, and a sympathetic chambermaid, thinking she was new and late for her shift, pointed her in the right direction.

She stepped into the kitchen, thinking she could snag a waiter to deliver the message she had written out, but was stymied immediately by the chaos around her. She had waitressed before, at the Red Lobster in Glens Falls, but that kitchen could have fit into a corner of the acreage of white tile and chrome racks that surrounded her here. She was perhaps ten steps in when a short man in front of an open blast furnace of an oven started screaming at her, first in a foreign language, then in English. "Get out! Get out, you! Get out!"

Lisa stumbled back, breathless, and was on the verge of bolting when a hand fell on her shoulder and a pleasant voice asked, "What are you doing here, kiddo?"

She was face-to-face with a faultlessly white shirt and an elaborate waistcoat. The man holding her looked like a riverboat gambler in a western. "Are you a waiter?"

"Sure am. Are you new?"

She shook her head. "No." Her throat threatened to close up, but she got her prepared story out. "I work for Mr. Shaun Reid. I have to get a note to him. It's important. It's about the, the mill. His mill."

"Where's he at? The banquet? The door's right over there. I can show you the way."

"Oh, no. I can't. I'll get in trouble. He, he doesn't want the other businessmen to know. That . . . there's a problem." She reached into her pocket and withdrew the tightly folded note. "Could you?"

The waiter smiled at her indulgently. "Sure, kiddo. Do you know where he's sitting?"

She had thought about that, driving in. "I think he's with the people from the big paper company."

"GWP? Okay, I'll see that he gets it." He held out his hand for the paper, but she unfolded it quickly and pulled her ballpoint from her pocket. *Meet me in the hallway outside the kitchen,* she scribbled at the bottom. She refolded the paper and passed it to the nice waiter.

"You better leave now, before Egoberto tries to fillet you."

She glanced over to where the ferocious cook was ramming rounds of helpless bread into the fiery inferno. "Right," she said.

So here she stood, chafing her hand over her arms in a futile attempt to rub away the cold seeping from her gut. It already felt as if she had been waiting for an hour. What if the waiter couldn't find Reid? What if he laughed and tore up the paper? What if he called the cops and they were already on their way to arrest her for blackmail? What if—

The kitchen door swung open again. Shaun Reid strode into the hall, brushing at his tuxedo jacket as if it had been soiled by his time in the kitchen. He saw her. His head went up. His black eyes and bruises startled her. He looked like a boxer. "Who are you?" he asked.

His age, his clothing, the authority in his voice—she almost blurted out the truth by sheer force of habit. The thing that caught her was that he didn't know already. She had been cleaning his house for a year now, and he didn't recognize her. Then she noticed the sheen of sweat across his forehead, the dampness on his upper lip.

It was quite cool in the kitchen passageway.

"I'm the person who has Millie van der Hoeven safe."

He glanced quickly over his shoulder, then back at her. "I don't know anything about that," he said.

"Fine. I'll go call my friend, and he'll take her to the cops. She's been dying to talk to them all day." She feinted, as if she were going to go around him.

He threw out his arm to stop her. "Open your jacket," he said.

She did.

"Pick up your sweater."

"Screw you. You want to see tits, go somewhere else, you perv."

"I want proof you're not wearing a wire before I talk with you, you little twit."

"Oh." She lifted her sweater and jacket as far as the underside of her breasts and turned around slowly, so he could see there wasn't anything snaking down her back. It was by far the weirdest thing she had done in a day full of weird things. It didn't feel real—more like she was acting in a TV show. The unreality emboldened her. "Here's the deal," she said, lowering her sweater. "You confess to having beaten up Becky Castle, and we'll make sure Millie van der Hoeven never has the chance to testify that you killed her brother."

Reid's eyes narrowed. He stepped toward her, and for a moment she was afraid. Then a crash from the kitchen reminded her that they were in a relatively public place. If he tried anything, she could bring the house down with her screams.

"It was you who put that dress and the makeup in my office, wasn't it? You little bitch." He hissed the last phrase so quietly she wasn't sure he had said it at all.

She forced her voice to remain strong and confident. "I'm sure you'd rather be arrested for assault than for murder."

"It was an accident," he snapped.

"So you want us to take Millie to the cops?"

"No!" He crossed one arm over his chest and propped the other against it. He covered his mouth and chin with one hand. Finally he said, "How do I know you won't let her testify to the police after I've pled guilty to the assault?"

"It's a balance. Like a seesaw. If you deny you beat up Becky Castle, we'll be in trouble. If we let Millie tell the cops, you'll be in trouble."

"Getting arrested for assault and battery is trouble, you idiot."

"You're a rich guy. You can afford a good lawyer. Tell him it was a lovers' fight, he'll probably get you off with a few years suspended and some domestic violence classes."

He looked at her closely. "Your friend is the person who really assaulted the Castle girl, isn't he?" He stared at her hand. She looked down and saw her wedding ring. "He's your husband," Reid said.

She folded her hand and pressed it against her leg. "Do we have a deal?"

"I have to finish the dinner," he said, tilting his head toward the kitchen. "I'm conducting some important business there. And I need a chance to call my attorney, to arrange to turn myself in."

"You have until midnight tonight."

"Just like Cinderella," he said. "All right."

She stood for a moment, not knowing what to do now. He had just . . . given in. She hadn't been expecting that. Finally she shook herself and walked off. He said nothing, so neither did she.

It wasn't until she had rounded the corner and was facing the stairs up to the lobby that she let herself smile, a wide, glorious, split-seamed smile. She did it. She was going to save her husband.

8:30 P.M.

Shaun waited until the young woman was out of sight before shouldering his way through the swinging kitchen door. He barged straight through the middle of the freewheeling choreography of chefs and line cooks and waiters, his face pricking even foul-tempered kitchen workers to jump out of his way.

The hushed roar of the banquet hall neither slowed him nor soothed his expression. He pistoned along the edge of the room until he spotted the sommelier, pulling bottles from the bottom of a well-loaded cart. He moved into her space, crowding her until she clinked against the cart. "Jeremy Reid," he said. "Where is he?"

"Um," she said.

"Where?"

She pointed toward the ballroom exit. "He's . . . he's . . ."

"*Where?*"

"The lobby bar," she squeaked.

Shaun sped toward the exit, moving as fast as he could without drawing undue attention to himself. He pushed through the doors into the lobby.

The lobby of the Algonquin Waters resort, for all its gleaming wood and arching spaces, was essentially a triangle whose point was truncated by a wide rectangle. The ballroom and smaller meeting rooms ranged along the bottom of the rectangle. One corner of the triangle hosted massive leather furniture in front of a riverstone fireplace that could have accommodated a whole deer on a spit. The other corner was the lounge bar. At the intersection of the triangle and the rectangle, the Oriental-carpet-covered floor opened to allow visitors to descend to the lower spa level via a polished cherry stairway. The same stairway where, if his guess was correct, his little friend was going to come out and cross the lobby to the parking lot.

He knew, from listening to Jeremy, that the hourly employees' entrance in the back was locked, day and night, accessible only to those who could punch in the pass code. To get in to see him, his blackmailer must have come in through the public entrance, a bank of double doors opposite the top of the staircase.

Shaun speedwalked across the lobby to the bar. Jeremy was behind the faux-distressed bar counter, going over a list with one of the bartenders while the other one watched a football game on the television.

"Jeremy, I need to speak with you right away," Shaun said in a low voice.

His son looked at him, clearly startled. "Dad? What's up?"

"Please," Shaun said, beckoning Jeremy with fingers flapping "urgent." Jeremy excused himself and stepped away from the counter. Shaun grabbed him by the shoulders and moved them into a position where he was partially concealed by an overgrown ficus. "Can you see the lobby?"

Jeremy looked past the green fronds. "Yeah."

"Okay." Shaun let out a breath. "In a moment, you're going to see a young woman come up those stairs. She's wearing jeans and a jacket that has NORTH COUNTRY HARLEY-DAVIDSON on it. I want you to trail her, discreetly, to the parking lot."

"What?"

"When she gets into her car, I want you to follow her. See where she goes. Then call me and let me know."

His son searched his face. "Dad? Are you drunk?"

"Listen to me. This is an emergency. That woman is blackmailing me. She's . . . she going to set up an accident at the mill and claim we're responsible. Somebody could get hurt."

"Are you kidding?" Jeremy looked toward the lobby, the bar, and the lounge before settling his gaze on Shaun's face again. "Dad, if that's so, call the police. Right now."

Shaun squeezed his son's shoulders tightly. "I can't." He cut off the start of Jeremy's protest. "I know it doesn't make sense to you. I know you're working right now, and I'm asking you to abandon your job."

"It's not that. Things are humming along. I'm practically redundant."

"Never." He stared into Jeremy's eyes, so like his own and his father's before him. "Please. I need you to do this for me now. Please." He saw Jeremy's gaze flick away from him. "Is that her? Do you see her?"

Jeremy nodded.

"Will you do it? For me?"

Shaun felt his son's shoulders relax beneath his hands. "Sure, Dad. If that's what you need."

"Go. Do you have your cell phone?"

Jeremy was already weaving his way between the tables, headed for the open lobby. He slapped his jacket in response. "Right here."

"Don't get too close to her. Don't lose her." Jeremy was moving out of earshot. "Thank you," Shaun said. But he didn't think the boy heard.

8:40 P.M.

Clare was watching when Shaun Reid made his return to the ballroom. He paused in the entryway for a moment and wiped his brow with a handkerchief. Her grandmother Fergusson would have approved. *Never trust a man who uses tissues,* she would say. *He will prove flimsy and unreliable.*

"Shaun Reid's back," she said, pitching her voice to slip under the lively conversations on either side of her.

Russ, across the table, nodded. He twisted his head slightly, as if getting the kinks out, and followed Reid's progress back to his table. "Shame," he said. "He's missed most of the dinner." Servers were circulating throughout the ballroom, collecting dirty plates and laying out dessert ware.

"*You* almost missed the dinner," Linda said, mock-elbowing him in the ribs. "I swear, you'd stop your own funeral for police business." She leaned on the table and spoke confidingly to Clare. "Listen to a woman who knows. Never marry a cop."

Clare felt hot color flooding her cheeks. She was saved from coming up with a response by Hugh, who took her hand in his and said, "I'll do my best to see she takes your advice." He kissed the back of her hand. Robert Corlew made an awkward harrumphing sound, and Lena and her mayor "aaaahhhhed" as if they were sinking into a vat of marshmallow goo.

Russ looked like one of the great stone faces of Easter Island.

Clare had never been entirely convinced of the doctrine of bodily assumption, but she found herself wishing it were true and that God would see fit in His wisdom to whisk her, dress, hand, flaming cheeks, and all, into His heavenly kingdom. Now. Right now. Any time now.

She gently withdrew her hand and smiled almost convincingly at Hugh. Apparently she still had work to do on earth. To escape the massed gaze of the entire table, she twisted away, looking to where waiters were rolling out a podium next to the head table. "What's on the schedule?" she asked no one in particular.

Jim Cameron answered. "The president of the ACC is going to give a little speech, introduce a few people, and make a plug for donations. Then the GWP folks and the van der Hoevens—" He tilted his head back, apparently just noticing the dearth of van der Hoevens at the head of the room. "Well, whoever else has to sign the deed of sale will do so. Then the dancing starts." Beyond the head table, Clare could see where a bandstand had been set up next to the glass wall.

As she watched, the sommelier and her assistant rolled a heavy wine cart to the head table and began unloading some familiar wooden crates. "Oh, no," she said. She couldn't remember the damn wine for more than five minutes. She turned back to the table in time to see Linda twine her arm around Russ's. On the other hand, perhaps she had good reason for her lack of focus.

"Excuse me." She pushed back from the table and stood. Hugh, Russ, and Jim Cameron all rose.

Robert Corlew looked at them. "What?" he said. "What? Guys still do that?"

Lena Erlander looked sympathetically at the nonentical Mrs. Corlew.

Clare wove her way through the tables, careful to control her skirts. She crossed the dance floor and caught up with the sommelier just as she was unlocking the cart and preparing to roll it away. The crates, with their van der Hoeven Vineyards labels proudly displayed, were stacked in a staggered pyramid in front of the head table. Clare thought she had never seen a sadder sight. "Excuse me." She touched the sommelier's arm to get her attention. "Mr. van der

Hoeven gave me two crates of his family's wine to deliver to the banquet to-night. I'm afraid I forgot and left them in my car. Is it too late to bring them in?"

The sommelier frowned thoughtfully. "Mr. van der Hoeven's instructions—" She caught herself, and Clare guessed that the news about Eugene van der Hoeven had already made the rounds at the Algonquin Waters. "His wishes," she amended, "were that all the principals get a case as a gift and that the re-mainder be uncrated and uncorked for the dancing." She tapped the side of her mouth with a white-gloved hand. "Yours will be awfully cold, but I suppose if we hold them back until the end of the evening . . . sure, go ahead. Bring them in. Do you need any help?"

"No. I'm right out front. My date and I will get them." She turned back to her table, paused, then turned again. She crossed to where the slim woman in gray was seated, staring listlessly into nowhere. "Ms. van der Hoeven?"

The woman blinked and looked up at Clare. "Actually, it's Tuchman. Well, no, I suppose it isn't anymore. Maybe this time I'll go back to being Louisa van der Hoeven. That sounds better than Louisa Tuchman, doesn't it? Or Louisa de Parrada. I always thought that sounded like a flamenco dancer's name. Who are you again?"

Eugene and Millie's sister was apparently drowning her sorrows the old-fashioned way. "I'm Clare Fergusson," she said. "I just wanted to say how very sorry I am about your brother."

Louisa van der Hoeven de Parrada Tuchman blinked slowly. "I think Gene is one of those people about whom you can say, 'His sufferings are over.'"

"Perhaps so." Clare chose her words carefully. "I only knew him briefly, but he struck me in that time as a man who cared deeply about many things. In-cluding your family and its history." She waved a hand at the rough wooden crates framed by snowy linen. "I think it's lovely that his last gesture will enable everyone to celebrate the van der Hoeven name with the van der Hoevens' wine."

Louisa looked down at the crates with a jaundiced eye. "No," she said. "That's just another example of how fake we are. Trying to impress everyone with money that was lost two generations ago."

"I'm sorry?"

Louisa flopped one bony wrist over the edge of the table. "This is that stuff you buy in California and get stamped with whatever label you choose. The van der Hoevens don't *have* a vineyard."

8:45 P.M.

Millie heard the door open. She hunched over her ankles, frantically jabbing the point of the door hinge into the stretched expanse of her duct-tape shackles. She had already punched ten, twelve, fifteen holes in the thing, but it still wouldn't tear apart.

"Millie?" It was Randy, of course. "Still back there?"

"I told you I'd wait right here," she called back, her voice as lighthearted and reassuring as she could make it. It wasn't as if she could go anywhere else. Still, if she could just separate the tape before he walked back and discovered what she'd been doing while he was away. . . . "Hey, when Shaun Reid brought me here, he said something about a box of wine near the door. Why don't you find it, and we'll have a drink? I don't know about you, but I could use one."

"Okay." The thin beam of the flashlight appeared. It bounced around near the narrow door Randy had used to leave and enter. In the light's backsplash, she could make out his silhouette. He had shoulders like a freaking gorilla. She thought of herself as a strong woman, but she didn't have any illusions. He could do just about anything he wanted to her. If she didn't get to him first. She redoubled her efforts, poking and tugging at the holes in the duct tape.

"I don't see anything."

"Try by the big door, the one that has the loading dock outside," she called.

"Are you okay? You sound kind of winded."

She took a deep breath. "Just feeling a little stressed. The wine will help."

The flashlight beam tilted toward the front of the building. Millie poked another hole into the tape. She thrust her fingers through and pulled, her arms shaking, her thighs cramping from the strain of keeping her ankles as far apart as possible. She felt something yield. She pulled harder. There was a moment's catch, and then a tearing sound, and her fetters fell into two pieces of tape, the ragged ends fluttering between her ankles.

She bit her lip to keep from howling. Then, for the first time all day, she stretched her legs wide, wide apart. The painful stretch was the most wonderful thing she had ever felt.

"Hey, I found it. Lemme see if I can get the lid off the box."

Millie slowly rose from the floor. She straddled a crate, rolling her pelvis forward and back, cracking her spine and flexing her arms. From near the flashlight's glow, she heard the distinctive sound of nails screeching out of wood.

"Phew! I hate to tell you, but this wine smells way bad. Like somebody stuffed old garage rags inside."

"Nevermind, then." Now she was free, she was anxious. She wanted to do what she had to do and get out. "Would you come back here, please? I'm feeling a little scared, all by myself in the dark."

"You want me to find some water or something? I got a couple bottles in my backpack."

"No. Please, I don't want to sit here alone."

"Okay." His voice had the resigned tone of every man baffled by a woman's changeable mind. "If that's what you want."

She wiped her palms against her pants. She wanted them to be hard and dry for this. "What did you and your wife decide to do?"

His voice, and the light, came closer. "Uh . . . she thinks you'd be better off coming home with us. In case Mr. Reid, you know, comes after you."

She thinks we need to keep you under lock and key, Millie translated. She brought her ankles together and hunched over so that her hands, folded in her lap, weren't visible.

The light played over her. "You okay? You look like you might be sick."

She nodded her head. "I think I might." She tightened her grip around the iron hinge pin. Its point, sharp and hard, pricked against her thigh. "Would you help me to the washroom?"

"Sure," he said. He was close enough so she could smell him, gasoline and sweat and the strong, cheap detergent his clothes were washed in. He opened his arms to lift her, and she sprang forward, her thighs, her back, her arms all working together, and she drove the iron spike into his gut.

For a moment, they stood like lovers, his arms half embracing her, his face inches from hers, staring into each others eyes. Then, afraid she had only lightly wounded him, she shoved against his chest. He let out a noise like a chainsaw caught in a tree bole and fell to the floor.

The flashlight bounced off the uneven wooden boards at an angle and smashed against the metal footing of an ancient pulping machine. Instantly, the unrelenting darkness swallowed them.

"You . . . stabbed me." Randy's voice held more amazement than pain.

Millie was shaking so hard she could barely move. She backed away from the voice below her. She tried to think of something to say to him, something to justify what she had done, but in the end, her justification was that she was free to leave, whether he or his wife or Shaun Reid wanted her to or not. She backed away another step.

Randy groaned. "Holy crap." He breathed shallowly, as if the movement of his lungs was painful. "Hurts."

"I'll call for help as soon as I'm away." She skirted around him as best she could, bumping into crates and feeling her way past tarp covered machines.

"Lisa," he moaned.

She moved toward the front of the building by touch and memory, fixing the location where she last saw Randy's light when he had found the wine bottles. She caught a whiff of something, something that smelled like mildewed cloth and crankcase oil, and remembered Randy's description of the case of wine. She must be getting close. "Don't worry," she called to the man in the darkness behind her. "We're both going to get out of here alive."

8:50 P.M.

Russ was watching Clare make her way back to the table when his phone rang. "Excuse me," he said to his dinner companions. "I have to take this."

"You didn't even check the number," Linda said in an undertone. "Can't they do without you for a couple of hours?"

He opened his mouth to explain that with two major investigations and a missing person, he shouldn't even be at the party, but he bit off the words. What was the use? "I'm sorry," he said, then retreated to the entryway and opened his phone.

"Van Alstyne here," he said.

"Hey, Chief, it's Eric, up to Haudenosaunee."

"Eric. How's it going? Find anything?" Russ watched as Clare arrived at the table. Instead of sitting down, she bent over and said something to Parteger. The view was so good he almost missed McCrea's next sentence.

"We found a few more of those Planetary Liberation Army pamphlets."

"Any correspondence? Anything that might be a threat to van der Hoeven?" Hugh rose from his seat and stepped back, gesturing for Clare to precede him. They began maneuvering between the tables, headed toward the entryway.

"No. It's all pretty generic stuff. But," Eric stressed, "we found something very interesting in the cellar. They were stacked up, nice and clean, but there were a dozen bleach jugs, the same number of empty detergent boxes, fifteen dry gas cans, and—get this—a half of a box of sawdust.

The ingredients for homemade napalm. "Holy shit," Russ said. Clare and Hugh walked past him. "Hang on," he said to Eric. He clamped a hand over the phone. "Are you leaving?"

Clare shook her head. "Hugh's helping me get the wine out of my car. We'll be right back."

"I want to ask you about your conversation with the housekeeper this morning."

Her eyes brightened with curiosity. "Okay."

Russ turned back to his phone. "Eric? Good work. I'm going to call Harlene and have her alert the state police and the Feebs that we have a possible terror weapon on the loose. I'm going to give out the number at Haudenosaunee. Stay within earshot of the phone, in case anyone needs to ask you questions."

He hung up and speed-dialed Harlene. Dammit, he didn't want to wait until Clare and Parteger got back. Besides, Clare shouldn't be lugging wooden crates around dressed like that. Didn't that pansy-shirted Brit have any sense at all?

"Dispatch."

He strode across the lobby toward the front doors. "Harlene, it's Russ."

"Hey, Chief. What can I do you for?"

"Listen carefully. I need you to notify the state police threat response team and the district FBI office that we may have a terrorist weapon situation."

Harlene, thirty-plus-year veteran of the dispatch board, didn't turn a hair. "They're going to want to know what type."

He pushed open one of the elaborate glass-and-pine doors. The lights around the portico were so bright they nearly drowned out the moon. "Eric's found evidence suggesting home-brewed napalm. Direct any questions to him up at Haudenosaunee. You got the number there?"

"Yep."

"We don't know the amount, but it looks as if it could be several dozen gallons. This may be associated with Millie van der Hoeven's disappearance. The stuff may be in the hands of a militant ecoterrorist group, the Planetary Liberation Army. You got that?"

"Got it."

He walked down the curving drive toward the guest parking. "Oh, and get

Kevin on the radio. Tell him to break the stakeout. I want him to have another talk with Lisa Schoof. We need to know everything about anything she might have seen and heard while at Haudenosaunee."

"Will do."

He spotted Clare's little red car beneath one of the sleek light poles dotting the lot. He broke into a trot. "Keep me informed," he told Harlene. "Anything at all, I want to know. Chief out." He beeped off without waiting for her reply.

Clare was overseeing Parteger, who was stuffed halfway into the rear seat of her Shelby. One crate sat on the asphalt near her feet—or where her feet would be if he could see them. Her upper body was wrapped in a fur that looked like something Mamie Eisenhower might have worn.

"What is that?" Russ asked.

She plucked at the thing. "A beaver jacket. It belonged to my grandmother. I don't have many occasions to wear it, but it's terrifically warm." Her voice was apologetic; whether for the existence of the fur or for not bringing it out more often, he couldn't tell.

Parteger wiggled out of the backseat without the remaining wine. "Oh, look," he said. "The police. What a surprise."

Russ ignored him. "When you were talking, did either Lisa Schoof or Eugene ever say anything to you about Millie transporting anything on or off the property?"

"No," she said. "What's up?"

"Eric McCrea's been doing the search of the house at Haudenosaunee. He's found dozens of empty bleach bottles, detergent boxes, and gas cans. Plus sawdust."

She sucked in her breath. "Oh, that's not good."

"What?" Parteger said. "What is it?"

"You combine them to make an accelerant," Clare said, still looking at Russ. "All you need is a triggering mechanism and boom, instant inferno."

Parteger looked at Russ skeptically. "And you think someone at this . . . Haudenosaunee has been playing junior chemist?"

"It's not difficult," Clare said. "It's not much different from an old-fashioned Molotov cocktail." She kicked the wine crate. Bottles clinked in emphasis. "You put the accelerant in a container, add some sort of basic fuse, and . . ."

She looked down at the crate.

She looked up at Russ.

"Oh, my God," she whispered.

Russ lunged for the crate, prying and yanking at the top until the slender nails holding it together groaned out of their holes and he toppled backward. A musky petroleum smell bloomed in the cold night air. Clare reached for one of the bottles. "Wait," Russ said. Climbing to his feet, he yanked his handkerchief out of his pocket. "Don't touch them directly. You may get some on you." Working quickly but carefully, he removed the dozen bottles and set them on the pavement.

Clare looked into the bare box. "Where's the fuse?" She dropped to her hands and knees beside the wooden crate. "I think the bottom on the *inside* of this box is higher than the bottom on the outside." Russ patted his jacket pockets. "I need something to pry it open." Clare rose from the pavement, turned toward her car, and reached inside. He heard the pop of a glove compartment, and then she was handing him a Swiss army knife. He slid the knife blade between the boards and pressed it up and in. The false bottom tilted up smoothly. Beneath it, twisted wires, a stripped-down cell phone, and an even layer of blasting caps had been composed into the arts-and-crafts project from Hell.

"Holy Mary, Mother of God," Clare said. He wasn't sure if she was praying or not.

"What's going on?" Hugh's voice was tight with fear. "What the bloody hell is going on?"

"These are bombs," Russ said. "The wine crates are bombs." He looked into Clare's eyes and saw his own horror there. She got it. First there would be the explosion. Then, in a moment too quick for human reckoning, a spray of shrapnel, deadly splinters embedding in unprotected flesh, and finally the sticky, liquid flame clinging to everything it touched.

"We have to clear the ballroom," he said, amazed, as he always was, at how matter-of-fact his voice could be despite his fear.

She nodded.

"We have to get this thing out of your car," Hugh said, turning to the backseat.

"Leave it," Clare said.

"But Clare, if it goes off—"

"Leave it!"

Hugh reared back. Unlike Russ, he had evidently never heard Clare unleash her command voice.

"The car can be replaced. You can't." She turned, snatched up her skirts, and ran for the entrance to the resort.

Russ pounded alongside her, trying to hit the speed dial for Harlene with his arm jerking up and down. "Harlene," he gasped, when he finally made the connection, "IEDs here at the resort." Improvised explosive devices. "We need fire, we need emergency, we need every unit in the county turning out for this."

"Copy that, Chief," Harlene said. "Do you have casualties?"

"They haven't blown yet, but when they do it's gonna be bad." Ahead of him, Clare flung open a door and leaned against it to let him run through.

"Bomb squad?"

"Hell, yeah," he said, knowing it would be futile. The nearest explosive ordinance team was in Troop G, an hour away in Loudonville. Clare had skidded to a stop in front of the registration desk and was trying to juice an obviously skeptical clerk. "Chief out," he said to Harlene. Pocketing his phone, he reached inside his jacket and pulled out his badge. He hung it in front of the desk clerk's face. "This is a police emergency. You listen to what this lady says and do what she tells you to do. Got it?" He glanced at Clare without waiting for confirmation from the wide-eyed bell clerk. "I'm going to evacuate the ballroom."

She jerked her chin down.

He ran to the entryway. At the head of the huge room, dwarfed by the moonlit mountains looming behind him, a tall, balding, academic sort was at the podium. He was talking about the preservation of the Adirondack wilderness, his amplified voice underscored by the clinking of dessert forks and coffee spoons.

". . . and so we want to recognize those for whom preserving the natural world has become a calling . . ."

Russ paused at his own table. He put one hand on Linda's shoulder and the other as close to the centerpiece as he could. "I want you all to get up right now," he said in a low voice. "Get your coats and go to your cars. Go home immediately."

"Russ!" Linda tipped her head back to look at him. "Honey, whatever on earth are you saying?"

"Bomb threat." He decided to underplay it. The words "There's a bomb in the room" tended to produce running and screaming. The only way they were going to clear this ballroom without someone getting hurt was to keep it low-key. Seriously low-key. Urgently low-key.

"Oh, for God's sake." Robert Corlew reached for his after-dinner coffee. "These things are always complete smoke. Some bored teenagers with nothing to do on a Saturday night."

Or maybe not so low-key. "Linda," he said, taking her by both arms. "Your life is in danger. If you love me, you'll leave. Now."

He looked into her big blue eyes. *Please, honey,* he thought. *Please.*

She rose from her seat and kissed his cheek. "I'll see you at home, then." Without a single look behind her, she walked out of the ballroom.

The table was dead silent. "Jim," Russ said, "I'm going to make an evacuation announcement. Will you come with me? Having the mayor there may make people a little less skeptical."

Cameron nodded. He took his wife's hand and kissed it. "Better go, *alsking.*" She nodded, pale-faced. "I'll wait for you in the car."

He glanced up at Russ, who shook his head, then back to her. "Don't," he said. "I'll find my own way home."

Robert Corlew abruptly shoved his chair back and bolted from the table. His wife looked to where he was disappearing out the entryway. "Excuse me," she said in her hesitant voice, and followed him.

Russ and Jim Cameron skirted the edge of the room. "What's the story?" Cameron asked quietly.

"See those wine crates stacked up by the head table?"

"Yeah."

"Their bottles are full of a home-brewed fire accelerant that works sort of like napalm. The timers are inside a false bottom."

Cameron's face drained of color, but he kept walking toward the front of the room. Toward the bombs. Russ's respect for the man went up a good five notches. "How do you know?"

"I took one apart a few minutes ago out in the parking lot."

"When's it set to go off?"

"I don't know. I can recognize the basic ingredients of an improvised explosive device, but I'm no expert at figuring out the mechanics." A waiter trundled out the kitchen doors, a silver coffeepot in each hand. Russ stopped him and showed him his badge. "There's a bomb threat," he said in a low voice. "We're clearing the building. Get back in the kitchen and tell everyone. Then leave."

The waiter peered at Russ's badge. "And you are?"

"Millers Kill chief of police."

The waiter's mouth formed the word "Oh." He turned and went back into the kitchen.

Russ and Cameron crossed the empty stretch of dance floor. The head of the ACC, who was still talking, saw them and made discreet shooing motions to clear them out of the audience's line of sight.

". . . of course, this great work cannot continue without the sort of support tha— What do you think you're doing?"

Russ crowded the man from the podium. "Good evening, folks. I'm the chief of police here in Millers Kill, and this is our mayor, Jim Cameron." Somewhere in the middle of the room, someone started to clap. The sound stopped immediately. "We've received a credible threat that bombs have been placed in this location. We are taking this threat absolutely seriously. I want you all to get up and leave the ballroom in an orderly fashion. Please exit the building and go to your cars. Emergency vehicles will be arriving shortly. Please do not impede them."

Maybe 10 percent of the people in the ballroom rose and began making their way to the exit. The rest sat where they were, looking at each other. A torrent of voices filled the air. Someone shouted, "What about our coats?"

Russ leaned toward the mike to tell him what he could do with his damn coat. From the back of the room, a voice that could bounce off the walls cut him off. "Staff members are taking all the coats outside. As soon as you're past the portico, you can collect your belongings."

"Isn't that Reverend Fergusson?" Cameron asked.

"Oh, yeah," Russ said, smiling slightly. "You." He turned to the head-table occupants. "Get out. Now."

Louisa van der Hoeven stood unsteadily. "Did my brother have something to do with this?"

Russ paused. He figured either Eugene, Millie, or a combination of the two was responsible for the explosives. What the hell did Louisa van der Hoeven know that would make her jump to the same conclusion? "We consider him one of the prime suspects," he said cautiously.

She turned to her dinner companions. "Then it's serious. Get the hell out before the place goes up like a tinderbox." She lurched around the end of the table and took off for the door. As more and more people rose and headed toward the entryway, the mood changed from skepticism to alarm to panic.

Russ saw Shaun Reid, cell phone clamped to his ear, dragged by his wife across the dance floor. Several people began running. A woman screamed. At the other end of the ballroom, there was a booming sound as the doors to the adjacent conference area were opened. A petite woman in a severely chic black suit stood next to one and yelled, "You may exit through these doors and then out into the lobby! You may exit through these doors and then out into the lobby!" As the human tide stopped, changed direction, and began to flow toward her, she fought her way to the now-empty dance floor.

"I'm Barbara LeBlanc, the manager," she said when she reached them. "We're clearing the hotel right now. What else can we do?"

He motioned toward the retreating crowd, shoving and pushing to get out the doors. "Let's start by getting as far away as possible from these crates."

She followed him toward the dwindling mass of people, looking over her shoulder at the floor in front of the head table. "That's them?"

"That's them."

"Could we move them? Some of those glass panels are doors to the terrace outside."

He shook his head. "We don't know when they're going to go off. I don't want anybody touching them." He glanced up at the ceiling. "You have a sprinkler system in here?"

"Of course."

"Is there some way to jimmy it so it starts without a fire? If we gave the crates a good drenching, it might help."

"I'll see what I can do." She turned toward the kitchen.

"Ms. LeBlanc," he said.

"Yes?"

"Why don't I hear a general evacuation klaxon?"

She looked embarrassed. "The system's not up and running yet. This is our opening night." She cut across the almost empty room and vanished through the kitchen doors.

"This is an opening night like the *Titanic* was a maiden voyage," he muttered. They reached the entryway. The last people in the ballroom, and thank God for that. "Jim," he said, "you better get out. You've done everything you can here."

"I'm trying," the mayor said dryly. "Unfortunately, these people jamming the lobby don't recognize that rank hath its privilege."

Russ was distracted from replying by the sight of Clare, free of her fur, shoving against the crowd to get back inside the doors to the ballroom. Away from safety. Toward danger. "Typical," he said under his breath. He slapped Cameron on the back and pointed to where the crush of bodies was thinnest. "Get on the phone as soon as you're safe," he said. "We don't need any foot-dragging or turf games among the emergency response units. You can help cut through that."

The mayor nodded. "Good luck." He slipped away.

Russ snagged Clare by the arm. "Why the hell aren't you outside?" He spoke loudly. It sounded as if the entire population of Millers Kill were jammed inside the lobby.

She laughed. "I didn't know we had all this time," she yelled. "Now I wish I had let Hugh get the wine out of—"

The ballroom behind them exploded.

9:00 P.M.

Shaun's cell phone burbled just as Russ Van Alstyne took the podium. He glanced at the number displayed and flipped the phone open. Usually, Courtney would have handed him his head on a platter for taking a call at the table, but she was staring, transfixed, at where Russ was going on about something and didn't seem to notice anything else.

"Hi, Jeremy," he said. "Where are you?"

"God, Dad, you were right! I followed her car, and she drove straight to the mill."

"The old mill? Or the new mill?"

Jeremy sounded confused. "The new mill. I mean, she can probably see the old mill from where she's parked, but it wouldn't do her much good to stage an accident there. What's that noise in the background?"

That noise was two hundred and forty chairs scraping, thumping, falling over as their occupants scrambled to get out of the ballroom. Courtney grabbed Shaun by the hand. "Come on," she said. "Let's go!"

"Dad?"

Courtney plowed through the crowd, elbows flying, hauling Shaun along in her wake. "I'm here, son," he said into the phone.

"What's going on?"

Christ, if he told Jeremy the truth, he'd do ninety all the way up from town to be here for the crisis. And Shaun needed him at Reid-Gruyn, keeping an eye on the blackmailing bitch, making sure they didn't move Millie van der Hoeven out of the old mill.

"It's sort of like intermission," he said. "Everyone's up and stretching their legs before the dancing starts." He and Courtney squeezed through the entryway shoulder to shoulder with at least ten others. The lobby was filling up rapidly. He clamped his hand over the phone. "Look, you head outside and get your coat. I'm going to step down the hall a ways and finish this call."

"Shaun, the police chief said to get out!"

"Honey, it's probably just a prank. Most of these bomb threats are. I'll be out as soon as I can."

She looked doubtful, but she released him. He strode quickly away from the noisy, panicked hubbub of the lobby.

"Jeremy?"

"Yeah. Are you sure everything is okay?"

"Yes. It's quieter now. People are going back inside. Look, have you seen anyone leave the old mill?"

"No." Jeremy's voice was equal parts confusion and suspicion. "Why would there be?"

"I think the woman you followed has at least two accomplices and that they're hiding out in there."

"Dad, are these employees? 'Cause if they are—"

"No, they're not." He looked behind him. The mob in the lobby was flexing like a living thing now, one part desperately trying to get out, the other part determined to stay put. He could see uniformed staff forcibly preventing guests from getting onto the elevators, presumably in order to retrieve their belongings. "But I suspect they're working with someone inside. If we're going to find out who, we can't call the police." He came down hard on those last words. "I want you to—"

But he didn't get out what he wanted Jeremy to do. There was a horrific sound, a death scream of wood and glass, a percussive wave that boxed his ears and shoved him against the wall, and then, swallowing it all, the hungry howl of a monstrous fire.

He was amazed to find he still had the phone pressed against his temple. Jeremy was screaming something. He lifted the phone higher. "What?" he rasped.

"Dad! Oh, my God, Dad! There's just been an explosion inside the old mill!"

9:00 P.M.

The explosion knocked Millie to the floor. She lay stunned and aching for a moment and then crawled to her hands and feet. She was scraped and battered but whole. Bracing her hand against the tarp-covered machine that had served to protect her from the blast, she got to her feet. The wide front door Shaun Reid had carried her through a lifetime ago was in flames. Fire splashed in all directions from it, clawing up tarpaulins, feasting on empty pallets, inching across the old wooden floor.

The light, after so many hours of darkness, was almost unbearable. Millie threw her hands up, blocking the worst of the blaze from view. A bomb. Shaun Reid had planted some kind of bomb. He had never intended to come back for her. He had left her here to burn to death. Despite the heat from the flames, she felt cold inside. As cold as the stone tower where her brother had died. Oh, God—what about Louisa? Was he after her sister, too? She had to get out. She had to.

"Help me." The cry from the outer edges of darkness shivered down her spine. "Please. Don't leave me."

There, at the far edge of the growing circle of flame, she saw what she was looking for. A narrow door. She looked behind her. If she went back for him, if she tried to carry him out, the fire would swallow the door before she could make it. *It's him or me,* she thought, desperation rising like vomit in her throat. *It's him or me.*

"I'll call the fire department when I get out," she yelled. "They'll help you."

"Please!"

She skirted the flames, refusing to look at the raging heart of them, focusing on avoiding the questing tendrils and embers pinwheeling through the air. There it was. The door. Within reach. The heat was already hammering at its surface, and she cried out in pain as she grasped the doorknob. She thought she heard a final "Please!" but that might have been the eager, air-sucking hiss of the fire.

She staggered out into the cool darkness, blind again.

She heard shrieking, and as her eyes adjusted to the faint light thrown off by the parking lot lights, she saw the outline of a woman, running and stumbling across the scrubland dividing the old mill from the new.

"Randy!" the woman screamed. "Randy!"

A brilliant bobbing light tore Millie's attention away from the sight. A car was jouncing down the rough drive toward them, bouncing up and down in the same pattern she had felt, locked in her captor's trunk.

"Where is he?" The woman scrambled over the last stretch of hillocky ground. "Where's my husband!"

"Where's Shaun Reid?" Millie demanded.

The woman looked at her as if she had gone mad.

"Where is he?" Millie strode to where the woman was standing. "I know you went to see him!" She grabbed her by the arms and shook her hard enough to rattle her back teeth. "Tell me where he is, and I'll tell you where your husband is!"

"At the new resort! He's at the new resort!" The woman burst into tears.

"What the hell is going on?"

Millie spun around. A young man she might have recognized as handsome stood there, his immaculate suit looking ridiculous in the lurid glow of the fire. Behind him, his car was still running, the driver's door open.

"My husband's in there!" The woman, still sobbing, pointed toward the now-burning mill door.

Millie made her decision in an instant. "He's hurt!" she said to the young man. "Please, please help him!"

He turned to look at the door and actually stepped toward it, which was more than she had thought he would do. Millie shoved him, hard, and was pounding toward his car before he had hit the ground. She slammed the door on his indignant shout, yanked the gearshift into reverse, and careened up the driveway. She spun around in the parking lot, tires screaming, and accelerated out the gate.

9:05 P.M.

Clare rolled into a sitting position. Her head felt as if she were the clapper in a bell, ringing so loudly she couldn't hear anything else.

Russ was pushing himself off the floor, rubbing the back of his neck. He turned to her, relief in his eyes. *Clare?* She could see his mouth move, but no noise came out.

She shook her head and pointed to her ear. He nodded and held out his hand, and together they staggered to their feet.

A table had overturned behind them, partially sheltering them from the brutal heat emanating in waves from the inferno that had been the dance floor. Only a few feet away, ragged tablecloths trembled from the violence of their destruction. Clare clutched Russ's hand. If he had been a little bit farther from the door . . . She had just enough time to witness one of the magnificent antler chandeliers plunging into the maelstrom before Russ jerked her past the entryway and into the lobby.

Guests were surging, clotting, battering at the exits. She heard them faintly, shouts and crying from very far away. Mostly she heard the high-pitched ringing. Staff blocked the elevators, and the emergency stair had been chained open. As she watched, a middle-aged Asian woman emerged from the stairway, wide-eyed and shaking. Clare remembered what she had been going to do.

"The staff needs help making sure everyone gets out of their rooms." Russ's wince told her she needed to tone the volume down. "I'm going to go help."

He shook his head and pointed to the reception desk, where four uniformed clerks were on phones. He turned her so she was facing him. *They. Do. Job,* he said.

"But what if the guests think it's a false alarm?"

His eyebrows went up. He pointed behind him to where the ballroom was going up like a Christmas tree on a February bonfire.

She took his point. "Still. I ought to help."

She saw rather than heard him sigh. Then he gathered her into his arms, held her tightly, and whispered into her ear. The ringing receded, and she heard him. "If you love me, you'll leave. Now."

Then he did something that amazed her. With dozens of people still struggling through the lobby, he kissed her, lightly, briefly, and then he put her away from him, stripped off his dinner jacket, and draped it over her shoulders.

"I can hear you now," she said inanely.

"Go on. I'm going to make sure Mom and Cousin Nane got out okay." She nodded. Turned. And found a frightened-looking elderly man, wearing dress shoes and pajamas and a black overcoat, watching her. She shrugged her arms into Russ's jacket and crossed the lobby. She took the old man's hand. "Father Aberforth," she said. "Let me help you."

J eremy allowed himself sixty seconds to curse, kick the ground, and imagine what a roasting his dad was going to give him: letting one of the blackmailers get away by stealing his own freaking BMW.

After a minute had gone by, he put it aside and focused on the task at hand. The small, dark-haired woman who had screamed that her husband was inside stood by the lazily burning doorway, sobbing and hiccupping and calling, "Randy! Randy!" in an aching voice.

Jeremy crossed to her side. She looked up at him, her face wet. "Please," she begged. "Help him."

"I will," he promised. "But I want you to help, too." She nodded fiercely. "Go up to the new mill. There's a phone inside the employees' entrance. Call 911." She nodded again. "Find the foreman. Tell him to have the men collect all the extinguishers we have in the building and bring them here. You got that?"

"Foreman. Extinguishers."

"Tell him Jeremy Reid told you so." Her wide-eyed shock at his name would have been comical under different circumstances. "That's right, Jeremy Reid. So lay off my father."

She bolted without another word. Jeremy looked toward the old mill. If he could get inside, he should be able to break through a window on the river side and jump. He was a strong swimmer, confident of his ability to keep even a scared and injured man afloat for the time it would take to reach the riverbank downstream from the building. If he could get past the fire. Into the water. Fire. Water.

He grinned to himself and dashed toward the river rolling past the old mill. He scrambled down the steep bank faster than he intended and wound up staggering the first few steps into the black water. It was dark down here, dark and fast-moving and steeply angled. He was afraid he would lose his footing or become disoriented if he waded in, so he forced himself to sit in the knee-deep water, sit, stretch out, and duck his head beneath the surface.

He came up gasping and yelping with pain. Christ, it felt like someone had taken a nutcracker to him. He staggered, dripping, up the bank, cupping his poor beleaguered balls. It would be a miracle if he was able to father children after this.

Facing the fiery door, he wondered if a good drenching was enough. Then he thought of the poor bastard stuck in there. It would have to be good enough. He took off his sopping suit jacket, draped it over his head, and ran inside.

Running through flame: crackling and hissing and a smell, not of smoke but of gas; heat coiling about him, his shirtsleeves crinkling, his pants legs stiffening; and then he was out, steaming but unharmed. He stumbled forward, side-stepping the antiquated machinery, wondering what was going to happen when the fire hit those monsters. Would they melt? Explode? "Hello!" he called. "Randy? Are you in here?"

Over the consuming growl of the fire, he heard a noise like a cross between a gulp and a cry. "Here! I'm over here!"

Jeremy followed the sound toward the back wall. He was expecting— He didn't know what he was expecting, but it wasn't a guy his own age, lying on the dusty floor, surrounded by a backpack and pieces of food, bleeding from an iron stake shoved into his gut. Jeremy dropped to his knees. "Jesus Christ!" he said. "What happened?"

"Millie. She had this thing . . ." Randy waved toward the wound. A palm's width of black iron stuck up from the side of his abdomen. "I didn't pull it out," he said weakly. "I thought it might bleed more."

Jeremy rested his hand gently on Randy's shoulder. "That was good, man. Good thinking." He glanced up and saw right away that his breaking-the-windows idea had a serious flaw in it. The casement-style windows facing the river were a good twelve or thirteen feet above his head. "You just take it easy, man. I'm going to get you out of here. I need to take a look around, but I'm not leaving you. You got that?"

Randy nodded. "I'm sorry," he said.

Jeremy rose and turned around. He considered the machines. Could he shove one under the window? To serve as a platform? He pushed against a few tarp-covered shapes and found they weren't going anywhere without the help of a forklift. He went closer to the fire, grabbed a pallet, and dragged it to the back wall. He returned, took another, and hauled it away. He got a third from the stack, but by then the fire had spread too far, and he lost the rest of them. He prowled the grotesquely lit floor, looking for more pallets amid the detritus of a hundred and thirty years of papermaking. There were maybe four that were sturdy enough to use. He mentally measured their height against the wall. Stacked up, they might boost him high enough to leap for the casement of one of the windows. They weren't going to allow him to bring Randy with him.

He had noticed the washroom as he circled through the building. Now he walled away the tiny hammer-beat of panic that was thudding against his ribs and went to check it out. It was small and stinking, as if rodents had died in the walls. The one window was another impossible-to-reach casement. But, he was amazed to see, the gravity-flush toilet still worked, and when he pulled the chain, water gushed into the bowl.

For a moment, he thought about wetting himself down again and making a break for the door. The fire had spread—to his eye, it seemed to be spreading faster than was natural—but one man, soaked and running at top speed, could probably still make it. One unburdened man.

He looked at the water, visible in flashes of firelight. This had probably been the executive washroom in his great-great-grandfather's day. He felt sad, and sick, and proud, all at once.

He returned to Randy's side. He could feel the heat now, even back here at the edge of the river-side wall, harsh and oppressive. He knelt down. Randy's eyes were closed. "Hey, man. Are you still with me?"

"Yep."

"Great." Jeremy tried to infuse his words with as much confidence as possible. "Look, we're going to wait this out until the fire trucks get here. They're on their way already. Your wife called them."

"Lisa?"

"Yeah."

"She's okay?"

"She's fine. We're going to be fine, too. Hang on, I'm going to pick you up. It may hurt."

Randy's whimper as Jeremy hauled him off the floor was almost lost in Jeremy's grunt. "Jeez, man," he gasped, staggering across the room. "You must be solid muscle."

"Yeah." Randy gritted the word out.

Jeremy squeezed sideways through the door of the water closet and laid the other man on the floor. "I'll be right back," he said, panting. He grabbed the first tarp he could find and dragged it off its machine and over to the water-closet door. He did the same with another tarp, hurrying, because he could see the fire, literally see it leaping and flowing, claiming more and more of his great-great-grandfather's mill. Finally he snatched up a pickle jar he had seen half-revealed by Randy's backpack. He unscrewed it, dumped the pickles and juice as he bolted for the water closet, and plunged it into the bowl. He poured water over Randy, over himself, over the floor, over the tarps. He poured and flushed, poured and flushed, until he realized that he could see the interior of the tiny room clearly by the light of the fire. The blaze had reached the far wall.

He abandoned the pickle jar in the toilet, heaved the tarps inside the water closet, and shut the door. Feeling his way in the dark, he edged to Randy's side, tugging the dampened tarps over them until they were both completely covered.

"This reminds me of pretend camping as a kid," he said. "You know, crawling under a blanket?"

Randy made a noise halfway between agreement and pain. Jeremy stripped off his jacket and, folding it, placed it under Randy's head. "Don't get discouraged, man," Jeremy said. "Help is on the way."

"I'm sorry," Randy whispered.

"For trying to blackmail my dad? You should be. When we get out of here, you're going to go straight, right?"

"I'm sorry . . . I thought you were a rich snot."

"I am a rich snot," Jeremy said, smiling.

"Why are you helping me?"

Jeremy thought for a moment. "Well, you know." He didn't know how to put it into words. "You, me, we're all human beings. We have to do right by each other."

There was a long pause. Jeremy listened to the muffled sound of the fire's roar. He didn't hear any sirens. He told himself he wouldn't be able to, over the other noise. Finally Randy spoke again. "If you get out of this and I don't, will you do me a favor?"

"You're getting out of this. Don't worry."

"Will you?"

Jeremy squeezed his eyelids tightly closed. He could feel the hot tears pressing against them. "Yes," he whispered.

"Tell Becky Castle I'm sorry."

"That's it?"

"Yeah."

Jeremy placed his hand over Randy's shoulder and pressed hard. Randy's hand fluttered up and patted Jeremy's hand. They waited, in the damp and stifling dark, two boys under the blanket. Less afraid because neither of them was alone.

9:10 P.M.

Ed Castle's beeper went off the same moment Lyle MacAuley's radio crackled to life. Lyle muttered an excuse-me and walked into the hospital hallway.

"What is it?" Suzanne asked quietly. Becky had finally fallen asleep again. She lay folded into her bed like the little girl she had once been. Her fragile whiteness would have blended in with the sheets if not for the purpling bruises blooming across her face.

"Fire," Ed said, checking the code.

"Do you have to go?"

"Lemme call in and check." He crossed to Becky's bedside phone and dialed the dispatch number. It rang, and rang, and rang again. Finally, the line picked up, but before he could say a word, he heard a blurted, "Holdplease" and was left listening to a recorded message giving him alternate numbers to call if he was looking for the town hall, the animal control officer, or the department of motor vehicles. By the time Dispatch came back on, he had worked up a good mad.

"Harlene, what the hell is going on over there? In all the years I've been a volunteer, I've never had to wait on a fire response call."

"Who is this?"

He raised his eyebrows. He thought Harlene could recognize every volunteer firefighter by voice. "Ed. Ed Castle."

"Sorry." She sounded flustered. He started to worry. He had never, ever heard Harlene flustered. "We got two major fires. The Reid-Gruyn mill and the new resort. Meet your team A.S.A.P. You'll be supported by Corinth, Glens Falls, and Hudson Falls."

"Wait—" he said, but she had already clicked off. He was left staring at the phone in his hand.

"Ed?" Suzanne looked questioningly at him.

"The Reid-Gruyn mill's on fire. And the new resort." He shook his head in disbelief. "Sounds like they're turning at least two counties out to respond."

"The new resort?" Suzanne sucked in a breath, turning toward their daughter. "Oh, lord, Ed. What if Becky . . . ?"

He caught her in a quick one armed hug. "Don't think about it. We've got her here. Whatever else happens, she's safe now."

Lyle MacAuley came back in from the hall. "You hear the news?"

Ed nodded. "Any idea what happened?"

Lyle's face was an outcropping of Adirondack granite. "Chief thinks some sort of ecoterrorism. Who knows, nowadays."

Ed turned toward his wife. "Suze—"

"Just go," she said. "We'll be here waiting when you get back."

9:20 P.M.

He kept calling and calling Jeremy's number, but the boy didn't answer. Shaun was starting to get worried. He had gotten the hell out after the explosion and now was milling around the portico. He wasn't sure what to do. Maybe he should get into the car with Courtney and head over to Reid-Gruyn. What the hell had Jeremy been on about? An explosion? It had sounded as if it were at the mill, but there was no way that could happen. Could it?

A firefighter shouldered him out of the way. "Excuse me, sir." They had started arriving a few minutes ago, hook and ladders and water trucks and emergency response vehicles. Lights whirling, hoses unrolling, men and women stomping around in bulky turnout suits. The fire fighter turned at the door and held up a megaphone. "Folks," he said, his voice electronically amplified. "Please move away from this area. Please move back into the parking lot. Please stay away from the fire equipment so we can do our jobs."

Like the nearby parking lot was safe. Shaun could see the burned and smoking ruins of one car already. He retreated downslope, instead, crossing the border of large riverstones demarcating the garden area, treading carelessly on the decorative heathers planted below the curving drive. He tried calling the foreman's desk on the mill floor, but no one answered. He tried Jeremy's number again. The cool edges of fear stroked his spine and coiled in his belly.

Then he saw Jeremy's car pull into the lower parking lot. He plunged through the newly landscaped garden, churning up plants and clots of earth. The BMW drove closer and closer to the portico, stopping only when it was blocked by a line of cones. Shaun galloped toward Jeremy, thanking God, promising to mend his ways, whatever they might be. His ankle almost turned on one of the riverstones, and he had to hop over them to catch his balance. The door swung open. "Jeremy!" he called out.

Millie van der Hoeven stepped out.

She seemed as shocked to see him as he was to see her. Then she laughed, a painful, racking laugh. "You thought you'd get away with it, didn't you?"

He was speechless.

"You thought you had me tied up tight in that godforsaken warehouse. One fire, and you get rid of the only witness who could link you to my brother's murder."

One fire?

"I was going to . . . I don't know, punch you in the gut or something. Bite you again. Let you know what a miserable, despicable failure you are. But you know what? I don't need to count coup on you." She turned away from him. Toward the car.

"What—" His voice cracked. "What are you going to do?"

She stopped. Looked at him disbelievingly. "What do you think I'm going to do, you murdering bastard?" She spun on her heel.

He scooped up a fist-sized rock. It was dark down here, below the light and tumult at the resort's entrance. But even in the dark, he could still throw. He was always good at throwing the ball.

The stone hit her hard, right behind her left ear. She went down with a thud. He strode over to her. Heaved her off the ground and threw her over his shoulder. He didn't hesitate, as he had done this afternoon. Clearly there was only one course. And what could be more fortunate than a deadly fire close at hand? Shaun moved past the fire trucks and emergency vehicles, toward the far side of the hotel. All he had to do was get inside, somewhere away from the main entrance, and dump her into the flames.

It took him no more than five minutes. Skirting the light and the action, he discovered a side door that had been propped open with a chrome-and-rubber stop. He swung Millie from his shoulders into his arms. It was heavier and a lot less comfortable, but it would present the illusion of a man carrying a woman to safety.

He walked down the hall. He could hear the fire—a smashing, sucking, howling noise. The air was hot and heavy with smoke. He passed a door, opened onto a meeting room, and recognized where he was. The hallway leading to the ballroom. Could he slip into the conference room beside the ballroom and give her a little shove through the door?

"Hey, you!" The voice was weirdly muffled.

Shaun looked up. A firefighter, his face obscured by mask and eye shield, blocked the end of the hall. He had an ax in his hand and an oxygen tank strapped to his back. "You need to get out of here. This area's not safe."

Shaun nodded. He turned and walked in the opposite direction. He'd wait outside the doorway until the firefighter moved on, then bring her back. Maybe go upstairs, put her above the ballroom. Bash her a few more times and call it smoke inhalation. Even if the fire didn't get her, who would know?

"Hey!" the muffled voice again. "That girl."

Shaun looked down. Millie's head had lolled back, and her long blond hair was swaying above the Oriental runner.

He kept walking.

"Stop!"

He walked faster. Behind him, he heard the thud of running feet. He broke into a run, but even his athlete's body couldn't function at peak with a hundred and forty pounds of young woman in his arms.

The firefighter's tackle knocked him to the carpet. The girl bounced and rolled, coming to rest on her back, her head tilted to one side.

A hand grabbed his jacket and flipped him over. The firefighter set his ax, blade side down, against Shaun's sternum. With his other hand, he shoved the face shield up and tugged his oxygen mask down.

Shaun frowned. It was . . . it was . . . He blinked. It was Ed Castle, the guy who supplied his pulp.

"What," Ed Castle said, "are you doing with my daughter's college roommate?"

9:40 P.M.

R uss had finished getting a radio briefing from Lyle MacAuley on the three-alarm fire that was consuming the old mill on the Reid-Gruyn property. He turned to the newly arrived Mark Durkee and Noble Entwhistle. "What's the flammable version of 'It never rains, but it pours?'" Mark shrugged his shoulders. "Okay," Russ said. "We're going to need some crowd and traffic control here. I want you to—"

Someone grabbed his shoulder. He looked around at John Huggins. "Hey," Huggins said. "I got a radio squawk from one of my guys. He's calling for paramedics and the cops." He pointed toward the edge of the hotel. "Go around there. The second door. It'll be open."

Huggins strode away before Russ could acknowledge the information. "You heard the man," he said, pointing to Mark. "Let's go."

From the corner of his eye, Russ saw two paramedics from the Corinth squad shouldering their rolled pallet and medical kits. He let Mark lead, trusting his younger, keener night vision to find them footing.

They found the door. The firefighter who called them in was close by.

"Lookit who I found," Ed said.

Mark knelt by Millie. "She's got a bloody laceration at the back of her skull," he said. "But she's alive."

Russ looked at Shaun a long moment. Then he looked at the man holding the ax. "Ed," he said. He paused. He didn't know what to say. "Thank you," he finally got out.

Ed nodded. "It was her hair caught my eye. Like Becky's."

Russ pinched the bridge of his nose beneath his glasses. "Mark," he said wearily. "Will you cuff Mr. Reid and inform him of his rights?"

9:45 P.M.

Clare and Deacon Aberforth sat in Hugh Parteger's car together, keeping warm.

"Do you think they'll stop it?" he asked.

"Oh, I'm sure they will." She looked through the window at the carnival of lights and hoses and moving reflective stripes. She sighed.

"I wonder if I'll be able to get back to my room?"

"You can bunk in the rectory tonight, Father."

He smiled at her for the first time. "You know, before all this, I would have said that was totally unacceptable."

"And now?"

"And now, I think I'll just say, 'Thank you.'"

Clare leaned back against the seat and closed her eyes.

"Ms. Fergusson."

She opened them again.

"I suspect you and I disagree on quite a number of things, including homosexuality, the proper degree of episcopal control of a parish, and, for all I know, the doctrines of immutable grace and virgin birth."

"I may be a liberal, Father, but that doesn't mean I've fallen under the sway of Bishop Spong."

"No. No, I suppose not. And we are called to remember what unites us in Christ, not what divides us in the world."

"Amen," she said. The car's heater kicked in again, and her skirt rustled in the blower's blast.

"What I'm trying to say is, I recognize I must seem like a hopelessly outdated fossil to you."

She prudently kept her mouth shut.

"But I have lived a good number of years. I've seen quite a lot of the world. It may surprise you to know that I served in the marines as a young man."

"You're kidding."

"In Korea."

"I'm impressed."

"And I'm a widower."

She paused. It was difficult to imagine Willard Aberforth in a marital relationship. "I'm sorry," she said.

"I'm not saying this to garner your sympathy but to let you know that I've attained a good deal of knowledge about human nature. And about men and women." He looked at her. His black eyes were a good deal less intimidating than they had been earlier. It was hard, she guessed, to keep your back up around someone wearing striped pajamas.

"I saw you, earlier."

She was silent.

"When I was at the bar, after you left, the man you . . . were with . . . came through the lobby. With a woman who acted very much like a wife. Was I mistaken?"

"No. You must have a good eye for body language."

He sighed. "Unlike you, I cannot offer confession and absolution."

"No," she said.

"But I can offer a quiet, listening heart. And whatever insight my years have left me with."

Clare closed her eyes. She felt . . . taut, as if her skin were stretched around this secret she was stuffed with. She tried to live her life with integrity. But integrity required her to be integrated. To be one whole person, whether alone in her house or in front of an entire ballroom full of people.

She opened her eyes. Beyond the crazy emergency lights she could see the mountains. And the moon.

"When I met Russ Van Alstyne, I thought of him simply as a friend," she started. "Our relationship seemed like"—she thought for a moment—"a meeting of true minds."

9:55 P.M.

He found her sitting in Parteger's car, her skirts practically up to her nose, deep in conversation with an old guy in pajamas and an overcoat. He knocked on the window. She rolled it down.

"Guess what?" he said.

"After tonight? I wouldn't dare try."

"We've found Millie van der Hoeven."

She smiled brilliantly. "Oh, Russ, that's wonderful. Finally, some good news."

"She's been resting up in one of the ambulances, but before she goes, she'd like to meet you."

"Me? Whatever for?"

"I told her about you being on the search party and talking with her brother and all. Will you come?"

She looked at the old fellow. "Will you excuse me?"

"Of course," he said.

She maneuvered her skirts out of the car. She was still wearing Russ's tuxedo jacket. "I see you found a replacement," she said, fingering the heavy parka he was wearing.

"I borrowed it." He turned his back, to show her the words FIRE CHIEF in reflective letters.

"Why am I not surprised you found one that says 'chief'?"

He smiled to himself.

"Did you find your Mom okay?"

"Yeah, She and Nane and the rest of the ACC gardeners were already out-side when the crates blew. They've all gone to the Kreemy Kakes diner to talk the evening over."

"How are the firefighters doing?" she asked.

"Not bad. The ballroom, the kitchen, and the conference room next to the ballroom are a complete loss, and there's serious structural damage to the floor above them, but they've managed to contain it."

"Thank God."

"Was Millie behind the bombing? Or the PLA?"

"No." He didn't elaborate on what the van der Hoeven sisters had already told him.

He pointed to where the Corinth ambulance was parked. Several people milled around the open back doors. "Are those the corporate honchos from GWP?" Clare asked.

"Yep. Millie and her sister insisted on signing the documents transferring Haudenosaunee before they left for the hospital."

"Wow. That's dedicated."

Ahead of them, the delegation from GWP finished bowing and shaking hands. Russ and Clare hung back a moment until they had cleared out. Then he urged her forward. "Millie, this is Reverend Clare Fergusson. Clare, I think you've already met Millie's sister, Louisa."

Clare shook hands with Millie, who reclined on the ambulance bed with a bandage on her head. Louisa sat next to her sister, holding her hand. One of them looked like a San Franciscan socialite, and the other looked like she'd come out of a brawl in a lumber camp, but their resemblance to each other—and to their late brother—was notable.

"Millie, I'm delighted to meet you. And find you safe and relatively sound."

Millie touched her bandage tentatively. "Thank you. Chief Van Alstyne told us about all you did to help me. And my friend Becky."

Clare shook her head. "I was just one of the search team." She hesitated. "I've already told Louisa, but I'm so very sorry about the loss of your brother."

Tears filled the young woman's eyes. She nodded.

"I understand your car is one of tonight's casualties," Louisa said. "Please al-low us to make restitution."

Russ thought of the twisted, smoking wreck that was her Shelby Cobra. "Oh," Clare said gamely, "I have insurance."

"Nevertheless." Louisa looked at her sister. "And we'd like to explain to you," she looked at Russ, "why we believe Gene was solely responsible for tonight's carnage."

There was a long pause. Clare looked at Russ. He shrugged. Millie had disclaimed the IEDs earlier, and he was pretty sure further investigation of the physical evidence was going to prove her statement, but he didn't know what this was about.

"I feel responsible," Millie said. "I was the one who brought the land sale up. I knew Gene was attached to Haudenosaunee, but I didn't realize . . ."

Louisa looked at Clare and Russ. "I believe it's common knowledge that Gene's lived a reclusive life at Haudenosaunee since the fire that destroyed the old camp and took his mother's life."

Russ nodded.

"What is not commonly known—in fact, no one outside the family knew— was that . . . Gene . . ."

"Gene started that fire." Millie's face was as expressionless as her inflection.

"His mother had gotten primary custody of him, and he didn't want to go. He loved to . . . tinker with things. Make things."

"Things that blew up?" Clare asked bluntly.

Louisa nodded. "I don't think he actually meant to hurt her . . ."

"Yes, he did," Millie said. "He hated her, and he didn't want to leave Daddy and Haudenosaunee. So he waited until she was alone in the old camp, and he set off his firebomb."

"Good heavens," Clare said, which was a lot milder than what Russ was going to say. "That's a pretty big secret to carry around for all those years." She searched both the sisters' faces. "Are you sure, though, that means Eugene was responsible for tonight's violence?"

"He locked me in the tower," Millie said. "He slipped something in my drink last night during dinner. I don't know what. I couldn't remember anything when I woke up this morning."

"Probably roofie. Rohypnol," Russ explained. "Makes you extremely susceptible to suggestion and wipes out your memory. He could have told you to walk to the tower and climb the stairs and you wouldn't recall doing it."

"He did it to keep me away from the ceremony," Millie said. "So I wouldn't get hurt."

"He didn't tell *me* to keep away," Louisa said. Her mouth drew taut, as if its strings had been yanked shut.

"Lou, I'm sure he had some plan up his sleeve. He didn't want to hurt you."

"No," Russ said, "just the leadership of the ACC and the GWP corporate brass." All three women looked at him.

"Oh, my God," Clare said. "This afternoon, when I agreed to deliver the cases of wine for him, Eugene told me to leave the ballroom and come outside at nine o'clock. And bring my friends. He told me he was going to set off fireworks."

Everyone looked out the open ambulance door, to where the night was alive with whirling lights and color.

"And so he did," Clare said, so quietly Russ doubted the van der Hoevens heard her.

His phone rang. He excused himself and jumped out of the ambulance. "Van Alstyne here."

"Russ? It's Lyle. I'm calling to update you on the Reid-Gruyn fire."

Russ listened while Lyle told him the news. He thought about Becky Castle, and Ed, and about Shaun and his new young wife, and about Lisa-the-housekeeper. He thought about Mark and Rachel Durkee. *It's true,* he thought. *We are all related. If not by blood, then by bonds we don't even realize. Until they're gone.*

He walked back to the ambulance in time to hear Clare saying, "Let's be thankful for at least this. No matter what the damage, it's been confined to things. Things can be replaced. At least no people have been hurt."

"I'm afraid that's not true." The ambulance dipped under his weight as he climbed in. "I just got off the phone with my deputy chief. He's been monitoring the fire over at the Reid-Gruyn mill. It seems Randy Schoof and Jeremy Reid were caught in the old mill. They've both been confirmed dead."

Millie van der Hoeven burst into tears.

10:00 P.M.

Lisa Schoof sat in the back seat of her brother-in-law's cruiser. It was dark, very dark, except where it was lit by the light of the still-burning fire. Every once in a while someone would come up to her and ask if she was okay, if she wanted to go to the hospital, if she could answer a few questions. She didn't reply; even if they opened the door, their voices remained behind thick glass, and eventually Mark spotted whoever was bothering her and shooed him away.

She tilted her head against the back of the seat. She was tired. So very tired.

Once, when she and Rachel were kids, they had spent the day sledding down a hill behind their grandfather's pasture. They had been cold, then colder, and finally their toes and fingers ached and pinched with the bite of it. But they had dared each other to stay out till dark, and Lisa had found that after a while, the pain went away, and she felt nothing at all.

That was how she felt now. Numb. And tired.

She had thought, when the firetrucks arrived, that would be the end of it. So many of them, and so many men, tossing hoses into the river, sending great sprays of water arching over the old mill. She stood on the scrubgrounds surrounded by Reid-Gruyn workers, the plant emptied out, and someone had said, "Thank God it didn't start in the new mill," and she had turned and said, "My husband's in there," and they all fell silent and drew away from her.

But still, she believed the firefighters would save him. Him and the man who had gone in to get him out. She believed, right up until the moment when, with a series of cracks and pops that echoed through the night like artillary fire, the joists and braces that had held up the old mill for one hundred and thirty years gave way. The roof collapsed inward with the flaming roar of a dying forest, blasting out great gouts of fire that scattered the firefighters and made the onlookers stumble back in shock and awe.

Randy was gone.

She couldn't remember what she had been thinking of when she ran, screaming, toward the fire. Someone had tackled her, several someones, and held her down while she thrashed and screamed and clawed, until the paramedics appeared and gave her a shot, one of them kneeling on her chest and another one immobilizing her arm.

Now she was numb.

Mark had asked her some questions—about Randy, and Becky Castle, and Shaun Reid. She had answered them because it was the quickest way to get him to stop bothering her. After that, he left her alone. And kept the others away.

Outside, she could hear someone crying, and Mark's voice, and then the squad car door opened and Rachel was there, saying, "Lisa. Oh, Lisa," in a tear-clogged voice.

Lisa let her weeping sister wrap her arms around her shoulders and hold her. She wanted to tell her it was okay. She wanted to ask her if she remembered that day sledding, and the sun going down, and the numbness. But she was too tired to talk. So she let Rachel choke and sob over her, and she closed her eyes against the darkness and the light.

Compline

Keep watch, dear Lord, with those who work, or watch,
or weep this night, and give your angels charge over
those who sleep. Tend the sick, Lord Christ; give rest to
the weary, bless the dying, soothe the suffering, pity the
afflicted, shield the joyous; and all for your love's sake.
Amen.

2:00 A.M.

Clare rolled to a stop and turned off the lights. "Here we are."

"Let's go," Russ said without moving. "You must be exhausted."

"I'm not, surprisingly. I think I've gotten my second wind." She had shuttled Hugh to the Stuyvesant Inn and Deacon Aberforth to the rectory before returning to the Algonquin Waters resort—or what was left of it—to pick up Russ. He had been adamant about getting a ride with one of his officers, but when she pointed out that they could drop her at the rectory first, and that he'd be doing her a favor by returning Hugh's car to him on Sunday, he agreed.

"How's Mark?" she asked.

"Okay, I guess. I took him off duty as soon as I found out about Randy Schoof. I think they were all planning on going over to his in-laws' house. I'm sure it'll help the girls, being with their parents."

"Mmm. I have to remember to call tomorrow and ask if I can do anything."

"You mean today. It's Sunday."

"Is it?"

"Has been for two hours."

She wrapped his dinner jacket, which she hadn't taken off yet, more tightly around her. She liked the smell of it. "Now you're fifty years and one day old."

"I've decided I'm not going to have another birthday until I turn sixty. Maybe by then the town will have recovered from this one."

"I wonder what you'll be like when you're sixty?"

"A geezer, just like everybody else."

She grinned into the darkness. "Nah. I bet you'll be all dashing and sexy, like John Glenn."

"John Glenn? The astronaut? You think he's sexy?"

"Yep."

"You have some serious father issues you're working out, don't you?"

She laughed.

"Clare?"

Something in his voice made her laughter die away. "Yeah?"

"I decided something tonight."

She took a breath. "What?"

"I've decided to tell Linda. About us. About my feelings for you."

Say something, Clare. Say something. "Oh."

"I can't be dishonest with her anymore. She's been beside me every step of the way for the last twenty-five years, and now I've walked so far afield we can't even find one another with a map. I need to do something about it. I've decided to start by being truthful."

"What do you think her reaction is going to be?"

He laughed briefly. "Damned if I know. Somewhere between shooting me and giving me her blessing, I think."

"What if she asks you to cut off all contact with me? That wouldn't be unreasonable, you know. A lot of marriage counselors would probably recommend it." She forced herself to consider, dispassionately, what might be best for Russ. "Maybe it would be better."

He looked at her in the darkness. "It wouldn't be better. It would kill me. The thing about all this is, Linda loves me. I don't think she'd ask me to do something that will"—he searched for the right word—"eviscerate me."

She reached for his hand. He interlaced his fingers with hers. *I'm going to have to be the one,* she thought. *When the time comes, I'm going to have to be the one to break it off.* She squeezed his hand, and he tightened his fingers in return. *Lord God, give me strength.*

"C'mon," he said. "Time to get you into bed."

She laughed. He paused, not getting it for a second, and then groaned. She opened the door, leaving the keys in for him. He held out his hand, and she went around the side of the car and caught it, interlacing her fingers in his again.

"Look at that moon," he said.

She looked to where it was riding, halfway to the horizon.

"We had dinner," he said, "but we never danced."

"Nobody danced. The bandstand blew up and the instruments melted."

He tugged her off the driveway and onto the front lawn. The frost on the grass was pure silver in the moonlight. She could feel it, chilling her feet.

"Dance with me," he said.

"You're moonstruck," she said.

He placed one hand at the small of her back and took the other in a proper dancing position. "No, I'm not. I'm alive, and you're alive, and we don't know where we'll be twenty-four hours from now. So let's dance while we can."

He began singing a melancholy, wordless tune. *"Dum-da-dum, da-dee-da-dumdum, dum-da-dum, da-dee-da-dumdum."* His free hand nudged her back, and the next thing she knew, they were waltzing, her skirts swishing through the frost, his feet crunching the frozen grass. She recognized the melody suddenly. "Ashokan Farewell," from the Civil War documentary.

She chimed in, her alto humming above his baritone, the sleeves of his dinner jacket falling over her hands, and they danced, beneath the November moon, to sad, sweet music they made themselves.

Don't miss out on these Clare Fergusson and Russ Van Alstyne novels